G

D0063882

SEMPRE

J.M. DARHOWER

Gallery Books

New York   London   Toronto   Sydney   New Delhi

G

Gallery Books

A Division of Simon & Schuster, Inc.

1230 Avenue of the Americas

New York, NY 10020

www.SimonandSchuster.com

First Gallery Books trade paperback edition February 2014

GALLERY BOOKS and colophon are registered trademarks of Simon & Schuster, Inc.

For information about special discounts for bulk purchases, please contact Simon & Schuster Special Sales at 1-866-506-1949 or business@simonandschuster.com.

The Simon & Schuster Speakers Bureau can bring authors to your live event. For more information or to book an event contact the Simon & Schuster Speakers Bureau at 1-866-248-3049 or visit our website at www.simonspeakers.com.

Designed by Jill Putorti

Manufactured in the United States of America

10 9 8 7 6 5 4 3 2 1

Library of Congress Cataloging-in-Publication Data has been applied for.

ISBN 978-1-4767-6075-9 (pbk.)

ISBN 978-1-4767-3419-4 (ebook)

PROLOGUE

BLACKBURN, CALIFORNIA

The building was in shambles, decades of dry desert weather taking a toll on the exterior. It had started out as a town hall, back when the mining companies had a stake in the land, but those times had long since passed. Now it stood alone, withering away in the dark of night—the sole lasting reminder that the area had once flourished.

What had been a place of assembly now held another gathering, one more sinister that seven-year-old Haven was learning about for the first time. Her legs shook and stomach churned as she followed her master into the building, staying on his heels but doing her best not to step on his shiny black shoes.

They walked down a dark, narrow hall, passing a few men along the way. Haven kept her gaze on the floor, the sound of their voices as they greeted her master sending chills of fright down her back. These were new men, strangers, people she hadn't known existed.

He led her through a door at the end of the hallway, and what met them made her stop in her tracks. The stale scent of sweat and mildew saturated the room, heavy cigar smoke burning her nose. Masses of men stood around, talking loudly, as the sound of crying echoed off the walls, hitting the child like a freight train to the chest. She gasped, her heart racing as her eyes darted around looking for the source of the pain, but she couldn't see past the sea of bodies.

Her master grabbed hold of her, forcing her in front of him. She cringed as his hands clamped down on her shoulders and walked again at his command. The crowd parted for them, giving the two a clear path, and Haven obediently made her way to the front. She could feel the men staring, their eyes like lasers that burned down deep, making her blood boil as her face turned bright red.

In the front of the room, on a small stage, a few young girls knelt in a line. Tags were pinned to their ragged clothes, a number scribbled on it in black marker. Haven stood as still as possible, trying to ignore her master's touch, and watched as the crowd tossed money around. One by one the girls were auctioned off to the highest bidder, tears staining their cheeks as men dragged them away.

"Frankie!"

Haven turned at the sound of her master's name and recoiled from the man approaching. His face was like cracked leather and mangled with scars, his eyes a blackened pit of coal. In her frightened mind, she mistook him for a monster.

Frankie tightened his grip on her, locking her in place as he greeted the man. "Carlo."

"I see you brought the girl," Carlo said. "You getting rid of her? Because if so—"

Frankie cut him off before he could finish. "No, I just thought it would do her some good to see her own kind."

Her own kind. The words fascinated Haven. She looked back at the stage as a new girl came out, a teenager who looked as if she'd been in a fight with some scissors. Dozens of holes peppered her clothes, and her blonde hair was haphazardly chopped in a pixie cut. She was gagged and shackled, the number 33 affixed to her shirt.

Haven wondered—Was she like her? Could they be the same?

Number 33 struggled when the man gripped her arm, resisting more than the others. A split second changed everything as she pulled away, the metal binding her ankles making escape difficult. She jumped off the front of the stage and managed to stay on her feet, bolting for the crowd.

Chaos erupted like a volcano, violent and sudden. Men shouted, and Haven held her breath as Frankie reacted, his movement fluid as he reached into his coat and pulled out a gun. A shot exploded beside Haven, and she jumped, her ears ringing from the sudden bang. Number 33 dropped, the bullet ripping through her forehead and splattering Haven's blue-jean dress with fresh blood.

Hyperventilating, Haven's chest painfully heaved as she stared at the body on the floor by her bare feet. Blood streamed from the wound, soaking into the cracked wood and painting the girl's blonde hair a deep shade of red. Her icy blue eyes remained open, boring into Haven like they could see through her skin.

Frankie returned the gun to his coat and bent down to Haven's level. She tried to turn away from the carnage, but he gripped the back of her neck and forced her to look at Number 33.

"That's what happens when people forget their place," he said, his voice as cold as the dead eyes she stared into. "Remember that."

He stood, resuming his earlier position as he clutched her shoulders. The auction continued as if nothing had happened—as if an innocent girl weren't slain in front of them all. Number 33 lay lifeless on the floor, and no one in the room gave her a second thought.

No one, that is, except Haven. The vision of it would haunt her *forever*.

TEN YEARS LATER . . .

1

The hot, dry air burned Haven's chest. She gasped, struggling to breathe, as the dust kicked up by her frantic feet made it hard for her to see. It wasn't as if it would help anyway, since it was pitch black out and she had no idea where she was. Everything appeared the same in every direction, nothing but desert all around.

Her feet felt like they were on fire as every muscle in her body screamed for her to stop. It grew harder and harder to continue with each step, her strength deteriorating as her adrenaline faded. A bang rang out, her footsteps faltering as she swung in the direction of the noise, spotting a faint glow of light in the distance. *A house.*

She darted toward it, trying to yell for help but no sound escaped her throat. Her body revolted against her, giving out when she needed it most. The light grew brighter the harder she ran until all she saw was a flash of white. Blinded, she tripped and collapsed to the ground, pain running through her in waves as the light surrounding her burned out entirely.

The basement was dark and damp, the only exit a set of metal doors locked with heavy chains. With no windows, it was sweltering, the air polluted with the stench of sewer. Dried blood tinged the concrete floor like old splatters of red paint, a grotesque canvas of prolonged misery.

Haven lay in the corner, her frail body unmoving, except for the subtle rise and fall of her chest. Her long brown hair, usually somewhat frizzy, was so matted it appeared only half its length. By society's standards, she was as sickly as they come. Jutting collarbones and limbs like twigs, her ribs could be counted through her bruised and bloodied skin. She thought herself to be healthy, though. She'd seen people worse than her before.

The day had begun like every other. Haven woke up at dawn and spent most of the morning cleaning. In the afternoon she spent some time with her mama, the two of them sitting against the side of the old wooden house. Neither spoke as the sound of the television filtered out of an open window above them. The news told of a hurricane brewing in the south and a war waging in Iraq, the significance of both lost on Haven.

Her mama said listening to it was a waste of time, because their slice of the world was barely a blip on the big radar, but Haven couldn't help herself. The five o'clock news was the highlight of her day. She needed to feel like she was real, that something—or someone—she'd had contact with still existed out in the world, somewhere.

Screaming started inside the house, interrupting the news as fighting made its way into the living room. Haven climbed to her feet, not wanting to be caught eavesdropping, when she heard something that stopped her in her tracks. "I want the girl gone!"

"I know, Katrina! I'm working on it!"

"Not hard enough!" Katrina was the lady of the house, a harsh woman with short black hair and wickedly pointy features. "Get rid of her already!"

Get rid of her already. The words suffocated Haven. The fighting moved from the living room to upstairs, their voices fading as tense silence crept in.

She was in serious trouble.

"This world's scary," her mama whispered. "People will hurt you. They'll do things to you, sick things . . . the kind of things I hope you never know about. And they'll trick you. They'll lie to you. You have to be on guard at all times, baby girl."

Haven didn't like where the conversation was going. "Why are you telling me this?"

"Because you need to know," she said. "You have to run."

Haven stared at her in disbelief. "Run?"

"Yes, tonight. There's more to life than this, and I'm afraid of what will happen if you stay here."

"But I can't run, Mama. I don't know what's out there!"

"People out there can help you."

Tears formed in Haven's eyes. "I can't leave you."

"It's the only way," she said. "You have to get away from here, find someone and tell them who you are. They'll—"

"Save you?" Haven asked, finishing her sentence. "Will they come here?"

"Maybe." Something sparked in her eyes. *Hope?*

"Then I'll do it," Haven said, "for you."

After nightfall, when Haven thought no one would look for her until morning, she quietly slipped away. She ran for the world outside of the ranch, determined to find help so she'd never have to return.

Waking up in the musty basement, she realized she'd failed.

A clanking jolted Haven awake, a blinding light assaulting her. Cringing, she noticed the doors open and someone standing a few feet away. A man with olive skin approached, his dark hair slicked back on his head. He wore black pants and a white button-up shirt, the sleeves rolled up to his elbows. Haven gaped at the silver gun holstered to his belt.

Her voice cracked. "Are you the police?"

The man knelt near her, setting a small black bag on the floor. He didn't answer but gave her a bemused smile as he pressed his large palm to her forehead.

Haven closed her drowsy eyes and got lost in the silence until the man finally spoke. She opened her eyes again, surprised by his gentle tone, but recoiled when she met a hostile glare.

Behind the stranger stood someone she knew well. Michael, or *Master* as he preferred to be called, scowled at her with his dark eyes, the whites of them dingy yellow. His lip was curled in a sneer, his wiry hair graying around the ears.

"Relax, child," the stranger said. "It's going to be all right."

She looked at him, wondering if she could believe it, and panicked when he pulled a needle out of his bag. She whimpered, trying to move away, but he grabbed her and jabbed it into her shoulder blade.

"I'm not going to hurt you," he said, letting go and handing the offending little weapon to Michael. "I'm only trying to help."

"Help?" Her mama had told her people out there would help, but she'd also warned her that some of them would lie. Haven wasn't sure which group this man fell in to, but she leaned toward the latter.

"Yes, help." The man stood. "You need to rest. Save your energy."

He walked away, and her master followed him without saying a word. Haven lay there, too drained to make sense of it, and her eyes closed when she heard their voices again.

"She looks horrible!" the man yelled, all trace of kindness gone. "How could you let this happen, Antonelli?"

"I didn't mean for it to," Michael said. "I didn't know she'd try to run!"

"This started before yesterday, and you know it! You should've been watching her!"

"I know. I'm sorry."

"You should be." Haven started to slip away, but before sleep took her, the man spoke once more. "I'll give you what you want for her, but I'm not happy about this. At all."

Haven awoke later, still on the concrete floor. Every inch of her ached, and she grimaced as she struggled to sit up. A throat cleared nearby, the stranger once again standing in the basement with her. "How do you feel?"

She wrapped her arms protectively around herself as he moved toward her. "Okay."

His voice was calm but firm. "The truth."

"Sore," she reluctantly admitted. "My head hurts."

"I'm not surprised." He knelt down and reached toward her, the movement making her flinch. "I'm not going to hit you, child."

He felt her forehead and grasped her chin, surveying her face. "Do you know who I am?" She shook her head, although something about him struck her as familiar. She thought she might've seen him from a distance before, one of the visitors she'd been kept away from throughout the years. "I'm Dr. Vincent DeMarco."

"Doctor?" They'd never gotten medical attention before, even for the severest of problems.

"Yes, I'm a doctor," he said, "but I'm also an associate of the Antonellis. I arrived after you went missing. You suffered a minor concussion, and you're dehydrated, but there's no permanent damage that I can see. You're lucky you were found. You could've died out there."

A sinking feeling settled into the pit of Haven's stomach, a small part of her wishing she would have. It had to be better than being killed at the hands of a monster.

Dr. DeMarco looked at his watch. "Do you think you can walk? We should leave soon."

"We?"

"Yes, you're going to be staying with me now."

She shook her head, cringing as her pain intensified. "I can't leave my mama. She needs me!"

"Maybe you should've thought about that before you ran away."

She tried to explain, her words sluggish. "They were going to kill me. I didn't have a choice."

"You always have a choice, child," he said. "In fact, you have one right now."

"You're giving me a choice?"

"Of course I am. You can come with me."

"Or?"

He shrugged. "Or you stay here, and I'll leave without you. But before you decide, tell me something. You ran away because you thought they were going to kill you. What do you think they'll do to you now?"

She stared at her dirt-caked feet. "So I either go with you or I die? What kind of choice is that?"

"One I suppose you won't like making," he said, "but it is a choice, nonetheless."

Tense silence brewed between them. Haven didn't like this manipulating man. "What do you want me for?"

She was used to being punished for speaking out of turn, but she had nothing to lose. What would he do, kill her?

"I never said I wanted you, but I'm a busy man. I can use someone to cook and clean."

"You can't pay someone?" She regretted the question immediately and backtracked. "At least it would be legal. I think this is illegal. Isn't it?"

Truthfully, she wasn't sure.

"I suppose it technically is, but—"

Before he could finish, shouts rang out above them in the house. Haven flinched at the loud thump and startled cry, tears stinging her eyes when she realized Michael was hurting her mama.

Dr. DeMarco sighed. "Look, I'm not going to wait around all night waiting for you. If you don't want my help, so be it. Stay here and die."

The man stood to leave. Haven climbed to her feet, muttering, "Why me?" She wanted to believe there was a point to it all, but she wasn't sure anymore.

He gave a slight shake of the head. "I wish I knew."

———

The soles of Haven's feet burned as Dr. DeMarco led her out of the basement. "I'm not chasing you if you run," he said, laughing bitterly when her panicked eyes darted to his gun. "I'm not going to shoot you, either."

"You're not?"

"No," he said. "I'll shoot your mother instead."

She gasped as he let go of her arm. "Please don't hurt her!"

"Stay where you are and I won't have to," he said, walking away.

Although her legs were weak and she felt dizzy, Haven refused to move an inch as he disappeared inside the house. The sky glowed bright orange as the sun dipped below the horizon, casting distorted shadows along the ground in front of her. She didn't know what day it was, had no clue how much time had passed. She scanned what she could see of the property, searching for some sign of her mama. She wanted to call out to her, to find her. She wanted to ask what she was supposed to do.

But her mama never appeared. The sun disappeared, and out of the darkness came Dr. DeMarco again. He didn't look at her as he opened a door to a black car. "Time to go."

Timidly, Haven slid into the rigid passenger seat and peered around as he slammed the door. The harsh stench of fresh leather in the confined space made her feel like a weight was pressing on her chest. She had trouble breathing, struggling to stay calm when he climbed in beside her. Dr. DeMarco frowned as he reached into the backseat for his bag. He pulled out another needle and stuck her without a word.

Blackness came again.

The small road cut through the dense forest, the painted lines so faded it appeared made for one car. A new highway diverted traffic from the area, so the only people who navigated there were locals and those who lost their way. Haven lay slumped over in the passenger seat of a car, woozy as she watched the trees whipping past in the darkness. She turned from the window, fighting sickness. Her eyes found the clock on the dashboard, the numbers glowing a quarter after twelve.

She'd been out for hours.

"I didn't mean to sedate you for so long," Dr. DeMarco said, noticing her movement. "You slept the entire flight."

"In an airplane?" He nodded. It was her first time even being near a plane. She wasn't sure whether to be glad it was over or disappointed she'd missed it. "Where are we now?"

"Almost home."

Home. Haven didn't know what that meant.

"Before we get there, I want to make something clear," Dr. De-Marco said. "You're going to have some normalcy living with us, but don't mistake my kindness for weakness. I expect your loyalty, and if you betray my trust in any way, there will be consequences. As long as you remember that, we won't have any problems." He paused. "I want you to be comfortable with us, though, so you can speak freely as long as you're respectful."

"I'd never disrespect you, sir."

"Never say never. Sometimes we don't realize when we're being disrespectful." Haven wondered what he meant by that, but he didn't explain. "Do you have any questions?"

"You said 'us.' Do you have a family?"

"I do. I have two sons, ages seventeen and eighteen."

"Oh." She was on the verge of panicking. She hadn't been around many people her age and had never had any contact with teenage boys. Studying him, she noticed the plain gold band gleaming under the moonlight on his left hand. *Married.* "And your wife, sir? Their mama?"

The moment the question came from her lips, Dr. DeMarco's demeanor shifted. His posture stiffened and his jaw clenched as he stared straight ahead, his foot pressing harder on the gas pedal. He gripped the steering wheel so tightly his knuckles turned as white as bone, conversation ceasing.

So much for speaking freely.

The car turned off the pavement and drove down a bumpy path that cut through the dense trees. They came to a clearing, and Haven gaped at the house that came into sight. The old planta-tion home stood three stories high, with columns spanning the height of the structure. The white paint was faded, tinting the exterior a dull gray. A large porch wrapped around the first floor, with smaller ones running the lengths of the second and third.

Dr. DeMarco parked between a smaller black car and a silver one, and Haven stepped out cautiously, taking in her surroundings. All she could see in the darkness beyond were trees, while a porch light made the gravel faintly visible beneath her feet. Dr. DeMarco grabbed his luggage before heading toward the front door, and she limped behind with empty hands, having nothing of her own to carry. She'd never had much, all of her clothes ragged hand-me-downs that she'd left behind without a choice.

After stepping onto the porch, Dr. DeMarco pressed his finger to a small panel on a rectangular keypad. It beeped before he opened the door. Haven stepped into the house, pausing as he closed the door and punched something into an identical keypad on the inside.

A green light flashed as a lock clicked into place, the door automatically securing itself. "It's wired into a computer network," Dr. DeMarco explained. "The house is impenetrable, the glass bulletproof and windows nailed shut. You need a code or fingerprint authorization to get in or out."

"What happens if there's a power failure, sir?"

"It's on a backup generator."

"And if the generator doesn't work?"

"Then I suppose you'll stay locked inside until power's restored."

"Will I have a code?"

"Maybe someday, when I feel I can trust you with one," he said. "After what you pulled in Blackburn, I'm sure you can understand my position. I'm a lot closer to civilization than they were."

She couldn't understand his position, refused to try. "What happens if there's an emergency?"

"There are ways around the system, but I don't foresee any situations that require you to know those tricks."

"But what if there's a fire and I need to get out?"

Dr. DeMarco gazed at her. "You're a crafty one, aren't you?" Before she could respond, he turned away. "I'll show you around."

Straight in front of them was the family room, with several couches and a television on one of the walls. A fireplace was tucked in the back beside a piano, the wooden floor shining from the glow of the moon streaming through the large windows. To the left was a kitchen filled with stainless-steel appliances, an island in the center with pots and pans hanging above it. The dining room behind that had the longest table Haven had ever seen, big enough to accommodate fourteen. She wondered how often all those seats were taken, unable to imagine cooking for that many people. To the right were a bathroom and a laundry room, as well as an office tucked underneath the staircase.

The second floor belonged to Dr. DeMarco—a bedroom and a bathroom, along with another office and a spare room. Some of the doors had keypads beside them, a sign Haven wouldn't be going into those rooms.

They continued up to the third floor, the stairs ending in a large open space. A window lined the back wall, in front of it stood a table with two plush gray chairs. The other three walls held doors leading to bedrooms, but the area itself was packed full of bookcases. Hundreds of dusty books lined the shelves. Haven stared in shock, having never dreamed of seeing so many before.

"Our library," Dr. DeMarco said. "It doesn't get much use and I imagine it still won't, considering Antonelli said you couldn't read."

Haven could feel his eyes on her, but she remained quiet and didn't meet his gaze.

A door opened nearby and a boy stepped out from one of the bedrooms. He was tall and lanky, with shaggy brown hair. Dr. De-Marco turned to him. "Dominic, this is, uh . . . She's going to be staying here."

Dominic eyed her curiously. "Hey."

"Hello, sir," she said, her voice shaky.

His laughter echoed through the room. "Oh, that won't do. Just call me Dom."

Dom headed downstairs as Dr. DeMarco led her across the

library, striding past the middle door without a word and stopping at the last. "This is where you'll sleep. Go in. I'll be back."

Haven hesitantly stepped inside. The furniture, the curtains, and the carpet were all plain, everything a dull white with dustings of wood. Most of the house held the same effect, the walls empty and rooms uncluttered. There were no pictures and no knick-knacks, nothing to hold any sentimental value. Nothing to give her any idea of what type of people she was dealing with.

She still stood just inside the doorway when Dr. DeMarco returned with a pile of clothes. "They'll be big, but at least they're clean."

She took them. "Thank you, sir."

"You're welcome," he said. "Get cleaned up and settle in. This is your home now, too."

He'd said it again. *Home.* She had lived with the Antonellis her entire life and never heard it referred to as *home.*

Dr. DeMarco walked away but stopped after a few steps. "Oh, and help yourself to anything in the kitchen if you're hungry, but don't try to burn down my house. Doing so won't get you a code any faster. I'll let you burn to death before I let you outsmart me."

––––––––

Haven ran her hand along the fluffy comforter. She'd never had a bed before, much less a bedroom of her own. Her nights in Blackburn had been spent in the stables, in a back stall on a worn-down mattress with some of the springs exposed. The temperature was comfortable there at night, so she hadn't had much use for blankets, one of the ratty covers they kept for the horses enough for the occasions it did get cold. She preferred not to use them, because they were itchy on her skin, nothing like the material against her fingertips now.

After stripping out of her old clothes, Haven went into the connecting bathroom. A large tub sat in the corner with a long counter and a sink across from it, a rectangular mirror on the wall above the sink.

Hesitantly, Haven surveyed her reflection, her sunken cheeks and the cuts covering her face. A bruise ran along the right side of her jaw while blood caked her hairline from a gash in her forehead.

It was like a layer of dirt had settled on her body, tinting her skin a slightly darker shade, but it wasn't enough to cover her scars. There were dozens she could see and even more on her back, constant reminders of what she'd been through. The bruises faded and sometimes so did the memories, but the scars . . . the scars remained.

She drew a bath and slid into it, hissing as the scalding water came into contact with her skin. She scrubbed every inch of her body raw as tears pooled in her eyes, overwhelmed and unsure about what would come of her. Dr. DeMarco had been civilized, but she wasn't fooled by his gentle voice and small tokens of independence. Nothing came without a price. While Dr. DeMarco might not have looked like a monster, she wasn't naïve enough to believe one didn't live inside of him, lurking under the surface.

Experience told her one always did.

She got out after the water cooled and found a towel in a small cabinet. It smelled like flowers and was soft against her skin as she wrapped it around her body. Heading back into the bedroom, she grabbed the clothes and slipped on the black flannel pants. They hung limp on her frail form, and she had to roll them up to keep them in place. She grabbed a white t-shirt and unfolded it, noticing the football on the front. Turning it over, she flinched at the big black number 3 covering the back.

———

Time passed slowly as sleep evaded Haven. She huddled under the blanket, trying to find comfort, but the stillness was unsettling. It was too new, too foreign. A prickly sensation crept across her skin as the walls closed in on her, hunger and anxiety taking its toll.

In the early morning hours, it got to be too much, and she quietly slipped downstairs. The hallways were dark, but she noticed a subtle glow of light in the kitchen. Tiptoeing to the doorway, she peeked inside and saw a boy in front of the refrigerator. He was a few inches taller than her, his skin the color of coffee with a lot of extra cream. A few days' worth of stubble accented his sharp features, and his thick hair was dark, shorter on the sides than on the top. His gray shirt hugged his chest, the short sleeves shoved up to his shoulders. Ink marked his right arm, a tattoo she couldn't make out in the darkness, and he had on a pair of pants identical to the ones she wore.

He drank juice from a glass, unaware of her presence, and Haven took a step back to flee. The movement caught his eye, and he turned in her direction, the drink slipping from his hand when he spotted her. It hit the floor and shattered, the spray of liquid soaking his pants.

Jumping back, he looked down at himself. "Shit!"

The curse sent Haven into a panic, and she darted forward to clean up the mess. He bent down at the same moment Haven dove to his feet, their heads colliding. The force knocked him backward, a piece of jagged glass stabbing him when he caught himself on the floor. He cursed again as blood oozed from the small gash and stuck his wounded thumb into his mouth. She noticed, as she looked at him, a scar running through his right eyebrow, slicing it in half.

His gaze lifted, a pair of vibrant green eyes greeting Haven, intense passion swirling in the color that took her breath away. She broke eye contact, her chest tightening as she snatched a towel from the counter to clean up the juice. Tears streamed down her cheeks as she pushed the glass into a pile, but she was disrupted when his hand seized her wrist. She yelped at the zap of static electricity, and he blinked rapidly, just as caught off guard.

"What's wrong with you?" he asked, gripping her tightly.

"I'm sorry," she said. "Please don't punish me."

Before either could get out another word, the overhead light flicked on and Dr. DeMarco's harsh voice rang out. "Let her go!"

The boy dropped her wrist so fast it was as if he'd been savagely burned. "Sorry," he said, the word barely audible as he climbed to his feet.

Haven struggled to breathe as Dr. DeMarco poured a glass of water from the faucet and handed it to her. "Drink," he commanded. She forced the water down and gagged, her stomach more interested in expelling its contents. "What happened here?"

They replied at the same time, answering in sync. "It was an accident."

"It won't happen again, sir," Haven continued. "I swear."

Dr. DeMarco blinked a few times. "It's not often *two* people accept blame around here."

As if on cue, the boy spoke again. "Yeah, well, it wasn't really my fault. She scared me. She's a fucking ninja or something."

Dr. DeMarco pinched the bridge of his nose. "Watch your mouth, son. Go get ready for school."

He started to argue, but Dr. DeMarco's hand shot up to silence him. The sudden movement startled Haven. She recoiled, bracing to be struck.

The boy eyed her strangely. "What the hell's wrong with—?"

"I said go!" Dr. DeMarco said. "I don't have time for you."

"Fine, what-the-fuck-ever."

Dr. DeMarco turned to her after the boy stormed out. "He isn't usually . . . well, never mind; that's a lie. He *is* usually like this. He's finicky and angry, but that's neither here nor there. He's set in his ways, and it doesn't matter what I do. Carmine is who he is."

Carmine. A strange name for a strange boy.

"Why are you up, anyway?" he asked. "I figured you'd sleep most of the day to recover."

"I didn't know what time I was supposed to get up."

"You get up whenever you get up," he said. "You can go back to bed now."

"But what about—?"

He didn't let her finish. "I'll handle this. Don't worry about doing anything today. Just rest."

2

"I need a favor."

Carmine stepped past his father, refusing to acknowledge he'd spoken. The scent of freshly brewed coffee was strong in the kitchen as Vincent cleaned the sticky mess from the floor. The knees of his newest Armani suit were soaked with juice, and Carmine got a tiny bit of satisfaction from that fact.

"Are you ignoring me now, son?"

"Oh, are you talking to me? I thought you didn't have time for me this morning."

Vincent stood. "I certainly don't have time for your attitude, but I do need a favor."

"Of course you do."

Vincent pulled a piece of paper out of his pocket and handed it to him. "Ask Dia if she'll grab this stuff after school today. I'd do it myself, but I know nothing about things teenage girls need."

Carmine laughed. "I don't think Dia knows shit about teenage girls, either."

"She knows enough," he said. "Just do it."

Carmine shoved it into his pocket. "Whatever. Is it for the ninja girl? Who is she, anyway?"

"Do you honestly care?"

"No." The word came out before he gave it any thought. He wasn't sure *what* to think.

"Then it doesn't matter who she is," Vincent said. "But she needs things, so don't forget to ask Dia."

"I heard you the first time," he said. "It would've been nice to have some warning you were bringing someone here, though. Where'd she come from?"

Vincent poured some coffee into his silver travel mug. "I thought you didn't care."

"I don't."

"Then again—it doesn't matter," he said. "All that matters is she's here now."

"Whatever."

"Whatever," Vincent mimicked him, shaking his head. "It's nice to see the money I paid to send you to Benton Academy made you more articulate."

Carmine shuddered at the mention of that place.

He'd landed in trouble the year before—trouble that could have ruined his life—but his father had pulled some strings to get him out of it. He hadn't exactly been forgiving, though, and had shipped him to a boarding school across the country for a semester. Carmine swore the moment he was on the plane heading home that nothing like it would happen again, but it was a lot easier said than done. He never went looking for it, but trouble found him every time he turned a corner.

And Carmine turned *a lot* of motherfucking corners.

"Yeah, well, you should've saved your pennies. Your life would be easier if you would've let me rot."

"I bet you truly believe that," Vincent said, glancing at his watch. "I have to get cleaned up for work. Just remember to ask Dia—"

"I already said I heard you. How many times are you going to remind me?"

"Until I know you won't forget."

"Well, I won't."

"Good," he said, "because if you do, we're going to have a problem."

Dia Harper drove an old Toyota, slate gray and missing two hub-caps. She'd bought it with money she earned freelancing, which meant she'd do nearly anything for a few bucks. Shopping, clean-ing, passing messages . . . She'd even written a term paper for Carmine for fifty dollars once. A leak in the exhaust system made the car emit strong gas fumes that she tried to cover with a dozen tree-shaped air fresheners. Carmine wouldn't be caught dead riding in it, but to Dia, the car was the Holy Grail.

She was perched on the hood of it in the parking lot that morn-ing when Carmine arrived at school. "I still don't get it," she said, shaking her head as soon as he stepped out. "Explain it again."

Carmine leaned against his black Mazda in the spot beside her. "There's nothing to get. It is what it is."

"What is it?"

"Sex," he said, laughing at the bewildered expression on Dia's face. Her blue eyes were hidden beneath layers of dark makeup, and she'd added some pink and purple streaks to her short blonde hair since yesterday. She defined eccentric in her mismatched clothes, her new bulky camera hanging by a strap around her neck. Noth-ing about Dia conformed, which was what had drawn Carmine to her in the first place. Although he was popular, there weren't many people he considered friends. He felt there were two types of people in the small town of Durante, North Carolina, where they lived—those who wanted him, and those who wished they could be him. Dia was different, though. She was honest and, living in a world surrounded by nothing but lies, Carmine appreciated that.

"But why Lisa?" Dia asked, refusing to drop the subject.

Carmine looked across the parking lot at where a group of girls had gathered and shrugged when he spotted Lisa Donovan. She had long blonde hair, her body slim and skin darkly tanned. She looked like every other girl in school—nothing to write home about.

Not that there was anyone at his home who gave a shit about his life . . .

"She's quick to get naked. Less work for me."

"Gross." Dia wrinkled her nose. "You need a decent girl to straighten you out."

"I don't need straightened out," Carmine said. "Why drown in love when you can have so much fun swimming around in lust?"

"But her?" Dia pressed. "Out of everyone in this school, you pick *Moanin' Lisa*."

Carmine chuckled, tugging on a chunk of Dia's colorful hair. "Looks like you're the painting today, Warhol."

"Hey, I'll take it," she said. "Andy Warhol was one of the best."

"He was crazy."

"Maybe, but he was still a genius." She nodded toward the group of girls. "Which Moanin' Lisa, clearly, is not. I don't think she can even string together a sentence. Have you tried to have an intelligent conversation with her? It's like talking to a brick wall."

"No, we don't do a lot of talking," he said. "She's not so bad from behind with her face shoved into a mattress, though."

Dia shook her head as Carmine laughed again. He had no real interest in Lisa, or any other girl for that matter. But while a relationship was the furthest thing from his mind, he'd realized there were benefits to keeping female company. They might not have been intellectually stimulating, but they did stimulate another part of him . . . often.

A silver Audi whipped into the parking lot then, coming to a stop beside them. Dominic hopped out from behind the wheel and Tess, his girlfriend, climbed from the passenger seat. Tess was Dia's twin sister, but the two couldn't have been more opposite.

They'd all known one another since they moved to the area in elementary school, but the relationship between Dominic and Tess was new. It was strange—the life Carmine had left wasn't the same one he'd returned to, and he had a hard time adjusting to the change.

"What are y'all up to?" Dominic asked.

"Trying to get Carmine to see the error of his ways when it comes to Lisa," Dia said. "It's not working."

"Can't say I'm surprised," Tess said. "No girl with an ounce of self-respect would want him."

"I'm not that bad. I'm rich, popular. I have a sense of humor. I'm good looking, and not to mention I have a really big—" They all groaned loudly before he could finish. He shrugged, thinking he'd summed himself up nicely. "Besides, it's not like I plan to date her. The only time you'll catch me asking a girl out is after I'm done with her, and I'm asking her to *get* out."

"See, that's why you'll always be alone," Tess said. "You only think about yourself."

"So says the vainest bitch alive," he said. "You better be careful throwing stones in your glass house, Tess. You're liable to get cut."

"Enough, you two," Dominic said, stepping between them. "Carmine's free to do whatever—or whomever—he wants, so get off his back. But, bro, you better watch yourself, threatening my girl."

"I didn't threaten her. I warned her. She ought to thank me."

Rolling her eyes, Tess stalked off, and Dominic followed behind, calling her name. The routine happened daily: Tess gets mad, stomps away, and Dominic chases her like a dog.

Carmine didn't see the appeal. "He's pathetic."

"He's in love."

"If that's what love does to you, you can definitely count me out." He couldn't imagine spending every waking moment of every day with the same person, doing the same shit they did the day before. "That has to be boring."

"And what you do isn't?"

He looked at her incredulously. "You think my life is boring? I get what I want, when I want it. I enjoy my freedom too much to give it away for some bitch."

Dia cringed. "Do you have to use that word?"

"What word?"

She glared at him but didn't respond. Carmine knew what word she meant, but he didn't see the big deal, considering it was just that—a word. Whatever happened to "sticks and stones can break my bones, but words can never hurt me"?

The bell rang in the distance, signaling the start of school. "Here comes Moanin' Lisa," Dia said, hopping down from her car. "And yeah, a girl would be lucky to have you, Carmine, but not like this. You're wasting your time, and it's not worth it. You need to find something that is."

She scurried away before he had a chance to reply.

"Hey, handsome," Lisa said as she approached. She leaned against his car, beaming, but he pulled her away from it. He hated people touching his things. She didn't notice, though, and ran her hand down his chest, fiddling with the buttons on his shirt. "You look good today."

"Thanks, but you know what would look *really* good today?"

"What?"

"*Bocchino.*" He brushed his pointer finger across her pink glossy lips. "That mouth on me."

———

A sharp pain ricocheted through Carmine's head as warmth streamed down the side of his face. Every ounce of rationality left his body in a whoosh. He was bleeding. *Again.*

Unacceptable.

A frantic voice rung out, adamantly apologizing, but the words seemed distant as Carmine's temper dangerously flared. He slammed the locker door that had struck him before pouncing, hurling a boy into another row of lockers, his clenched fist landing straight into his stomach.

Someone stepped between them, and Carmine nearly swung again until their eyes connected. Coach Woods towered over him, nostrils flaring. "Principal's office!"

"Me? This is bullshit!"

Coach Woods glared at him. "Don't speak that way in my locker room! I'll bench you!"

As starting quarterback for the varsity football team, Carmine was usually afforded a bit of leniency, but he could tell from his coach's expression that today was an exception. He grabbed a towel, holding it to his forehead to soak up the trickle of blood as he stormed out.

The secretary in the front office barely glanced at Carmine when he busted in, throwing himself down in a chair to impatiently wait. She casually radioed the principal, notifying him someone was waiting. Principal Rutledge came out, merely casting Carmine a look that told him to join him. Carmine took his usual seat in the cracked brown leather chair in the small office, still clutching the towel to his head as he sprawled his legs out in front of him.

"What happened this time?" It was a question Principal Rutledge seemed to have asked Carmine every week since his freshman year.

"Someone hit me with a locker door."

"Intentionally?"

Carmine shrugged. "Might as well have been."

The principal picked up his office phone, dialing a number he'd long ago memorized. Carmine glanced around the small space while he waited. He noticed a new picture frame on top of a filing cabinet with a photo of the man's daughter, a curvy sophomore with brown hair and hazel eyes.

"Your daughter's looking good these days."

"Leave her alone, Carmine."

He chuckled but didn't have time to respond before the principal focused on the call. "Dr. DeMarco, Jack Rutledge here . . . Yes . . . I'm doing well, how about you? Yes, well, there was an incident . . . He is injured . . . No, I don't think the other boy is . . . He's still in my office . . . No, he hasn't been seen by the nurse."

Principal Rutledge looked at him. "Do you think you'll need stitches?"

Carmine shrugged, but the man didn't wait for him to respond. "Yes, we do have a procedure in place for injured students . . . I understand that . . . With all due respect, I don't think it's that serious . . . No, you're right; I'm not a doctor." He paused, his eyes bulging. "Yes, the school's insured, but I don't think this is a case of negligence."

Carmine slowly smirked. Most people didn't know what type of man his father truly was, but he managed to terrify the shit out of them anyway.

"I'll send him right over." The principal hung up, eyeing him cautiously. "You need to go to the hospital to be checked out. I should've sent you right away. I don't know what I was thinking."

Carmine stood. "Yeah, I don't know, either."

Carmine went through the emergency room entrance at the hospital, bypassing the nurse's station for his father's office on the third floor. Vincent sat at his desk with his arms crossed over his chest. He motioned for Carmine to come closer and checked his wound. "You should get a few stitches."

"Nice."

Vincent removed his glasses and pinched the bridge of his nose. "What were you thinking?"

"He started it."

His father shook his head. "It's never your fault, is it? There are only going to be so many 'get out of jail free' cards, Carmine. Someday you're going to get yourself in a situation that has no way out, and you're finally going to have to learn to live with the consequences."

Carmine scoffed. "Right back at you."

Vincent walked him down to a room in the emergency room, and Carmine took a seat on one of the stiff beds as he waited to be sewn up. After a few minutes, the door opened and a young blonde-haired woman in hot pink scrubs stepped in. "My, my . . . look who it is."

"Jen." Carmine nearly gagged as he said her name. If ever the term *gold digger* was to make it into the dictionary, Carmine was sure her picture would be plastered beside it. Even *he* wouldn't touch her, but his father had. He'd walked in on them one day. The memory of what he'd seen was something he often tried to drink away.

Three stitches and a stolen double dose of Percocet later, Carmine strolled toward the exit, feeling like he was floating on air. Vincent cornered him in front of the building, still scowling. "Go straight home. We'll talk when I get there."

Carmine mock-saluted him as he made his way to the parking lot. His car was parked in a spot reserved for a doctor, right in the front near the building. Reaching into his pocket for his keys, his brow furrowed when he felt a piece of paper. "Fuck."

He'd forgotten about the list, after all.

He climbed into the car, debating for a moment before driving through town. He bypassed the road that led toward home and instead took the highway to Lisa's.

Since he was going to be in trouble, he figured he might as well make it worth it.

———

Haven hummed while she worked.

It was a habit she'd had all of her life. Her mama used to say that before Haven could talk, she hummed, mimicking the lullabies she'd sung to her at night in the stables. It had calmed her as a baby, soothed her, and as she went about her work, it had a similar effect.

The words to the songs were long forgotten, but the melodies continued to play in her head. It brought Haven back to an earlier time—a time when things were still innocent. She'd hum, and suddenly the sun shined a bit brighter, the world around her not as dark as she knew it could be.

Used to having every detail of her life controlled, she had a hard time sorting through things on her own. She should've gotten clarification, because nothing should be assumed, but she was so afraid of making a mistake that she couldn't force the questions out. She'd already upset Dr. DeMarco once asking something. How many chances would she get before he snapped?

So she did whatever came naturally to her. That afternoon, she scrubbed the hardwood floors and cleaned the bathrooms. She dusted and vacuumed, but stayed away from every room with a lock. She found a clear bottle in the supply closet, labeled in black lettering that it was for the windows. They were the only dirty part of the house, so she cleaned them as high up as she could reach.

By three o'clock, Haven was fresh out of things to do.

She was sorting through the pantry when the alarm in the foyer beeped and the front door opened. Footsteps headed her direction and her heart thumped wildly. Panicked, she darted for the doorway, irrationally planning to hide, and collided with Dominic when he stepped into the kitchen. "Whoa, Twinkle Toes. Warn me next time you wanna dance."

Instinctively, she backed up a few steps. "I'm sorry."

"No biggie," he said, heading for the refrigerator. "You hungry?"

Haven watched the doorway for his company, realizing after a moment he was talking to her. She stammered, her stomach growling before she could get out a coherent thought.

He laughed. "I'll take that as a yes."

He slapped some ham and cheese between two slices of bread and grabbed a paper towel, holding it out to her. She stared at the sandwich with surprise but took it carefully. She couldn't recall the last time she'd eaten anything, too nervous to touch their food on her own.

Haven took a small bite as Dominic cleaned up, the entire exchange surreal. She couldn't believe he'd served her, the servant.

3

Haven sat on the edge of her bed, her hands folded in her lap and her gaze trained on the floor. She could see Dr. DeMarco's shoes from the corner of her eye, a small trail of dirt on the carpet behind them that he'd dragged in. The impulsive urge to clean it hit her, but she remained still, not wanting to offend him.

It was a few minutes past six in the evening. She'd slipped up to her room after eating her sandwich earlier in the day, feeling out of place downstairs.

"You cleaned."

"Yes, sir."

"But I told you to relax."

She tensed. Was that disrespectful? "I was awake and didn't know what else to do."

"I appreciate the effort," he said. "In all honesty, I can't recall the windows ever being free of grime. You did clean them, right?"

"Yes, sir."

"And you used the correct cleaner?"

"I think so," she said. "The clear bottle from the closet."

He took a step toward her. She flinched when his hand shot out, but her reaction didn't stop him. Grasping her chin, he forced her to look at him. "I don't expect perfection, child. Make sure the house is decent, the beds are made, and the laundry is done, and we shouldn't have any problems. Dinner is to be on the table at seven every night, unless I tell you otherwise. Got it?"

"Yes, sir."

Dr. DeMarco let go of her, and she looked away, eye contact uncomfortable. He turned to walk out of the room but stopped in the library when he realized she was right on his heels. "Is there something you need?"

"It's already after six, so I thought I should start dinner."

He sighed. "Tomorrow. Take the night off."

She stood there as he walked away, leaving her alone in front of the stairs. *Take the night off.* The words ran through her mind but refused to sink in, as foreign to her as another language.

Who are these people?

———

1:47 A.M.

The glowing red numbers on the alarm clock taunted Haven. It was too quiet, the silence deafening. She'd never been on her own for so long before. Even at night in the stables the animals had kept her company while she slept. She usually had her mama, and she realized, as she lay in the dark room, that she'd taken her for granted. She had no one now. She was alone.

2:12 A.M.

She thought about her mama, wondering what she was doing and if she was okay. Did she know what happened, or was she imagining her out there somewhere, getting help? Haven pictured her standing on the front porch of the ranch, gazing out at the desert and waiting for a sign. Waiting for rescue. Waiting for *her*.

3:28 A.M.

Haven wondered what would've happened had she found someone to save them. Would they be somewhere together? She imagined them having their own house, with a backyard and a fluffy white kitten to keep them company. They'd name her Snowball and she'd climb their tree at Christmas, tearing down the lights

and scattering pine needles. They'd have presents and hot chocolate, and there would be snow outside. Haven had only ever seen
snow in pictures, but her mama talked about it sometimes. She
told her how beautiful it was when it blanketed the ground, how
the cold flakes tasted when they landed on your tongue. Haven
asked how she knew, since she'd never had a life other than the one
they had. "I dream about it," she'd said. "When you dream, you can
go anywhere. I always go to the snow."

4:18 A.M.

Haven pictured her mama, skin flushed from the cold. Flakes
stuck to her hair, and she glowed, smiling as she twirled in the
snow. She was happier than Haven had ever seen her before, living
a normal life . . . the kind of life she always should have had.

5:03 A.M.

Her cheeks were stained from tears and her eyes burned like
grains of sand were caught in them. She felt like she was running
again, the air suffocating as she struggled to breathe, but no matter
how hard she fought, she'd get nowhere.

5:46 A.M.

The faint sound of music filtered into the room, a welcome
disruption from the agonizing silence. The soft melody comforted
Haven. She relaxed as the tension left her body, but it did nothing
to shut off her mind. She lay awake, listening as she stared at the
clock, wishing for relief.

6:30 A.M.

The time they'd gotten up at the ranch. Haven climbed out of
bed after the music stopped and wiped the tears from her face. She
quietly slipped into the library and wandered along the tall stacks,
running her fingertips along the spines of the books. She kept the
light off, but the window let in enough of a glow for her to see. A

strange sense of peace settled over her. For the first time in a long time—possibly ever—Haven almost felt safe.

Almost.

She walked to the window and gazed out, the sky lightening as the sun rose. The backyard was lush and green, trees scattered throughout the clearing with the edge of the forest a few hundred yards away. Haven wondered how far the trees went and which direction the closest town was, how long it would take someone to get there on foot.

Eventually, a quiet cough warned her she was no longer alone. Carmine strolled toward the stairs with a white bandage on his head that hadn't been there yesterday. The sight of him made something inside of Haven twist.

His gaze shifted to her, and he jumped, grabbing his chest. "Christ, what are you doing?"

"Just looking," she said, motioning toward the window.

"In the dark? You couldn't turn on a light?"

She tore her eyes from his. "Sorry."

"It's fine," he said. "Just try to make some noise next time. You're worse than a damn cat sneaking around. Maybe you need a bell."

Traitorous tears formed. *Don't let him see you cry,* she silently chanted. "I'll try."

"Who are you, anyway? What are you doing here?"

"Haven," she said quietly, peeking at him.

He gazed at her peculiarly. His eyes were bloodshot, dark bags under them. "Heaven? No, this definitely isn't Heaven. But I get why you're confused, since I'm standing in front of you." She stared at him, and he cracked a smile. "I'm kidding. Well, kinda . . . I have been told I've taken a girl to Heaven a time or two."

"Haven, not Heaven," she said, louder than before. Nothing about the conversation made sense to her. "My name's Haven. It means—"

"I know what it means." His sharp voice cut her off. She recoiled from the tone and pressed her back against the cold glass of the window. His moods changed too quickly for her to get a read on his frame of mind. "So, what happened to you? I mean, no offense, but you're kinda fucked up. Looks like you've been to Hell and back."

She reached up to touch her bruised face when it dawned on her what he meant. "I fell."

"You fell? If you don't wanna tell me, say so. No need for a bullshit response."

"Honestly, I fell! I tried to, uh . . . I was . . ."

"You don't have to explain. It's none of my business, anyway."

"But I did fall," she insisted. He still didn't look convinced, but she wasn't sure what else she could say. She pointed to his bandage. "What happened to you?"

He touched his injury like she'd done and shrugged. "I fell."

"Did you really?"

"No," he said, laughing as he disappeared down the stairs.

She frowned. "But I did."

When Carmine was ten years old, his father brought home a cat, its fur scraggly and tail chopped off. It infested the house with fleas and clawed up the furniture. Two weeks later the cat disappeared. Carmine never asked what happened to it. Frankly, he didn't care.

When he was fourteen, it was two dogs. The first was a little ankle biter with kinky yellow fur and three legs. It pissed all over the house before chewing up Vincent's favorite shoes. It didn't last a week. The second dog was a pit bull with one eye and deformed ears. His father tied it up in the backyard, and it barked all night, keeping them awake. Carmine could barely function in school the next day, and when he got home, the dog was gone.

So Carmine wished he was shocked when his father brought home a girl, but he wasn't. He figured he was just picking up strays again. But Carmine could tell something was different, and he didn't know what to make of it. His father was buying the girl things. He hadn't even bought the last dog any food.

That fact weighed heavily on him as he strolled down the

stairs. He told himself it was sheer curiosity fueling his thoughts, but the truth was, in just one day, the strange girl had gotten under his skin. He couldn't pinpoint why or what to do about it, but he didn't like the nagging feeling in the pit of his stomach. It irritated him, keeping him awake all night long, like a tiny little hammer chipping away at his insides. *Fucking conscience.*

He paused on the second floor in front of his father's office. "Hey, do you want me to—?"

"No."

Vincent's sharp voice made Carmine stop midsentence. "You didn't let me finish. I was gonna ask—"

"I don't need you to finish," Vincent said, remaining hunched over his laptop with his reading glasses low on his nose. "I don't want you to do anything for me."

"But what about the—?"

"Don't worry about it." Vincent laughed humorlessly. "Not like you'd actually worry about it. You don't care about anything that doesn't benefit you."

"That's not true. I care about—"

"No, you don't."

"Christ, can I get out a full sentence? I'm trying to help."

"I don't need your help," Vincent said, shaking his head. "I asked you to do one thing, and you couldn't do it. Lesson learned, son. I now know I can't count on you."

Ouch. The list.

"I forgot," he said. "I'll make it up to you."

"It's too late. I already asked someone else."

"Who?"

"Jen."

He grimaced. "Why her?"

"Well, she knows the sorts of things girls need, since she is one."

With some effort, Carmine refrained from making a crack about Jen's age, but he couldn't hold back his opinion entirely. "If by that you mean they need birth control and a heavy dose of penicillin, I agree."

Vincent shot him a disapproving look. "You can't judge, given the company you keep."

"True, but I'm not exactly role model material, am I? Would you want me doing the shopping?"

"Absolutely not," he said. "You'd come home with underwear no bigger than dental floss."

"And you think Jen won't? She doesn't even wear underwear."

Vincent glared at him. "Aren't you late for school?"

"Whatever."

He turned to walk away, but his father called after him. "If you really want to make it up to me, there's something you can do."

Carmine glanced back at him. "What?"

"Stay out of trouble."

"I'll try, but I'm pretty sure wreaking havoc is in my genes, Dad."

———

An hour and a half later, Carmine waltzed into his second period classroom and disrupted the American history teacher, Mrs. Anderson, in the middle of a lecture. She smiled curtly. "Mr. DeMarco, you're just in time to give your presentation on the Battle of Gettysburg."

He groaned, having forgotten all about them having oral presentations today. She motioned toward the front of the room, and he begrudgingly took his place as she sat behind her desk. "You can begin any time."

"Uh, the battle happened in Pennsylvania. It was, like, 1800s."

Mrs. Anderson corrected him, "1863."

"Yeah, what she said. General Lee led his army up from the South; they met the North in Gettysburg. A bunch of people died on both sides, hundreds of thousands."

"Tens of thousands."

"Same difference," he said. "The South lost and the North won. Abraham Lincoln came and gave the Emancipation Proclamation."

"The Gettysburg Address," Mrs. Anderson said. "The Emancipation Proclamation was delivered six months before the battle."

He gave an exaggerated sigh. "Who's giving the report here?"

She waved her hand. "Proceed."

"Like I said, the North won. The slaves were all freed. *Hurrah, hurrah.* The end."

He bowed jokingly, and everyone laughed as Mrs. Anderson shook her head. "Did you even read the material?"

"Of course I did."

"Who was the leader of the North?"

"Lincoln."

"No, he was the president."

"Yes, which means he was the fucking leader of everyone."

Mrs. Anderson's face clouded with anger. *Oops.* "You won't use that language in my classroom."

"Could've fooled me," he said. "I thought I already did."

A collective gasp resonated among his classmates as Mrs. Anderson stood, and Carmine started toward the door before the words could come from her mouth. "Principal's office," he muttered, mocking her at the same time she said it.

In no rush to see the principal again, Carmine headed out of a side exit, going for his car in the student parking lot instead.

The house was silent when Carmine made it home. He headed to the third floor and paused at the top of the stairs. In the library, in the same spot she'd been hours earlier, stood Haven. She stared out into the backyard with a vacant expression, her arms wrapped around her chest.

He cleared his throat to get her attention, and she flinched but didn't look his way. After a moment, he strolled over and stood beside her. Her body grew rigid as she held her breath, tension rolling off of her when their arms brushed together. The simple contact wouldn't have registered with him if not for her reaction. "Have you even moved today?"

"Yes."

He waited for her to elaborate, but no more words came. It wasn't until then that he realized she had on his shirt and pants, vaguely recalling his father taking them from his room. "You're wearing my clothes."

Carmine didn't think it was possible, but she managed to grow tenser. "I can take them off."

He stifled a laugh. "You're offering to take off your clothes for me?"

"*Your* clothes. I have none of my own."

And just like that, she made him feel a twinge of guilt. She'd have had clothes if he had done what his father asked. "What happened to whatever you came here in?"

"They were bloody, so Dr. DeMarco got rid of them."

"Whose blood?"

"Mine."

He tilted his head and stared at her. There was something strange about the way she stood motionless but still managed to seem like she was fidgeting. It made him uneasy.

"Keep the clothes," he said, wanting away from her to clear his head. He didn't like feeling uncomfortable in his house. "I'm gonna take a nap, Heaven."

"Haven," she corrected him.

"I know," he said. "I kinda like Heaven, though."

She turned to him, their eyes meeting for the first time since he'd walked in. "Me, too."

Despite Carmine's fierce protectiveness over his belongings, he wasn't careful about what he did with things. His bedroom was cluttered, everything haphazardly strewn around the floor. Shoes were scattered among heaps of dirty clothes, his hamper sitting empty in the corner of the room. His desk was covered with papers and books, a laptop buried somewhere in the mess.

It never bothered him. He was used to it, nothing about his life neat or tidy. He felt safe tucked into the chaos, surrounded by the things only he controlled. It was that he craved—control over his life—because it was the one thing Carmine never had.

A loud succession of bangs pulled Carmine from his nap, and he staggered to the door to find his father there. Vincent barged into the room, stumbling over some stuff lying on the floor. Grumbling, he kicked it out of the way. "Where are your keys?"

Carmine rubbed his eyes, his guard going up with someone in his personal space. "What?"

"Your car keys," Vincent said as he started searching through the desk, furiously pushing things around and tossing half of it on the floor.

"What the hell do you want my keys for?"

"Just give them to me!" Vincent opened the top right drawer and grabbed Carmine's wallet. Fumbling through it, he pulled out the silver American Express credit card and shoved it into his pocket before tossing the wallet aside, going right back to searching.

Carmine's blood boiled. "What do you think you're doing?"

"I tried to be your friend," Vincent said. "I cut you some slack, hoping it was a phase, but you only got worse. So I sent you away. After what you did last year, so help me God, I hoped you'd get the message. But no, you come back and start the cycle all over again. The fighting, the back talking, the disrespect . . . I can't take it anymore."

"What the hell did I do?"

"The better question would be what *didn't* you do." He slammed a drawer and grabbed the bottom one, but it wouldn't budge. "What's in here?"

Carmine didn't answer, watching as his father yanked on it.

"Where's the key to open it, Carmine?"

"You're not getting it. You're not getting *any* of my keys."

Vincent stood up straight at his words. "I am getting your keys. You're on restriction. You'll go nowhere but to school, and you'll stay there. No more cutting class. You'll do your work, you'll watch your mouth, you'll keep your hands to yourself, and when that last bell rings, you'll come straight home. Nothing else!"

"I can't," he said. "I have football."

"You don't tell me what you can't do. I tell you!"

Carmine clenched his hands into fists. "So you're gonna take football from me?"

"You brought this upon yourself."

Carmine narrowed his eyes as his father moved from the desk to the dresser. "I'm just living the life you gave me!"

"You can't blame me for this," Vincent said, opening the top dresser drawer. Carmine groaned as he pulled out his set of keys. "Your brother turned out fine."

"My brother didn't go through what I went through! But you know what? I don't care. Go ahead and take football. You might as well. I've lost everything else because of you!"

There was a moment, when those contemptuous words hung in the air between them, that it seemed like time stopped. It was a low blow, and Carmine almost felt guilty when he saw the hurt in his father's eyes. "You'll always blame me."

"You're damn right I will," Carmine said. "Give me my keys back."

"No."

Every ounce of sensibility Carmine had slipped away when his father turned his back to him. "If you don't give me my keys, I'll call the police."

Vincent turned back around so fast the movement startled Carmine. "You wouldn't."

"I would."

"You'd risk everything over a car?"

"Yes," he said. "You would, too, if it was all you had left."

That flicker of hurt returned but faded as fast as before. Vincent threw the keys at Carmine, hitting him in the chest with them. "Keep the car, and go play your precious football, but the credit card's mine."

"I don't care. I don't need your money."

Vincent laughed dryly. "We'll see about that."

———————

A dozen overflowing shopping bags littered the bedroom floor, splashes of brilliant color against the dreary carpet. Dr. DeMarco had brought them in, saying they were necessities, but Haven had gone her whole life without so much stuff. "All of this is for me?"

"Yes." Dr. DeMarco stood in the doorway behind her, rocking on his heels. He was irate, though she wasn't sure why. "If you find there's something missing, let me know."

Haven mumbled her thanks as he left, leaving her alone with her new belongings. She unpacked carefully, hanging the clothes in the closet and putting the bathroom items away. Used to having a bar of white soap, she had no idea what things like bath salts and pumice stones were for. She found a brush, though, and ran it through her hair, cringing as she snagged on the massive knots.

She changed into some fresh clothes, taking off what belonged to Carmine, before heading downstairs to start dinner. Cooking hadn't been her main job in Blackburn, as her mama usually worked in the kitchen, but Haven had helped her whenever she got the chance.

Cooking, according to her mama, was an art. Recipes and instructions were unnecessary, because the best meals were made with intuition and heart. Her mama always put her all into her food, even if she hadn't been allowed to taste it. It was a trait Haven had picked up, one that was coming in handy as she stood in the DeMarco's kitchen.

Dr. DeMarco walked in as she finished a pot of spaghetti, and she stood back, nervously awaiting his reaction. He scanned the meal before nodding. "Will you be eating with us?"

Instinctively, she shook her head.

"You don't have to, but I do insist you eat something every day. I won't allow you to starve under my roof."

Even something as generous as offering food sounded like an order coming from him.

4

Living in Blackburn hadn't been easy for Haven, with an over-abundance of work and a lack of food, but she always found a way to get by. It was a dismal life, but it had been hers, and it was the only one she'd ever known.

Durante, on the other hand, with its slow pace and down time, intimidated her.

By the third day, she fell into a routine. She cleaned during the day and cooked at night before hiding away until everyone went to bed. She'd slip downstairs then and eat something in the dark dining room, before retreating to the bedroom. She'd climb into bed, the music always starting not long after. She wasn't sure where it came from but the sound of it would ease her to sleep, and she'd stay there until everyone left the house for the day.

While easier, little things knocked her off-kilter. The strong mint of real toothpaste, hot bathing water, and eating with silverware were small amenities, but each made her stumble a bit. She had been deprived of things everyone else took for granted. Even wearing shoes made her feet hurt. She didn't like them a bit.

It was a few minutes past three on her third day when Haven encountered Dominic again. He came into the house and dropped a backpack on the floor before taking a seat in the family room. She considered fleeing upstairs, but that made her feel guilty. He'd been overwhelmingly kind to her.

She stepped into the family room, nervously picking at her brittle fingernails. "Can I do something for you?"

Dominic shook his head. "I'm cool."

"Are you sure? There has to be something I can do."

"Uh . . . I could always eat something, I guess."

She smiled. "Eat what?"

"Surprise me."

Haven headed for the kitchen and made a peanut butter and grape jelly sandwich before grabbing a paper towel. She walked back into the family room, and Dominic took it. "You seriously didn't have to do this."

She averted her gaze. "But you made me one . . ."

She went to the kitchen before he could respond and wiped down the counters. A little while later, as she defrosted chicken for dinner, she spotted Dominic lugging his hamper downstairs. She stepped into the foyer, directly in his path. "Can I get that for you?"

He laughed. "You're offering to do my laundry?"

"Yes."

Dominic hesitated but let go of the hamper so Haven could pull it to the laundry room. He followed, pausing in the doorway. "Look, Twinkle Toes, I don't know who you are . . ."

She chimed in. "I'm Haven."

"Haven. The point is I make it a habit to stay out of my father's dealings. It gives me plausible deniability, which means I have no idea what's going on with this"—he waved his hands all around them—"situation. The way I see it, since you're staying here, it's only right for me to be hospitable. So if I get you a sandwich, don't feel like you have to make it up to me. It's just a sandwich."

She said nothing, but he was wrong. It wasn't just a sandwich. It was more than that to her.

"And I appreciate the offer to help with my laundry. Thanks, Haven."

He walked away as she whispered, "No, thank *you*."

———

Dinner was ready again at a quarter to seven, and Haven kept it warm as she folded Dominic's clothes. The front door opened while she was in the laundry room, and she stepped out to greet Dr. DeMarco.

Was she supposed to? She wasn't sure.

"Smells terrific in here," he said.

"Thank you, sir. The food's ready."

"Great. Carmine should be home from football practice in a few minutes."

Her pulse quickened at the mention of Carmine. She hadn't seen him since their awkward encounter in the library, and she wasn't sure she wanted to see him so soon again.

She set the table, placing the food in the center for them to serve themselves, before grabbing Dominic's hamper and heading upstairs. She made it to the second floor when the front door swung open, Carmine's voice hitting her instantly. "*Cazzo*, what smells so good?"

She smiled to herself and resumed walking, placing Dominic's clothes outside his bedroom door before shutting herself away to hide.

———

The next evening, Dr. DeMarco arrived home as Haven was looking for something to make for dinner. "I forgot to tell you. You have the night off."

She closed the pantry door. "Okay."

"It's Friday, so the boys will be at the football game, and I'll be gone this weekend on business."

Confusion set in. He was leaving? "Are you sure you don't want me to make you something before you go?"

"Positive." He reached out, and she flinched, but it didn't discourage him from grasping her shoulder. "Come with me. I want to show you something."

She followed him into the family room, where he picked up a cordless telephone. "I had a phone installed in case you need anything when I'm away. Speed dial number one goes directly to my cell phone. If I don't answer and it's an emergency, speed dial number two is Dominic."

"Is Carmine number three?" The words flew from her mouth before she had enough sense to restrain them.

"Yes, but any trouble you encounter won't be as bad as the trouble that follows my youngest. So if you need anything, call the first two."

"Okay." She stared at the phone. "How do I do that?"

Sighing, Dr. DeMarco gave some quick instructions on how to place a call. A flurry of thoughts hit her as she listened, but Dr. DeMarco cut them off. "I'll know any time it's used, so don't get any bright ideas like calling 911."

Her brow furrowed. "Who's 911?"

He stared at her as if he thought she might be joking. "Let's just say calling 911 is the last thing you want to do, child."

Dr. DeMarco left, and those words ran through Haven's mind as she wandered the empty house. She ended up in the family room after a while, standing in front of the white telephone again.

Picking it up, she turned it on like Dr. DeMarco had shown her. She hit the 9 button before pressing the number 1, her finger hovering over the 1 again. She stood there, her heart pounding rapidly, before pressing the button to turn off the phone.

She did it three more times before placing the phone into its cradle and leaving the room, too frightened to press the last number.

The sun was setting when Haven ended up in the library. She came across some paper and swiped a few pieces, finding a pencil before eagerly running to her room. She lay down in bed and sketched, her mama's face emerging on the paper. With no pictures, Haven was desperately afraid she would forget what her mama looked like, afraid her memory would fade with time.

Drawing came naturally to Haven. When she was little, around the age of seven, her first mistress, Monica, gave her paper and crayons. It was the first time she'd given her anything, and it turned out to be the last, but Haven cherished the gift until the last shred of crayon disappeared.

As she grew older, she'd sneak supplies from the ranch house, but afterward destroyed all evidence so no one would find out. She usually folded the sketches and stuck them in her pocket, burying the papers the first chance she got.

Haven lost track of time as she immersed herself in the drawing of her mama, and it was nearing midnight when the sound of music captured her attention. It was earlier than the other nights. Curious, she set the drawing aside and crept to the door to peek out.

Carmine sat in the library, holding a tan acoustic guitar. Darkness obstructed Haven's view of his face, but the glow from the moonlight illuminated his hands as he plucked the strings.

She took a few steps forward, entranced as the music smoothed out and grew louder. It swirled all around her, goose bumps springing up as the melody seeped into her skin. Her stomach fluttered and limbs tingled, warmth spreading throughout her body. She closed her eyes, reveling in the foreign sensation, until the music stopped.

Haven's eyes snapped back open, and she could see his face then, still partially encased in the shadows. He frowned, staring at her with questions in his eyes, but she had no answers to give.

Turning on her heel, Haven ran back into the room and closed the door, pressing her back against it as the music started up once more.

———

The next morning, Carmine woke up earlier than usual and grabbed a bowl of cereal, his footsteps faltering in the family room. Dominic sat on the couch reading a *Sports Illustrated*, and Haven was beside him, neither of them speaking.

Before Carmine could utter a single word, Haven leaped to her feet and scurried away. He watched her retreating form before taking the seat she'd vacated. "She acts like I'm diseased and she's gonna catch something by coming near me."

Dominic nodded. "I noticed."

"I haven't done anything." He paused. "I don't think, anyway."

"You don't realize how abrasive you come off," Dominic said. "It's the way you look at people."

Carmine shrugged. There wasn't anything he could do about that. "Whatever. There's obviously something wrong with her."

"Have you taken the time to ask her what it might be?"

"Haven't had a chance," he said. "Like I said, she runs from me."

"Well, maybe if you took an interest in her, she wouldn't act sketchy around you."

"Is that what you did—took an interest?" Carmine asked. "I'm not sure Tess would be happy about that."

Dominic shoved him, spilling some of his cereal. "I was nice to her, bro. You should try it."

Carmine brushed some of the stray Lucky Charms from his lap, glaring at the wet patch where the milk had soaked into his pants. "Asshole."

———

Vincent DeMarco was an easily recognized man. The people in Durante knew him as the talented doctor and the dedicated single father, the wealthy bachelor women rigorously pursued. He'd accumulated a few wayward gray hairs, but he looked younger than his forty years. He was like his father that way. Antonio DeMarco had died at fifty when he looked more like a youthful thirty-five.

Genetics, Vincent thought, was a peculiar thing.

Although he was well known, few people saw the man behind the mask. Vincent felt like he lived two different lives, both equally real yet at odds with each other. He liked to believe he was the family man that others saw, but he was also deeply committed to a different type of family.

A family not bonded by genetics, instead forged by spilled blood and sworn oaths. LCN, the government called it, short for *La Cosa Nostra*, but it was known by many different names: *la famiglia, borgata*, outfit, syndicate. It all meant the same. The Mafia.

He'd taken a step back from the life years ago, moving away from Chicago and the center of the action, but there was no leaving the organization once it had you in its brutal grasp. He was kept on as an unofficial *consigliere* to the Don, Salvatore Capozzi. Vincent's job was to play the middleman, to give advice when asked and come when called, and he did this obediently, taking care of whatever needed to be handled. But just because he was good at what he did, didn't mean he enjoyed it.

Vincent sat in the smoky den of the mansion in Lincoln Park, holding a full glass of scotch as he listened to the swarm of men debate business. There were twenty of them, but Vincent wasn't sure why half were there. They had no say in how things were run, some of them so new they hadn't earned their buttons. There was no reason to trust them—no reason to confide in them—considering there was no blood on their hands.

Not to say he *wanted* them to be murderers. He envied their clear consciences and wished he could warn them all to turn away. Get out while they still could, because someday it would be too late . . . and that someday would probably end with a lengthy prison sentence.

Or a hollow-point bullet to the brain. Vincent hadn't decided which outcome would be worse.

But he couldn't warn anyone. He'd sworn an oath to put the organization first, and if the organization wanted these dime-a-dozen thugs, Vincent would deal with his ill feelings silently. He'd initiated young—one of the youngest made men in history. Usually guys struggled for decades trying to prove themselves worthy, most never surviving long enough to see it happen. But not Vincent. He'd slipped right in the door while his father was in control.

He wasn't the youngest to do business with them, though. Kids were recruited fresh from high school, molded into vindictive soldiers to do the family's bidding. The young ones incurred all the risk, while those at the top lavished in the fruits of their labor.

Blood money. Hundreds had died to pay for the mansion in which they sat.

"We cannot tolerate these things. They are savages."

Giovanni was speaking, his thick accent making Vincent strain to pay attention. Sicilian by birth, he'd immigrated to America a decade before and moved up in rank to become their highest-producing *Capo*. Some of his crew was present, sitting off to the side. Vincent had a hard time remembering the names of the *soldati*, but one he was familiar with was Nunzio.

Nunzio had been lurking around for years. They called him Squint because of the way his eyes always seemed to be half-closed, his face frozen in a roguish scowl. He kept his head buzzed, a light dusting of brown hair showing, and his eyes were the dull color of cracked earth. The Don's brother had taken him in as a baby, so Salvatore had a soft spot for the boy.

The men argued back and forth as Vincent swirled the scotch around in his glass, having no intention of drinking it. He remained quiet until the unmistakable voice of the Don chimed in, speaking directly to him. "What do you think, Vincent?"

I think I want to go home. "I think being hasty will backfire. I don't like the way the Russians conduct business, but they've yet to hurt any of our people."

"They will," Giovanni warned.

"If they do, it'll be handled," Vincent said, "but until that time comes, who are we to police another group?"

Vincent looked across the room at where the Don sat in his favorite chair. In his late sixties, Sal was shaped like a balloon and sounded perpetually full of helium. He'd been the underboss when

Vincent's father ran things and succeeded rule after he died. Antonio had dubbed him Salamander. "If you scare a salamander, he'll drop his tail and run," he had said. "No skin off his back. Two weeks later, he's good as new."

Sal mulled over Vincent's words. "You're right. Maybe they'll take themselves out with their stupidity."

Squint laughed dryly, but tried to cover it with a forced cough when everyone looked his way. The guy beside him seemed annoyed by the outburst, another *soldato* whose name eluded Vincent. He thought it might be Johnny, one of about a hundred other Johnnys running around the streets. His looks certainly fit the name—generic, undistinguishable. Another number in the crowd, easily replaced, never missed. A tail, Vincent thought. Sal would drop him and keep going.

When Sal dismissed them with a wave of the hand, Vincent was the first out of his seat. He dumped the scotch and headed for the door, but Giovanni cut him off. "I think we are making a mistake, Doc. It will do us no good ignoring them now."

"We're not ignoring them," Vincent said. "We're just not going to instigate a fight. The last thing we need is violence on our streets over things that have nothing to do with us."

Vincent headed for his rental car when Giovanni's voice rang out once more. "Just because we do not know of anything does not mean they have not violated us. There will be war."

5

Carmine pulled the last clean shirt off the hanger in his closet. The small piles of laundry had morphed into mountains, every piece of clothing he owned now dirty on the floor. Usually it wouldn't have gotten that far, as he would have taken them to the local laundry service, but he had a problem—he was broke.

He strolled through the library to the other side of the floor and grabbed Dominic's doorknob, his brow furrowing when it wouldn't turn. He could hear voices inside and pounded on the door.

Dominic opened it. "What?"

Carmine noticed Tess lying across the bed in one of Dominic's shirts, and cringed at the mental image of what he'd interrupted. "I need some money. My clothes are dirty."

"You want money?"

"Yeah, a loan."

"You have a funny way of asking, bro," Dominic said. "And how are you going to pay me back when you don't have a job?"

Carmine shrugged. "I'll figure it out."

"Yeah, you will," Dominic said. "You'll figure out how to do your own damn laundry."

The door slammed in Carmine's face. Tess laughed inside the room as Carmine punched the wall before heading back to his bedroom. He grabbed his cell phone and dialed Dia's home number, breathing a sigh of relief when she answered. "What do you want, Carmine?"

"What makes you think I want something?"

"Because I know you," she said. "You don't call to chitchat."

He sighed. "My laundry needs done."

"You want me to do your laundry?"

"Yes. I don't know who else to ask."

"Well, how much money do you have?"

"None."

All he heard was the sound of laughter before Dia hung up.

Irritated, he picked up armfuls of clothes and tossed them in the hamper before dragging it downstairs. As soon as he reached the laundry room, he heard the humming, soft and sweet like a lullaby. Haven stood in front of the dryer, folding clothes. She glanced at him apprehensively as she quieted, her eyes darting from him to his overfull hamper. He lugged it into the room and opened the washing machine hatch, shoving all the clothes into it. It overflowed, and he had to push on them to get the door closed. He looked around for some detergent and caught Haven's eyes again as she gaped at him, holding a pair of pants.

He wasn't sure what her problem was, but he was too aggravated to deal with it. Another week had passed with her avoiding him, dodging from rooms before he could say hello.

"So, where's the soap?" he asked. "You know, the Tide or whatever we use around here?"

Haven reached behind her and opened a small cabinet, pulling out a jug of laundry detergent. Carmine opened the washer again as he took it from her, and he was about to pour it straight in when Haven sharply inhaled.

The intake of breath stalled him. "What?"

"Shouldn't you put in the water first?"

He wavered. "Should I?"

"I was taught to start it, put the soap in, and add laundry to the line."

"What line?"

"The line that tells you how far to fill the machine."

"There's a limit?" He set the jug of detergent down before pulling his clothes back out. Haven returned to folding as he glared at the front of the washer. "Where's the start button?"

"There isn't a button," she said. "You choose your setting and pull the dial."

Her nonchalance at doing laundry annoyed him. "What exactly is my *setting*? It looks to me like the setting is the goddamn laundry room and the plot is I don't know how to fucking turn this thing on."

Her brow furrowed. "Should I . . . do it for you?"

The question caught him off guard. "I don't know."

She reached over and turned the dial to colors. It filled with water, and she measured some detergent before putting in half his clothes. She worked briskly, pushing the hamper with the rest of the laundry off to the side before turning back to folding hers.

Carmine stood there, anxious, unsure of what to say. All week long he had invented conversations in his mind, shit he'd say to her when she stopped eluding him, and now that she was in front of him, he drew a blank. "So, you're good at that shit."

Awkward.

She smiled softly. "I've been doing it my whole life."

"Yeah, well, this is a first for me," he muttered. "So, who are you?"

She looked confused. "I told you my name."

"I know, but that doesn't tell me who you are. Do you have a last name?"

She continued to fold her laundry. "Antonelli, maybe."

"Maybe?"

"I don't really have one, but that's his."

He cocked his head to the side, studying her. "Whose?"

"My master's."

"What do you mean your master?"

"You know, my master where I came from."

No, he didn't know. "Where did you come from?"

"Blackburn. California, I think."

"You think? Did you live there long?"

She nodded. "Until I came here."

"And you're not sure where it is?" He was stunned. "Did you hate the place or something?"

"Depends on what you mean by that."

"Explain it to me."

She sighed. "I didn't like my master, but I had someone there who understood me."

"What about here?"

"Here I have food to eat and clothes to wear."

"But no one understands you?"

She shook her head. "My masters treat me nicely, though."

"Whoa." Masters? That rubbed him the wrong way. "Why the hell do you keep saying that? It sounds wrong, like you're a servant or a slave or something."

She peeked at him as he spoke. "Aren't I?"

"How . . . ? What the fuck?"

"It isn't bad here," she quickly explained. "People like me wish for the kind of place where they don't have to fear paying for someone else's mistakes with their life."

"And wherever you came from, you worried you'd be killed for no reason?"

"No, there's always a reason," she said. "Just not one you caused."

Carmine was taken aback by how much he understood the strange girl. She may not have seen it, but Carmine knew what it was like to pay for others' mistakes. He knew what it was like to live knowing your life could end because of something that had absolutely nothing to do with you.

But *masters*? *That* he didn't get.

She finished folding her clothes in silence before making a move to leave, but Carmine remained in the doorway, blocking her only exit.

"Do you need anything else?" she asked.

"I need to know why you hate me."

Her brow furrowed. "What do you mean?"

"You run from me; you won't look at me or talk to me. The only reason you're doing it now is because you don't think you have a choice. You have no problem being around my brother, so why the problem with me? Am I that horrible?" She stared at him as he rambled in frustration, her muteness putting him more on edge. "Christ, now I'm fucking yelling at you, like that's going to fix anything. Is that what's wrong? Is it my temper?"

"I don't hate you. I just . . . don't understand you."

Something about those words was like a dagger striking his chest. No one had understood him before, but he wanted her to. He needed her to, because for the first time in years, he wondered if someone finally could.

The ringing of his phone thwarted his response. He pulled it out of his pocket, and she took the opportunity to slip past him.

"Haven," he called, stepping out of the laundry room behind her. "I think you'll find we're a lot alike if you take the chance to get to know me."

He turned away from her to answer the call. "Yeah, Dia?"

"I shouldn't have hung up," Dia said. "Do you still need your laundry done?"

"No, I got it," he said. "Someone showed me how to do it."

He realized, as he glanced into the laundry room, that he hadn't even thanked Haven for her help.

———————

Carmine burst into his father's office and plopped down in the chair in front of the desk. Vincent put down the medical journal he'd been flipping through and removed his glasses. "Come in, son. You're not interrupting at all."

Not in the mood for a lecture, Carmine dived in to what was on his mind. "Why's that girl here?"

Vincent sighed. "Haven't we already had this conversation? You said you didn't care."

"I care now." His own words caught him off guard. Did he?

Vincent eyed him suspiciously. "Why?"

Good fucking question. "She says some weird shit."

"I wasn't aware you cared to talk to her."

"Yeah, well, she's staying in my house . . ."

"*My* house," Vincent corrected him. "Your grandfather left this place to me when he died. And the girl's here because I brought her here."

"Willingly? Because it doesn't seem like she's on vacation, cooking dinner and cleaning up after people. She didn't even own anything."

"You're right—it's no vacation for her—but it's a big step up from her last home."

"California," Carmine said. "Or so she thinks. She lived with a master who could've killed her."

Vincent's eyes widened. "I'm surprised she told you so much."

"I asked, and apparently she feels like she can't deny anyone anything when they ask."

"Oh, that's where you're wrong," Vincent said. "If the child didn't want to tell you, she wouldn't. She might be trained to serve, but she knows how to keep secrets. She wouldn't have survived as long as she has otherwise."

Carmine had no idea how to respond to that. "So, what? She's going to stay here indefinitely?"

"Yes," Vincent said, putting his glasses back on. "And she isn't to leave the house without my permission, so get used to her."

"Get used to her? Really? There's seriously something wrong with the way we live."

Vincent shook his head. "I know how you can be, so unless you need more help with your laundry, I suggest staying away from her."

"How do you know she helped me with my laundry?"

Vincent motioned toward the computer monitor on his desk. Carmine realized he'd watched the exchange on the surveillance cameras. There were a few in the house, mostly in the common areas. "I wasn't watching because of you. There still aren't any cameras in the bedrooms."

"And it better stay that way," Carmine said.

"I don't want to see what goes on in that pigsty any more than you want me to see it," Vincent said, picking up his medical journal again. "Just be mindful of what I said. I'd appreciate it if you were polite and didn't try to meddle. The last thing she needs is you making things harder for her."

Carmine stood. "In other words, don't be myself."

"Precisely, son."

Carmine arrived at school Monday morning to find Tess and Dominic arguing in the parking lot. He climbed out of the car as Dia strolled over, plopping down on the hood of his Mazda. He shoved her off, and she laughed as she took a seat on her clunker instead.

"What's gotten into those two?"

Dia shrugged while Tess laughed dryly, pushing past Dominic. "What's gotten in to us is the fact that your father's an idiot!"

"Knock it off, Tess," Dominic said. "It's not that big of a deal."

Tess glowered at him. "Dr. DeMarco moved a teenage girl in, and you not only fail to tell me, your girlfriend, but when I find out you say it's not a big deal?"

Dia leaned toward Carmine. "There's a girl living with you?"

"Yes, but she's blowing it out of proportion," Carmine said. "She's just some girl."

"Just some girl living in a house with Mr. I'll-fuck-anything-that-walks!" Tess said.

"Give me a break," Carmine said. "Don't act like you're upset because of me. It's not my fault you don't trust your boyfriend."

Tess gave him the middle finger before storming off, but Dominic stood there, for once not following.

"That was interesting," Dia said. "You're not really banging the girl, are you?"

Dominic chimed in. "They don't even get along."

"It's not that we don't get along," Carmine said. "It's just she runs every time I come near her."

Dia laughed. "If you'd relax, I'm sure she'd come around."

"You've never met her," Carmine said. "Hell, you didn't know she existed until a minute ago. You aren't exactly an expert on the subject."

"She's just some girl, right? We're not that complicated. Besides, I'm not saying you should bang her, but there's nothing wrong with making friends."

Carmine rolled his eyes. "No one says *banging* anymore, Dia. The nineties are over. People fuck."

"Not always," she said. "Sometimes they make love."

"Not me."

———

Forty-five minutes later, Carmine was strolling through the school's corridor toward his second-period class when he spotted his brother in the library. Dominic sat at a computer, furiously typing away at the keys. Curiosity grabbed Carmine and he slipped through the glass doors into the room.

"Christ, it's bright in here." Carmine shielded his eyes as his voice echoed through the silent room, but no one was around to scold him.

"First time in the library?" Dominic asked.

"I've been in here for English class," he said defensively. "I even checked out a book once."

"Which book?"

"*The Count of Monte Cristo*. I had to do a report last year."

"So you actually read it?"

"Yeah," he said. "I read the first page before I rented the movie."

Dominic laughed but said nothing, too busy pulling up files on the computer. Carmine leaned against the desk beside him, trying to decipher what all the coding meant. "What are you doing?"

"Changing your grades for you, bro."

His eyes widened. "Really?"

"No, but I did look at them. You'll never make it out of high school at the rate you're going."

Carmine shook his head. "You have some nerve hacking the school's servers and going through people's records like this shit isn't illegal. And they say I'm the one who's gonna turn out like Dad."

"I don't intentionally hurt people, so you still have me there," Dominic said. "Besides, have you seen your disciplinary record?"

"I think the better question is have you seen it, Dom."

"You're damn right I have. It was like reading a true-crime novella. Your permanent high school record is longer than Uncle Corrado's arrest record, and that's saying a lot."

Their aunt Celia's husband, Corrado Moretti, had been arrested more times in his life than he had had birthdays, but none of the charges ever stuck. Whether it was a missing witness, a dirty judge, or a bribed juror, Corrado always found a way out of trouble.

A reporter once dubbed him the Kevlar Killer. No matter what he was hit with, he came out unscathed.

"Uncle Corrado's the Man of Steel," Dominic said. "Faster than a speeding bullet."

"Did you seriously just compare him to a superhero?"

"Yeah, guess I didn't think that one through."

Glancing at his watch, Carmine pushed away from the desk. "I have to get to history before Mrs. Anderson sends a search party out for me."

"Yeah, you do that," Dominic said. "From what I saw, you're not passing the class."

"You're really not gonna change my grade for me?"

"Sorry, no can do. What does Superman say? With great power comes great responsibility?"

Carmine smacked his brother on the back of the head as he walked past. "That's *Spider-Man,* dumbass."

———

Carmine got home after football practice that night in just enough time to see Haven bolt up the stairs. He washed his hands and went into the dining room where dinner waited, his father already bowing his head to pray when he sat down. "*Signore, benedici questi peccatori che essi mangiano la loro cene.*"

Lord, bless these sinners as they eat their dinners.

Carmine was eating before they could say, "Amen."

Vincent tried to make conversation during the meal, and Dominic humored him, but Carmine remained silent. It was well after dark when Vincent's pager went off, and he dismissed them, needing to head to work. Carmine made his way upstairs and hesitated when he saw Haven in the library, gazing out the window with her palm pressed against the smooth glass.

He expected her to flee, but she instead motioned toward the small flashes of light sparking in the darkness. "What are those things?"

Carmine turned to see if someone else was there, taken aback that she was attempting to talk to him. "Fireflies. Some people call them lightning bugs."

"Why do they glow?" she asked. "Is it so they can see?"

He strolled over to her. "I think it's how they talk to each other."

"Wow."

"You've never seen them before?"

She shook her head. "We didn't have any in Blackburn."

"Ah, well, we have plenty here," he said. "They're like flying beetles with asses that light up."

She smiled at his description. "They're beautiful."

"They're just bugs. Nothing special."

"They're alive," she said. "That makes them special."

He had no comeback for that. Haven continued to gaze out the window while he watched her, seeing the childlike wonder in her expression. She looked as if she were seeing the world for the first time, like she had been blind until now but suddenly could see. He wondered if she felt that way, too, if everything in front of her was brand-new.

He tried to think back to when he saw fireflies for the first time, but he could barely recall that point in his life. He vaguely remembered catching some in a jar once.

"Do you wanna see them up close?"

The words were out of his mouth before he realized what he was asking. He'd heard his father, but at the same time, he didn't see the harm.

She turned from the glass to look at him. "Could I?"

"Sure."

Excitement sparked in her eyes. The sight of it made Carmine's heart skip a beat. It had been years since he felt anything close to that, and for a moment, he wished he could steal it for himself.

"You mean go outside?"

"Yes."

"But I'm not allowed."

He shrugged. "Neither am I."

Technically true, since he was grounded, but he'd never let that stop him before.

"I'd like that," she said, pausing before adding, "If you're sure."

He smiled. She was trusting him. He wondered if maybe she shouldn't do that, but it was a vast improvement from avoiding him. "Wait here. I'll be back."

He ran down to the kitchen, glad his father had already left, and returned to the third floor after finding an empty mason jar. Haven stood in the same place, her hand still pressed to the glass.

"Come on," he said, heading to his bedroom. Turning on the light, he noticed she lingered outside the doorway, surveying the mess. "Are you coming in? I know it's a disaster . . ."

"Oh no, it's not that." She looked panicked. "I didn't know if I should."

"Well, we can't go out the door, because my father will find out. We have to go out up here."

Her brow furrowed. "From the third floor? How?"

"You'll see."

He watched her locked in an internal debate before ultimately taking a step into the room. Careful not to trip over any of his belongings, she made her way to where he stood. Carmine pulled up the blinds before shoving open the large window. It squeaked a bit but gave little resistance.

Haven gaped at it. "I didn't think the windows opened."

"They don't," he said. "Dom disabled this one from the system so I could pry it open and sneak out at night. My father's never caught on since it doesn't set off any alarms."

Carmine held the curtains aside, motioning for her to climb through, and she stepped out onto the small porch that wrapped around the floor. Carmine joined her, and she carefully followed him along the balcony to a massive sycamore tree. Thick branches extended toward the corner of the house, so close Haven touched some of the green leaves, the tips fading to brown with autumn on the horizon.

Carmine tossed the jar down from the balcony, holding his breath as it landed in the grass with a thud. Gripping the branch closest to him, he stepped over the banister and climbed into the tree. "Come on, it's easy."

She peeked over the edge. "I don't want to fall."

"You won't."

"You swear?"

He chuckled. "All the fucking time."

She hesitated before grabbing the branch like he'd done and pulling herself over the banister. Carmine expertly navigated the tree, having done it dozens of times, and Haven carefully followed his path. A minute after he jumped to the ground, she landed beside him on her feet.

"See, that wasn't so bad, huh?"

A hint of a smile graced her lips. "I didn't fall."

Carmine grabbed the jar as Haven wandered a few steps away, her eyes darting around. Fireflies continued to flash in the darkness, the brief glows illuminating her awestruck face. Her smile grew as she reached out for one, but she pulled her hand back quickly. "They won't hurt me, right?"

"Right," he said. "You're probably ten times more dangerous than fireflies are."

Dangerous. The word made his heart rate spike. Something told him this girl was a danger to his fucking sanity.

She gently captured a firefly in her palm and stared at it with awe as the bug ran across her hand and took off from the tip of her middle finger. Soft giggles erupted from her as it flew away, catching Carmine off guard. It was the first time he'd heard her laugh.

Shaking himself out of his stupor, he handed her the jar. "Here, catch a few."

Carmine sat down on the ground as she took off, chasing fireflies through the yard. He laughed as she fought to catch them, the little bugs evading her grasp. Soon her laughter mixed with his, her excited cheers sounding out in the night when she managed to wrangle some into the jar. She spun and twirled, jumped and ran; all the while a smile graced her lips.

As he watched, Carmine thought she looked different from the girl he'd encountered that first day. There was no awkwardness, the tension that radiated from her a distant memory. Out in the yard, under the shine of the moon, she seemed relaxed and carefree.

———

Haven sat down and spread out her legs, the lush grass tickling her feet. She inhaled deeply, the cool night air a far cry from the dusty shallow breaths she forced into her lungs growing up. It smelled different here, clean and crisp. Everything was green. She'd never given the color much thought before, but she realized it was more than something to see. It was a feeling, a taste, a smell. It was the dampness of the grass and the shelter of the trees. It was fresh. It was comforting. Green was happiness.

Green made her belly rumble, and the feeling terrified her.

The few trees she saw in Blackburn were barren, deformed sticks jutting from the ground, but here they were giant umbrellas of leaves towering above her.

She stared at the jar in her lap, the half-dozen fireflies trapped inside flickering at regular intervals. She found it strange the way they blinked in harmony, a silent melody she yearned to hear. "I wonder what they're saying," she said, shattering the silence that had settled between them.

Carmine pointed at the jar. "I'm pretty sure this one just told that one it had a nice glowy ass."

"And the others?"

"Ah, well, that one's jealous, because it wanted the one with the nice ass," he said, pointing again. "And the others are gossiping. You know—who did who, why, where, when, what-the-fuck."

"I didn't realize bugs were so scandalous."

He laughed. "It's nature. They can't help themselves."

She stared at the jar, having no idea what to make of it.

Carmine stood after a few minutes, brushing the grass from his pants. "We should head inside before we get caught. You can bring the bugs with you."

Shaking her head, she unscrewed the lid. "They should be free," she said quietly, watching as the fireflies flew away.

Carmine grabbed her hand, pulling her to her feet, and her fingertips tingled from his touch. The sensation alarmed her. It was like electricity under her skin, running through her veins and jolting her heart. Her pulse raced as she averted her gaze, not daring to look him in the eyes.

His eyes—green, like the grass and the trees.

Haven felt like she, too, was suddenly glowing.

6

Evasion became a way of life for Haven again during the next few weeks, but deep down she knew it couldn't last. As she headed downstairs one Friday to do her work, she heard the television playing in the family room, although everyone should have been gone for the day. Her pulse quickened. Every weekday she had been left alone until three o'clock. She didn't like her routine being disrupted.

Quietly, she walked to the family room and saw Dr. DeMarco sitting on the couch. He addressed her without even looking up. "Good morning, child."

Bewildered, she mumbled, "Good morning, Master."

Dr. DeMarco shook his head. "Calling me that is unnecessary. It makes me feel like you place me on the same level as Antonelli, and I like to think of myself as a better man than that."

"Sorry, sir."

"No need to apologize. Call me Vincent, if you'd like."

She was shocked he would ask her to use his first name. "Can I get you something?"

"No, I was waiting for you. I've been putting it off, but your checkup needs to be done today."

Her eyes widened.

"It shouldn't take long," he said, finally looking at her. "And on the bright side, you get to leave the house for a bit. You haven't been outside since you've gotten here."

Not true, but she didn't dare correct him.

He drove her to a small brick building about ten minutes away, a white sign reading DURANTE CLINIC adorning the front above the main entrance. Unlike the busy hospital, which could be seen from the parking lot, the clinic was dark and vacant, not a soul anywhere.

"They're closed today, so we shouldn't have any interruptions," Dr. DeMarco said as he unlocked the front door.

"What will we be doing?" she asked.

"Just the basics."

Haven didn't know what the basics were, and Dr. DeMarco didn't take the time to explain.

He ushered her into the building, her nerves growing with each step. They went straight to an exam room with a brown cushioned table, and Dr. DeMarco flicked on a single light. She stood in place as he explored the room, pulling out supplies and turning on machines. He grabbed her arm, wordlessly stabbing a needle into her vein. She continued to stand still while he filled vial after vial with her blood, every second that passed making her woozier.

She grew so light-headed she nearly fainted.

Dr. DeMarco weighed and measured her next before leading her to the exam table. "You're going to have to take off your clothes." She stared at him, fear coursing through her, and he sighed with frustration at her terrified expression. "It's going to happen whether you cooperate or not, and I'd prefer it be on good terms than from me forcing you."

Dr. DeMarco strolled over to the window as Haven carefully stripped and climbed up on the table. Her feet hung off the side, nowhere close to reaching the floor as she shielded herself with a flimsy paper gown, clinging to it as if it could protect her.

Dr. DeMarco spoke without turning around. "Lie back and scoot to the end of the table. Place your feet in the metal stirrups and try to relax."

She did as she was told, closing her eyes as the sound of his footsteps slowly neared.

"You're going to feel something cold down below," he explained, pulling a stool closer and sitting down as he slipped on a pair of latex gloves. "It'll be uncomfortable, but it'll be over quick."

She squeezed her eyes shut tighter when he touched her, a tear slipping through and falling down her nose. She counted in her head, trying to distract herself, and as soon as she reached ten he let go.

"You appear fine, as far as I can tell," he said, disposing of his gloves. Her vision blurred from the tears when she opened her eyes, but she could see Dr. DeMarco beside her. He injected her with a few syringes, some stinging worse than others, before he headed for the door. "Put your clothes on so we can leave. I'll wait for you in the hall."

Standing, she held on to the table as her legs shook, and redressed.

Haven lay in bed that night, listening to the soft music drifting in from the library. It was the same melody as every other time, one that usually lulled her to sleep, but tonight she couldn't relax. Her skin felt taut, her muscles strained and tensed as anger and disgust crept through her. Despite scrubbing and scrubbing in the shower, she still felt *dirty*.

She'd never been so confused before.

She'd kept her distance from Carmine, wanting the strange feelings for him to stop. She didn't get why her chest felt like it would burst when he spoke, why her skin got prickly whenever he came near, or why she felt dizzy when she heard his light laughter. She barely knew him—she'd made a point not to—but it didn't make a difference, because the feelings came anyway.

Grabbing some paper, Haven sketched a picture of Carmine, every detail of his face etched in her memory: the shape of his jaw, the curve of his lips, the arch of his eyebrows, and the angle of his nose. She remembered his eyes, the way they sparkled in the light.

He had some freckles on his nose and cheeks, and a small blemish on the right side of his bottom lip.

As she lay there, she found herself wondering how she'd noticed all of those things.

After she finished, she held the drawing up to look at it in the light. Something was off, the sketch flat and colorless. It didn't hold a fraction of the emotion the music carried.

Frustrated, she balled up the paper and tossed it aside.

———

Haven was avoiding him again . . . Carmine just couldn't figure out why.

He tried to wait it out, giving her time to relax, but he was low on patience. Insomnia plagued him, and as Carmine strolled downstairs the next afternoon, still exhausted and sore from his football game, he was determined it wasn't going to happen anymore.

Groggy, he hesitated in the foyer when Haven stepped into the doorway from the kitchen. He ran his hand through his messy hair, having not bothered to brush it. "What's up?"

"Nothing." She glanced around. "Should I be doing something?"

He shrugged. "You tell me."

"Are you hungry? I could make you some food."

"No."

"Do you need laundry done?"

"No."

"I've cleaned," she said. "I don't think I've forgotten anything."

"I wasn't implying you did. I was making conversation."

"Oh."

She continued to stand there, looking at him with apprehension. As the tension mounted, he regretted getting out of bed. "Look, let's watch a movie or something."

She seemed startled by his suggestion. "Okay."

"Is that an, 'Okay, I wanna watch a movie with you, Carmine,' or is it an, 'Okay, I'll do whatever the fuck you say because I think

I have to?' Because you can disagree with me, you know. You can even yell at me if it'll make you feel better, but don't say 'okay,' because I don't know what you mean by it."

"Okay."

They were getting nowhere. "Look, I'm gonna sit my ass down on the couch. Whether or not you join me is up to you."

He turned away when she spoke again. "Do you want something to drink?"

His footsteps stalled. "Uh, sure."

"What do you want?"

"Just a Cherry Coke will be fine."

"Cherry Coke?"

Sighing, he ran his hands down his face. It was too early for this. "Yeah, you know, it's cherry-flavored Coke. Hence the name, Cherry Coke."

She slipped into the kitchen as Carmine went to the family room and turned on a movie. He saw movement from the corner of his eye after a few minutes, and Haven stopped in front of him, purposely avoiding his gaze as she held out a glass of soda. He took it as she sat down beside him, keeping a bit of distance between them on the couch.

He surveyed the drink with confusion, wondering why she hadn't brought him the can, when he caught sight of the cherries floating in the glass. He took a sip of it, realizing she had *made* him a cherry Coke.

Dazed, he couldn't find the words to thank her. His mom had made them for him when he was a kid.

Haven watched the movie intently, pulling her feet up on the couch with her head cocked to the side. "Have you seen this?" Carmine asked.

She looked at him like it was a dumb question. "I haven't seen anything. This is the first time I've ever been invited to watch television."

His brow furrowed. "You don't watch TV?"

"I wasn't allowed."

"How the hell did you pass the time? Reading?"

"I wasn't allowed to do that, either. They didn't think it was appropriate."

He gaped at her. "Teachers constantly shove books down my throat, and you had people telling you reading was inappropriate?"

She smiled sadly. "They didn't want me to get any ideas."

"Ideas? How much harm could a book do?"

"A lot. They thought I'd get it in my head that the outside world was somewhere I belonged."

"The outside world? You make it sound like you were living in a different universe."

She shrugged, her gaze still fixed on the television. "It feels like it sometimes."

––––––––

The forty-five-foot white Riviera yacht floated on Lake Michigan, just east of the Navy Pier. The glow from the moon reflecting off the calm waters gave Vincent just enough light to see. Nothing but blackness was visible below the surface, but he'd been around long enough to know what was down there. Algae. Fish. Shipwrecks. Sunken cars. *Bodies.*

Yes, he was aware of four people who lay at the bottom of the lake . . . or what was left of them, anyway. They'd been tossed in from where he stood, the back of the hull of *The Federica*. The words were etched in black on the stern, named after the Don's long-dead sister. The half-million-dollar yacht was Sal's, although as far as the government knew it belonged to Galaxy Corp., a company out of Chicago that manufactured GPS chips. It was a cover for his more shady business practices, most of his extravagant possessions written off as company property. That way, if the IRS came knocking, he wouldn't have to explain how he could afford such things. He'd simply borrowed them.

Tax evasion—Vincent admired how Salvatore made manipulation an art.

A throat cleared behind him. He remained still, staring out at the water as Sal approached. "Motion sickness?"

Vincent wished that were his problem. "No, just enjoying the view."

"It's nice out here, isn't it? Peaceful."

He nodded. Peace wasn't something he experienced often, and now that he'd been interrupted, he'd lost it again.

Sal clasped him on the shoulder. "Come inside. I'd like to get this over and get back to land."

Vincent begrudgingly followed Sal, seeing two men sitting on a black leather couch as soon as he stepped into the yacht. One he was well acquainted with—his brother-in-law, Corrado. Corrado was a man of few words, his silence often speaking volumes. *Mezza parola*, they called it. *Half word*. He could hold an entire conversation with nothing more than a nod of his head.

A few years older than Vincent, Corrado's thick, dark hair showed no sign of gray, a slight curl to it that gave him a boyish look. He was sturdy, lightly tanned, and statuesque. Women tended to find him attractive, but he'd never shown interest in any except Celia. Corrado's mind was always on business.

Family or not, Corrado's presence put Vincent on edge. It meant something had gone terribly wrong, but the boy beside him hadn't been around long enough to learn that.

The boy fidgeted, jittery. The doctor in Vincent surmised he was likely on something. Cocaine, he thought, but meth wouldn't surprise him. He'd witnessed too much to be shocked by anything anymore.

Salvatore looked at the boy. "You've been doing things for us for how long now?"

"A year." Excitement radiated from his words, pride for the work he'd done. He wasn't much older than Vincent's children, which meant he'd gotten involved the moment he turned eighteen. *Dumb young Turks.*

"A year," Salvatore repeated. "From what your *Capo* says, you've pulled in quite a bit of money for us . . . more so than a lot of the guys working the streets."

"Yeah, man. Just doin' my part, ya know? Gotta make that paper."

From the corner of his eye, Vincent saw Corrado grimace.

"I heard you've been asking about more responsibility," Salvatore said. "You think you have what it takes?"

"Hell yeah," the boy said. "I've been ready since I was born."

Salvatore pulled out a bottle of scotch, pouring four glasses. Vincent stood back, swirling his in the glass and listening as the boy bragged about the jobs he'd done. Hijackings and robberies, shakedowns and gambles, but never once did he mention where the bulk of his cash came from.

"Drugs," Vincent interrupted, tired of the charade. "You forgot about the drugs."

The boy blanched. Even working at such low ranks, he knew *Cosa Nostra*'s policy: Don't get caught with drugs. Ever. "What drugs?"

"The ones you've been selling out of your house," Vincent said. "We have an insider who says the police caught wind of the location."

"I, uh . . . I haven't . . ."

He didn't have time to come up with an excuse. Corrado reached into his suit coat and pulled out his gun, pointing it at the back of the boy's head. Vincent looked away as Corrado pulled the trigger, the silencer muffling the gunfire as the bullet tore through his skull. The room was void of emotion as Corrado returned his gun to his coat, Sal continuing to drink his scotch like it hadn't happened. Sickness stirred within Vincent the moment he saw the dead kid's frozen expression of fear. Bolting from the room, he ran to the deck and threw up over the side of the yacht.

Sal joined him, eyeing him strangely, and Vincent sighed. "Motion sickness got me, after all."

Corrado dragged the body up on deck, wrapping it in a tarp and chains before tossing it overboard. Vincent watched as the boy sank, disappearing into the blackness of the water.

Make that *five* people on the bottom of the lake.

7

Haven's head brutally thumped when she opened her eyes the following Saturday. One, two, three seconds passed before sickness rushed through her like a waterfall. Jumping up, she ran for the bathroom and collapsed in front of the toilet just in time.

An hour passed before she was well enough to get back to her feet. Clothes wrinkled and hair disheveled, she made her way downstairs, coming face-to-face on the second floor with Carmine and a girl with wildly colored hair.

She'd seen Carmine a few times the past week but could never tell what he was thinking, his expression curious as he gazed at her. The attention caused her chest to swell with that unknown sensation, one she was still too afraid to confront or name.

Escaping from them before they could speak, she almost fell down the steps in haste as she went straight for the kitchen. She tried to calm her racing heart as she washed a few dishes, but an unexpected voice from the doorway only startled her more. "Hey! I'm Dia!"

The glass she was holding slipped from her hand as she turned around, hitting the floor with a clank but thankfully not breaking. "Uh, hello."

Dia raised her eyebrows. "Are you okay?"

Haven stared at her. Of course she wasn't okay. She was alone and missing her mama, so confused and emotionally spent that she didn't know which way was up anymore.

Not to mention she felt like she was going to be sick again.

"I'm okay," she whispered, looking away. She took a few deep breaths, woozy, and headed for the stairs without another word. Breathing heavily, she had to pause when she reached the top of the staircase. Her vision blurred, her chest burning as she lost her breath. Everything grew hazy as her legs gave out.

She collapsed, her head slamming into the wall as she hit the floor with a thump, the sound of a freight train rushing through her ears.

———

"Haven?"

Haven pried her eyes open at the familiar voice, incredibly close, and made out the set of green eyes hovering in front of her. She blinked a few times as Carmine backed away. "*Maledicalo!* You can't do that to me!"

Confused, her vision blurred again from unexpected tears. "What?"

"You can't pass out like that! You looked like you were dead. Christ, I thought you were dead!"

She stared at him. He'd worried she was dead?

"Dom called my father to come check on you. You hit your head pretty hard." He brushed his hand across her forehead. His fingertips were cool against her feverish skin. He spoke again, his voice so soft she barely heard it. "*Bella ragazza*, you scared the hell outta me."

She gazed at him. "What does that mean?"

"What does what mean? I said you scared me."

They sat in silence, Carmine stroking her cheek with the back of his hand as he stared into her eyes. It was uncomfortable, but Haven couldn't break from his gaze. "I'm sorry this happened," she said. "Especially with your girlfriend visiting."

His brow furrowed briefly before he laughed. "I don't have a girlfriend, but if I did, it definitely wouldn't be Dia. I have the wrong equipment for her."

Haven wasn't sure what he meant by that. Her cheeks reddened from the intensity of his stare, but before she could get her thoughts in order, Dominic's voice rang out. "*Colpo di fulmine.*"

They both jumped, glancing toward the doorway. Carmine pulled his hand away. "What?"

"*Colpo di fulmine.*" A slow grin spread across Dominic's face. "I don't know why I didn't see it hit sooner."

Carmine's expression shifted. "No fucking way."

"Yep," Dominic said. "Kaboom!"

Carmine stormed from the room as Dominic laughed, taking a seat on the bed where his brother had been. "That boy is full of surprises."

Colpo di fulmine. The thunderbolt, as Italians call it. When love strikes someone like lightning, so powerful and intense it can't be denied. It's beautiful and messy, cracking a chest open and spilling their soul out for the world to see. It turns a person inside out, and there's no going back from it. Once the thunderbolt hits, your life is irrevocably changed.

Carmine never believed in it. *Colpo di fulmine,* love at first sight, soul mates . . . he thought it was all bullshit. Love was just people deluded by lust, pussy blinding men from using common sense.

He still wanted to think that. He wanted to deny it existed. But a twinge of something deep inside of him—past the thick steel-reinforced, Kevlar-coated, barbed-wire fence surrounding his heart—suggested otherwise. And when he saw Haven's limp body on the floor, he couldn't ignore it anymore. This peculiar girl had come out of nowhere, and he was afraid she'd leave as quickly as she'd appeared. That she'd vanish from his life before he had a chance to *know* her. His chest ached at the thought, his insides on fire, and the girl who caused it was oblivious to it all.

In other words, Carmine was royally fucked.

He bolted out of the house and drove to the next town, scrounging up enough change in his car to buy a cheap fifth of vodka with his fake ID. He pulled over alongside the road and drank alone in the darkness until his mind was fuzzy and he felt nothing.

He passed out eventually and awoke the next morning, his head pounding viciously. Throwing on his sunglasses, he drove home doing the speed limit, not wanting to get pulled over since alcohol likely still coursed through his veins. He was sure his father would be about as thrilled to post bail in the middle of the afternoon as the cops would be about the loaded Colt .45 pistol concealed under his driver's seat.

When Carmine walked into the house, he found Haven asleep on the couch in the family room, and something twisted inside of him at the sight of her. She had goose bumps on her arms so he grabbed a blanket from the closet and carefully covered her before going upstairs to shower.

He grabbed some crackers from the kitchen to put something in his stomach and headed back toward the family room when Haven called his name. He ran his hand through his damp hair as their eyes met. She looked at him imploringly, and it was an invitation he couldn't refuse.

He took a seat beside her. "You feeling better today?"

"Yes," she said, shifting a few inches away from him. "Dr. De-Marco said it was a stomach virus. I might be contagious, though, so you should keep your distance."

"I'm not worried about it," Carmine said. "If you give it to me, I'll get a few days off school."

"Aren't you supposed to be in school now?"

"Yeah, but I'm not really known for doing what I'm supposed to do."

She smiled. "Rebel."

It surprised him how relaxed things were between them. He expected tension. Haven was quiet for a bit, her gaze drifting to his bare chest. Carmine realized she was staring at his tattoo. "Time heals all wounds."

Her eyes shot to his. "What?"

"My tattoo. *'Il tempo guarisce tutti i mali.'* Time heals all wounds."

"Oh, I didn't mean to stare."

"It's fine. The one on my arm is a cross draped with the Italian flag, and *'fiducia nessuno'* is on my wrist. It's usually covered." He pulled off his watch and turned his arm over so she could see the words scrawled across the veins in small script. She lightly traced the ink with her fingertips. Tingling shot up his arm from her touch, and he closed his eyes briefly at the sensation.

"What does it mean?"

He pulled his arm away and put the watch back on. "Trust no one."

"Did they hurt?"

He shrugged. "I've felt worse pain."

Images flashed in his mind at those words, and he absentmindedly rubbed the scar on his side. He got lost in the memory until a rumbling sound brought him back to reality. He looked at Haven, realizing it was her stomach. "Do you ever eat?"

She nodded. "Every night."

"Really? You never eat with us."

She hesitated. "Master Michael said someone like me shouldn't sleep in the same house as someone like you, much less sit at the same dinner table."

"Christ, they did a job on you. Were you always with Michael?"

"He was always around, but he didn't become my master until his parents died."

"Were his parents just as bad?"

"Frankie scared me, but he didn't hit much, and Miss Monica sometimes played with me when I was young. Michael ignored me at first, but it got worse when my mistress realized that he, uh . . ."

"He what?"

"He made me."

Carmine's eyes widened. "Michael's your father?"

She picked at her fingernails, ashamed. "He didn't mean to be."

8

For the first time since coming to Durante, there hadn't been any music last night.

Right away, Haven could feel something wasn't right, that she was intruding on a moment and seeing something she wasn't supposed to see. Something sacred. Something intimate.

But she couldn't look away.

Restless and exhausted, she had been too anxious to sleep. She rose from her bed and found Carmine in a trance in the family room. A faint glow of moonlight from the window illuminated the silent room as he sat at the piano, slumped forward and staring down at the keys.

Carmine laced his fingers through his hair as he dropped his head down, a strangled cry echoing through the room. Holding her breath, her chest constricting, Haven took a step back and treaded lightly upstairs, relieved when she reached her room undetected.

Confusion nagged at her. She didn't know what she felt for Carmine, but seeing him in pain upset her. Her alarm grew at that realization, her heart hammering in her chest. Vulnerability would do nothing but get her hurt.

Only when Haven heard Carmine come upstairs did she gather the courage to venture back down. She made breakfast as a distraction, finishing the food when Carmine appeared. He opened the refrigerator and grabbed the jug of orange juice, brushing past her to get a glass.

"Smells good," he said quietly, no spark to his words, none of that passion Haven was used to hearing. Haven fought the urge to try to smooth away the heavy bags under his bloodshot eyes.

As the boys ate, Haven figured out how to make coffee, knowing Dr. DeMarco drank it every morning. It was brewing when he walked in, his footsteps faltering a foot away. He stared at the pot before turning to her, his tone accusatory. "You made my coffee."

"Yes, sir," she said. "Are you hungry?"

"I'll be home today," he said, ignoring her question. "Don't bother me unless it's an emergency."

He stalked out without pouring any coffee.

———

Besides a load of Dr. DeMarco's laundry, there wasn't much work to be done that day. By noon, Haven had finished and lugged his clothes upstairs. Dr. DeMarco left his door open the days he wanted her to clean since he hadn't given her the codes to open any doors.

She pulled the hamper inside the room and opened a dresser drawer, her movements halting when she saw his shiny silver gun lying on top, across the clothes. She grabbed it by the handle, using both hands, to move it out of her way as her stomach churned. It was heavier than she expected.

The sound of a door latching captured her attention, and her head snapped in the direction of the noise. Dr. DeMarco stood just inside the room, having shut them in together. Intense fear ripped through her at his expression. His face was his usual mask of serene, but his eyes glowed with rage.

She dropped the gun as a reflex, and it landed on top of the dresser with a thump. The fire in Dr. DeMarco's eyes sparked more at the sound. He reached behind him, so careful and deliberate it was almost slow motion when he grabbed the deadbolt and turned it smoothly.

Haven's heart raced with the click of the lock. She knew it then. She had made a grave mistake. She had never seen him look like this, his eyes darkening like a tornado in the distance, tumultuous and clouded. A spark of unpredictable evil lurked beneath. Staring at him, Haven finally saw a glimpse of Vincent DeMarco. *The monster.*

He took a step forward. Instinctively, Haven stepped back. She backed up against the wall as Dr. DeMarco stopped in front of the dresser and carefully picked up the discarded gun.

"Such beautiful things." He reached into the dresser drawer and pulled out a gold bullet, holding it up. "It's fascinating how much devastation something so small can cause. Do you know anything about guns?"

The detachment in his voice frightened Haven more, her body violently trembling. She tried to sound strong, but her voice shook as much as the rest of her. "No, sir."

He returned the bullet and shut the drawer, staring at the weapon. "This is a Smith & Wesson 627 Revolver, .357 magnum, eight rounds, hollow-point bullets. I have plenty of guns, but this has always been my favorite. It has never let me down." He paused. "Except once."

He pointed the gun at Haven as he closed the distance between them, thrusting the muzzle against her throat. She gasped as the force cut off her airflow. "A flick of my finger on the trigger will blow a hole through your neck. You'd die without a doubt. If you're lucky, it might even be quick, but there are no guarantees. Most likely, you'd be unable to speak or breathe but capable of feeling everything until you suffocate to death."

He pulled back, letting her take a deep breath, before pressing the gun to her throat again. Her chest felt like it would burst when he spoke again. "Shall we see what happens when I pull the trigger? I think we will."

She tried to cry out as she braced herself for the pain. It was the end. She was going to die. She squeezed her eyes shut, waiting for the explosion, and jumped at the loud click. The pressure against her neck disappeared and she collapsed to the ground in sobs, unable to stand on her feet.

"Look at me," he demanded, reaching down and roughly grasping her chin. "You're lucky it wasn't loaded or you'd be dead now. Understand?"

She nodded frantically, hyperventilating.

"Good. Now go to your room for your punishment. It's time you learn what happens when people forget their place."

Dr. DeMarco unlocked the door and stormed out with the gun. His words bounced around her frightened mind as images hit her, flashes of dead eyes gnawing at her aching chest. *That's what happens when people forget their place.*

Death happened. Number 33 happened. Frankie had told her to remember, and she was sure she would never forget. How could she?

She pulled herself up on shaky legs and made her way to the third floor, fear overriding all logic. Bolting straight for Carmine's room, Haven tore open the window and climbed through. Running along the balcony, she held her breath and forced herself not to look down as she scampered into the tree and shimmied down to the yard.

The moment her feet hit the ground, she ran. Trees and brush scratched her limbs as she navigated the dense forest, her heart thumping wildly. She moved as fast as her legs would carry her, having no sense of direction as she once again ran for her life.

Eventually, the forest thinned. Haven saw the clearing beyond the trees and turned in that direction, shoving branches out of her way as she broke through to the road. The squeal of tires made her stop in her tracks, and she gasped when she saw the familiar black car.

No, no, no . . . She backed away, shaking her head, but it was too late.

Dr. DeMarco grabbed her and dragged her toward the idling car. Haven begged him when she saw the open trunk, but he picked her up without much effort and threw her in with no regard. She stared at him, horrified, and his furious eyes bore into her before he slammed the trunk.

Haven flinched as she was encased in darkness.

He accelerated, the force flinging her around the trunk, her head slamming against the side of it. Sobbing, she frantically felt around for some way out. A small light came on whenever he hit the brakes, illuminating the space enough for her to see. She found a small lever and pulled it, stunned when the trunk popped open. She jolted again as Dr. DeMarco slammed the brakes, but she managed to climb out quickly. Her feet carried her a short way down the road before she was seized from behind, an arm circling her throat as a hand roughly pressed against her head. She flailed around, but his hold was too strong.

In a matter of seconds, her vision faded.

When Haven regained consciousness, she was on the floor in her bedroom, bound to the post of the bed. Dr. DeMarco stood a few feet away, watching, waiting. She let out a sob as reality slammed into her, but Dr. DeMarco raised his hand to silence her cries. "Did you really think you could get away? Didn't you learn your lesson last time you tried to run? I've told you before—you can't outsmart me."

"I didn't . . . I, uh . . ." Her cries muffled her words. "I don't want to die."

Dr. DeMarco grew rigid before snatching a roll of duct tape from the nightstand. She shook her head frantically as he tore off a piece, but it didn't deter him from covering her mouth. "I want you to think about how good you have it here. Think about how lucky you are to still be alive."

He walked out, leaving her alone.

Nine years.

Nearly a decade had passed since the fateful day that changed Carmine's life—the day none of them talked about—and it still affected him like it was just yesterday. Nobody knew, though. No-body knew he cried, or that he still couldn't sleep at night, but for the first time in nine years, Carmine wished someone did.

The moment he walked in the door from school that after-noon, he knew something had happened. It was a feeling in the air, a stifling silence, a sense of danger that made his adrenaline pump overtime, charring his nerves as it ran through his veins.

Carmine headed upstairs, looking around, and found his bed-room door open when he reached the third floor. A cool breeze swept through his room, the window wide-open and curtains rus-tling. His heart rate spiked. This was bad. *Real fucking bad.*

The voice behind him was icy, detached. "How did she know?"

Carmine turned around, seeing his father near the stairs, non-chalantly leaned against the wall with his silver revolver tucked into his pants.

"How did she know what?"

"How did she know your window opened, Carmine? Because it's my house, and I didn't know!"

Carmine turned back to the window. *Oh, shit.* "Where is she?"

"Does it matter?"

"Yes."

His father stared at him hard. "Why?"

Carmine blanched. *Why?* "Because it does. You're a lot of things, Dad, but . . . Christ, this? I didn't think you were *this* fucked up!"

Vincent's eyes narrowed. "Do you have something to say?"

"Yeah. Nothing's gonna bring her back."

Vincent's calm mask slipped. "What?"

"You heard me. It's not gonna change anything! She's still gone!"

Those words broke something inside Vincent, severing his ten-uous grip with sanity. He grabbed his gun and aimed at Carmine's head.

"You won't shoot me," Carmine said. "I look too much like her."

Vincent's hand shook, confirming it. "Stay away from the girl."

He meant it as a threat, but Carmine only felt relief. It meant that Haven was still there, somewhere . . . but he had no intention of keeping his distance from her.

Time went by torturously slow for Haven as she held her position in the dark bedroom. Her muscles ached, nothing alleviating the tension. She cried until exhaustion took hold, sleep whisking her away.

A noise startled her awake later, the pain explosive the moment she opened her eyes. She faintly saw a form lurking in the shadows, her brow furrowing when she made out the sorrowful green eyes. Carmine knelt in front of her and wiped her tears before running his fingertips across the duct tape covering her mouth. "*La mia bella ragazza*, I'm sorry this happened to you."

She studied him, her head tilted as if it would help her understand.

"It's the anniversary of, uh . . . fuck! Why can't I say it? It's the day my mom . . ." He trailed off, leaving her confused. None of them spoke of Carmine's mama. Haven didn't even know her name. "I wish I could let you go, but he'd kill me. No, he'd kill *you*. He told me not to come near you, but I had to know you were okay. But, Christ, look at you! What's wrong with him?"

He tucked some of her hair behind her ears, his fingers grazing over the duct tape once more. "I'll be back in the morning. Stay strong, *tesoro*. I'll never let anything like this happen again."

"Are you awake?"

Haven's eyes opened at the sound of Dr. DeMarco's voice the next morning, his tone not as callous as it had been yesterday. Squatting down in front of her, he peeled up the corner of the duct tape and ripped it off. She winced, her lips throbbing like the beat of a drum.

Dr. DeMarco freed her from the restraints, and she rubbed her burning wrists. She sat there after he left with her head slumped forward, wiping her nose on her shirt as she flexed her limbs, trying to get the cramps out.

After a few minutes, Carmine knocked and stepped in with a glass of water. He knelt beside her. "You should drink this."

She took the water and tried to smile at his generosity but couldn't manage it. Everything hurt.

Carmine held out a small yellow pill. "Take this. The kids at school would eat this shit like candy if they could. It'll take away the pain."

She took the pill and swallowed it, her voice gritty as she whispered, "Thank you."

"You're welcome. Do you think you can get up?"

Carmine held his hand out to her and pulled her to her feet, but the moment he let go, her knees gave out. He cursed and snatched her before she hit the floor, his grip firm as he pulled her into his arms.

His face softened as he carried her to his room and placed her on his bed. Confused, she lay as still as possible as Carmine disappeared into his bathroom, returning with his arms full of first-aid supplies. He dropped it all on the bed beside her and sat down, a washcloth in his hand. "I need to fix you up. You don't want any of this getting infected."

Carmine washed her cheeks, the cool cloth feeling good against her skin. He brushed it across her mouth, being extra gentle, and washed the dried blood from her wrists. Haven did her best to ignore the pain, keeping her attention on his face, strained with concentration.

The pain receded as the drug kicked in. "You're good at this."

He smiled. "Now, *this* I've been doing my whole life."

9

Carmine paused beside the bed and stared down at Haven, her face nuzzled into his pillow. He smiled unconsciously at the sight of her as he sat down. "Do you wanna talk about what happened?"

"There's nothing to talk about," she whispered. "I survived. That's what I do. I'll keep surviving until I don't survive anymore."

"So, you're saying you're a survivor?"

Her cheeks flushed. "Yeah, that didn't sound smart. I think I need a thes—uh, one of those books with words."

He laughed. "A thesaurus?"

"Yes."

"I'll get you one if you promise to use it."

"Okay, I will." Recognition flickered across her face as her smile fell. "You'll have to read it to me, though. I can't read."

"Truthfully?"

She hesitated. "I can a little bit. People taught me, and I picked up some from closed captioning when my mistress watched the television . . . so I guess you can say I watched some television, too."

He shook his head. "I still don't understand why it mattered to that Michael guy."

"Because smart people try to escape," she replied. "They think they can make it in the outside world. The ones who don't know anything are easier to control, and they needed to control me."

He gaped at her, surprised by her sudden seriousness. "Okay."

Haven laughed, her carefree expression returning. "Is that an, 'Okay, I get your point, Haven,' or is it an, 'Okay, I'm just going to agree with you, because I don't know what else to say?'"

She'd mocked him. *Him.* "You did that all fucking wrong. You didn't even curse."

"I don't curse."

He cocked an eyebrow at her. "Why not?"

"I've seen too many people have teeth knocked out from saying bad words."

"So not cursing kept you all your teeth?"

"No, luck did that. As many blows to the face I took, I should be more disfigured than I am."

He scoffed. "You aren't disfigured."

"My nose is crooked," she said, matter-of-fact. "There's a bump."

He squinted a bit, looking at her nose, but saw nothing wrong with it. "How'd you get this supposedly horrific bump?"

"My mistress kicked me in the face."

He cringed. "Why did she kick you?"

"Because I scuffed her high heels when she tripped me."

"Why did she trip you?"

"For fun? I don't know."

His brow furrowed. "The bitch tripped you for laughs, got pissed because she scuffed her shoe, and decided to kick you in the nose as punishment?"

She nodded. "Do you want to know the color of the shoes? You've asked everything else."

His eyes widened at her sarcastic tone.

Haven noticed his stunned expression and covered her mouth. "I'm sorry."

"Don't be," he said. "And if you wanna tell me the color of the shoe, by all means, tell me. If you're sick of my questions, tell me to shut the fuck up."

"The shoe was red, and I don't mind your questions," she said. "I can't believe I had an outburst like that."

He smirked. "It's the drug. It's why, in the past half hour, you've mocked me, gotten fresh with me, and confessed to me."

"So when it wears off, I'll be in pain *and* embarrassed? Probably even in trouble, too."

"No reason to be embarrassed," he said. "And nothing will top you escaping out my window, so I wouldn't worry about being in trouble anymore."

She picked at her short brittle nails. "Did I get you in trouble, too?"

"No more than I get myself in daily," he said. "He came up here in the middle of the night and nailed it down, though, so no more scaling trees for either of us . . . until I get it open again."

"I panicked," she said. "I thought he was going to kill me."

"He wouldn't . . ." He wouldn't kill her? Carmine wasn't sure if he believed those words. "Why did you think that, anyway?"

"He said the same thing my master said when I saw him murder a girl."

Carmine didn't know what he'd expected to hear, but that wasn't it. "You saw a girl die? Is that the worst thing you've seen?"

"Maybe. I've seen a lot."

"Like?"

She averted her eyes. "Like my mama being raped."

As much as those words sickened him, Carmine was immensely grateful for whatever pharmaceutical company cranked out those potent little yellow pills that made her open up. "That'll never happen to you here. You know that, right?"

She nodded but didn't appear to be convinced.

"Look, sex can be great between people who want it, but I'd never touch a girl unless she wanted me to. None of us would. That's wrong."

"Do you love those girls you touch?"

"No." He felt bad about admitting that.

"Have you ever been in love?"

He stared at her, unsure of how to answer. "I don't know. I'm still figuring out what love is."

"Me, too," she said. "It's confusing."

He pursed his lips in thought. Could she feel what he felt? He couldn't ask her, though. Even if she said yes, he couldn't be sure it wasn't drug-induced.

Leaning back on the bed, Carmine stared up at the ceiling as Haven spoke, her words slurring from exhaustion. "Carmine? What's the worst thing you've seen?"

He contemplated whether to answer. It was a story he'd never told anyone. His family knew the technical parts, the shit that made the newspaper, but he never talked about what he saw.

Could he tell her?

He looked at her and smiled when he saw her eyes closed, lips parted as she lay there, fast asleep. He would have told her, he realized. He would have told her everything.

———

When Haven woke up, muscles throbbed she hadn't been aware of. The intoxicating scent of cologne invaded her lungs, assaulting every cell in her body when she took a deep breath. It reminded her of the smell of the air in Blackburn when a storm came and it rained for two days.

Haven sat up, needing to clear her head, and stretched her back as Carmine retrieved a bottle of Tylenol. He sat down and gave her the pills before grabbing a half-full bottle of water from his nightstand. "I promise I don't have any diseases."

She took it from him and drank the rest of it before handing the empty bottle back to him. He shrugged as he tossed it onto the floor in a pile of dirty clothes. The room was somehow messier than the last time she saw it. "I could clean your room for you."

"I'm not gonna make you do that."

"I know, but you've been nice. I'd like to do something in return."

He raised an eyebrow. "Nice? Don't say that shit too loud. It might ruin my reputation. And maybe I'll ask for help with my room someday, but not today."

"Someday, then."

They were both quiet again, the silence awkward. Haven tried to think of something to say to lighten the mood, but his eyes were watching her, and she couldn't focus on anything but them.

She looked around the room again, needing to break from his gaze. "I should try to move around. The longer I lie around, the harder it's going to be when I do have to get up."

Carmine helped her to her feet—putting weight on her legs was not easy. He held her arm the whole way downstairs, hesitantly letting go when they reached the family room.

They sat together quietly on the couch as night fell. Carmine offhandedly flipped through channels, watching a program until commercials came on and then turning to another. A few minutes past seven, he settled on an episode of *Jeopardy!* "This popular pasta dish consists of wide, flat noodles layered with meat, cheese, and tomato sauce."

"Lasagna," Haven and Carmine said at the same time. She smiled. "What is this?"

"Useless trivia," he said, "like the bullshit they teach us in school."

She turned back to the television, eyes wide, and soaked up every question asked during the next thirty minutes. When the show came to an end, she turned to Carmine. He appeared bored, his head propped up with his fist on the arm of the couch, as he flipped through channels again.

"Thank you," she said. "I liked that show."

"It's on every night at that time," he said. "You know, in case you wanna watch it again."

The front door opened a few minutes later, and Haven tensed when she heard footsteps. She could feel Carmine's gaze on her, could sense it powerfully, but she couldn't look at him. She didn't want to see his expression. She didn't want his pity. He had treated her like an equal, and she didn't want to feel like less than him again.

Dr. DeMarco walked in, an uncomfortable tension entering with him. Haven fought back a bout of sickness, focusing her attention on a smudge on the floor.

"Can you go to your room, Carmine?" Dr. DeMarco asked. "I'd like to talk to her alone."

Haven's heart raced as she picked at her fingernails, trying to keep her composure as Carmine left. Dr. DeMarco crouched down in front of her, blocking the spot she'd been focused on, so she stared at a loose thread on his shirt instead.

He raised his hand, and Haven recoiled, wrapping her arms around herself protectively as she moved as far back from him as possible. The queasy feeling flared, and Haven bit her bottom lip to keep it in.

"You should stay off your legs for a few days," Dr. DeMarco said as he ran his fingers across the tops of her knees and squeezed them.

She winced. It hurt. "I'm fine, sir."

"You have bursitis. It's when the little sac above the kneecap fills with fluid. You need to rest and ice them so the swelling goes away."

He let go of her knee but didn't get up. It was uncomfortable, him staring at her. She wanted nothing more than for him to go away.

"Listen to me," he said, his voice softer. "Do you know what a GPS chip is?"

She shook her head.

"It's a tracking device, sometimes as small as a grain of rice. My car has one in it. If someone steals it, I can find its location. It's a security measure, so no one takes what belongs to me." He paused. "You're no different, child. You have one in you, too."

At those words, Haven met his gaze. Sympathy shined from his eyes, which made her sicker.

"I injected you with one in the basement that first day, so no matter what happens, I'll be able to find you. It's how I knew where you went yesterday."

She couldn't speak, afraid if she opened her mouth, she'd lose it. She'd never had these reactions toward Master Michael. She endured years of abuse from him and could keep going, battered but strong, intact . . . but in one second, without raising his hand, Dr. DeMarco had shattered a part of her.

10

Durante fell under autumn's clutch. The lush green faded, giving way to rich, warm hues scattered among the tall pine trees. Leaves fell in heaps on the ground, covering the earth like a crisp blanket.

With the emergence of fall came Homecoming, a big extravaganza in town, with spirit week and a pep rally, a parade, and a football game, the week's activities culminating in a dance. Carmine should have been excited, but he had been dreading it all week.

Haven had been cold again, hiding out whenever he was home. He heard her crying at night as he sat in the library, whittling away the hours by plucking the strings on his guitar. He wanted to go to her, to console her, but he didn't know what to say. Sorry you're here? Sorry you're trapped? Sorry my father is a sick motherfucker? How could he explain it, make it all right, when nothing about the situation made sense to him?

It was close to six in the evening when Haven opened her bedroom door and came face-to-face with Dr. DeMarco. He stood in the hallway with his fist raised to knock, and she took a step back as he dropped his hand. "May I come in?"

She nodded, confused why he would ask permission in his own house.

He entered nonchalantly, as if he were there for casual conversation, and looked around for a moment before addressing her. "How do your knees feel?"

"Fine," she said quietly.

"Do you think you're up for a trip out of the house?"

The question alarmed her. A voice in the back of her mind screamed, *It's a trick!*

"Only if you say so, sir," she said, eyeing him warily.

Dr. DeMarco reached out to her. She recoiled, her heart pounding rapidly as she braced to be struck, but he dropped his hand without touching her. A frustrated sigh escaped his lips as he turned away, pinching the bridge of his nose. "We're going to Carmine's football game. Make yourself presentable."

She stood there when he left, having no idea what he considered presentable. She eventually changed into a pair of khaki pants and a sweater and brushed her frizzy hair, but nothing could tame the natural curls. She pulled it back with a rubber band and forced her feet into a pair of shoes before heading downstairs. Dr. DeMarco waited in the foyer with his hands shoved in his pockets, rocking on his heels. Hearing her approach, he scanned her. She awaited his assessment, but he said nothing as he pulled out his keys and opened the front door. Haven stepped onto the porch as he locked up the house, ushering her into the passenger seat of the car.

Durante High School's parking lot was packed when they arrived, cars lining the road and covering the field beside the school. Haven gawked at them as Dr. DeMarco parked on the grass.

"I've gone about things the wrong way," he said. "I've kept you in the house until you could prove you'd act appropriately in public, but there's no way for you to do that until I allow you around people. So I'm giving you a chance, and I expect you to be on your best behavior."

"Yes, sir."

Her knees wobbled as they made their way into the stadium.

People surrounded them on all sides, shoving past and blocking their path. Dr. DeMarco glided through the crowd fluidly, while she followed, feeling like she was drowning. They encircled her, voices and bodies swallowing her like a current. Dr. DeMarco paid her no mind as they headed up the packed bleachers.

A voice carried over the loudspeaker as a band played, and cheerleaders chanted something Haven couldn't hear over the roar of the crowd. She covered her ears as everyone took their seats, only dropping her hands when it calmed down.

Familiar laughter rang out, and Haven looked in the direction of the sound. Dominic walked toward them with his arm draped around a girl, Dia begrudgingly following them.

Dominic took a seat in front of them and introduced Haven to his girlfriend. Tess stared at Haven for a moment, her gaze intense, but said not a word as she sat down beside him. Dia wedged herself between Haven and Dr. DeMarco. It startled Haven, but Dr. DeMarco simply slid over to give the girl room.

Haven turned her attention to the game, trying to ignore the people all around. She scanned the field silently as a player was hit and knocked onto his back. She winced. Ouch.

"Looks like number three took a hard hit," the announcer said. "Let's hope he's okay."

"He's fine," Dominic said dismissively. "Carmine's tough."

Her eyes darted back to the field. *Carmine?*

He climbed to his feet and flexed his fingers, his white number 3 jersey smudged with grass and dirt. Her mouth went dry as she gazed at it. So that was what the big black number meant.

"You don't know shit about football, do you?" Dominic asked, glancing back at her. "I can see it on your face."

She smiled sheepishly. "No."

Dominic was rattling off the basics of the game, most of it lost on her, when Carmine pulled off his helmet, his skin glowing with sweat under the stadium lights. As she watched him, her breath hitched.

Carmine turned toward the bleachers, his eyes drifting in their direction as he scanned the crowd, and Haven could have sworn his gaze lingered on her for a moment.

———————

The rest of the game rushed by, the energy in the stadium making Haven's skin tingle. People occasionally approached Dr. DeMarco, not one inquiring as to who she was. She could see it in their eyes, though, could see it in their expressions as they surveyed her from a distance, trying to make sense of her presence.

When the final whistle blew, the crowd descended upon the field. Haven followed Dr. DeMarco to the surrounding fence, her footsteps faltering on the outskirts.

Dr. DeMarco paused. "Don't move from this spot. Remember what I've told you."

The voice in her head screamed again, *He's testing you!*

Someone approached while she stood there, their voice an unfamiliar southern drawl like none she'd heard before. "Lost?"

Haven turned to see a boy with sun-kissed skin, his blond hair concealed under a baseball cap. He wore a pair of cargo shorts and a blue t-shirt. Haven was immediately drawn to his nearly bare feet. She smiled at them—he had on flip-flops.

Her own feet felt stifled. What she wouldn't give to have a pair.

"I'm not lost," she said politely. "I'm waiting for someone."

"I'm Nicholas."

"Haven."

"So, tell me something, Haven. What do you call a deer with no eyes?"

"Excuse me?"

"No-eye deer." Nicholas grinned. "Get it? No idea."

She smiled when she realized it was a joke.

"Ah, a smile!" he said, playfully squeezing her arm.

Haven's smile fell when he touched her, but he didn't seem to notice.

———

Murderous rage shook Carmine. He'd been looking for Haven, seeking her out in the crowd, but his vision narrowed in on Nicholas Barlow instead. Carmine's feet moved on their own as he dropped his helmet on the field, running as fast as his fatigued legs would carry him. Shouts rang out as someone chased behind, but he didn't slow down. He couldn't.

He leaped over the chain-link fence and landed on his feet as Nicholas and Haven heard the commotion. Confusion played in Haven's expression, while Nicholas narrowed his eyes.

For as much as Carmine didn't like the boy—and Carmine fucking despised him—Nicholas hated Carmine, too.

Nicholas backed up a few steps, but it was too late. Carmine rammed into him, tackling him to the ground. His knee landed in Nicholas's crotch and he drew back his fist to punch him, but someone snatched the back of his jersey before he could, yanking Carmine to his feet.

Vincent jumped between them, shoving his son farther away.

Nicholas looked shell-shocked as he got to his feet, hesitating for a fraction of a second before running off. Carmine would have laughed at his cowardice if it weren't for the look on his father's face. "Do you know what I went through to get you out of trouble last year?" Vincent asked, fuming. "I'm not going to do it again!"

His father stormed away, grabbing Haven's wrist and yanking her in front of him. Tears streamed down her cheeks as they disappeared into the crowd, and Carmine's gut twisted.

He'd fucked up. Again.

———

Homecoming the year before had been significantly different. Only a sophomore at the time, Carmine was just a spectator at the varsity football game. He'd sat in the bleachers, surrounded by his classmates, with his best friend—Nicholas Barlow—at his side.

Best friend. The words felt venomous to Carmine now.

While the circumstances had changed this year, Carmine had every intention of ending the night in precisely the same way: fucked up beyond belief. Only this time, he was alone.

People packed the after-party when Carmine arrived, dozens of bodies crammed in the small house. He slipped through the crowd, grabbing some vodka from the kitchen before heading down the hallway. The den was dark except for a small, dim lamp in the corner, the stereo playing mellow rock music.

Everyone looked up when he entered, and a boy named Max nodded in greeting.

"You got any blow?" Carmine asked him, sitting down on the couch. With the week he'd had, he needed a major lift.

Max left the room, returning a few minutes later with a small baggie of cocaine. Carmine poured some of the powder out onto the table in front of them, enough for two lines. He snorted one straightaway, his nose numbing as his heart raced. After inhaling the second line, he closed his eyes and leaned back against the couch. Euphoria coursed through his body, warmth starting in his chest and radiating out through his limbs. He felt lightweight, invincible, without a care in the world.

A little while later, Lisa plopped down on his lap. Carmine's euphoria took an instant hit. "If you're gonna sit on me, you ought to at least get naked first."

Pushing her aside, he made two more lines and snorted them, desperate for the sensation back. Wiping his congested nose, he dumped the rest of the power onto the table and offered it to Lisa. She inhaled it like a vacuum.

"I got you a tie," she said, leaning back on the couch beside him. "It matches my dress."

"A tie?"

"Yeah, for the dance."

The dance. Carmine didn't even remember asking her to go with him. "What color is it?"

"Fandango."

He glanced at her. "What the hell is fandango?"

"It's kind of like fuchsia but darker."

"So, what, purple or something?"

"Yeah, purple."

He shrugged as he looked away. He didn't care as long as it wasn't pink.

The night was a haze of alcohol and drugs, like a movie in fast-forward that he couldn't slow down. He drank, he smoked, and he snorted, and then he popped a few pills before doing it all over again. The cycle continued, round and round, until he finally passed out where he lay.

———

The next morning, Carmine suffered the worst hangover of his life. His head pounded so hard his eyes pulsated. Wincing, he staggered out of the house into the sunshine, putting on his sunglasses as he climbed into his car.

The moment he pulled up in front of the house, a warm trickle streamed from his nose. Snatching down the visor, he looked in the mirror to see the blood. He pulled off his shirt and held it up to pinch his nose as he walked into the foyer, spotting his father holding a black duffel bag.

"Going away?" Carmine asked, heading for the stairs, but Vincent stepped in his path.

"To Chicago, yes." He pulled Carmine's hand away to survey his bloody nose. "If you keep snorting that stuff, you're going to damage your septum."

Carmine moved away. "How do you know I didn't get punched?"

"Because if someone had punched you in the nose, you would've broken theirs." Vincent started toward the door with his bag. "Lay off the coke. It'll get you killed."

———

Carmine fell asleep the moment his head hit the pillow and was woken up by a knock on his door. He pulled himself out of bed, groaning, and swung it open to see Dominic. He thrust a bag at Carmine. "Your date's here."

Fuck. He'd already forgotten about the dance.

He showered, trying to wake up, and dressed in a black suit and black shoes before grabbing the bag. Pulling out the tie, he held it up and glared at it. It was shockingly pink. *Fandango, my ass.*

He slipped it on, knowing he didn't have time to argue. After unlocking his bottom desk drawer, he filled a flask with vodka and slipped it into his pocket. He headed out, but paused in the library when Haven came up the stairs.

Carmine tried to think of something profound to say, something to make it all right again. "This tie makes me look fruity, doesn't it?"

That isn't it.

Haven burst into laughter. "Like the cake."

He shook his head when she disappeared into her room. She didn't even know what he meant.

. . . Or did she?

———

When they reached the school, Lisa ventured off with her friends while Carmine stood along the side, drinking heavily. They danced a bit, but by the time his flask was empty, he was drunk and ready to leave. Lisa smiled seductively, and the two of them went straight to her house. Her parents were out of town for the weekend, and Lisa hit up the liquor cabinet, handing him a bottle of Southern Comfort.

She took him to her bedroom, where he drank even more.

She kissed his neck and snatched the bottle away before pushing him down on the bed. He lay there and let her strip him, watching as she slipped off her dress. Climbing on the bed, she hovered over him and leaned in for a kiss.

Turning his head, he muttered, "I'm not that drunk."

Her touch was uncomfortable, too intimate. She went too slowly, her hands gentle. Nothing felt right about it, her body wrong. Squeezing his eyes shut, feeling himself softening, Carmine wished he could enjoy it. He'd compromised and worn a pink tie, and now his body rejected a guaranteed lay. He didn't recognize himself anymore. It was driving him nuts.

As soon as that thought ran through his mind, laughter erupted from him. Lisa moved away, startled. "What's wrong with you, Carmine? You're crazy!"

"I know." He stood and grabbed his clothes. "Nutty like a fucking fruitcake."

She stared with disbelief. "Wait, you're leaving? Why?"

"I don't love you," he said as he headed for the door. "I'm never gonna love you, Lisa."

Saint Mary's Catholic Church looked like a medieval castle tucked into the heart of bustling Chicago, with its pointy towers and strong tan bricks. The grass surrounding it was withered, the sidewalk cracked, but the church was still immaculate. High arches and golden walls accented the wooden décor, the ivory marble floor sparkling from the sunlight streaming through the stained glass windows. When Vincent was young, he felt like he had stepped inside a treasure chest. Every Sunday, without fail, Saint Mary's made him believe he truly belonged.

Today, however, as he strolled through the vacant pews, he felt like an outcast in the place of worship. The sound of his footsteps bounced off the walls, alerting the priest to his arrival. He headed straight to the confessional and sat down as Father Alberto took a seat on the other side.

Vincent pushed the screen out of the way, knowing it was senseless to shield himself from the priest. He would know it was him—he always did. "Bless me, Father, for I have sinned. It's been three months since my last confession."

Father Alberto made the sign of the cross before he spoke, his Sicilian accent still present even though he had lived in America for decades. "What sins have you committed, my child?"

Since his last confession, Vincent had lied, stolen, and been an accessory to murder in the name of *la famiglia*, but one sin weighed heavily on his mind. "I hurt someone . . . a girl."

"Did you intend to cause the girl harm?"

He hesitated. "Yes."

"Are you remorseful?"

Another pause. "Yes."

"Have you told her of your regret?"

He ran his hands down his face in frustration. "No."

Father Alberto was quiet for a moment. "Was it *her*?"

Vincent needn't answer. They both knew it was . . . and they both knew it wasn't the first time.

"I was angry," Vincent said. "The pain that morning was the worst it's been in years. I wanted someone else to hurt for once. I wanted someone else to feel what I felt. I had to get it out of me before I exploded. I needed to feel better."

"And did you?"

"No," he said. "I'm still angry—so angry, Father—but on top of it, now I'm ashamed. I want to stop feeling this way, but I don't know how to make it go away."

"Ah, but I think you *do*," Father Alberto said. "Judge not, and ye shall not be judged. Condemn not, and ye shall not be condemned. Release, and ye shall be released."

"Luke 6:37." Vincent recognized the Scripture. "But what if I can't stop? What if I can't let go? What if I can't forgive?"

"But if ye forgive not men their trespasses, neither will your Father forgive your trespasses."

"Matthew 6:15."

Father Alberto smiled. "Your hate is poison, Vincenzo. It eats you from the inside out. You must find it in your heart to let go. Then, and only then, will *you* be forgiven."

11

Haven stared at the alarm clock as the numbers rolled past midnight. Her broken hours of slumber had been interrupted by nightmares for days, and the thought of closing her eyes terrified her. She desperately wanted some peace, but she'd only been offered deafening silence.

There was no music tonight. Nothing to distract her.

After the boys left for the dance, Haven spent the evening drawing and thinking about her life. As much as she didn't want to admit it, she'd allowed herself to grow jealous. She longed to be the pretty girl in the pretty dress, going to a dance with the other teenagers.

Tired of wallowing, she crawled out of bed to go downstairs. She headed to the kitchen for a drink but froze when she turned on the light and realized someone was there.

Carmine sat on the counter beside the fridge, his shoulders slouched and a bottle of liquor in his hand. Their eyes met, and even from across the room she could see the passion. A lot of soul lurked beneath his hardened exterior.

"I didn't mean to interrupt," she said.

"You're not interrupting, Haven. It's not like I'm fucking doing anything. I'm just sitting here, drinking myself into a coma." His tone startled her. She considered walking away, but he spoke again before she could. "I sounded like a dickhead, didn't I?"

Without answering, she brushed by him to open the refrigerator door. She pulled out the jug of orange juice and set it on the counter, reaching past Carmine to grab a glass from the cabinet.

He spoke then, his breath fanning out against her. "Get me one, too."

A shiver ripped through her as she grabbed a second glass, unable to stop her reaction. Haven poured them both some juice and put the jug back in the fridge.

Carmine's behavior confused her, but a naïve part of her craved his company. Now that he was there, she had a distraction. And maybe she'd even have the music again.

He tipped his bottle of liquor, grunting after he pulled it from his lips. "Ugh, that's rough," he said, his voice gritty. He poured some in his juice, hesitating before dumping a bit in hers. "I don't like drinking alone."

Alone. Haven knew how that felt.

She sniffed the drink, scrunching up her nose. "What is it?"

"Why ask me? You can read, so fucking read the bottle." Her eyes widened, and he groaned. "I sounded like a dick again. I didn't mean it like that."

Irritated, she chugged her drink. It still tasted like orange juice, but a bitter edge to it burned her throat. Carmine stared at her as she set her empty glass onto the counter.

"*La mia*-fucking-*bella ragazza*." He chuckled, guzzling his drink. "You have potential, *tesoro*."

She smiled. "Thanks, I think."

"It's a compliment," he said. "And you'll get more where that one came from if you do it again."

He hopped down from the counter and poured two more glasses of juice, adding some liquor to both. Haven took a deep breath as she picked hers up. It was a lot stronger the second time, the burn harsher. She barely got half of it down before pulling the glass away with a cough. "Goodness, that's strong."

"Yeah, I loaded that one," he replied. "Don't chug anymore. If you do, you'll pass out, and I'd really like some company."

A swell of emotion shot through her, the longing returning. He wanted her company, too.

He held the bottle up. "And it's Grey Goose vodka, in case you're still wondering."

———

They went up to the third floor to Carmine's bedroom. He set his drink on his desk and sat in the chair, but Haven hesitated in the doorway, unsure of what to do.

"You can sit anywhere you want," he said, sensing her dilemma.

She took a seat on the edge of his bed and anxiously took a sip of her drink.

"So let's play a game or something," Carmine suggested. "How about twenty-one questions?"

Her nerves flared. She had no idea what that was.

He took notice of her bewildered expression. "We take turns asking each other questions until we hit twenty-one. Only rule is you can't lie. I don't give a shit what it's about—just no lying."

"Okay." She took a deep breath. "You go first."

Her hand trembled as Carmine gazed at her from across the room. He sighed and stood, taking her glass and setting it on his desk. After pulling out his keys, he unlocked his bottom desk drawer. "How do you feel about drugs? And that doesn't count as my question. I just wanna know before I do this."

"Uh, I don't know much about them."

He pulled out what looked to her like a cigar and lit it, the room filling with a pungent woodsy odor. He brought it to his lips and inhaled as he crouched down in front of her. "The weed will relax you, okay?"

She nodded, transfixed by his proximity.

"I'll make it easy on you," he said. "Just inhale and hold it as long as you can."

He brought it to his lips and sucked in deeply as he leaned toward her. Haven's heart raced as he cocked his head to the side, pausing with his lips an inch from hers. She inhaled as he exhaled, the smoke from his lungs infiltrating her system. She closed her eyes as everything clouded, only letting go when she needed air.

Exhaling slowly, she opened her eyes to see Carmine still in front of her, his staggering expression burning more than the smoke. "Question one—how did you practice reading if you weren't allowed to have any books?"

She blushed. "I took a book that belonged to my first master."

"That embarrasses you?"

"I confessed to being a thief."

He sat down again. "Yeah, well, you live with a career criminal. Thievery doesn't faze us."

"You're a career criminal?"

He looked at her with confusion. "No, I meant my father. You know, with what he does in Chicago." She didn't know, and that struck him. "Shit, I figured . . . It doesn't matter. Ask something different."

Still confused, she pulled out something random. "How'd you get that scar on your side?"

"Christ, you're not gonna take it easy on me, are you?" He ran his hand through his hair. "I got the scar when I was eight, bullet ripped through my side."

Haven thought maybe he'd fallen or cut himself—but she didn't think he would say he'd been shot.

"Like I said, we're more alike than you think," he continued. "I shed blood over shit that wasn't my fault too."

Could they really have things in common? "Why were you shot?"

He shook his head. "It's my turn. Do you have any secret talents?"

"Well, I like to draw, but I don't know if it's a talent."

"Will you draw something for me?"

She smiled. "You already asked your question."

He waved her off. "Fine, your turn."

"Why'd you get shot?"

"Can't say, because I don't really know," he said. "Ask something else."

She hesitated. "Well, why did you attack that boy at the game?"

"Because Nicholas deserved it. But knocking him down is nothing compared to what happened last time we saw each other." He muttered something under his breath before continuing. "So will you draw a picture for me?"

"Maybe someday."

"Someday? What does someday mean?"

"I'll draw for you the same someday you let me clean your room," she said. His mouth flew open like he was going to argue, so she cut him off by asking her next question. "What did you do to Nicholas before that was so bad?"

"Shot at his truck. The gas tank sparked. They accused me of attempted murder, but whatever. I honestly didn't *try* to kill him."

Haven was stunned he'd been so violent toward the boy when he'd seemed nice to her.

"What did he say that made you smile?" Carmine asked.

"He told me a joke about a deer."

He rolled his eyes. "That doesn't count as my question. Have you ever been kissed?"

She shook her head slowly, feeling inadequate. "That probably makes me seem immature . . ."

"Not at all. I shouldn't have asked that one." He nervously shifted around in his seat. "Hell, I haven't either, technically speaking, since I don't kiss on the lips." He paused again. "And that probably makes me seem like an asshole, that I can have sex with them but not kiss."

"How many girls were there?"

He dropped his head at her question. "A dozen and a half plus two or three, maybe."

"So twenty or twenty-one?"

He peeked at her. "You're quick at math. And that's ridiculously high, I know."

He looked upset by his own answer, and she couldn't help but wonder if he regretted some of those girls. She smiled, trying to be reassuring, but he just groaned. "New subject. Question number . . . whatever fucking number we're on. When's the most afraid you've been?"

"Maybe in your father's room."

Carmine nodded like he expected that answer and turned away to grab his drink. "Your turn."

"Where's your mama?"

She blurted it out, and her hands covered her mouth as Carmine froze, his glass midair.

"Chicago," he said, setting his glass down without taking a drink. He turned back to her, his blank expression surprising her as much as his answer.

"Chicago?"

"Actually, it's Hillside, a few miles outside of Chicago."

"Oh."

"Anyway," he said, "what's your favorite color?"

"Green." Her cheeks flushed as she answered. She lay back on his bed to avoid his gaze.

The bed moved as he sat beside her. Her eyes shot to his as he stared down at her. "Your turn."

"What's your favorite color?" She was too flustered to think of anything else.

"I'm torn between deep brown and this shade of pinkish red right now. Looks kinda like my tie."

Her blush deepened, and she had to look away from him as her heart raced.

"My turn," he said. "Why's green your favorite color?"

"Pass," she said.

"You can't pass."

"But you didn't answer some questions."

"Fine, I'll ask something else. Why are you embarrassed about your favorite color?"

Her brow furrowed. "I passed on that question."

"No, you passed on why green was your favorite color. Now I wanna know why green being your favorite color is embarrassing. Two completely different things."

He spoke matter-of-factly, as if it were just that simple.

"I think you're cheating," she said. "So I pass again."

Carmine laughed as he relit his cigar. Haven was mesmerized at the calmness of his expression as he inhaled, and goose bumps popped up on her skin at the sight of him. Maybe it was the intoxicants, but something made her feel at ease. She felt safe there, and as frightening as that was she basked in the sensation. Because never in her life had she truly felt safe with someone—not even her mama. She couldn't protect her.

She trusted him, when she'd never trusted anyone in her life. And she knew she shouldn't, especially him. He was the son of the man who controlled her—his family held her life in their hands. They could kill her, and she'd be defenseless to stop it. But she trusted him anyway. She could feel it in every inch of her body, every beat of her frenzied heart.

Something about this boy had burrowed under her skin.

Carmine leaned forward, pausing an inch from her mouth. She parted her lips, inhaling everything he gave her, and closed her eyes as she tasted his breath.

His face grazed her cheek, the sparks from his skin sending tingles through her body. She could feel the slight stubble of his facial hair, rough and scratchy, as he inhaled deeply. He breathed her in, and she allowed herself to wonder if maybe— just maybe—this frightening creature could want the same thing she craved.

She held on as long as she could, not wanting to let go, but her body's need for oxygen won. She exhaled as Carmine got up, but she kept her eyes closed. She didn't want to face reality yet.

Carmine slipped out of the bedroom, needing to put some space between them. She had him twisted. Up was suddenly down, left was now right, and everything surrounding him was a blur. It was difficult for him to admit he was as inexperienced as her. He could fuck a girl senseless, but when it came to loving one, he had no clue what to do.

Love. The word perplexed him. He wasn't swimming in lust anymore. This was uncharted territory, and he was fucking drowning.

Carmine walked over to the library and flicked on the light. Blinking a few times, he scanned the titles on the bookshelves, grabbing one before heading back to the bedroom. Haven lay on her stomach on his bed, her feet up by his pillows. He gave her a small smile and shut the door behind him, holding the book out to her. "*The Secret Garden.* Thought you might like it."

She took it. "What's it about?"

He shrugged. "A garden, maybe? A secret? I don't know. Read it and tell me."

"Uh . . ." she started, her brow furrowing as she eyed the cover.

He chuckled. A book flustered her. "Look, you don't have to. I'm not gonna make you write a book report. Just thought it would give you something to do."

"Oh, I want to! It's just . . . what if your father finds it?"

"Don't worry about him," he said. "I got you covered."

Her eyes glossed over with tears as she opened it halfway. "I don't think I can read this. There are a lot of different words."

"Well, I think you can do it," he said. "Besides, you have help now."

"Help?"

"Yeah. I mean, if you don't want help, fine, but I'm happy to do what I can."

She looked down at the book again. "Okay."

"Okay," he echoed her word. "Is that an, 'Okay, I'd like to do this reading shit with you,' or is it an, 'Okay, you're really fucking nuts if you think you can help me?'"

She merely smiled, the sight of it telling him it was probably a combination of the two.

He kicked off his shoes and sat down next to her, playing a few chords on his guitar as she read the book. It made him warm inside, and for a while, it felt like it was normal . . . like they were normal. Just a boy and a girl, both of them a bit fucked up, but they were just themselves.

And he savored it.

He tried to keep his attention off her, not wanting to make her uncomfortable, but from the corner of his eye he could see the look of concentration on her face as she sounded out words. "What's *tyr*—uh, this word?"

He set his guitar down and rolled onto his stomach, peeking over to see what she pointed at. His chin rested on her shoulder. "Tyrannical. It's like a tyrant. You know, like a master."

She turned to him, their faces so close the tips of their noses touched.

12

Haven stood in the kitchen, her mind wandering as she made cookies. She'd slipped out of bed an hour ago, her nerves on edge about last night. Her body controlled her when she was around Carmine, her heart taking the lead over her mind. Her mind told her it was ridiculous, dangerous to spend time with him, but her heart told her it was right.

She'd preheated the oven and put a batch in when there was a knock on the front door. Glancing out the window, she saw a small white car in the driveway. Whoever it was knocked again, more forceful the second time.

She couldn't open the door. The alarm was enabled, and she still didn't have a code. Quietly locked in a dilemma, she was relieved when Carmine stomped down the stairs. "Whoever's at the fucking door better have a search warrant."

Haven strolled to the doorway as he answered the door. Before he could say a word, someone shoved into him, barging into the house. "You're such an asshole!"

While Haven was stunned, Carmine's expression remained blank. "Lisa."

"How could you do that to me last night?" Lisa spat, glaring at him, the look on her face reminiscent of Mistress Katrina yelling at Master Michael. She wondered what Carmine could have done to ignite such fury, but he wasn't giving any indication of a response.

Carmine glanced toward the kitchen as Lisa repeatedly cursed at him, and he smiled when he spotted Haven watching. Lisa noticed the exchange. "Is she the reason, Carmine? That bitch?"

Carmine's smile fell. "If you know what's good for you, you'll shut up right now."

"I thought you were better than that! Look at her!" Lisa glared at Haven. "How much is Dr. DeMarco paying you to screw his son?"

Her words set Carmine off. He grabbed Lisa's arm and swung open the front door with so much force it slammed into the wall. He pulled her out to her car while she continued to yell, flailing and trying to strike him, but Carmine ducked out of the way. He yelled back—Haven couldn't hear him, but she could see his mouth move furiously—and slammed his hands against the hood of her car.

The oven beeped, the cookies done. Haven pulled them out as the front door slammed, rattling things on the kitchen counter. Carmine walked in and paused beside her at the window. "You should have answered it and told her I wasn't home."

"I couldn't. I don't have a code."

He looked at her peculiarly as he grabbed one of the peanut butter cookies from the rack. Taking a bite, he turned away. "Eat a cookie, Haven. They're good."

Dr. DeMarco arrived home as Haven was putting the cookies in a container. He walked right to her in the kitchen, stopping so close his arm brushed against hers. Her skin crawled, his presence alarming, and she fought back a shudder.

Dr. DeMarco snatched a cookie before she could put the lid on. "Morning, *dolcezza*."

"Good morning, sir." She paused. "What does that mean?"

"*Dolcezza*?" He took a bite, smiling kindly. "Sweetheart."

Sweetheart?

Dr. DeMarco made a pot of coffee, something Haven hadn't dared to try since the morning everything went terribly, horribly wrong, and poured a cup before walking out. She brushed the flour from her clothes and finished cleaning before heading into the family room, where everyone had gathered. Carmine glanced at her from the spot he had taken on the couch.

"Dad," he said, his eyes remaining on her. "I'm gonna teach Haven how to read."

Fear shot through her. Dr. DeMarco raised his eyebrows. "I assumed to teach someone to read, you'd have to know how."

Carmine rolled his eyes. "I can read."

"Yeah," Dominic interjected. "Didn't you know? He read the first page of *The Count of Monte Cristo*."

"*Vaffanculo*," Carmine said.

Dr. DeMarco sighed as he turned his attention to Haven. "Take a seat, child."

She couldn't tell whether it was an offer or a demand, but it was safer to just do what he said. She took the empty seat beside Carmine, folding her hands in her lap, tense and nervous. Carmine, on the other hand, had his feet casually kicked up on the coffee table as he slouched with boredom.

There was a knock on the door after a while, but no one got up to answer it. They knocked again before the door opened, a female's voice ringing through the downstairs. "None of you can answer the door for me?"

"Hello, Tess," Dr. DeMarco said as the girl strolled into the family room. Tess glanced around at all of them, her eyes lingering on Haven for longer than she was comfortable with, before squeezing in the chair with Dominic.

Haven turned to the television and tried to focus on the movie, but Carmine kept inching closer to her, his presence clouding her mind.

"Doc, did your son tell you he beat up Lisa's car this morning?" Tess asked.

"I hit it once," Carmine said. "It only left a small dent."

"Well, you better find a job to pay for that dent," Dr. DeMarco said. "I'm not forking the bill for you anymore, remember?"

"I shouldn't have to pay for *anything*. She deserved it, busting in here like a damn interrogator."

Those words drew Dr. DeMarco's attention from the movie. "Why did she interrogate you?"

"She wants a relationship or something."

Dr. DeMarco laughed. "That's what happens when you lead girls on."

"Whatever, I don't lead them on. And regardless, maybe I deserve the shit, but Haven didn't deserve to get dragged into it."

Dr. DeMarco's eyebrows rose. "How did that happen?"

Carmine shrugged. "Wrong place, wrong time."

"I don't think she meant any harm," Haven said quietly.

"Bullshit," Carmine said. "Lisa knew what she was doing."

Dr. DeMarco shook his head. "You shouldn't be put in the line of fire with Carmine's *puttani*."

Haven had no idea what *puttani* were, but she had a feeling it wasn't nice. "I've survived worse."

Dr. DeMarco's gaze was intense. "Yes, you have."

Everyone turned back to the television, but Haven fidgeted in her seat. Uncomfortable, she wanted a reason to leave the room and leaned toward Carmine. "Do you want something to drink?"

He shrugged. "You can bring me something."

She stood up, taking a few steps toward the kitchen. "Do you need anything, Dr. DeMarco?"

"No, thank you."

"I'll take a bottle of water," Tess chimed in. "Thanks for asking."

Haven paused, frightened she had made a mistake, but Dr. DeMarco alleviated her worry. "You're capable of getting your own water, Tess. There's nothing wrong with your legs."

Haven made a cherry Coke for Carmine and grabbed a bottle of water for herself, hesitating before getting a second one. She headed back into the family room and handed it to Tess. Tess raised her eyebrows as she took the water without saying a word.

Haven sat back down and handed the soda to Carmine. "You didn't have to do that. Actually, you didn't have to do any of it." He brought his glass to his lips and took a sip. "I appreciate it, though."

"You're welcome," she said as something from the corner of her eye caught her attention. Dr. DeMarco was staring at her again.

The home phone rang then, and everyone jumped at the shrill sound. Haven hadn't heard it ring before. Her heart raced as Dr. DeMarco stood to grab it.

"What the fuck is that?"

Haven saw the baffled expression on Carmine's face. "It's the telephone."

"No, I get that, but where did it come from?"

She shrugged as Dr. DeMarco answered the call. "DeMarco residence . . . Wait, slow down . . . How many hits did you say you had?" Haven tried not to listen, but he spoke loudly. "How is that possible?"

"Seriously," Carmine said. "When did we get a phone?"

Dominic laughed. "Weeks ago."

Dr. DeMarco raised his voice more. "Do it again. If it comes out the same the second time, we'll redo the entire thing, but it has to be wrong. There's no way it's true."

"Why didn't anyone tell me?" Carmine asked.

"The better question, bro, is why didn't you notice?"

"Keep it off the record," Dr. DeMarco continued, speaking over all of them. "I don't want this getting out until I can make sense of it. *Capice?*"

He tossed the phone down, ending the call, and pinched the bridge of his nose. His gaze drifted to Carmine and Haven, his expression unreadable, but the raging fire was back in his eyes. Standing, he snatched the cherry Coke right out of Carmine's hand, spilling some on the floor as he stalked out of the room. A moment later something crashed in the kitchen, the sound of a glass smashing as it was thrown into the metal sink.

Stunned, Haven glanced at Carmine. "What happened?"

He shrugged, staring at his empty hand. "Beats me. I didn't even know we had a damn phone."

———

The door to the office on the second floor was uncharacteristically left open. Vincent sat behind his desk, his glasses low on his nose as he rummaged through files. Carmine stood in the doorway, watching him. "Who jizzed in your coffee?"

Vincent's head snapped up. "Excuse me?"

"What's your problem?" Carmine elaborated as he stepped into the room and took a seat, not waiting for an invitation. "You were fine and then suddenly it was like you swallowed someone's bitter junk."

Vincent shook his head. "Must you always be crass?"

"I don't know," Carmine said. "Must you always be evasive?"

"Only when you ask questions you really don't want the answers to," Vincent said. "Did you need something? I have things to take care of."

"Well, for one, I wanna know why you took my drink."

"I was thirsty."

"So you drank it?"

"No," he said. "Any other questions?"

"Yeah, why do you have Haven locked in here like she's on house arrest?"

"She's been outside," Vincent said, casting him an incredulous look. "She seemed to enjoy herself at your game until you had one of your episodes."

"One of my episodes? Is that what we're calling them?"

"Unless you have a better name for it."

"Whatever," Carmine said. "The point is she rarely leaves. She doesn't even have a code."

Vincent sighed exasperatedly. "Why do you suddenly care?"

"Because she's a person."

"So is Nicholas Barlow, but you never seem to be concerned about him."

"It's different. Someone ought to lock him up, but she's just a girl. She's harmless."

Vincent looked up again at those words, blinking a few times. "Are you suggesting you've never hurt a girl before, Carmine? Because I think a few would say differently."

The room remained silent. Carmine had no response. Vincent pushed his files aside and took off his glasses, sighing. "Look, she's locked inside because I don't have the time or the energy to take her anywhere, and there's no one else to do it."

"Yeah, maybe you're right," Carmine said. "I don't even have enough gas in my car to take myself anywhere right now."

"How do you plan to get to school?"

Carmine shrugged. "Siphon the gas from your car while you sleep."

Contrary to the tension in the room, Vincent actually laughed at that. "You probably would."

Carmine smirked. He would.

Vincent opened his top desk drawer and pulled out the silver American Express card. "I tell you what—I'll make you a deal."

Carmine eyed him skeptically. "I'm listening."

"I'll give you the credit card back if you make more of an effort."

"What, like keeping my room clean?"

"I said an effort, not a miracle. And what I mean is straighten yourself out. Stop the fighting, stop the drugs, pass your classes, and when I ask for a favor, I want you to actually do it."

"Fair enough," Carmine said, grabbing the credit card before his father could change his mind. "I'll make an effort."

"Great, because I need a favor."

Carmine stared at him, not at all surprised.

"We need groceries," Vincent said. "Enough stuff to last a while."

"Like food and shit?"

"Just food, Carmine. But yes."

"And you want me to get these groceries? On my own?"

"Of course not," Vincent said. "Since you're so concerned, take the girl with you."

Carmine looked between his father and the credit card. "Is this a test? Because not two goddamn hours ago you said I was still cut off."

"Things change, son."

"What changed?"

Vincent shook his head—evading again. "You want a chance to prove yourself? Do it. But don't screw up this time, Carmine. If something happens to the girl, there will be more dire consequences than being cut off financially."

Carmine stood up, figuring he needed to leave the room before his father came to his senses. "Does this mean I'm no longer grounded?"

Vincent sighed. "You've been grounded since you were thirteen, and you'll continue to be grounded for as long as you live under my roof. Not that being grounded has ever stopped you before . . ."

"So basically, I'm not really grounded."

"Were you ever?"

Carmine laughed. "No."

13

Sunny Oaks Manor, located in the Hyde Park neighborhood of Chicago, looked like an upper-class apartment complex. The only thing that gave away its true nature was the staff, wearing the typical medical scrubs. Everyone was friendly, the facilities modern, but none of that mattered to Gia DeMarco.

Vincent had done everything in his power to make her comfortable, insuring she had the biggest apartment and as many luxuries as allowed, but she held resentment that she'd been forced to move. Sunny Oaks wasn't her home, she'd told him, and as far as she was concerned, it never would be.

Gia sat in her chair at the window in her front room, dressed impeccably in a blue dress and black pumps as she gazed out at the courtyard. Vincent perched on the arm of the chair across from his mother, not surprised in the least when she refused to greet him. Same story, different day.

"It's nice outside," he said, attempting conversation. "We could go for a walk."

"I haven't seen you in months, Vincenzo," Gia said, her voice venomous. "Months."

Vincent sighed. "It's been three weeks."

"Three months, three weeks," she said. "May as well have been three years. You don't care."

"I do care, but I don't live in Chicago anymore, remember?"

"Don't remind me," she said. "I hate thinking my only son abandoned his family."

Vincent knew by *family* she didn't mean blood relatives. She was referring to *la famiglia*, where her true loyalty lay. If ever there was a stereotypical Mafia wife, dedicated to the lifestyle until death, it was his mother.

"I didn't abandon anyone," Vincent said.

"You abandoned me," Gia said. "You stuck me in this hospital."

"It's not a hospital. It's a retirement community."

"I don't belong here," she said. "I'm not sick! Your father, God rest his soul, would be ashamed of you."

That was nothing new. "How about that walk now?"

"I don't care what these quacks say," she said, ignoring his suggestion for the second time. "They can't be trusted. They're all probably working for the government. Kennedy always had it out for your father, you know. He tried to bring him down."

"Kennedy's dead," Vincent said. "Has been for a long time."

"I know that," she spat. "I'm not crazy."

Vincent laughed dryly. The jury was still out on that. The doctors suspected Gia DeMarco suffered from early onset dementia, but Vincent leaned toward her simply refusing to move past her glory days. She didn't want to admit life went on without her, that the world didn't stop turning the day her husband died.

Usually lucid, every now and then she'd slip back to those times when Antonio DeMarco was the most powerful man in Chicago and Vincent still cared about making his parents proud.

"Some fresh air would be nice, don't you think?"

Gia reached up and rubbed her right ear, ignoring Vincent for the third time. "My ear's ringing. That old hag Gertrude next door must be talking about me."

"Did you take aspirin today? That can cause ear ringing."

"It's not the medication," she said. "It's her."

His mother was nothing if not superstitious. "Gertrude doesn't seem like the gossiping type."

"Like you could tell, Vincenzo. You have the judgment of an imbecile! You and your Irish—"

"Don't start, Ma." Vincent raised his voice as he cut her off. "I'm not going to listen to it again."

Gia was quiet, as if considering whether or not to finish her thought, but finally changed the subject. "Your sister visits me all the time. I see Corrado more than I see you."

It was a lie, but Vincent let it roll off his back.

"Now that's what I call a good man," she said. "Corrado's loyal. Always has been. His only flaw is he never gave your sister any babies. I always wanted grandchildren."

"You have grandchildren," Vincent said. "Two of them."

Gia scoffed but managed to keep her opinion to herself. She stared out the window, shaking her head. "You don't care about me, Vincenzo. You never even take me outside anymore."

———————

Since the DeMarcos had moved to North Carolina, the boys had thrown a Halloween party every year. Vincent was hesitant to agree this year, but after a bit of pestering and a lot of promising, he caved with one strict rule—Haven was to be watched at all times.

The house smelled like Pine-Sol when Carmine arrived home that afternoon, the aroma so heavy it stung his eyes. He stopped in the doorway of the kitchen, seeing Haven scrubbing the marble floor. She hummed, oblivious to his presence, and he listened as he tried to place the song.

She stood and turned around, the humming cut off by a yelp. "You're home!"

He chuckled as she dropped the sponge. "Didn't mean to interrupt, hummingbird."

"You didn't. I was only . . ." She trailed off as she eyed him peculiarly. "Hummingbird?"

"Yeah, hummingbird. *Colibri*. You kinda remind me of one."

He felt like an idiot as those words hung between them.

She looked bewildered. "Why?"

"I don't know," he said. "They're these little colorful birds that flutter around and hum. And, you know, you're kinda the same way."

Her cheeks flushed. "You heard me?"

"I've heard you a few times. It's, uh . . ." He didn't know what to say. "What song is it?"

"It's something my mama used to sing."

She fidgeted, averting her eyes. Her sweatpants and tank top were splattered with soapy water, her hair all over the place.

"You should get dressed," he suggested. "We have somewhere to go, and I'm sure you'd rather put on something else."

She eyed him skeptically. "Okay."

She lingered for a moment before heading upstairs. He rolled his tense shoulders as he silently berated himself, wishing he'd loosen up around her. His anxiety fueled hers, and the last thing he wanted was for her to avoid him again.

It only took Haven a few minutes to return, wearing a pair of jeans and a t-shirt. He opened the front door, and Haven hesitated in the doorway before stepping on the porch. After engaging the alarm and locking up, he helped her into his car. She thanked him softly when he climbed into the driver's side, her eyes darting around as they drove. "Where are we going?"

Carmine opened the center console, looking for his list, before motioning toward the glove compartment. "Check in there for a piece of paper."

She did what he said, shifting things around, and blushed when she pulled out a small black box. Carmine groaned, realizing she'd found the condoms he kept in the car.

"Christ, I forgot they were in there." He snatched them from her hand and rolled down the window in a panic, tossing them out along the side of the road. He ignored her incredulous look, not wanting to have to explain, and waved her back to the glove compartment.

Haven searched again, grabbing a piece of notebook paper. "Is this it?"

"Yeah, that's it. Read it."

Wide-eyed, she stammered over some of the words. "Uh, chips . . . pret—uh, pretzels . . . soda . . . Are we going to a store?"

"Yes. That's what we need for the party. While we're there, we'll stock up the house. You know, kill two birds with one stone."

When they made it to the store, Haven's footsteps faltered as the doors opened on their own. She surveyed them, almost as if she was afraid to go through. Carmine waited for her to grab a cart, but she just stood there.

"Have you been grocery shopping much?" he asked.

She shook her head. "I've never been inside a store."

"Never?"

"Never."

This would be more complicated than he thought. "I can't say I've ever done this either. I'm not usually trusted, so I guess we'll figure this shit out together."

Haven tried to hand him the paper, but he instead handed her a pen. "You do the list. Practice makes perfect, right?"

Before she could argue, he grabbed a cart and led her to the produce section. "I have another confession. I can't say I've ever cooked either, so I have no idea what half this shit is." He picked up a green stalk and eyed it skeptically. "What the fuck is this?"

She smiled. "Those are Brussels sprouts."

"Definitely not buying them," he said, throwing the stalk down on the display.

It was quiet so early in the afternoon, only a few shoppers in the store other than them. Carmine was grateful for the privacy. Haven was clearly out of her element, clutching the list tightly as her eyes monitored everything. "What should we get?"

"Whatever you wanna cook," he said. "I don't know if you've

noticed, but Dom will eat anything. Hell, he'd eat Brussels sprouts. And my father isn't hard to please."

"And you?"

He shrugged.

"Finicky," she said to herself.

He blinked a few times. "What did you call me?"

She looked guilty as she repeated the word. "Finicky."

"My father taught you that, didn't he?" he asked. "He's been calling me that for years."

"Dr. DeMarco did mention it, but I didn't mean any disrespect."

"I know," he said. "But whatever, let's shop. We look like idiots just standing here, like we've never done this shit before."

"We haven't," she reminded him.

"I know that, and you know that, but the rest of these fuckers don't need to know it."

They made their way through the aisles. Carmine did most of the work, packing the cart full of junk food while Haven picked up the essentials he bypassed. He watched her those moments, as she grabbed milk and eggs and bread, her shoulders relaxed and movements confident.

She handed the list to him once everything had been crossed off, and they headed to the register. He put their stuff on the conveyer belt and reached toward the display of candy. Haven flinched as his arm shot out so he slowed his movements as he threw a chocolate Toblerone bar on the conveyor belt.

After paying, Carmine stuffed the trunk with all of the bags while Haven stood in the vacant parking lot beside the car. He wasn't paying her any attention as he returned the cart to the store, and his stomach sank when he turned around. Haven wasn't standing there anymore.

Panic erupted inside of him as he scanned the parking lot, searching for some sign of her. His father was going to kill him.

All it took was ten seconds—ten measly fucking seconds of his guard being down—and she'd slipped away, vanishing.

He hastily ran to the car, movement inside of it nearly buckling his knees. Haven sat in the passenger seat, seatbelt clipped in place and hands folded in her lap. He had to take a moment to collect himself, to savor the feeling of relief, before climbing in beside her with his candy bar.

He opened the Toblerone and pulled off a triangle for her, watching with confusion as she gawked at his hand. "Don't you like chocolate?"

"I've never had it."

He thrust it at her. "Christ, girl, take this shit, then."

She laughed at his enthusiasm and took it, biting off a small corner of the chocolate. Her expression brightened, her words escaping as a moan. "Wow, that's sweet."

Pulling off a few triangles for himself, Carmine handed the rest of the Toblerone to her. "I know. Fucking amazing."

———

It was drizzling when they arrived at the house, so Carmine parked as close to the porch as possible. "Unlock the door, okay?" She started to interject, but he cut her off. "The code's 62373. Punch it into the keypad and hit the big-ass button. Can you remember that?"

"62373," she repeated.

She ran to the door, pressing the numbers as the rain came down harder. Once she had the door open, he climbed out and grabbed some bags. Haven tried to head back outside when he reached the foyer, but he threw his hand out to stop her. Her arms flew up protectively in front of her, so he quickly withdrew his hand. "Shit, I didn't mean to scare you. I just don't want you to get wet."

She gave him a look that seemed to be a mixture of confusion and amusement before she took the groceries into the kitchen. He unloaded the car and tried to help, tossing things where he figured they went, but he only made the job harder by getting in her way.

Dominic brought pizzas home for dinner, and Carmine grabbed a box of pepperoni before plopping down on the couch. Glancing at Haven, he patted the cushion beside him. Her eyes darted toward the stairs, and he cocked an eyebrow at her as if to say, *Don't fucking dare.* He would have dragged her back. There was no reason for her to not eat with them.

———

Carmine awoke the next afternoon to a house in total chaos. Tess and Dia stood on chairs in the family room, tacking streamers around the window, while Haven sorted through a box of fake flowers. Dominic ran from one room to another, following orders barked at him from Tess.

Sneaking into the room, Carmine grabbed Tess's chair and vehemently shook it, startling her. Yelling, Tess leaped off the chair, and he covered his head as she punched him in the back. "You're such a jerk, Carmine!"

"Yeah, well, you hit like a little girl." The words barely left his mouth when her fist shot out, punching him right in the chest. He winced. "Damn!"

Tess smirked. "Who's the little girl now?"

"Apparently me," he said, rubbing his chest as he eyed his brother, arranging flowers he'd gotten from Haven. "I'm starting to feel like one, anyway, in a room full of bitches."

"What did you call me?" Haven's voice had an edge he'd never heard from her before.

His brow furrowed until it dawned on him what he'd said. "Ah, shit . . ." *Bitch.* "Nothing."

She turned back to the flowers without a word, handing more of them to Dominic, and Carmine watched her before approaching. Leaning close, his lips beside her ear, he whispered, "I'm sorry. I didn't mean it that way."

She said nothing. Guilt tugged at his chest. He couldn't tell if she believed him.

———

After the house was decorated, Carmine put on his pirate costume, sliding on the black pants and boots before buttoning up the white ruffled shirt and tying the red bandanna around his head. Grabbing the big black hat, he headed down to see Dominic in the foyer, wielding a sword.

"Which dumbass gave him a weapon?" Carmine called out, barely evading the plastic blade as his brother swung it at him. "You people should know better by now."

"No one gave it to him," Tess said, stepping out of the family room in her devil costume. "He found it on his own."

Shaking his head, Carmine headed toward the office under the stairs, punching in the code to unlock the door. The room looked like a normal office, with a wooden mahogany desk and a black leather chair. A Persian rug covered the floor, and Carmine folded the corner, exposing the hidden door. He opened it and headed down the flimsy stairs into the basement, flicking on the light. A subtle glow came over the room, revealing dozens of wooden crates.

Using the front of his shirt to cover his hand, he pulled the top off the one closest to the stairs and grabbed a few bottles of liquor. He didn't go any farther, having no desire to venture to the back.

He wasn't sure if it was subconscious fear or if his father had shown him at some point, but he never left his fingerprints down there.

Once he had the liquor, he headed upstairs in time for the guests to arrive.

———

Haven sat on the edge of her bed, picking at her fingernails as sickness stirred in her stomach. She felt out of place, afraid to go downstairs, worried that with one look they'd all know what she was. They'd all know she didn't belong in their world with them.

There was a soft knock on the door before Dominic peeked in. "Can I come in, Twinkle Toes?"

"Of course," she said.

He strolled in, using a sword like a walking cane, and sat beside her on the bed. He leaned back on his elbows and things grew quiet as Dominic stared off into space. She wondered why he was here instead of at his party, but she remained silent and let him speak first.

"*Nella vita: chi non risica, non rosica,*" he said. "In life: nothing ventured, nothing gained. My mom used to tell us that. It's been a long time, but I can still hear her."

He smiled to himself, remembering, as Haven conjured her own mama's voice in her mind, never wanting to forget what she sounded like.

"Mom taught us a lot, but that's what I remember most. You shouldn't be afraid to take risks. It might not work out, you might fail miserably and get hurt, but you'll never know unless you try." He paused, sighing. "You can play it safe, Haven, and I wouldn't blame you for it. You can continue as you've been, and you'll survive, but is that what you want? Is that enough?"

Haven had no answer for that.

"Or you could take a risk," he continued. "I know you have it in you. I can't promise you'll get everything you want, but I can promise nothing will change if you don't try."

She stared at him, absorbing his words, as Dominic's expression turned somber. "Carmine wasn't always such an asshole, you know. He used to be like Mom, couldn't hurt a fly, but all that changed. Carmine will take physical risks—sometimes I wonder if he has any regard for his life—but anything emotional is out of the question. You're good for him that way. You're the first girl he's looked at as a person and not an object."

Her eyes widened. "Why am I different to him?"

"I think you remind him of Mom, but he's the only one who can really answer that." Dominic stood. "So, tell me. Are we going to play it safe, or are we going to put ourselves out there?"

The party had been going for more than an hour, and there had yet to be any sign of Haven. Carmine strolled through the crowd searching for her and found Dia alone in the kitchen. She had on a colorful dress and bright blue tights, a yellow beak on her nose that matched her sneakers.

"Hey, Polly," he said, nudging her. "How come you look the most normal on Halloween?"

She rolled her eyes. "Har-har-har. Funny."

A group of girls burst into the room then, and Carmine groaned when he saw Lisa dressed like a cat in a black bodysuit. "Who invited her?"

Dia grabbed his arm and pulled him out of the kitchen before Lisa could corner him. "I'm pretty sure you did when you were going out with her."

"I didn't go out with her," he said. "It was more like getting into her a few times."

She cringed. "Gross."

"Yeah, well, I blame you. You should've warned me against doing it . . . or her. Whatever."

"I tried! You wouldn't listen."

The two of them stepped into the foyer just as Haven emerged from the stairs, wearing a shiny gold dress. Fake coins hung from the edges, costume jewelry hanging around her neck with a small crown in her hair. "She's my treasure?"

Dia patted Carmine's cheek condescendingly before walking away.

Haven paused in the foyer as Carmine stepped forward, taking her hand. "*Bella ragazza.*"

Her eyes sparkled as she gazed at their hands. "What does that mean?"

He smirked, pulling her toward the kitchen without an answer to mingle with the crowd. She was attentive, smiling and greeting people like she'd been entertaining company her entire life. Watching her fascinated Carmine, the way she adapted easily to her surroundings. He couldn't help but think they'd done the world a grave injustice by keeping her locked away.

They were in the kitchen getting drinks when somebody turned the music louder. Carmine grabbed Haven's hand to twirl her around. She laughed, losing her balance, and Carmine pulled her to him. Buzzing from the alcohol, he wanted nothing more than to feel her close. He gripped her hips and swayed her tense body to the music. "Relax, *tesoro*."

The anxiety in her expression lessened. "Will you ever tell me what anything means?"

"*Tesoro*'s kinda like sweetheart, but it means treasure . . . which, right now, you literally are."

She blushed, shyly looking away from him, and he took the opportunity to dip her backward. Yelping, she wrapped her arms around his neck and giggled when he pulled her back up. Their noses rubbed together, and he froze when Haven cocked her head to the side and softly brushed her lips against his.

Her strawberry gloss smeared on his mouth, and he licked his lips, too stunned to do anything but stare. Haven backed up a few steps, retreating, and he grabbed her arm when he realized she was about to run. Yanking her to him, he eagerly kissed her without another thought.

It was passionate and messy, seventeen years' worth of kisses rolled into one stolen embrace. Haven kissed him back, her lips parting as they moved with his. Running her hand along the back of his head, she laced her fingers in the hair by his neck as she trembled, but whether from nerves or excitement, Carmine wasn't sure.

"Holy shit!"

They broke the kiss at the sound of Dominic's voice. He stood in the doorway to the kitchen, gaping at them. Haven slipped away, bolting from the room before either of them could stop her.

"I didn't mean to barge in." Dominic smacked Carmine on the back. "But, man, I didn't expect to see that."

Carmine shook his head, dazed. He hadn't expected it either.

———

Haven stared in the bathroom mirror, bringing her hand up to her mouth, lips tingling from the force of Carmine's kiss. Her mind worked rapidly as she tried to sort it out. Did it mean he felt the same sparks she did?

Someone pounded on the door, saying they needed to use the bathroom, and Haven slipped back out, wanting to look for him. She asked Dia, who pointed her to the stairs.

She ran up to the third floor and spotted Carmine in front of her room with a group of boys. A smile tugged her lips as she approached him, and he returned her smile, but it faded fast when the boy standing next to him whispered, "Fresh meat?"

It happened as fast as the flicking of a light switch, smile turned to scowl as hands clenched into fists. Without saying a word, Carmine grabbed the boy and shoved him into the wall, punching him straight in the mouth. People shouted, heading straight for the chaos, as Carmine kicked and hit, unleashing his rage on the boy.

"If you even look at her again," he spat, "I'll fucking kill you!"

Haven gasped and ran into her room, locking the door behind her.

———

The pounding on the door vibrated the walls, ripping Haven back to another time.

Bang. Bang. Bang. Haven lay huddled in the corner stable, covering her ears, but it did nothing to muffle the sounds. She didn't know what was happening—her mama was gone when the banging woke her up.

Bang. Bang. Bang. It grew louder with time. Where was her mama? Haven squeezed her eyes shut, counting in her head to make it go away. She made it to six before she lost her place, starting over but never reaching ten.

Bang. Bang. Bang. There was whimpering and crying, but it didn't come from her. It felt startlingly close but so far away, a place Haven couldn't reach in the darkness.

Bang. Bang. Bang. She heard the voice then, malicious and low. He hissed like a snake as he spoke the scathing words, "If you tell anyone, I'll fucking kill you." She didn't know who said it or what they shouldn't tell, but the crying grew louder at the sound of them. "I promise I won't," another voice spoke, this one heartbreakingly familiar. "Just please—I beg you—leave my baby girl alone."

Bang. Bang. Bang. It faded, but the silence did nothing to comfort her. She opened her eyes, hoping it was a nightmare, but the first thing she saw was her monster's vicious face. He stood just outside the stall, buckling his pants as he ogled her.

Her stomach felt as mangled as her monster's deformed skin. Her chest ached from crying, a void deep inside her. Her mama came back that night, trembling as she hugged her, but she wasn't there now to calm Haven's fears.

"Haven?" Carmine's voice was soft, his banging now a subtle tap on the door. "Fuck, I'm sorry. I didn't mean to scare you."

14

Vibrant red blood splattered the white wall in the library. Haven was cleaning it with a rag when Carmine's bedroom door opened. Disheveled, he glared at her. "What are you doing? You shouldn't be doing that!"

He snatched the rag from her hand as her eyes welled with tears. Overwhelmed and exhausted, she couldn't take him looking at her that way, disgust and anger shining from his eyes. His hand flew in her direction and she recoiled, moving out of his reach. She stumbled and plopped down on the floor.

His face clouded with confusion as he dropped his hand. "I can't get anything right with you."

"I'm sorry," she said, not understanding. She was only trying to clean up the blood.

He groaned, throwing the rag down as his voice rose with passion. "You're sorry? For what? *Ciò è scopare pazzesco!* I'm gonna lose my mind if we don't stop doing this dance!"

Dance? "What are you talking about?"

He grabbed her arm, and the zap of tingles coursed through her. She wondered why he was touching her, an irrational part of her wishing he'd never stop. When he touched her, she didn't feel so alone. When he touched her, she felt alive for once.

"Tell me you don't feel that, and I'll back off."

She stared at his hand. "You feel it too?"

"Of course I feel it. I kissed you last night!"

She blinked a few times. "But I kissed you. I shouldn't have, because you told me you didn't . . ."

"You barely grazed my lips. I practically assaulted your mouth." He shook his head. "And you're right—I don't do that, which is what makes it so crazy. I've been trying to tell you that."

He ran his fingers through his unkempt hair as he stared at her, his eyes imploring her, but for what she didn't understand. "Tell me what?"

Her question was met with silence. He slumped against the wall and brought his knees up, wrapping his arms around them. "I would've cleaned up the blood," he said. "I caused it."

"Was the boy okay?"

"He's like a cockroach. I could cut his head off, and he'd still run around."

She sighed at his unwillingness to give her a straight answer. "I know I have no right to tell you what to do, but I don't like people being hurt because of me. If you want to blame anyone, blame me. Punish me. But please don't keep hurting them. They didn't do anything."

He stared at her, his mouth hanging open. "You think I look at you that way?"

"When you attack people, it's like you're upset they're messing with something that's yours."

He laced his fingers in his hair, tugging on a handful of the locks. "I have a problem with my temper. It's just, I feel . . ." He hesitated, taking a deep breath. "Look, it's not because I think you belong to me—it's because I want you to be mine."

Her brow furrowed. "Is there a difference?"

"That didn't sound right. Christ, I care about you, okay? I overreact because I don't want anyone to hurt you. And maybe that doesn't make sense, considering I'm hurting you more than any of those assholes, but I don't do it intentionally. You're not like anyone I've ever met. You can understand me the way no one else ever could." He scooted closer to her. *"La mia bella ragazza."*

"You know I don't know what that means," she said, blushing from the intensity of his stare.

He ran the back of his fingers along her flushed cheek. His touch was soft, and she leaned her head in his direction. "My beautiful girl," he said.

She took in his expression. "You think I'm beautiful?"

"I don't think you're beautiful, Haven. I know you are."

His words flustered her. "You are, too."

He smirked. "You're saying I'm beautiful?"

She nodded. "A beautiful person."

"I've been called everything under the sun, but a beautiful person was never one of them."

———

Never in Haven's life had she encountered a disaster like the one that met them downstairs. Trash was scattered throughout the rooms, beer cans and empty bottles littering the tables and counters. Food was smashed into the floor, the house smelling wretchedly like the inside of a trash can. There was broken glass in the family room, furniture moved, and things out of place.

Haven stood at the bottom of the stairs, scanning the mess, as Carmine disappeared into the laundry room. He returned with some black trash bags. "You start in the kitchen, and I'll go deal with whatever got broken. I know not everything survived the night intact."

"You don't have to do this," she said. "I can get it."

"I know you can, Haven," he said. "Just let me try to help."

She went into the kitchen and cleared off the counter, hearing noises every few minutes as Carmine tossed things around the family room. She got all the cans picked up and lugged the bag over to the side of the room. She was washing the dishes when Carmine appeared, dropping a second trash bag on the floor.

"You don't have to do those by hand," he said. "We have a dishwasher."

"I don't know how to operate it."

Carmine opened the dishwasher and pulled out the top rack. "Get your hands out of that nasty water and fill this up."

She looked at him cautiously. Considering he couldn't operate a washing machine, she had a feeling he didn't know what he was doing, but she conceded and loaded it with the dishes. When it was filled, he smiled proudly—whether proud of himself or of her, she wasn't sure.

Carmine squeezed in some soap and latched the door, narrowing his eyes as he pressed a few buttons. It made noise right away and he snatched his hand away with surprise.

Haven laughed as soon as he walked out, knowing she'd been right—he was guessing.

She did some laundry before walking back into the kitchen. The moment she neared the sink, she hit a slippery spot, and her feet came out from under her. She grabbed the counter to stay upright and looked around, her eyes widening at the bubbles pouring out of the dishwasher.

"Carmine!" There was no way that was normal. Footsteps hastily approached as he sprinted into the kitchen. She opened her mouth to warn him, barely getting the words, "Watch out!" from her lips before he hit a patch of sudsy water and slid.

"Fuck!" he said, treading through the soapy mess to the dishwasher. Frantic, he pushed buttons and yanked on the door, trying to get it to stop. It continued to ooze bubbles, and he groaned as he slapped the front of it. Temper flaring, he kicked the door, and Haven winced as his foot left a small dent on the front.

He cursed and hobbled, smacking the buttons again until the dishwasher abruptly stopped.

"I think we have a little problem here," Haven said, the entire thing too much for her to take. The kitchen floor was covered, and they'd managed to make a bigger mess than they'd started with. She cracked a smile, fighting to keep a straight face, and covered her mouth to quiet her impending giggles.

Carmine cocked an eyebrow at her. "Are you laughing at me?"

She laughed, her body shaking with amusement at his expression. She stepped away from the counter, not paying attention, and lost her footing in the suds. Carmine shot forward to catch her but skidded too, his feet coming out from under him. He knocked them both to the floor. She landed on her back with a thud, losing her breath as Carmine landed on top of her.

He pulled himself up, horrified. "Christ, I didn't mean to knock you down! Are you hurt? Did I hurt you? Huh? Did I? Say something!"

She pushed herself up as he sat on the floor in front of her. Covered in bubbles, her back was soaked, and Carmine stared at her like she'd grown a second head. She shook again and covered her mouth to hold it in, but it was fruitless. She laughed uncontrollably, so hard her sides ached. "I think you did something wrong with the dishwasher, Carmine."

He grabbed a handful of soap bubbles and flung them at her. She turned her head so they splattered her chest and cheek, and she didn't hesitate before flinging some right back. They hit him directly in the face, and he closed his eyes as he wiped the bubbles away.

"I can't believe you did that!" He lunged at her with a determined look on his face. She scampered backward, but he caught her before she could get away. He pushed her back on the floor and hovered over her, pinning her down in the hot sudsy water.

She flicked more bubbles at him, a little clump hitting his nose, but it backfired. Leaning down, he rubbed his face against hers, transferring them onto her. Haven cocked her head then, feeling brave, and kissed him. His lips were soft and wet, the flavor of him sweet but minty. There was a bitter tang there, and she wrinkled her nose. "You taste like soap."

Chuckling, he grabbed her hand to pull her up and brushed some bubbles out of her hair. "How about we clean this mess up so we can talk." He glanced around. "And nap. I'm definitely gonna need a nap."

15

After the house was together, the kitchen floor so clean Carmine could see his reflection in it, the two of them headed upstairs. Haven went to her room to shower as Carmine stripped, tossing his clothes onto the massive pile of dirty laundry. He desperately needed them washed, but he felt like an asshole asking her to do it. Did girlfriends do that kind of stuff for their boyfriends? He wasn't sure, considering he'd never had one before.

Hell, he wasn't sure if she was his *girlfriend*. All he knew was she'd stolen his heart, and there was no way he could ask for it back. In such a short time she'd taken him over, as much a part of him now as the air he breathed.

Fucking thunderbolt.

He pulled on a pair of shorts and grabbed his stereo remote, scanning through stations as he plopped down on his bed. He was exhausted, his eyelids closing, and he drifted into a light sleep until the bed squeaked. Haven sat beside him, so he pulled back the comforter and motioned for her to join him.

"I didn't mean to wake you," she said, lying down.

"I was resting my eyes," he said. "You look better, by the way. Not to say you looked bad to begin with, just that you look good after your shower. Yeah, that didn't sound right. Ignore me."

She laughed at his tongue-tied rambling and reached out, hesitating with her hand midair. He smiled reassuringly and closed his eyes, enjoying her light touch as she explored his face. She ran her fingers down his nose and across his forehead before threading them through his hair.

When he looked at her again, her expression stunned him. She looked awestruck, her hand stilled on his cheek, her eyes glassed over with unshed tears. "Is something wrong?" he asked.

"Do you . . . ?" She stroked her thumb across his cheek, sending tingling through him. "Do you really feel that?"

"It's like you have static under your skin."

"What do you think it is?"

"*Colpo di fulmine*?" he suggested. She stared at him, and he smiled. "I guess you're gonna want a translation."

"Please."

"It's when you're drawn to someone so forcefully that it's like being struck by lightning."

She stared at him. "Okay."

"Is that an, 'Okay, you're an idiot, Carmine, but whatever you say,' or is it an, 'Okay, that shit makes sense?'"

"It makes sense," she said. "I don't know what to make of it. It's all new, and I don't know what you expect."

"I don't expect anything, *tesoro*," he said. "I can't lie, I'm attracted to you, but we're only gonna do what you wanna do. We'll be whatever you want us to be. But I just want a chance. I'm *asking* you for a chance."

"A chance to what?"

A chance to what? A chance to prove himself? To be happy? To be trusted? To be loved? To love her? To finally be someone worthwhile? "Just . . . a chance. I can't promise it's gonna be easy, or that it's gonna be all happiness. I've never done any of this before, so I don't know what I'm doing. But I'll try to be good to you."

"I don't know what I'm doing either," she said.

"We can learn together. Just tell me what you want from me, and we'll figure the shit out."

She smiled, but he could sense her apprehension. "You make me happy. I, uh . . . I don't like being here when you're not around."

That had to have been hard for her to admit. "I can't predict the future, but I'll do anything I can for you. You're taking a chance on me. I appreciate it, and I'm not gonna take that shit for granted."

He pressed his lips to hers softly, and she smiled when he pulled away. "Wow." She ran her fingers gently across his lips. "Your mouth is surprisingly sweet for saying such naughty things."

He burst into laughter. "I think you're delirious. How about we take a nap before you tell me I smell like sunshine or something."

"You do smell like sunshine."

"And how does sunshine smell?"

"It smells like the outside world. Warm. Happy. Safe." She paused. "Green."

"Green?"

She nodded. "Definitely green."

Tarullo's Pizzeria was a small establishment, owned by second-generation immigrant John Tarullo. He was what they called an *omu de panza*, a man with a belly, and *La Cosa Nostra* rewarded him for it. He minded his own business and looked the other way, and in exchange for his silence they made certain he thrived. Tarullo didn't like relying on the mob—in fact, he'd told Vincent many times he detested the organization—but if it weren't them, it would be someone else. Someone would come around expecting something from him, and it was better that that someone at least be a familiar face.

Vincent, personally, felt protective of the pizzeria. Tarullo had been the one to find Carmine the night he'd been shot, and Vincent would forever feel indebted to the man for saving his son.

It was something Tarullo would rather forget, though.

They never had much trouble at Tarullo's Pizzeria, since everyone knew it was under protection after what Tarullo had done for Carmine, so Vincent was shocked when he received a call to go to the place years later. The moment he stepped inside the restaurant and heard the loud, disruptive voices, his hand settled on the gun concealed in his coat.

He stood still, surveying the men at the front counter, both Caucasian with sandy hair. Vincent assessed them as they bickered, their voices slurring. He wasn't sure why he'd been called in for such a petty situation, but when the drunken men's focus shifted to Tarullo, he took a step forward anyway. He barely made it three feet from the door when it opened, a single word booming through the pizzeria. *"Zatknis!"*

Shut up. It was one of the only words Vincent knew in Russian. He'd heard it barked many times in his life from the lips of the man now standing a few feet from him.

Vincent glared at him. He was tall and built like a linebacker, his gray hair concealed under a black cap. Although he was pushing seventy, the man had the mind-set of a psychopathic twenty-year-old assassin.

"Ivan Volkov," Vincent said. "You're not welcome here."

Ivan stared at him blankly for a moment before turning around and walking out of the pizzeria. Before the door could close, he stepped back in. "I do not see your name on the sign."

"I don't need to own the place," Vincent said. "You have no business being in this part of town."

Despite the fact that Vincent was fuming, Ivan had the audacity to smile. "Why are you always serious? We have only come for pizza."

"Go somewhere else."

"But I wish to eat here."

The two men stood at an impasse, Vincent's hand still hovering near his gun. Ivan was unaffected, though, and appeared impatient as he scanned the price menu on the wall.

The door opened again as Corrado walked in. He didn't look at Ivan as he stepped around him. "Volkov."

"Moretti."

"Leave."

"Why?"

"Because I'll be forced to kill you if you don't, and I'm wearing my favorite shirt. It'll ruin my night to get your filthy blood on it."

Ivan said nothing in response as Corrado casually strolled up to the counter. The two men moved out of the way when Corrado reached into his coat. Everyone tensed, a suffocating silence blanketing the room, but instead of pulling out his gun, Corrado retrieved his wallet. "I need a small deep dish with sausage and mushrooms. Light on the sauce. You know how I like it."

Tarullo rang him up, the chime of the register magnified in the edgy restaurant. "$17.78."

Corrado handed him a fifty and told him to keep the change.

Ivan sighed, motioning for his guys to leave before turning to Vincent. "We will see each other again."

Vincent nodded. "I'm sure."

The Russians left, their voices loud once more as they stepped into the street. Vincent looked at his brother-in-law. Corrado eyed him peculiarly as he leaned against the counter, waiting for his pizza. "They're trying to provoke us."

"I know," Vincent said. "Did you get a call to come here too?"

"No, I wanted some pizza."

Vincent stared at him. "You know we're expected to meet Sal for a sit-down, right?"

"Yes," Corrado said, looking at his watch. "But I'm hungry."

———

Sit-downs to *la famiglia* were nothing like the movies. When he was growing up, Vincent envisioned elaborate meetings held like court, and he'd laugh, imagining his father in a black robe with a gavel, sitting on a bench while the parties argued their sides. The guilty man lost and justice was served, another case put to rest.

No, sit-downs were nothing like that. They more than often happened while on a casual stroll, sometimes adjourning with no words spoken. You didn't plead your case, and it didn't matter if you were innocent. Judgment had been passed before you showed up.

Vincent stood near the pier overlooking Lake Michigan. *The Federica* floated not a hundred feet from him, a woman moving around on deck. She looked young, maybe late twenties. A *goomah*, a mistress, attracted to the lifestyle and turned on by the power they held. Vincent thought them to be nothing but glorified prostitutes, exchanging sex for gifts and trips abroad.

"Is Carlo coming?" Giovanni asked. Vincent turned away from the yacht, glancing around at the men gathered. Giovanni looked frozen, bundled up in a thick coat.

Sal shook his head. "He's gone back to Vegas."

Carlo had taken over their operations in Las Vegas a few years back, so he rarely appeared in Chicago anymore. Vincent resented him for the special treatment he received. He'd moved away, too, but was still expected to show up.

"So, fourteen pinched," Sal said, getting down to business. "Two stool pigeons singing."

There was collective grumbling among the men. Fourteen members of *La Cosa Nostra* had been arrested and two had turned state's evidence, cooperating with the government.

"You gonna silence them?" Squint asked.

Vincent looked at him, still wary the boy was invited to these meetings. "There's too much heat. They're being guarded."

"So?" Squint said. "Take out the families. They'll get the message."

Vincent and Giovanni both opened their mouths to interject, but Corrado's voice rang out before they could. "No."

He leaned against his Mercedes, clutching the box of pizza and devouring it like he hadn't eaten in weeks. He said nothing else, no explanation, but that didn't surprise Vincent. He'd said all he needed to with that one word.

"Corrado's right," Sal said. "Just lay low until we know more."

Squint grumbled to himself while Corrado continued to eat. Giovanni shivered, and Vincent grew impatient as Sal's attention drifted to the yacht. They spoke a bit more as Vincent's mind wandered, only returning to the conversation when the Russians were mentioned.

"They were at Tarullo's tonight," Vincent said.

"Did they hurt anyone?" Sal asked. "Or did it get handled?"

"It was handled."

He nodded. "No reason to dwell, then."

Giovanni tried to interject, but Sal gave him a look that closed the subject. He waved his hand, silently dismissing them, and Corrado was in his car without having spoken another word. Vincent turned to walk away but was stopped by the Don's voice. "How's my godson?"

Vincent's blood ran cold at the question. "He's fine."

"Is he doing well in school? Passing?"

"He's squeaking by. Still skipping a lot."

Sal laughed. "Doesn't surprise me. This business, *la famiglia*, is in that boy's blood. And that's everything, you know. *Famiglia.* That's what matters."

Vincent had nothing nice to say about that, but Sal didn't wait for a response. Reaching into his coat, Sal pulled out a thick manila envelope and held it out to Vincent. "Give this to *Principe* for me. A little something from his godfather."

Begrudgingly, Vincent took it before heading to his car. Once inside, he shoved the envelope of cash into his glove compartment. He had no intention of giving it to his son.

Haven took a seat at the library window while Carmine grabbed his guitar, joining her. Wordlessly, she picked up a book from the small table between them. Carmine smiled when he saw it was *The Secret Garden*. "So you haven't given up on that?"

"No," she said, opening it to a page about a quarter of the way in. "It's good. She searches for the garden and makes friends with this little robin. It reminds me of . . ."

She trailed off as Carmine plucked the strings of his guitar, random notes sounding out in the room. "Reminds you of what?" he asked when she didn't continue.

"It reminds me of when I was little and talked to the animals," she said. "They had a few dogs, but it was mainly horses. I stayed in the stables with them."

Caught off guard, his finger plucked the wrong string. They both cringed from the sharp note. "You slept with the fucking *horses?*"

"Yes, but it wasn't so bad. They kept me company."

His jaw clenched as he held back his temper. She could say it wasn't bad if she wanted, but Carmine couldn't think of a more inhumane scenario.

He continued to strum his guitar, playing around with sounds as she quietly read. Her eyes would occasionally drift over the top of the book, settling on him. "Can I ask you something, Carmine?"

"Of course you can."

"Why did you shoot at Nicholas last year?"

Another sharp note rang out. Of all the things she could ask, she wanted to talk about Nicholas? "We had a falling-out after I messed around with his sister. He got mad and ran his mouth, said something about my mom, and I snapped."

"Your mama?"

"Yes."

"And she's in Chicago?"

He sighed. "Hillside."

"What's she doing there?"

He hesitated. "Nothing. She's gone."

"You mean like . . . dead?"

Carmine cringed at the word and nodded.

He played again as Haven went back to her book. He felt no judgment, no disappointment, no pressure to explain. It wasn't until that moment that he realized how much he craved that acceptance. She'd changed him. He wasn't sure how, but he felt different. He was Maura's son again, and not so much Vincent DeMarco's heir.

"Look at the Suburban."

Corrado's voice was nonchalant, but Vincent knew better than to believe he wasn't on alert. He waited a few seconds before turning, seeing the black Chevy Suburban parked along the curb half a block away.

The darkly tinted windows obstructed the inside view, but Vincent could manage a guess or two at who was there. "FBI, you think? Doesn't seem like locals."

"Anything's possible," Corrado said. "FBI, DOJ, CIA . . ."

Vincent shook his head. "What did you do to have the CIA working on a Saturday night?"

"You never know," Corrado said. "Maybe they're looking to recruit me."

Vincent laughed, although he wouldn't put it past them. Wouldn't be the first time the government showed up, wanting to exchange services.

"They were parked near the club this morning," Corrado said. "Then at the restaurant tonight."

"And you're just now pointing them out to me?"

"You should've spotted them yourself."

"You don't think it's someone like the Irish, do you? Russians?"

"No, it's law enforcement."

"Must be a rookie on his first stakeout," Vincent said. "Or else they're intentionally letting themselves be seen."

"Either way, I'm offended. What do they take me for? An idiot who wouldn't notice or a coward who would be intimidated?"

"Maybe they aren't here for you," Vincent said. "Maybe they're watching me."

Corrado shrugged. "It would make more sense."

"Why?"

"Because you're the idiot who wouldn't notice."

If Vincent weren't a mature man, and if his brother-in-law wouldn't punch him for it, he would have certainly rolled his eyes then.

"I'll tell Sal," Corrado said. "If they're lurking, we'll want to take precautions."

Corrado headed inside his house with a nod while Vincent strolled down the block. He pulled a set of keys from his pocket as he stepped onto the porch of the white two-story house, using the worn copper key to unlock the front door. The smell of mothballs was strong, dust tickling his nose when he stepped into the corridor. Heat wafted around him, the place muggy from being closed up for so long.

Vincent strolled through the empty downstairs, the sound of his feet on the wood echoing off the barren walls. An ache in his chest made it hard to breathe, and although Vincent blamed it on the thick air, he knew it was emotional torment eating him up instead.

In the front room, he leaned against the wall and closed his eyes. He could see it then, the sunlight streaming through the open windows, air blowing in and stirring the blue curtains. The house was cluttered with furniture and knickknacks, family photos covering every inch of space.

And he could hear it, footsteps running in the hall upstairs, the squeals of excited children as they played hide-and-seek. Music streamed from a small radio, the sounds of Mozart and Beethoven.

And Vincent could feel it, the warmth and love, the happiness he craved. It was pure chaos, but it was his peace. It was his home. There was nothing else like it.

And there she was, like always, fluttering around the house in her flowing summer dress, bare feet on hard wood, toenails painted soft pink. She smiled at him, green eyes twinkling.

But when Vincent opened his eyes again, it all faded away. He was left with nothing but darkness, silent except for his strangled breaths in the vacant room. He still slept there sometimes when he visited, even though there was no electricity or furniture. He would lie on the bare floor and stare at the white ceiling, time wasting away as he wallowed in memories.

Not tonight, though. He couldn't stay.

The black Chevy Suburban was gone when he went back outside.

Haven lay awake that night, unable to sleep. She had spent her life belonging to other people, but for the first time she felt like she actually *belonged*. It wasn't about being a possession—it was being a part of something. People never cared what she thought before, but Carmine did. He asked, and Haven found she wanted to tell.

She gave up trying to sleep around dawn and headed downstairs, surprised to hear noises in the family room. Dominic lay on the couch in his pajamas, the lights off but television playing. He sat up when he spotted her, patting the cushion beside him. "Join me."

She sat down, folding her hands in her lap. "I'm surprised you're awake so early."

"Couldn't sleep," he said. "Why are you up?"

"Same," she said. "I thought I'd come downstairs and make sure the house was clean."

"No rush," he said. "It'll probably be a few days before my father shows up again."

She eyed Dominic curiously. "He's gone a lot."

"Yeah, been that way for as long as I can remember," he said. "There's always something for him to do somewhere that isn't here."

"What does he do when he's gone?"

He laughed wryly. "Don't know, and don't want to know. Dad moved us here years ago so we wouldn't be a part of that. Said he wanted us to have a normal life, so we could live like normal kids, but there's nothing normal about raising yourself, you know? Nothing normal about the situation with you. We've all suffered because of the things he's done, and I hate to think how much more we'd suffer if we knew the shit we don't know."

She stared at him, confused, and he smiled at her expression.

"In other words, Twinkle Toes, ignorance is bliss."

———

Vincent slipped a hundred-dollar bill into the collection plate and sighed as his mother waved it on. She hadn't donated to the church in years, convinced the altar boys were stealing the money for drugs and prostitutes, even though most of them were still in grammar school.

Celia and Corrado put in their share, and the four of them sat silently as the collection plates made their way through the crowd. Corrado remained standoffish as usual, while Vincent's sister was her typical poised, smiling self. Celia was a tall, slender woman, her face with a soft, round look. She had sleek black hair, the color of night, and dark eyes to match.

The pews were packed. Vincent scanned the congregation. Most of the ranking members of *la famiglia* were there, dressed in their best suits in the front of the church. It was a big production for them, the one day of the week where they could flaunt their money and pretend to do good. It made the honest men—the *galantuomini*—feel protected, men who respected them, who trusted them, who were less likely to rat them out.

After donations were collected, people made their way into the aisle. A long line formed for communion, but Vincent stayed in his seat. Corrado eyed him peculiarly, but didn't say a word as he got in line.

The rest of the service passed quickly, everyone standing as the final prayer was spoken. Father Alberto made the sign of the cross when he finished. "May you go in peace."

They were headed to the exit when Father Alberto called Vincent's name. The hair on the back of his neck bristled like a child being reprimanded. "Yes, Father?"

"You didn't take communion," Father Alberto said, his face etched with genuine concern. "You haven't taken it in weeks."

It had really been months, but Vincent didn't correct the priest. "I keep forgetting to fast before service."

Father Alberto knew he was lying. "The church never closes. You don't need an appointment. God is always here for you."

"I know, Father. Thank you."

Vincent left before Father Alberto could press the matter and joined his family on the front steps of the cathedral. Corrado and Celia stood along the side as Gia infused herself into the crowd. *Mafiosi* surrounded her, listening as she rambled away about the past. They smiled and laughed, urging her on, but not a single person mocked her. She was a former Don's widow, the mother of a *consigliere*, and an in-law to another made man. The men respected her, bat-shit crazy or not.

And while she lived in Sunny Oaks, *respected* was something Gia didn't feel.

Vincent waited as his mother finished telling a story about Antonio and one of their adventures back when Vincent and Celia were young. He found himself smiling as he thought about those days. It was before tragedy had struck. Before Maura and the kids. Before the Antonellis and the girl. Before Salvatore's family had been murdered. Before the world had imploded around them.

Gia turned to him when she finished, the crowd disbursing and saying their good-byes.

"Ma, are you ready to—?"

"You didn't take communion."

He sighed. He'd planned to ask if she was ready to head back to Sunny Oaks, but it was senseless now. She wouldn't go until she had said everything she wanted to say. "I couldn't."

Gia smiled. "I'm proud of you."

He stood frozen as those words sunk through his thickened skin. Never in his life had he heard them from her. *She must be demented.* "You're proud of me?"

She nodded. "You see it now, don't you? After all these years, you understand."

"Understand what?"

"That you were living in sin. Your marriage wasn't recognized by the church."

Vincent's smile fell. *Not demented, just evil.* "It was recognized."

"You were young, Vincenzo. And she was Irish! She wasn't even like us!"

Celia responded before Vincent could. "Maura was Catholic, Mom. It was sanctified. Father Alberto was the one to marry them."

Gia glared at her daughter before waving her hand dismissively. "How was I supposed to know? I didn't even get invited."

She'd been invited, of course, but she had shunned the service. Antonio had shown up out of respect for his son, but Gia refused. In her mind, if she didn't see the wedding, she could go on acting as if the marriage didn't exist.

"You were invited," Vincent said. "You chose not to come."

"That's ridiculous," Gia said. "I didn't know anything about it until it was over."

"If that's true, Ma, how did Dad know to come?"

"What does that have to do with anything? Your father always snuck around, never told me anything. What makes this any different?"

Vincent tried to keep his anger at bay. "Because I handed you the invitation. You took one look at it and tossed it in the trash."

Gia scoffed. "And the quacks say *I* have memory problems. That never happened."

Corrado strolled over, his hands in his pockets. "What are we arguing about now?"

"Vincent marrying Maura," Celia said. "Again."

"Ah," Corrado said. "I regret I wasn't there."

Gia laughed. "They didn't invite you, either?"

"Oh, I was invited. I just didn't think it was appropriate for me to attend."

"See!" Gia looked at Vincent. "I told you it wasn't a real marriage. Corrado agrees!"

Corrado started to correct her, but Vincent shook his head. Although it stung that his brother-in-law had skipped the wedding, sending Celia to the ceremony alone, Vincent understood. Unlike Gia, Corrado meant well.

"It doesn't matter what anyone else thinks," Vincent said. "I know it was real."

————

Haven spent the morning cleaning and finished near three o'clock when she heard cars outside. The alarm beeped and the front door opened as she stepped into the doorway to the kitchen, a few voices carrying through the house. Dr. DeMarco walked in with two men behind him. The hair on the back of Haven's neck stood up at the sight of them.

Dr. DeMarco's eyes met hers. She realized these men were probably like Master Michael—uncaring and cold, with no regard for people like her. They were like that part of Dr. DeMarco she'd seen in his bedroom. They were dangerous. More monsters.

Taking a deep breath, she stepped forward to gauge his reaction. The corner of his lips turned up, and she took his reaction to mean she should stay. Her legs trembled as she walked into the family room, where they gathered, the men taking notice of her right away.

"Bring us a bottle of scotch and some glasses," Dr. DeMarco told her with a flippant wave. Haven scuttled to the kitchen. She searched the cabinets until she located the alcohol, and she scoured through the bottles, finding a brown one in the back with GLEN-FIDDICH SINGLE MALT SCOTCH WHISKEY written on it. She wiped off the unopened dusty bottle and juggled three glasses on her way back to the family room. She delivered the drinks, too nervous to make eye contact with any of them.

"So this is the girl."

Haven chanced a peek at the man who spoke, his voice grating like metal scraping against glass. An air of authority surrounded him as he sat in the center, the others flanking him. He was clearly older than them.

"Yes," Dr. DeMarco said. "It's her."

"I'm curious, Vincent," the man said. "Do you think she was worth it?"

Dr. DeMarco's bitter laughter sent chills down Haven's spine, putting her more on edge. "Personally or as business?"

"Personally."

"Of course she wasn't worth it."

She lost her breath, his words striking her hurt. Had she been that much of a disappointment?

"But speaking as a businessman," Dr. DeMarco continued, shrugging, "she's a hard worker."

"So she wasn't a bad investment?" the other guy asked. Haven looked at him. *Investment?* Their eyes met, his the cold drab shade of a knife's blade. Her skin crawled at their interest in her. She had to look away.

"You could say that." Dr. DeMarco shifted position and cleared his throat. "Why don't you start dinner, child? My guests will be joining us tonight."

———

Haven's heart raced as she fled into the kitchen, leaning against the counter to take a few deep breaths. Dominic arrived home while she stood there, and he greeted the men in the family room before joining her. "You look worried," he said, grabbing a soda from the refrigerator.

"Nervous," she admitted.

Dominic sighed, opening his drink as he leaned against the counter. "Does it help to know they make me uncomfortable, too?"

It did help a bit, but not enough to eliminate her fears. "Do you know why they're here?"

"Business, I guess. Like I said, I don't get involved." He took a drink, shaking his head. "I do know the man in the gray suit, Salvatore, is in charge."

"And the other?"

"His name's Nunzio. We used to hang out when we were kids, but he's no friend of mine now."

————

Footsteps approached an hour later as Haven cooked dinner, and the man named Nunzio appeared in the doorway. His eyes lingered on her as she deliberately concentrated on the food, ignoring the crawling of her skin, hoping he'd go away after he saw what he came to see.

He strolled toward her as she stirred the pasta. The tension in her body made her muscles ache, her hands trembling more with each calculated step. Repulsed shudders tore through her when she felt his breath on her skin. "You're prettier than I expected you to be," he said, running the back of his fingers lightly down her exposed arm. "I think we could have some fun together."

His hand came to rest on her hip. Haven squeezed her eyes shut, wanting him to remove it.

At that moment, something struck her from the side, a shove hurling her into the stove. Her hand slammed against the pot of boiling water. Blistering pain made her eyes snap back open, and she grabbed her burned palm as Dr. DeMarco pinned Nunzio against the counter beside her, the serrated edge of a kitchen knife pressed to his neck.

His voice was hard. "Don't touch my property, Squint."

Nunzio scowled at him. "I hear you, Doc."

The blade of the knife came close to piercing the skin where

Nunzio's neck pulsated, his heart pounding. Dr. DeMarco took a step back, and Nunzio glared at Haven before storming from the room.

The knife dropped onto the counter with a clang as Dr. De-Marco marched in her direction. She recoiled from him. "I'm sorry."

Ignoring her flinching, he snatched her hand and barked a few orders on how to care for her burn. He turned then to leave the room but hesitated, eyeing the pot of boiling water. "You'll be eating dinner with us tonight, so be sure to set yourself a place at the table, too."

———

Carmine pulled in the driveway after football practice, seeing the black rental sedan parked out front. The sight of it put him on edge. His father hadn't come back from Chicago alone.

He heard Salvatore's voice the moment he hit the foyer. Carmine gave Haven a quick glance in the kitchen before making his way to the family room.

Salvatore smiled as he entered. "Ah, *Principe!*"

Carmine kissed the back of Salvatore's hand when he held it out, fighting off a cringe. If ever there was a custom that made his stomach turn, it was that one. "Great to see you, Sal."

"You too, dear boy. We were just talking about you."

"Good things?" Carmine asked.

"Your father was telling me what you've been up to."

He chuckled. "So not good things, then."

Vincent stood, shaking his head as the others laughed. "If you'll excuse us, I need to speak with my son."

Sal waved them away, and the color drained from Carmine's face at his father's rattled expression.

16

Carmine slumped in the leather chair in his father's office, trying to act nonchalant while inside anarchy reigned. He drummed his fingers on the arm of the chair as Vincent took a seat at his desk with his laptop. "Do you like the number thirteen, Carmine?"

Carmine's brow furrowed at the question. "Uh, it's just a number."

"I never understood the fascination," Vincent said, typing away at the keys without looking up. "There's even a psychological disorder over the fear of the number, triskaidekaphobia. In southern Italy, *tredici*—the number thirteen—is slang meaning someone's luck has turned bad."

He stopped speaking, and the room grew silent. Carmine drummed his fingers some more. "I appreciate the random trivia, and I'm sure if I ever go on *Jeopardy!* it'll come in handy, but I don't understand what the fuck it has to do with me."

Vincent's typing stopped. *"Lasciare in tredici."*

"Are you telling me my luck ran out?"

"Not just yours." Vincent turned back to his laptop. "I need another favor."

"Of course you do."

"I need someone to keep an eye on the girl."

Carmine looked at him incredulously. "You want me to spy on her?"

"Not exactly," he said. "I need to make sure she stays safe. I caught Squint touching her."

Carmine's rage boiled over. He stood so quickly his chair flew back. "He *touched* her?"

"He didn't harm her, although she did burn her hand," Vincent said casually, ignoring Carmine's outburst. "I handled it."

"You handled it?" Carmine clenched his hands into fists as he fought back the urge to pummel something.

"Yes, I handled it," Vincent said again. "What's gotten into you?"

Carmine glared at his father as he flopped back down in the chair. "I don't like that shit."

"I know, but you need to control your temper. I'd get rid of Squint if I could, but Sal's blinded by the fact that he's technically family. Sal has no blood relatives left, since his brother's and sister's families were all murdered. That's why he's always been fixated on you. You are the closest thing to a son he had—his godson. Getting him to believe Squint's untrustworthy won't be easy."

"Do you think he could be a danger?"

Vincent sighed. "Trouble's brewing, so there's little focus on things going on within the walls of the fortress, so to speak. I think Squint's more than happy to take advantage of that."

"Why's he interested in Haven, though?"

"Probably because it's wrong for him to be."

Carmine's heartbeat thrashed in his ears. *Wrong?* "You mean it's wrong for someone like her to be with one of you?"

"I was referring to him having no right to touch what isn't his," Vincent said. "Although, that is a good point."

"So you do think that's wrong?"

"Of course it is," Vincent said. "Rape is always wrong."

"I mean consensual."

Vincent shook his head. "Do you really think a girl in her position has the right frame of mind to consent? It would take a strong woman to look at him as a man and not a master, to see him for who he is and not what he is. But just because it could happen, doesn't mean it should. It's asking for heartache for everyone involved."

Carmine sat quietly. He'd never given any of that much thought. To him, she was just a girl.

"Regardless, Squint's advances were unwanted," Vincent said. "I should've figured this would happen, but I couldn't have done anything differently. I couldn't have kept her hidden. Sal would've asked about her because of who she is."

Carmine's brow furrowed. "Who is she?"

"Excuse me?"

"Is her father important or something? Michael Antonelli?"

Vincent gaped at him. "I don't recall telling you Michael was her father."

He shrugged. "Haven may have mentioned it."

"I'm surprised," he said. "He didn't claim her, so not many people know that information. His own wife only just recently found out. She wasn't very happy."

Carmine laughed dryly. "Haven mentioned that, too."

Vincent raised his eyebrows. "Have you told her you know them?"

Carmine stared at his father. "I don't."

"You do," Vincent insisted. "Or, well, you know Katrina's brother. We're related to him."

Silence permeated the office. It took a minute for that to click with Carmine. "Katrina *Moretti*? Are you telling me the bitch who tortured Haven is Corrado's sister?"

"Yes."

"That motherfucker! Does he know what they were doing?"

"Possibly, but none of that matters right now," Vincent said. "Squint has his eyes set on the girl, so she needs to be watched for that reason."

It didn't make sense to Carmine, but he knew his father wasn't going to tell him anything more.

———

"Just relax," Carmine said softly, pulling out a chair for Haven as they made their way to the table for dinner that night. He took the seat beside her, and Haven remained still as they bowed their heads for a prayer. They helped themselves to food but Haven only took a little, too anxious to eat. She scooted the food around on her plate with her fork, alarmed, as she tried to ignore Nunzio's gawking from across the table.

"So, Carmine," Salvatore said, attempting conversation. "You'll be eighteen in a few months. Any plans for the future?"

Haven peered at him, curious. She, too, wondered what his plans were, but Carmine merely shrugged, offering no answer.

Dr. DeMarco cleared his throat. "Carmine can do what he wants with his life, but I like to think he'll hang around here until he graduates."

Nunzio laughed mockingly. "School's useless. What's a diploma gonna get you these days—a job at McDonald's? There's money to be made out there, and no piece of paper from some school will matter a bit when it comes to it."

Dr. DeMarco spoke up again, his voice sharp. "A diploma may not matter in our line of work, but it's not about a piece of paper. It's about finishing what you started, being dedicated and not selling out. Nothing is worse than an opportunist."

"I wouldn't call it being an opportunist," Nunzio said. "It's wising up and changing priorities."

"Your priorities shouldn't change when you're on a path you swore you'd stay on," Vincent said. "Carmine's mother would want him to see it through."

Nunzio shrugged. "But Maura's not here anymore, so why does it matter what she'd want?"

Dr. DeMarco jumped to his feet, his chair crashing to the floor. "Don't even say her name, *scarafaggio*! You never disregard your family!"

Haven tensed, her heart feverishly pounding and making her dizzy. Salvatore grabbed Dr. DeMarco's arm and forced him to sit down. They went back to eating without another word, strained silence overtaking the room.

"So, Haven . . ."

Her name spoken in the high-pitched voice made the fork slip from her fingers. It clanged against her plate, and she winced at the sound. Taking a deep breath, she glanced at Salvatore. She wanted nothing more than to blend into the background, wishing she could be overlooked.

"You don't have to be nervous," Salvatore said. "I'm just curious how you're finding life with Vincent. As hidden away as you were, I wondered if you were a figment of the imagination."

"The DeMarcos are kind to me, sir," she said quietly. "They treat me fairly."

Salvatore nodded. "That's great to hear. If I had known the Antonellis acted so cruelly, I would've stepped in. By the time Vincent informed me, it was too complicated to intervene."

Before Haven had the chance to make sense of what he had said, Carmine interjected. "What the fuck are you talking about?"

Dr. DeMarco groaned. "Mind your manners, son."

Salvatore shrugged. "Perhaps I've said too much. Forget I brought it up."

"You can't say some shit like that and then say, 'forget about it,'" Carmine said. "If you knew one of your own abused a kid, why didn't you do anything?"

Salvatore glanced at Dr. DeMarco, who subtly shook his head.

"Michael Antonelli is hardly one of our own," Salvatore said, turning back to Carmine. "There are certain rules that govern this life—rules you can't disregard because you don't like something that's going on. Personal feelings have no place in business."

Nunzio let out a bitter laugh from his seat but offered no opinion.

The strained silence returned as Carmine glared at Salvatore and his father. They seemed oblivious to the looks, both of them instead focusing on Haven.

She cleared her throat, unable to take it. "Thank you for your concern, sir."

Under his breath, Carmine mumbled, "Don't fucking thank him."

Haven lay with her head on Carmine's shoulder later that night as the two of them watched a movie in her bedroom. She ran her fingers down his forearm and stroked the back of his hand before turning it over and tracing the creases of his palm. His fingers twitched as she grazed the tattoo on his wrist. "Do you really believe that? Trust no one?"

"I used to," he said. "Until you came along."

She picked her head up to look at him. "You trust me?"

"Yeah, why does that surprise you?" he asked. "I let you sleep in my bed and be around my stuff. You think I'd do that if I didn't trust you? That's not me at all."

"That's right," she said. "You're finicky."

He chuckled, shaking their bodies with the motion. "Am I that bad?"

"No," she said. "You still won't let me clean your room, though."

He sighed exaggeratedly. "That has nothing to do with trust or being finicky. I feel like an asshole having you clean up after me. I mean, you're my girl—you aren't supposed to do that shit."

A swell of hope surged inside her when the words *my girl* rolled from his lips. "But don't you see? That's one of the only things I can do for you. I have nothing to offer, Carmine. No way to make you happy."

He stared at her, his expression intense. Self-conscious, Haven looked away, but Carmine grasped her chin and pulled her gaze back to him. "Don't feel like you have to do things to impress me. Being yourself is enough to keep me interested."

Staring at him, she wondered if it could really be that simple.

"You're pure," he said, as if he could sense her reservation. "After everything I've done, I just hope I can be good enough for you."

She blinked a few times, stunned he'd say such a thing. "You're *too* good for me."

"Me?" He scoffed. "Are we talking about the same person? The selfish fucker who curses and yells and beats up people because he can't control his temper? You know, the one who drinks like a fish and fries his brain with drugs? That person is too good for you?"

She shook her head. "I'm talking about the boy who shared his chocolate bar with me when he probably never shared anything before, who gave me his mama's favorite book because he thought I deserved to read. I'm talking about the boy who treats me like a regular girl, the one who desperately needs his bedroom cleaned and laundry washed but chooses to live in a mess and wear dirty clothes because he's too polite to ask the girl he kisses for help."

"Wow," Carmine said. "I'd like to meet that motherfucker."

Haven smiled as he pulled her toward him again, and she rested her head on his shoulder. Carmine took her hand, running his fingers along it much like she'd done his, being careful to avoid the fresh wound.

17

Haven headed out of her bedroom at a quarter after eight in the morning and collided with Dominic outside her door. She recoiled, but he just stood in front of her, holding a DVD and a bowl of popcorn. "About time you wake up, Twinkle Toes. Now turn around and head back into the room."

Dominic took a step forward, and Haven instinctively took one back. He found it amusing and did it again, continuing until they were both inside the bedroom. He shut the door and put the bowl on the table before turning on the DVD.

Grabbing the remote, he flopped down on the couch and kicked his feet up on the table. He started the movie, chewing noisily as he munched on the popcorn. "You just gonna stand there? Your feet might get tired."

Haven tentatively sat beside him, her brow furrowing when she realized he'd put on a cartoon. She was about to ask him what they were watching when he thrust the bowl of popcorn into her face.

She cowered from the sudden movement, and he froze. "Scared of popcorn?"

"No," she said as he pushed the bowl closer to her. She took a small handful and turned to the television. "What are we watching?"

"*Shrek!*" He threw a handful of popcorn into his mouth. "I love this shit."

She watched for a bit. After getting to know Dominic, she

wasn't surprised he enjoyed such a movie. "It makes sense we're watching cartoons. Isn't that what people do when they babysit?"

He laughed, startling Haven when he playfully tossed a piece of popcorn at her. "Look at you making a joke! You're funny. No wonder Carmine fell in love with you."

She stared at him. "Uh, I don't know if I'd say he was . . . in love." She whispered the last part, having a hard time getting the words to leave her lips.

"Please, girl. He's given up all of his *puttani* and that's something I never thought I'd see. His favorite pastime was always busting a nut."

"A nut?"

Dominic ruffled her hair. "Oh so innocent. Ask Carmine what a nut is when he gets home. I wanna see him try to explain it to you."

After the movie finished, Haven followed Dominic out into the backyard. She sighed as the warm sunshine hit her face. Dampness lingered in the air, a cool breeze wafting across her bare arms and flushed cheeks.

She paused a few feet from the door. "Are you sure I'm allowed out here?"

"I'm positive," he said. "I asked."

The two of them strolled toward the thinning trees, the brittle, fallen leaves crunching under her shoes. She was apprehensive when they headed into the forest, the same ones she'd tried to escape through months before, but she wanted to believe he wouldn't lead her astray.

The sound of rushing water met her ears as they walked, the two of them coming upon a small creek. She knelt down, dipping her hand into the frigid water. "It's beautiful out here."

"I guess," Dominic said. "I'm not fond of nature. Carmine's the one who plays in the woods."

"Carmine comes out here?"

"He hasn't since he got back from the boarding school, but he used to when he wanted to be alone. He got into funks, so he'd come down by the water or run along the trail."

Dominic sat down and leaned against a barren tree as he gazed at the water. Haven mulled it over before pulling off her shoes and wiggling her toes in the thick grass. Rolling up her pant legs to her knees, she stepped into the freezing water.

"There are all kinds of creatures in there," Dominic warned. "Fish. Bugs. Snakes."

She smiled as the mud squished between her toes. "I'm not afraid of what's in this water."

"I thought all chicks were afraid of snakes."

"Not me." She laughed. "I grew up with scorpions."

"Are you afraid of anything?"

"Of course. Everyone's afraid of something."

"So what are you afraid of?"

She paused, considering how to answer. "Hope."

His brow furrowed. "Hope scares you?"

"I try not to hope for anything," she said. "If you expect nothing, you aren't disappointed when you get nothing."

"That's . . . sad," he said. "You don't have any hope?"

"I guess I do a little bit now." She kicked around in the mud, not wanting to dwell on the fact that she now had the one thing she told herself she'd never succumb to. "What are you afraid of?"

"Losing my dad," he said. "I already lost my mom to this life. I don't want to lose him, too."

An ache strangled her chest as she thought through his words. Her mama was still alive, but she felt as though she'd lost her forever.

"You should always have hope, you know," Dominic said.

"My mama used to say that all the time."

"Smart woman," he said. "You knew her?"

"Yes. I spent my whole life with her. She told me to run, to try to escape, but I got caught. That's when your father took me."

Dominic stared at her. "My father took you from your mother? Does he know that?"

"Yes, he knows."

They were quiet for a while, Dominic sitting in thought as she stomped around in the creek. "I'm sorry you're here," he said eventually. "It stumps me that he'd take you from your mother. That's wrong."

"It was scary to leave her, but I wouldn't call it wrong," she said. "Compared to where I came from, my mama would say he did me a favor."

Dominic stared at her in silence for a while before telling her they needed to get back. Although she hadn't wanted to go inside, she tentatively stepped out of the water. Her feet were covered in mud so she cleaned them off, figuring Dr. DeMarco wouldn't be happy with a dirty-footed servant scampering around when he had company.

They strolled toward the house in silence, finding a large white box truck now parked in the backyard. The men from last night were unloading boxes, taking them into a door in the side of the house, hidden under vines and green growth, blending into the surroundings.

"I didn't know a door was there," she said.

"It leads to the basement," he said. "Trust me when I say you don't want to go down there."

Nunzio stepped from behind the truck with a box then, his eyes drifting toward her. Haven moved closer to Dominic and focused her eyes on the ground, not wanting to give him the wrong impression.

———

Dominic went to take a shower when they made it inside, while Haven gathered Carmine's laundry, intending to start her daily cleaning. A foot or so from the top of the steps, she froze when she saw someone heading toward her. Fear ripped through her, so powerful she lost her breath.

Nunzio.

What she saw in his eyes alarmed her, hatred and lust thrown into a big frenzy of excited emotion. Her heart pounded fiercely, that voice in the back of her head telling her to get away. She took a few steps back and dropped the hamper, the clothes spilling out into the library as she sprinted to her room. She could hear him behind her as she flung the door closed, his foot blocking it before it could latch.

She backed away, looking around for some protection when he stepped into the room. Nunzio closed the door behind him, and Haven's knees nearly buckled when the lock clicked into place.

She was trapped.

Nunzio calmly pulled off his coat and tossed it on the table, the nonchalance when he spoke making it sound as if they were old friends. "Alone at last."

Loosening his tie, he pulled his shirt from his pants and let it hang as he sauntered toward her. Haven let out a scream for help, but Nunzio backhanded her before it could echo from the room. The strike stunned her into silence. "Behave, and I'll make it worth it for you."

Tears flowed from her eyes as she stepped back once more, her legs colliding with the footboard of the bed. "Don't touch me."

"Aw, don't be like that." He smiled vindictively. "Don't you like making people happy? That's all you gotta do. Be a good girl and please me. After all, that's why you exist. It's all you're good for. It's not like anyone could actually love someone like you."

He closed the distance between them as he unbuckled his belt. She fought the urge to heave, her body trembling. Stepping to the side, she tried to dart around him, but he blocked her path.

"Don't bite, or I'll knock your teeth out," he said, his voice gritty. Grabbing her head, he tried to force her to her knees as his other hand snaked into his pants. Out of time, panicked, Haven snatched his gun from his waistband. Using every ounce of strength she could muster, she swung and smacked him across the face with the butt of the gun. Nunzio stumbled, stunned, and let go of her.

It was all Haven needed to slip away.

Throwing the gun across the room, she sprinted for the door. Nunzio recovered and came after her, yelling. Her hand grasped the knob as she unlocked the door, but he grabbed her before she could open it. She screamed Dominic's name as he turned them around, pushing her roughly toward the bed. She fell and scurried away as he stalked toward her, the bang of the door being forced open her saving grace. Dominic ran in, a towel around his waist but still dripping water from his shower, and shoved Nunzio out of the way before helping Haven to her feet. "Are you okay?"

"It's fine." Haven wiped her tears. "I'm fine."

"He didn't hurt you, right?"

She shook her head as Nunzio scoffed. "Me, hurt her? That bitch attacked me!"

Dominic's face twisted with rage as he snatched the gun from the floor. "Haven, leave. I need to have a talk with my old friend."

Haven ran out and hesitated in the library before darting for Carmine's room. Locking herself in there, she sat on the edge of the bed and covered her ears to drown out the fighting.

———

Carmine knew something had gone terribly wrong when he made it home from school and walked into a house filled with fighting. Curses and insults flew around in multiple languages, the anger and hostility coming from the kitchen palpable. Stunned, Carmine paused in the doorway, seeing his father sewing up a cut on Nunzio's face. "What the fuck happened?"

Dominic walked up behind Carmine, eyeing him warily. "I should've watched Haven better. Nunzio cornered her."

Carmine's stomach dropped as he fought to keep his composure. "Where is she?"

"Up in your room," Dominic said. "She said she was okay."

Sighing, Carmine glanced back at his father in the kitchen as Nunzio snickered and pulled away. "That bitch begged for it."

Carmine's control slipped at those words. "What did you say?" Nunzio glared at him. "I said she wanted me."

Carmine leaped right for him, and Vincent blocked the path when Nunzio tried to move. Swinging, Carmine's fist barely connected with the man's nose when Sal intervened and dragged him away.

"You're sick!" Carmine yelled as Vincent shoved Nunzio into the counter to continue sewing him up. Sal pulled Carmine into the foyer, not letting go of him until they were near the stairs. "This isn't right!"

"I know, *Principe*, but didn't we have a conversation yesterday about feelings having no place in business? He'll face the consequences for disrespecting your father, but this isn't a major violation."

Carmine stared at him hard. "So she's worth nothing to you people? Is that what you're telling me? Oh, who gives a fuck if he hurts a girl? She's no one special, because she wasn't lucky enough to be born into a powerful family!"

Sal's expression twisted with anger, the sight of it silencing Carmine. "That girl means more than you understand, but things are black and white to *la famiglia*. You need to learn how to distinguish between what's personal and what's business. You need to learn to follow the code of conduct here"—he smacked him in the back of the head—"and quit following *this* so much." He punched Carmine in the chest, over his heart. "The moment you cursed at me yesterday, I knew she'd gotten to you here"—another punch in the chest—"and you're going to cause problems if you don't start using *this*."

A final smack to the head sent Carmine over the edge. "Quit hitting me!"

Sal shook his head. "You know I think of you as a son. I've always treated you like you were my own, and I want what's best for you. I want you to succeed, to have a good life, the life you're supposed to have. I'm not telling you not to let the girl in here"—he tapped him lightly on the chest—"but I am telling you not to let those feelings override everything else. You need balance."

Carmine ran his hands down his face, frustrated. "I get it."

Sal clapped him on the shoulder. "You're enamored. These things happen, but it's a fragile situation that shouldn't be flaunted. Trust me when I say it's not the time to ignore reason."

"I just . . . I didn't realize it was obvious."

"It's a complicated situation," Sal said. "Your father has a similar problem. I've spent years trying to get him to recognize boundaries, but he still finds himself blurring lines." A loud bang rang out in the kitchen, and Salvatore sighed. "Now likely being one of those times."

———

Haven stared at the clock, counting the minutes as they passed. Three. Five. Eight. Twelve. Sixteen. Twenty-two.

After thirty agonizing minutes, frantic footsteps bounded into the library. Someone tried to turn the locked doorknob, but Haven refused to open it, terrified to move. Keys jingled as the door opened, and Carmine rushed into the room.

He pulled her into his arms, tears still streaming down her cheeks. She wasn't sure how long he held her before Dr. DeMarco's voice rang out from the doorway. "Is she okay?"

Haven's vision was blurry, but she could make out his stern expression. He looked irate. She hoped that anger wasn't directed at her.

"She will be," Carmine said. "Is Nunzio gone?"

"Sal's driving him to the airport now."

"The airport," Carmine repeated. "He got off too easy. I would've killed him."

All was quiet for a bit, and Haven closed her eyes. She began to wonder if they were alone when Dr. DeMarco's voice rang out once more. "I would've killed him, too."

Carmine lay beside Haven in bed, brushing the hair from her face. Her cries had quieted, her face blotchy from tears. "I'm sorry," he said. "I should've been here to protect you."

"It's not your fault," she replied, her voice scratchy. "I'm the one who's sorry for being so weak."

"You aren't weak," he said. "You have every right to be shaken up. Fuck, *I'm* shaken up. No one touches my girl unless she wants to be touched. That's something my mom made sure we understood—a woman's body is a temple, and you should never enter it without an invitation."

He paused and ran his fingers through his hair. It was difficult to talk about, but he wanted to share this with her. "I don't know details, but my mom was raped when she was young. She spent time volunteering as an advocate after that. My father still donates money to the center in Chicago where she worked."

Haven scooted closer to him. "Wow."

"That's the reason I don't want you to feel like we have to do anything. Your body is your temple, and I won't come in it unless you want me to." The moment the words left his lips he laughed to himself. "That sounds so fucking wrong. I didn't mean it that way."

Haven lifted her head to look at him. "What's wrong about what you said?"

Of course she wouldn't get the perverted connotation. "I don't think now is the time to explain."

She shrugged and laid her head back down.

The room was quiet except for the air whistling as it blew from the vent in the ceiling. Haven took one of Carmine's hands and linked their fingers together, resting them at her chest. He felt her breath as her lips brushed across his swelling knuckles.

He smiled at the feel of her kiss. "What are you thinking, *tesoro*?"

"I'm wondering if, uh . . . It's stupid."

His curiosity grew. "Nothing you think is stupid."

"Well, do you think . . ." She paused to take a deep breath. "Do you think you could ever love someone like me?" She whispered the question, and he froze. Before he could gather his thoughts and answer, Haven cut in again. "I told you it was stupid."

Devastation shook her voice as she took his hesitation as rejection. She found the nerve to bring up a subject he wasn't brave enough to broach, to utter the word *love* that terrified him so much, and instead of reassuring her he clammed up. "Haven, I could never love someone like you, because there isn't anyone else like you. You're one of a kind."

———

The haunting melody filtered into Carmine's subconscious, taunting him, as he watched his mom under the flickering streetlight of the vacant alley. Her words filtered past the gloomy song, her voice soft. "My *sole*," she whispered. *Her sun*. She called him *sole* because he shined so brightly.

She laughed, drowning out the tortuous notes. It was such a beautiful night that she wanted to walk home, and Carmine trusted her so he didn't argue. His mom was infallible. He would always believe in her.

It came out of nowhere, the chaos and mayhem. Images flashed before him, so fast and frenzied he could barely keep up. Tires screeching. The terror on her face. Voices cold, their words brutal.

"Run, Carmine!" she yelled. "Run, baby, and don't stop!"

Her screams were loud in the night, but no one was around to help. Carmine stayed frozen, because he couldn't leave without her. He didn't want to go alone. He was her *sole*, her sun . . . He couldn't bear to leave her in the dark.

"If you love me, Carmine Marcello, you'll run," she said as tears spilled from her eyes. He hesitated, terrified, but at the last second he fled.

"Shut her up!" a man yelled. "Do it quick!"

The petrifying, bone-chilling scream rang through the alley. Carmine's steps waned, and he turned back around. They were hurting his mom. She needed him.

The men were shrouded in black, but in the flicker of the streetlight, he saw the flash of a face. It was a blur, a mosaic of scar tissue and hate as the loud bang of the gunshot ricocheted in his mind.

Startled, Carmine sat upright and clutched his chest as he tried to get his heart to slow down. Glancing beside him in the dim room, he saw Haven's eyes were wide-open, her expression layered with concern.

Falling back onto the bed, he ran his hands down his face. Sweating and shaking, his breathing erratic, he half expected Haven to run when he reached out to her. She didn't, though. Instead, she allowed him to squeeze her in a hug.

Tears built up as he cleared his throat. "I was eight, and it was my first piano recital. It was late when it was over, and my mom wanted to walk home. She didn't want to wait for a car to pick us up. We took a shortcut through an alley, and a car pulled up—a black car with dark windows."

He could still see it. Generic, another undistinguishable black sedan, but it stood out to him.

"I saw it and thought my father sent it for us, because he didn't like us out without protection. But my mom knew. I don't know how, but she did. She told me to leave, to go straight home. I didn't want to, but she said if I loved her I'd run. And I fucking loved her, so I did. I ran."

Hot tears burned his cheeks. He didn't fight them—they'd come whether he wanted them to or not. "I made it to the end of the alley when she screamed, and I turned around in enough time to see him pull the trigger. She dropped as the second guy pointed a gun at me. The burning tore through me. At first, I seriously thought I was on fire. I hid behind a Dumpster at a pizzeria around the corner, too scared to go on. I thought they were following me. I thought I was gonna die."

He paused to clear his throat, taking a deep breath. "The next thing I remember is waking up in the hospital. I'd never seen my father cry before that day. He just sat beside my bed, chanting, 'It's my fault,' and fuck, I felt the same way. I ran. I left her there to die."

He let out a shaky breath and squeezed Haven tightly, feeling her warmth and life. Her hand stroked his chest as she looked up at him, her face streaked with tears. "I ran, too, you know. My mama told me to run away and leave her. I only did it because she asked me to."

"So you know the guilt I feel."

She nodded. "But you didn't let her down, Carmine. You did what she needed you to do."

Carmine brushed away her tears. "And what's that?"

"You survived."

18

Time wore on, weeks passing as the chilly southern autumn spawned an unusually frigid winter. The football season ended so Carmine spent more time at home, he and Haven growing closer every day. Despite the coldness outside, despite the dreary weather, warmth and passion flourished inside the old plantation home as young love blossomed, unable to be contained.

Carmine and Haven would lie together, holding hands and embracing in the darkened bedroom after nightfall, away from prying eyes, away from a reality that couldn't understand how two kids, broken and yearning, could find a way to somehow feel whole together.

One night, Carmine brought his lips to her ear. *"Ti amo tantissimo, mia bella ragazza."*

Haven didn't know what he was trying to say, but the sound of it made her heart beat wildly.

He kissed her as she lay on her back, his body moving with her, lips working frantically. She gripped his shoulders, trying to pull him closer, but he held back. Carmine stared into her eyes, searching for an answer to an unasked question. Haven wanted to know what he sought, but before she could ask, he seemed to find his answer.

The corner of his lips turned up, and he kissed her sweetly before whispering into her ear. "Let me make you feel good. *Prometto di non danneggiarlo.* I'll only touch."

She trembled at his words, her body igniting in a fire she'd never felt before. "I trust you."

Carmine reached toward the nightstand and hit his stereo remote, soft classical music instantly filling the room. "Tell me to stop any time and I will."

She laced her trembling fingers through his thick hair. Carmine's lips moved down to her neck as he softly stroked her sides before pulling off her shirt. Haven closed her eyes, trying to relax, and shivered when she felt his warm breath against her bare stomach. He tasted her flesh, his tongue dipping inside her belly button, and she gasped as tingles coursed through her lower half.

Carmine took his time, kissing and caressing every inch of exposed skin. She squirmed, her moans mixing with the song pouring from the speakers. She had no idea what it was, no idea who performed it, but the melodic notes washed through her, accentuating every calculated touch of Carmine's fingertips. His hands roamed her thighs, stroking her soft skin, before making their way up her torso. He slipped them beneath her, undoing her bra clasp with one swift experienced flick.

Surprised, Haven opened her eyes again and peeked up at him as he sat back on his knees. He smiled sheepishly as he pulled off her bra, discarding it on the floor. His eyes remained on hers for a moment before slowly, carefully, drifting down.

She tensed self-consciously as she thought of her scars. He could see every mark and blemish, the remnants of the countless beatings she'd endured at the hands of the first people who were supposed to protect her. She felt so raw and open, having never been so exposed to someone before.

She waited for him to react, for him to be repulsed and turn away, but instead he trailed his pointer finger down her chest, from the dip in her throat to between her breasts. He traced the small scars with his fingertips, drawing a pattern on her quivering stomach. "*Bellisima*," he whispered. "You're so fucking beautiful."

The sound of his voice put her at ease. Sparks danced across her chest, her skin pebbling under his touch. The hand resting on her stomach drifted farther down, slipping under the waistband of her shorts. Haven could think of nothing and feel nothing but his touch, the sensations overwhelming her from head to toe. It only grew stronger when his hand rubbed the space between her thighs that, until that moment, she hadn't realized desperately ached for his attention.

He pressed his lips to hers again as she swallowed a cry and arched her back. Jolts of electricity ran through her veins, tiny pop rock explosions igniting inside her. Her legs shook, her breathing erratic as the softest of whimpers forced their way from her throat.

Fisting the bedsheets, she squeezed her eyes shut tightly, the sensations more intense than she imagined a simple touch could evoke. Her entire body was on fire, lava pooling beneath the surface and rushing through her bloodstream, warming her skin to a light pink flush.

Carmine whispered into her neck, his voice gritty. "Just feel it, hummingbird. Enjoy the flutters."

The buildup intensified, growing stronger and stronger as Haven moved her hips, seeking more friction. Her body craved it, cried out for it, begging for more.

Groaning, Carmine pulled his mouth from her neck, his lips meeting hers as her body seized up before erupting in pleasure. Shockwaves went off inside her, shooting down her legs and up through her stomach as she convulsed with her first orgasm. She stammered, trying to call his name, but nothing coherent passed between their connected lips. The feeling faded as quickly as it came, the tension receding from her muscles like a wave.

19

Two in the morning and Carmine couldn't sleep. He slipped downstairs, jumping when his father appeared in the doorway to the kitchen. Carmine hadn't expected anyone to be up at this hour, much less him. Vincent's gaze followed Carmine as he brushed past him to get something to drink. "Insomnia?"

Carmine shrugged. "You could say that."

"Is it nightmares again?"

"You could say that." Carmine was annoyed he would bring that up, but he could see the genuine concern in his father's expression. He didn't want to dwell, though, so he quickly changed the subject. "So, why are you up?"

Vincent sighed. "I'm leaving for Chicago."

"I didn't know you had to go this weekend."

"Neither did I until Sal called," he said. "I wasn't supposed to fly out again until next weekend, but the trouble with the Russians is escalating."

Carmine's brow furrowed. "You have a problem with Russians?"

"We've had one for a while. They impede on our territory, which is something we can't tolerate."

Carmine was surprised he was telling him that much. His father wasn't one to offer extra information. "Well, good luck with that, I guess."

"Thanks. I'll be back on Sunday night . . . hopefully." He hesitated like he had something else to say but eventually shook his head. "Have a good weekend, son."

Vincent left the kitchen. Carmine stood there, looking at the spot where his father had been standing. He chugged the last little bit of juice in his glass before heading upstairs, lying silently in bed and staring at the ceiling.

When Haven woke up the next morning, he wrapped his arms around her waist. "Morning, *bella ragazza*. How about we get dressed and do something today?"

She smiled sleepily. "Like what?"

"Whatever you want," he said. "We could go to the movies or the park, maybe get some dinner."

He had no clue what people did. The closest he had ever been to a date before was going through a fast-food drive-through on the way to drop some girl off after sex. He wasn't sure he could count even that, considering he usually made them buy their own food.

An odd expression flickered across her face. "In public?"

He laughed. "Yes, in public. With other people around, even."

"Uh, okay." She smiled excitedly. "I'll get dressed."

He let go of her and watched as she scampered away, amazed something as trivial as a movie could make her light up so much.

Carmine showered and sifted through his clothes, choosing a pair of faded jeans and a green long-sleeved button-up shirt, since green was her favorite color. He rolled up the sleeves, feeling stifled, and pulled on a pair of Nikes before grabbing his things. Heading out, he noticed Haven standing in the doorway of her room, wearing a pair of tight jeans and a blue sweater, fidgeting. "Do I look okay?"

"You look more than okay," he said, holding his hand out to her.

Leading her downstairs, he helped Haven into the car and

fiddled with his seat and mirrors for a few minutes. Haven giggled. "Finicky."

He rolled his eyes and started the car, scanning through radio stations as Haven stared out the side window, a small smile playing on her lips. They held hands and chatted about nothing in particular during the drive. She never ceased to amaze him with her knowledge about things she had never experienced.

He drove straight to his favorite Mexican restaurant and slowed to pull into the parking lot until his gaze fell on a white car. He accelerated again to pass the place, knowing they couldn't eat there if Lisa was working. He pulled into a steakhouse about a block away and shut off the engine as Haven turned to him. "You knew someone there, didn't you?"

He sighed and ran his hand through his hair. "Yeah. I don't want you to think it's because I don't wanna be seen with you, because I do. It's just, it's Lisa, and she—"

Haven placed her pointer finger against his lips. "I understand."

———

They were quickly seated in the restaurant, and Haven picked up the laminated menu, her brow furrowing and lips moving as she sounded out the words. When the waitress came to take their orders, Haven looked at Carmine, expecting him to speak for her, but he just sat patiently.

She got the hint. "I'll have the stuffed chicken breast with a side salad, please."

Carmine smirked. "A twelve-ounce New York strip steak for me."

"How do you want it?" the waitress asked.

"Rare," he said. "Barely cooked."

Haven gazed at him peculiarly when the waitress walked away. "I didn't know you like it that way. I always cook your meat well done."

"Yeah, two things in life I prefer bloody—my steak and my enemies."

She shook her head. "You're too young to have enemies."

"I wish," he muttered. "I was born with enemies. My last name alone gives me more than I could ever earn."

It only took a few minutes for their food to be brought out. Carmine expected things to be edgy since she wasn't often around people, but she surprised him again. He wondered if there would ever be a time when she didn't.

He paid the bill before they headed across town to the movie theater. The two of them stood on the outskirts of the waiting crowd, and Carmine took Haven's hand as he scanned the list of movies. "What are you in the mood for?"

"I don't really know much about any of them."

"Well, there's one about a drugged-up rock star, one about a family with a whole bunch of kids, and one about some kids who get sucked into a game." She looked at him with confusion on the last one, and he chuckled. "Don't ask. There's also some chick flick."

"Chick flick?"

"Yeah, you know, the lovey-dovey romantic sharing bullshit." She laughed. "Any of them are fine by me."

He led her up to the window and bought two tickets. At the concession stand, he bought a soda and a box of Sour Patch Kids before leading Haven into the packed theater. She hesitated, glancing around, and it dawned on him that this was her first time. It was easy for him to forget sometimes that she was still new to the world and hadn't experienced the things he took for granted. He squeezed her hand, trying to be reassuring, and chose a seat near the exit in case she felt the need to escape.

She relaxed as he pushed the armrest out of the way and pulled her close to him. The theater finished filling as it significantly darkened. Haven tensed at the thunderous noise coming from the speakers but relaxed again by the time the movie started. He popped a few Sour Patch Kids into his mouth, and Haven eyed the candy before pulling out a piece. Her face contorted as soon as it hit her tongue, and he chuckled. "It's sour, huh?"

"Yes, but it's good."

She took a couple more and watched the movie intently while Carmine spent most of the time focusing on her. They shared the soda and munched on the candy like it was no big deal, but to both of them, it was. Carmine was giving, and Haven had no qualms taking from him.

He felt no anger as she snatched a piece of candy right from his hand, only pride that she had grown so brave. Her guard was down, and little by little, Carmine felt himself cracking too.

He took her hand when the credits rolled, and the two of them slipped out of the theater before everyone else. Haven enthusiastically chatted the entire way home. He had no clue what she was talking about, but he smiled anyway, her happiness making him content.

Nine men. Nine guns. Almost ninety bullets. One delivery truck full of electronics.

This wasn't how Vincent had expected to spend his Saturday night.

They were outnumbered two to one. A run-of-the-mill Glock was pointed at Vincent's chest while he stared down the barrel of a Beretta. The hand of the man holding the Glock shook, telling Vincent he was nervous. For that reason, Vincent chose to aim his revolver at the other one. If Vincent had learned anything, it was that a man with a steady hand wouldn't hesitate to pull a trigger.

Corrado stood a few feet away, in the midst of a showdown with Ivan Volkov. The two men glared, neither one moving or speaking, with their guns pointed at each other's heads. Corrado seemed unaware of everyone else around them. Vincent wasn't sure if that was good or bad.

Giovanni held his ground despite the armed men zeroing in on him. The box truck idled, the cramped alley filling with the thick, suffocating fumes. It burned Vincent's nose and distorted his vision, but he fought to keep his focus. They had been called out by Sal a few minutes earlier, saying a truck Giovanni's crew had hijacked on the east side of the city was stolen from them by thugs. They had tracked it down, expecting to find amateurs, but came head-to-head with the Russians again.

The man with the Glock was the first to crack. He lowered his weapon and frantically took a step back. Shaking his head, he wordlessly ran out of the alley.

One by one they surrendered, their lack of loyalty astounding. They fled, leaving the three of them with an unruffled Volkov. There was no fear in his expression, no concern in his eyes, no surprise that his men had abandoned their posts.

They were nothing like the Italians. If one of them abandoned *la famiglia*, they wouldn't live to see another sunrise.

After a moment, Volkov lowered his gun and slipped it into his coat. "You may have the truck," he said, as though he was simply being gracious under the circumstances.

He tried to walk away, but Corrado stepped in his path. "Next time I see you, I'm going to kill you."

Volkov paused. "Is that a threat?"

"No, it's a guarantee."

A tense second passed, then another, and another. Finally, Volkov's stone-cold face flickered with the hint of a smile. "I look forward to our next meeting, Moretti."

———

Haven sat cross-legged on Carmine's bed, *The Secret Garden* open in her lap. Carmine strolled through his room and kicked a schoolbook lying on the floor, stubbing his toe. He yelped as he grabbed his foot and plopped down on the bed beside her, the jarring losing her place. Before she could find it again, the book closed as Carmine pulled it from her hands. For a second, irritation flared inside her at the interruption, but it faded when he laid his head in her lap.

She ran her hand across his cheek, gazing down at him with a smile as he spoke. "My bedroom needs cleaned."

She jolted them both with her laughter. "Yes, it does."

Haven ran her fingers through his hair, and he sighed contently. "Tomorrow. Cleaning can wait."

"I look forward to it."

He chuckled. "You should be terrified."

The two of them drifted into a light sleep, but when Haven awoke later, she was alone. She slipped out of the bedroom, surprised to find the library empty, and made her way downstairs to search for Carmine.

The house was eerily silent, but on the first floor she heard the faint sound of music, the haunting dark melody laced with sadness. She walked slowly toward the family room, spotting Carmine sitting at the piano. His posture matched the song, his body collapsing in on itself, and the music grew louder as he furiously pressed the keys.

Haven sat down in the doorway and leaned against the wall in the shadows, watching him play in a trance. She was mesmerized hearing so much emotion pouring from his fingertips. It was the same tune in a continuous loop—as soon as it would wind down, he'd start it up again.

She recognized it. Though different in tone, the notes louder and fluid on the piano, it was the same one he strummed on his guitar at night.

Her eyelids grew heavy as she listened, but she fought sleep, captivated by the music. She eventually lost the battle, and the next thing she knew she was being jolted around. Her eyes snapped open, startled when her gaze fell on Carmine. They were on the second floor, and she was cradled in his arms. She gave him an apologetic look, hoping he wasn't upset she'd spied on him, but he merely smiled. "We have beds, *tesoro*. You don't have to sleep on the floor."

20

Haven stood in the doorway of Carmine's bedroom, exhausted from broken sleep and wanting nothing more than to take a nap, but much more pressing things needed to be dealt with.

Scanning the mess, Haven contemplated where to start.

"Look, I have no idea what you'll find," Carmine said. "I'm gonna apologize in advance for it all, so I don't have to keep saying it as we go."

He walked over to his dirty clothes and tossed them in his hamper as Haven tentatively navigated her way through the room. "Don't you want to separate them?" she asked.

He froze, holding a pair of pants. "Separate them how?"

"A pile of whites and a pile of colors will work."

"Yes, ma'am." He mock-saluted her. Her smile disintegrated, and he sighed at her fallen expression. "I'm kidding. I can handle separating clothes . . . just forgot I was supposed to."

He dug the clothes back out of the hamper and made two piles as Haven picked up his schoolbooks. She set them on his desk and shifted the stacks of paper around to organize a bit.

"So, uh . . ." Carmine held up a white shirt with navy blue stripes. "Would you consider this a color or a white?"

"Color," she said, looking at the piles. "That white shirt with the green design is a color too."

Carmine picked up the shirt and tossed it on the other pile. "How can you tell?"

"The tag says not to use any bleach."

"You read my tags?" His voice was serious, like they were discussing something scandalous.

She smiled. "Yes, I read them when I do your laundry."

"And you remember that?"

"Of course."

"Well, you didn't tell *me* to read the tags."

Haven held back her laughter, knowing it would only make his irritation worse. When Carmine finished separating the clothes, she took the hamper of whites downstairs to start a load. She pulled out a few things that were obviously not bleachable and set them aside to wash with the next load, not wanting to make it a big deal.

She dragged the empty hamper up to Carmine's room and found him sprawled out on his stomach on the bed. She stared at his back, mesmerized by his sculpted muscles and the way his tattoos stood out prominently on his skin. He shifted around to look at her and smiled lazily. "I forfeit. This shit's hard."

All he'd done was sort clothes, and he'd done a pretty bad job of it, at that. "It's easy to me."

He rolled his eyes as she gathered the second load of laundry.

He put a few CDs away as she stripped his bed.

He took a break. She fetched fresh linens.

He put on some music. She made his bed.

He plopped down at his desk as she walked around the room, grabbing random things and putting them where she assumed they went. Carmine watched her closely, the attention making her hyperaware of every movement. She didn't mind that he wasn't much help, considering she'd do a better job on her own, but his gaze made her nervous. Occasionally, he'd grind his teeth, trying to contain his irritation when she touched certain things.

The floor was cleared before long, all except for the edge of a book sticking out from under his bed. She got on her knees, surprised by how cluttered it was under there. She pulled out books and magazines, as well as some movies. A few shoeboxes were stored under there, but she didn't touch them. She put the comforter back down and glanced at her pile, gasping when she saw the naked woman on the front of one of the DVD cases. She covered it up, but she wasn't quick enough—Carmine had already spotted it.

"Knew you'd find the porn." He laughed, grabbing it. "Wanna watch it?"

There was a mischievous twinkle in his eyes. She vehemently shook her head, and he tossed the DVD into a drawer in his desk as she picked up a packet of pictures. Carmine pointed toward a drawer to show her where they went. "You can look at them if you want. I'm pretty sure everyone has clothes on, but no promises."

He winked playfully as she pulled out the pictures. She flipped through them and smiled at the familiar faces, surprised to see Nicholas in a few of them. They all looked young and happy, but in most of them something was off about Carmine. His eyes were dull, the spark she was used to missing. He'd clearly been broken back then, the pictures telling a story no words could do justice.

She opened the drawer he had said they went in and froze. Sitting on top of everything was a tiny doll made out of tan string, no more than a few inches tall. It had short hair made from yarn, felt clothes glued to the body of what was clearly a little boy. She wondered why Carmine would have such a thing as she picked up the tiny doll, careful not to harm it.

Her chest ached as she gazed at it, remembering a time long ago when she had seen a similar one. She had been young, five or six years old, as she ran through the yard of the Antonelli ranch. Her bare feet kicked up dust as her laughter rang out, loud and blissful like the faint church bells they could hear on Sunday mornings. The tiny doll was clutched tightly in her hand, the long brown yarn flowing in the wind as Haven raced to the stables.

"Mama!" she yelled. "Look, Mama!"

Her mama sighed as she turned around, her face soaked with sweat. "I'm busy, Haven."

"Look, Mama," she said again, stopping outside the stall her mama stood in with the horse. Haven held up the doll, laughing wholeheartedly. She had never felt so overjoyed in her life. "It's me!"

Her mama's eyes widened with panic at the sight of the toy. "Where did you get that? You have to give it back."

"No, Mama."

Her mama stepped out of the stall and tried to take the doll. "Give it to me. You know better."

"No."

"Haven Isadora, give it to me right now!"

She held it behind her, shaking her head wildly. She wasn't overjoyed anymore. Now she was heated. She had never had a toy before, and no one was taking this one from her—not even her mama. "No, it's mine! Mine! She gave it to me! Not you!"

"Who gave it to you?"

"My angel, Mama. She gave me a present!"

Her angel. Haven had dreamed of her for years, the beautiful woman in white that glowed under the hot desert sun. She strained to conjure up the image of her again when a throat cleared nearby, ripping Haven from her thoughts. She glanced up, seeing Carmine right beside her.

She set the doll down and shut the drawer. "I'm sorry. I shouldn't have touched your stuff."

He was quiet as her nervousness grew. She chewed on her bottom lip, afraid of his reaction. His hand shot out toward her abruptly. She flinched, but he merely brushed his fingertips across her mouth, pulling her lip from between her teeth.

"You're gonna make yourself bleed if you keep that shit up," he said as he reopened the drawer. "My mom used to make these dolls for the kids who came to the center she worked at. Most of them moved around a lot, so they didn't have a lot. She said the dolls were easy to keep up with since they're small."

Easy to hide, too. Haven had kept the doll concealed for years without her master knowing.

"She always thought personal was best."

"She's right," Haven said. "It is."

He sighed, gazing at the little doll. "A few months ago, I would've disagreed with that."

"And now?"

He closed the drawer again. "Everything's different now."

21

Haven lay across her bed, clutching a pencil as she sketched on the top paper of a pile in front of her. She paused, surveying the gray lines, before balling it up and tossing it on the floor.

She had been at it for hours, the floor littered with balls of white paper. She felt guilty for wasting so much. Paper was made out of wood, and although there wasn't a lack of trees in Durante, they weren't to be taken for granted. Trees lived and breathed, enduring so much and still surviving, growing stronger and bigger no matter the conditions.

Was it silly to think so highly of nature?

She put the pencil aside and gathered up the crumpled pieces of paper, tossing them into the trash can before heading downstairs. It was a Friday in the middle of December, Carmine's last day of school before winter break. Christmas was fast approaching, and all Haven could think about was her mama in Blackburn. She remembered the look in her eyes as she would sit in the stables and gaze at the ranch decorated in lights, wishing she were a part of something bigger. She would never admit it, but at Christmas, her mama didn't want to be on the outside looking in.

Haven knew the feeling well, and now she was torn—sad for not being with her mama but excited about finally being a part of it all.

The DeMarcos didn't decorate much, except for a flimsy fake tree put together out of a box, but Haven helped Carmine string on the lights. A few colored ornaments had been added in the days that followed, and Tess hung mistletoe in the doorway.

Dr. DeMarco's presence had been scarce during the past weeks. Most nights he didn't come home until after the sun had risen and only stuck around long enough to shower and change clothes. Haven didn't ask any questions, but she found it odd he left her on her own so much.

Did he finally believe she wouldn't try to run again?

She still cooked every night, even though Dr. DeMarco usually wasn't around for it, and she started eating at the table with the family. The nights Dr. DeMarco came home he never acknowledged her. She would occasionally catch him giving her uncomfortable looks, like he was preparing for something to happen that never did.

Haven had grabbed a soda from the kitchen and taken a sip when a car pulled up outside. The familiar Mercedes parked near the porch, and Dr. DeMarco headed straight into the house. His voice filtered inside as he stepped into the foyer, his phone to his ear. He shrugged off his coat, and his eyes fell upon her. His gaze lingered there as he ended the call.

"Can you go to my office? I'll be up in a moment."

He posed it as a question, but it wasn't negotiable. She nervously made her way to his office and sat in the chair across from his desk. The room was silent, except for the ticking clock on the wall behind her, and it seemed like forever before she heard his footsteps on the stairs. Her heart beat erratically as he neared, and she held her breath instinctively when Dr. DeMarco stepped inside.

He stopped in front of her, holding a large cotton swab and a plastic container. His knees cracked loudly as he crouched down in front of her, the harsh sound making her wince.

She watched him warily as he smiled, something off about his expression. There was a hint of worry, maybe even a bit of aggravation, but it was mostly sadness, which surprised her. She stared at him, wondering what made him that way, but she couldn't ask. It wasn't her place.

"Open your mouth," he ordered.

She obliged, and he ran the cotton swab along the inside of her cheek. He stood when he finished, placing the swab into the container as he leaned against his desk. "You don't look—"

His words cut off abruptly when his phone rang. Dr. DeMarco closed his eyes. "You're excused, child."

––––––––

Haven went straight for the family room, sitting on the couch and longingly gazing at the flimsy tree. The boys arrived home from school, their animated voices ringing through the house. Her eyes fell upon Carmine, and he winked as he sat in a chair across the room. Dominic grinned and plopped down beside her, so close he practically landed in her lap. He flung his arm over her shoulder. "What's up, Twinkle Toes? Did you miss me while I was at school?"

"Uh, yes," she said. "I guess."

Carmine shot him an annoyed look, and Dominic laughed, pretending to whisper. "I think my brother's a wee bit jealous."

Haven heard footsteps coming downstairs and went to pull away, but Dominic held on to her. Dr. DeMarco walked into the room, his brow furrowing when he looked at them. "Don't let Tess see you. You'll start a war, and I'd hate to have to step in."

Dominic laughed. "Whose side would you take?"

"I didn't say anything about taking a side. I have a policy of staying neutral."

"Okay, but let's say you were betting on it," Dominic said. "Who would you put money on?"

Dr. DeMarco sighed. "Are you asking who I think would win in a fight?"

"Yeah, I guess I am."

Carmine groaned across the room.

"Well, Tess is good at cheap shots, but the child has a knack for survival. She's not helpless either, as Squint can attest to. Tess is used to having help, while the girl's used to trudging through it alone. One on one, I have to say she'd take Tess easily." Haven's eyes widened, stunned he would say that. "But don't tell Tess. She might try to prove me wrong."

"I wouldn't tell Tess that if my life depended on it," Dominic said. "She'd kick my ass."

"She could probably take you, too," Dr. DeMarco said. "I know the child could."

Haven's cheeks reddened as they looked at her. "Uh, I don't know about that, sir."

"Don't underestimate yourself. I certainly don't." Haven stared at him, unsure of what he meant, but he looked away without elaborating. "I have stuff to do, so I probably won't be home until tomorrow. Have a good night."

He walked out, an awkward silence lingering in his wake.

"That was fucking weird," Carmine said before turning to his brother. "And get your damn arm off my girl before I break it."

Dominic leaned in her direction again. "Told you he was jealous."

"Whatever," Carmine said. "And what's wrong with you? Who would win in a fight? What kinda question is that?"

"It was a good one," Dominic said. "But why are you mad? He picked your girl, not mine."

They were listening to music later that night when Carmine blurted out something that caught Haven off guard: "What do you want for Christmas?"

What did she want? She had never thought about it. "I don't expect anything."

"Well, you're getting something."

"But I can't get you a present."

"You already gave me my present, Haven. *You.* Best gift ever."

She sighed as he lay down beside her. "I still wish I could buy you something."

"I don't need anything," he said, "but there will be plenty more holidays in the future for you to spoil me rotten."

Hope swelled through her. Christmases. Presents. A future. It was all too much to fathom. "Do you guys have big celebrations?"

"We used to when I was young, but now it's just us. My aunt Celia always comes for a few days. Other than her and her husband, we don't have any family. My grandfather's dead, and we don't see my grandmother. She has dementia or something. I don't really know."

"What about your mama's family?"

He was quiet. She wondered if she had asked the wrong question, but he finally spoke in a soft voice. "I don't know of any. She immigrated here."

"Have you thought about finding them?"

"No," he said. "They never came looking for my mom, never wondered what happened to her, so why should I care about them? Hell, I didn't know she was born in Ireland until I saw a stack of government papers in my father's office a few years ago."

"Does it make you sad that you don't have a big family?"

He shrugged. "I don't really think about it. I figure I have enough."

"I used to dream about having a big family," Haven said. "I used to pretend like I had one. Mama said I was always having conversations with imaginary people. I used to even talk to an angel."

"Like with wings and a halo and shit?"

"That kind of angel, yes, but she didn't have any of that," she said. "Mama said angels watched over me and someday I'd be one, so I imagined them as people. My angel told me about life. She said I could be free like her when I grew up and have anything I wanted. I guess she didn't want to crush me with the truth."

Carmine pulled her closer to him, burying his face in her hair. Despite it being early, Haven was exhausted. She was on the brink of falling asleep when she heard Carmine's quiet voice. "You can have a big family, *colibri*. She wasn't lying to you."

22

When he was growing up, Christmas had been Carmine's favorite time of year. He loved everything about the holiday—watching *Rudolph* and *Frosty* and *It's a Wonderful Life*, singing Christmas carols and playing *Jingle Bells* on the piano. *Magical* was the only way Carmine could describe it, but even that word didn't do the experience justice.

After his mom died, though, it changed. He lost interest in most things in life, but especially holidays. Christmas reminded him of her, and all he felt after she was gone was grief.

It was now Christmas Eve, and for the past week Carmine had watched Haven get into the holiday spirit. He hadn't seen such enthusiasm for it since his mom's last Christmas. A part of him still wanted to forget it all, push it aside and go back into his hole, but a bigger part of him couldn't help but be happy. He had finally found his light in the darkness, the spark that snuffed when his mom died reignited in Haven.

But Carmine feared the light would go out on him again.

Carmine's nerves were on edge as he drummed his fingers on the arm of the couch, steadily watching the clock, hardly able to pay attention to the television. After about twenty minutes, a car pulled up out front, and from the corner of his eye, he could see Haven go rigid. The front door opened and Vincent's voice ricocheted through the house, followed by soft feminine laughter.

Aunt Celia.

Dominic jumped up, picking Celia off the ground to swing her around. She glanced at Carmine once Dominic set her back on her feet. "You look more like her every time I see you, kiddo."

She didn't have to specify—Carmine knew what she meant. He hugged her, not bothering to respond. It was the truth, and Celia was the only person not afraid to talk to him about his mom.

Celia pulled back. "Have you been good?"

"I haven't blown anything up lately, if that counts."

"It's a start."

Vincent cleared his throat, his eyes focused on Haven standing in front of the couch. She stared at the floor as she picked at her fingernails. Seeing her look so frightened tugged at Carmine's heart.

Celia approached her. "Haven?"

"Yes, ma'am."

"I've heard a lot about you," Celia said. "It's a pleasure to meet you."

Haven's voice was barely audible. "You too, Mrs. Moretti."

"Call me Celia, dear. Mrs. Moretti is my mother-in-law and quite the wicked witch, at that."

Haven's eyes widened as Vincent laughed, but he shook his head, not interested in sharing whatever he found funny. He shared a knowing look with Celia, the corner of his lips still fighting to turn up.

"Anyway, I'm hungry and exhausted from traveling," Celia said, "so don't expect me to be good company tonight."

Haven's eyes darted to the clock. "I should make dinner."

She started out of the room, but Vincent stepped in front of her. A look of fright flashed across her face as she gasped, and he held his hands up when she recoiled.

It was a train wreck. As much as Carmine hated it, he couldn't do anything but watch it unfold.

"Relax, child," Vincent said. "I was going to tell you not to worry about cooking."

Haven wrapped her arms around her chest. "May I be excused then, mas—uh, sir?"

Carmine cringed at the exchange.

"Yes, you're excused." Haven bolted out of the room before the words were completely out of his mouth, and he shook his head. "I should've figured."

"You couldn't have known," Celia said. "It didn't cross my mind."

Carmine watched them suspiciously. "Couldn't have known what?"

A small surge of panic coursed through Carmine when his aunt let out a surprised laugh. She could read him easily, and he hadn't considered that beforehand.

"It doesn't matter," Vincent said, turning away. "We'll deal with the girl later."

––––––––––

Carmine didn't see Haven again that night. He hung out in the library in hopes she would surface, but dawn broke with no sign of her. Giving up, he went downstairs and sat at the piano, ghosting his fingers over the keys in the darkness before hitting the opening notes of *Moonlight Sonata*. He played for a few minutes, the mellow tones swallowing him whole, until a floorboard creaked behind him.

Cutting off midnote, he swung around to see Haven. Her wild hair hung loose, framing an exhausted and solemn face. He patted the piano bench, inviting her to join him, and she sat down.

"You really play beautifully." She gazed at the keys as he played again, picking up on the same note he'd stopped. "Is that the only song you know?"

He rounded out *Moonlight Sonata*. "I know a few more. Not as well as I know that one, but I can play a bit of the others."

"Are they all sad?"

"No."

"Can you play something happy for me?"

A sudden rush of irritation struck him at her request, but he fought it back, knowing he needed to control his temper with her. He roughly played "Jingle Bells," only vaguely remembering the right keys. Entranced, Haven's eyes sparkled as she watched his fingers.

The room fell silent when he finished the song. "Merry Christmas, *bella ragazza*."

She smiled, whispering, "Merry Christmas," back to him. He stared into her eyes and leaned forward to kiss her when a throat dramatically cleared behind them. He pulled back swiftly. *Damn near busted.*

"Am I interrupting?" Celia asked, the smile on her lips telling Carmine she knew she was. He started to speak, but Haven ran from the room before he could say anything. He sighed as she disappeared, and Celia sat down beside him on the bench. "So talented."

He rolled his eyes. "I butchered that song. I haven't tried to play it in years."

"Haven thought you played it great."

"That's because she's never heard it before. She thought my fuck-ups were intentional."

"You're being self-deprecating. Your mother was always proud of her little Mozart."

He didn't respond. She knew he wouldn't, though. He never did.

"She recognizes me," Celia said. "That's what your father and I were talking about. She saw me when I visited Blackburn."

Carmine sat still as that sank in. "Did you ever think about helping her when you were there?"

"Believe me, kiddo. I wanted to. I talked to Corrado about it, but it was out of my hands. It's their business and—"

"Yeah, yeah, yeah." He cut her off. "Keep business and personal separate, the code of conduct, and all that bullshit. I've heard it all before."

"I see you've been talking to Salvatore," she said. "Anyway, if you'll excuse me, there's a girl hiding somewhere I should have a talk with."

23

Haven sat on the edge of her bed, feeling out of place. She'd never spoken to Celia before last night, had merely seen her in passing, but her presence made those two worlds converge. Her old life, the one of pain, was mixing with her new life, where she'd finally started to feel comfortable.

It made her uneasy. She wanted that feeling to go away.

There was a light tap on her door. Her stomach felt queasy as she gripped the knob with a sweaty palm. Opening it slowly, she was alarmed to see Celia. "Can I speak to you?"

Haven nodded. Celia took a seat on the bed, and Haven tried to stop her hands from shaking as she sat beside her. "I wanted to tell you a story. Would you be opposed to that?"

A story? "No, ma'am."

"Back in the seventies, when I was around eleven, an underground war ignited between, uh, groups. Safe houses were set up around the country for men to get their families out of the line of fire. This place was one of them—it was where my father sent us. It also happens to be where we met my husband, Corrado, and his sister, Katrina. Our fathers were friends. Vincent and I never liked Katrina. She's an evil twit who gets pleasure from hurting people. I'm sure you know that."

Haven nodded. It was true.

"Corrado was the opposite of his sister. He stayed out of the way and kept to himself. One day we were all out by the creek, and

Katrina was throwing rocks at me. Corrado just stood there and watched. We thought he was a pushover. Vincent wouldn't stand for it, though, and threw a rock back at her. Smacked her in the face and left a big welt."

Despite herself, Haven smiled.

"Katrina tattled and my mother was about to whip Vincent when Corrado spoke up out of nowhere. This little boy hadn't said a word for days, and the first time he opened his mouth, he spoke with such authority. He said, 'You shouldn't hit him.' He said a person shouldn't be punished for protecting their family. My mother was so surprised that she let Vincent go."

Celia laughed to herself. "That's my husband. When he speaks, people listen." She paused. "You're probably wondering where I'm going with this."

"Yes, ma'am."

"I just want you to know I'm not like the people in Blackburn . . . my husband isn't like them. We too deal with people we don't want to. It's something you understand when you involve yourself with a man in this life. They do horrible things—things most women would be ashamed of their husbands doing—but we know it's ingrained in them, just as things are ingrained in us. I've accepted Corrado for who he is, as I'm sure you accept Carmine, bad attitude and all."

Haven was alarmed at the mention of Carmine and tried to keep her expression blank. "I accept both of the DeMarco boys."

Celia smiled. "I'm sure you do, Haven. I don't worry about Dominic. Despite everything, he's pretty well adjusted, but Carmine's unique. He has a gentle soul underneath that ugly armor he wears, and it's nice that someone finally cracked through it."

Her heart pounded frantically. "He's . . . " She didn't know what to say. ". . . different."

"Yeah, he is," she said. "Although I think what you mean by that isn't the same as what I mean. But anyway, I should start dinner."

Haven jumped up, having forgotten about dinner. It was the

reason she'd gone downstairs so early in the first place. "Oh no, I should've already done it!"

"Relax. Christmas dinner's my gig. I look forward to it every year. Your job's to enjoy yourself today."

After Celia left, Haven headed for the door when Carmine burst into the room, holding a small present. He headed straight for her, no hesitation in his steps. He caught her off guard, and she took a step away, the backs of her knees hitting the bed.

He stopped in front of her, forcing the gift into her trembling hand. "Open it."

It was hard for her to find a spot to start since he had used so much tape, but she managed to tear a corner. After the paper was off, she stared at the thick blue book with MERRIAM-WEBSTER'S DICTIONARY AND THESAURUS written on the front. "This is for me?"

"Yeah," he said. "I remember you said you needed a thesaurus. And I know you were joking, but I thought, you know . . . it might be useful or whatever." He sighed. "I suck at this gift thing."

She stared at him as he rambled, realizing he was nervous. "Thank you."

"It's not what I wish I could give you . . ."

"It's great, Carmine."

She walked to the other side of the bed and briefly reconsidered what she was doing, but he'd put himself out there and she wanted to do the same. "I drew something for you."

A smile spread over his face. "I thought you forgot our deal."

"I never forget things."

He chuckled, all trace of nervousness gone, even though hers had skyrocketed. "I'll keep that in mind later when I fuck up."

Opening the drawer on the stand, she pulled out a piece of paper and held it so he couldn't see. "It's, uh . . . it's not that great."

He held out his hand. "I'm sure it's wonderful."

Resigned that it was too late to back out, Haven handed him the drawing. She swallowed a few times, trying to push back her nerves as she sat beside him. Besides her mama, no one had ever seen anything she drew. Carmine's silence as he stared at it flustered her. "I told you it wasn't good."

"*Tesoro*, this is amazing! I'm speechless, and you think it sucks?"

She glanced at the picture in his hand. Although she'd never seen one in person, she'd looked up a hummingbird in a book in the library. It was the only sketch she'd made that looked right to her. "Really?"

He laughed. "Yes, really. This is the best thing anyone's ever done for me. I told you I wanted you for Christmas, and you gave it to me. This is beautiful. You're beautiful, *colibri*."

Haven stood frozen in the family room as she stared out the window. The backyard was encased in a thin layer of white, thick flakes continuing to fall from the sky like confetti.

"We don't get much snow around here," Carmine said. "It never lasts long, but it's nice."

To her, *nice* didn't begin to cover it. It was beautiful. She walked to the window and pressed her hand to the frosty glass, her stomach fluttering as her eyes burned with tears. She thought of her mama then, the vision of her dancing in the snow. It was her happy spot, the place she went whenever she dreamed. Haven understood now. She yearned to go there, too.

A throat cleared behind her, and she turned to see that everyone had gathered. Dozens of presents of all shapes and sizes huddled under the fake tree, decorated in shiny paper with big bows. Haven sat on the couch, her nerves flaring as she gazed at them. Carmine hesitated but sat down beside her.

Dr. DeMarco handed out presents, and Haven was stunned when he set two in front of her. Dominic's name was written on the top one, and she glanced at the second to see unfamiliar handwriting. "Celia," Carmine said, the same time Haven read the name on the tag.

The gift from Dominic was filled with art supplies, paints and paper and markers, while Celia's box contained an empty picture frame. Overwhelmed by their generosity, Haven could do nothing but whisper her thanks. She felt almost normal as she watched the others with their gifts, like she was simply a girl enjoying the small things in life. It warmed her heart to feel like a part of them.

Despite that, there was still that other part of her that felt guilty. As she gazed around at the living room littered with wrapping paper and plates of cookies, she felt like she was betraying her mama. There would be no gifts for her. No sweets. No laughs. No family. No snow. No love.

She had been so lost in thought that she hadn't noticed the room emptied until Carmine squeezed her knee. She jumped, startled, and he looked at her questioningly. "What's wrong?"

"Just thinking about my mama."

Carmine put his arm around her, pulling her to him. "I miss mine, too."

––––––––

Tess and Dia showed up a few minutes later, and everyone gathered in the family room once again while Haven lingered by the doorway. Dr. DeMarco and his sister laughed together over some whispered secret, and Tess sat on Dominic's lap as he squeezed her in a hug. Dia was telling a story, making Carmine chuckle. The love in the room was so pure and powerful that Haven's eyes misted from the intensity of it.

Carmine spotted her and patted the cushion beside him. "Why are you standing there?"

"Habit, I guess," she said. "I'm used to being on the outside looking in."

"Well, we're gonna break that habit. You belong on the inside with me."

She gazed at him, smiling, before looking over his shoulder. A pair of dark eyes met hers, the penetrating gaze paralyzing. Dr. DeMarco was watching them, and he didn't look happy anymore.

"Time to play in the snow!"

Everyone jumped up at once as Dominic shouted those words, and Haven just sat there when they ran from the room. Celia laughed. "Aren't you joining them?"

"Am I supposed to?" Haven asked, looking to Dr. DeMarco for direction, but he said nothing, his expression giving her no hint.

"If you want to," Celia said, "but you'll need to bundle up."

"Yes, ma'am."

She headed upstairs, finding Carmine waiting for her. Haven put on some extra clothes before grabbing her coat. She wore so many layers she had a hard time walking down the stairs. The group headed for the back door, and Dominic collapsed to the ground right away, sending white stuff flying everywhere. He formed snowballs to pelt Carmine with, and Haven laughed as he threw some back. The fighting got out of control quickly. Haven ducked as Dia ran, snowballs barely missing them both. Tess wasn't lucky, though, and one slammed her in the chest.

Dia wandered off to snap pictures as Haven crouched down, running her hand through a pile of snow. She could feel the coldness through her gloves, the air chilly against her flushed face. She watched it drift through her fingers, captivated by the way it crunched when she made a fist.

The burden on her heart lessened. Just for a while, she allowed her guilt to ease.

Carmine strolled over to her. "Wanna go for a walk, *tesoro*?"

She nodded and trudged through the snow behind him. They hit the tree line, and Carmine took her gloved hand as they walked out toward the creek. He paused a foot away from it and glanced down at the rushing water, a look of longing embedded in his features. She stared at him, and he must have sensed her gaze, because he smirked after a second. "Like something you see?"

She nudged him. "You know I do."

They stood under the trees, hand in hand, as two squirrels ran by. Haven watched as they chased each other through the snow before scaling the tree beside them and leaping onto a branch. She ducked, realizing what they were doing, but Carmine was too slow. He looked up in time for one of the squirrels to hit a pile of snow and send it flying into his face.

"Son of a bitch!" he said, pulling his hand from hers to brush the snow away. She laughed as she watched him, and he cut his eyes to her. "Something funny?"

She bit her lip to hold in the laughter. The moment she finally got herself under control, the squirrel came running along the tree again, more of the snow falling onto Carmine.

There was a mischievous glint in Carmine's eye when Haven laughed again. She turned to run as he started toward her, recognizing the expression from the fiasco with the dishwasher, but she only got a few steps away before her foot caught on something. She fell into the snow face-first, a rush of cold instantly overtaking her body.

"See?" Carmine said. "*That's* what happens when you laugh at me."

She rolled over to look at him and tossed a handful of snow at his chest. "And that's what happens when you laugh at *me*."

He chuckled, pulling her to her feet. "You're covered now."

She shrugged. "It's just water."

"Just water? You can get frostbitten, or sick, or even pneumonia. Fuck, there's hypothermia. All sorts of things could happen. You might lose a toe."

"Carmine, I was born prematurely in the horse stables, and I survived. I've had the daylights beaten out of me, and I survived. I've had a gun shoved against my throat, and I survived. It's frozen water . . . I'll survive."

"So you're saying you're a survivor again?"

"Yes," she said. "And I just got my thesaurus, so I haven't had time to find other words for it."

"Carry on," he said. "Keep living. Remain alive."

"Aren't they definitions?"

"Synonym, definition . . . same difference. It's just a technicality."

Staring at him, Haven fought back her laughter again. "I don't think that's the word you want."

He ignored her. "You know, I was premature too. A few weeks early. My mom always wanted a bunch of kids, but they stopped after me. I never understood why."

His voice was wistful. Haven closed the distance between them and wrapped her arms around his neck. "Maybe they realized they created perfection with you and didn't need any more."

"I'm far from perfect, Haven," he said. "I have more flaws than I do good parts."

"You have flaws, but that's part of what makes you wonderful. You are perfect—perfect for me." She reached up on her tiptoes and kissed him softly before whispering against his lips. "Besides, flaws, no flaws, perfect, not perfect . . . they're probably just *technicalities*, too."

The sound of Carmine's laughter warmed her frozen skin.

24

Vincent stood in the family room, gazing into the backyard at the kids playing in the snow. He couldn't recall the last time he saw both of his boys happy at the same time. For years he watched his youngest in a perpetual state of turmoil, his soul broken and heart torn. Vincent blamed himself for that, for not doing more to ease his worries.

His child, so much like Maura—Vincent had failed him long ago.

Celia stood beside Vincent. "Carmine was playing the piano this morning."

"*Moonlight Sonata?*"

"No." Vincent could hear the smile in her voice. "*Jingle Bells.*"

"Interesting."

"Interesting is right," she said. "I can't believe you didn't tell me!"

He knew what she was referring to by the look on her face. "What did you want me to say? That my son is an idiot?"

Celia jabbed him in the ribs with her elbow. "Don't call him that. He cares about her."

"She's a novelty," Vincent said. "The newness will wear off, and he'll move on."

"Oh, give me a break. Even you don't believe that."

"One can always hope."

She shook her head. "They make each other happy."

"They're both idiots."

"Vincent!" Celia pushed him. He stumbled a few steps and

snickered as Celia grabbed his arm again. "So, what are you going to do about it?"

"I don't know." It was the truth; he had no idea how to handle the situation. "I considered sending her to Chicago."

"We would've taken her." He looked at Celia skeptically, and she smiled. "I would've convinced Corrado somehow."

Vincent doubted even Celia could have talked him into getting involved. He'd been refusing to intervene for years, and Vincent couldn't blame him. It was a disaster.

"It doesn't matter now. I missed my window of opportunity."

"Vincent, you're a fool if you believe you ever had a window of opportunity."

He didn't respond. There was nothing to say. His sister was right, but he didn't want to admit it.

He'd known for a while what was happening. He'd feared the worst that first morning until he heard what his son said when he let go of Haven's wrist. It was such a simple word, a word most people used needlessly, but a powerful word to people like them. It was something Carmine hadn't said since he was an innocent eight-year-old child, ignorant of the world's troubles, but he'd uttered it that morning so casually, so nonchalantly, that Vincent wondered if he knew what he was saying.

The word was *sorry*.

It was a word even Vincent couldn't bring himself to say. His sister would say he was a good man, a decent man with a heart full of compassion, and Maura would have said the same thing. She never saw the evil inside him. Neither of them did.

When his wife was stolen from him, the blackness took over. He became possessed by it, consumed by anger and guilt. No matter how many people he killed in his quest for vengeance, his thirst for blood never went away. That timid brown-haired girl, the one his youngest had grown fond of, almost became a casualty in his need for retaliation.

Vincent pulled away from Celia and sat down, rubbing his face in frustration. Celia sat across from him and laughed. "It's cute how slick they think they are. Reminds me of how you and—"

"Stop!" he said. Celia cut off midsentence and playfully pretended to zip her lips. "There's nothing cute about any of this."

"Oh, come on. It is cute! And why can't you let them be?"

"You know why," he said. "You can't honestly think it's smart for them to be together."

Celia glared at him. "Shouldn't that be their decision?"

"They don't know any better."

She raised an eyebrow. "Maybe you should explain. Tell him the truth."

He laughed bitterly. "The truth, Celia? Exactly which truth are you talking about? Do you want me to tell him all of it, even the part that's going to hurt? He's a lot like me now, and you have to admit there's a possibility he might snap. Carmine and I barely have a relationship as it is, and this could ruin the last bit we have left. Is that what you want?"

"You know it's not."

"Right, you want me to tell him enough of the truth to make him believe it's okay for them to be together, but I can't mislead him with bits and pieces. It's all or nothing."

She frowned. "I wish there was a way."

"I know," he said. "I've been trying to find some middle ground in the whole thing, but I'm not seeing a way out of this. I know what I'm supposed to do, but the potential wrath that might come down on us is too much to bear. Not to mention it would be throwing the girl to the wolves. And if that happens, I can't imagine the lengths my son will go to for her."

"You can't dwell on the what-ifs, Vincent."

"I always dwell on them," he said. "I barely sleep at night, wondering how one little thing could have changed it all. What if I hadn't taken Maura that weekend? What if we had gone earlier? What if we had gone later? Why did we have to be at that exact spot at that exact moment?"

"If that day hadn't happened, that girl outside would be dead. You're saving her, and she's healing him."

He shook his head. "If we hadn't been there, Celia, my son wouldn't need to be healed."

Vincent would never forget the day that started it all, and how he felt driving down that long, vacant road in the desert for the first time. He'd been miserable, sweat dripping from his brow. The car was completely silent besides the sound of the rumbling engine. Maura knew he hated the silent treatment. He'd rather be yelled at than for her to sit there as she was, staring out the window with that blank expression on her face.

He had no idea, as he slammed his hands against the steering wheel, that it was just the beginning of a vexing day. "If you don't say something, Maura, I'm going to spontaneously combust."

She exhaled sharply but still said nothing.

"What do you want me to do? Huh? It's my responsibility!"

His outburst was met with her scathing voice. "It's our anniversary. It's Valentine's Day!"

"I know that, but they don't care. When my father says go, I have to go."

She knew when he took the oath that he'd vowed to be there anytime *la famiglia* called on him, twenty-four hours a day, seven days a week, three hundred and sixty-five days a year.

Vincent slowed the car when they neared the cutoff in the desert that led to Frankie Antonelli's property. They climbed out when they reached the house, but Maura lingered by the car. Vincent stepped onto the porch and knocked on the door at the same time a high-pitched squeal rang out. Swinging around, he saw a frail little girl running straight at Maura, knee-high and skinny as a toothpick, her hair matted in dreadlocks. She looked like a sewer rat, covered in filth.

The girl, oblivious to the presence in her path, slammed right into Maura without slowing down. Maura stumbled from the force, and the little girl flew backward onto the ground. Her dirt-smudged nose scrunched up as she eyed the human road-block.

"You're awfully dirty, little one," Maura said.

The little girl looked down at herself. "Where?"

Maura laughed as she crouched down. "You're dirty *every-where*."

It only took Vincent thirty minutes to handle business that day, but it was a half hour that changed everything. The girl had come barreling into his life, turning everything upside down.

At Maura's insistence, Vincent inquired about her a week later, but Frankie informed him she wasn't for sale. No matter how much money he offered, the man wouldn't budge. Vincent hoped Maura would drop it, but the child became an obsession to her.

And he had been oblivious to it all, living in his shell of ignorance. He was a keen person, but his wife had spent her entire life wearing a mask of secrecy. He had no idea what she was up to, although he should have been aware.

He should have known she would see it as a second chance.

Vincent stood up. "When they come inside, tell her to come on up to my office."

"Who?"

"You know who, Celia."

Before he turned around, he saw his sister shake her head. "I still don't understand why you never say her name."

————

Vincent was typing an email when there was a timid tap on the door. It opened slowly, and she stepped inside. She was a tough girl, the type who kept secrets well. A lot like his wife that way. That thought made him feel like he had been kicked in the gut.

He motioned for her to sit down. "Are you having a good day, child?"

"Yes, sir. Thank you."

"Good. May I ask you a question?"

"Of course."

"Before I brought you here, do you recall ever seeing me?"

Her face scrunched up, and he smiled involuntarily. It reminded him of the look she gave Maura that day. "No, sir," she said hesitantly.

"The first time I met you, you were six years old," he said. "Well, you told my wife you were six, but you held up four fingers."

She looked startled. "Your wife?"

"Yes, my wife," he said. "I suppose you wouldn't remember her, either."

"I'm sorry, sir."

"An apology is unnecessary," he said. "Anyway, the reason I asked you up here is because I have something to give you."

He opened his desk drawer and pulled out the photograph, sliding it across to her. "I saw your mother a few weeks ago while on business and snapped that picture."

Haven picked up the photo with a trembling hand, her composure slipping. She traced her mother's outline with her pointer finger. "Thank you for showing me."

"You're welcome. That's all I wanted, so you can rejoin the festivities." She stood up and glanced at the picture briefly before holding it out to him. He shook his head. "Keep it. It's the reason Celia gave you a frame."

————

Carmine climbed out of the shower and wrapped a towel around his waist, surprised to see Haven sitting on the edge of his bed. She clutched a picture, her focus squarely on it. "What's that?"

She glanced at him, her eyes bloodshot. "My mama."

Intense dread rushed through him. "Your mom? Did something happen to her?"

"No, it's a picture of her. Your father gave it to me."

"Well, that was awfully nice of him." He ran a hand through his wet hair as he sat down beside her. He reached for the picture, but she automatically gripped it tighter in response. "I just wanna see, hummingbird. I'll give it right back."

She smiled sheepishly, handing it to him.

He surveyed the photo of the skinny woman with short hair, standing in front of a large wooden house. Beside it was a row of old horse stables, behind them a greenhouse and some storage buildings.

Haven rested her head on his shoulder. "Now you see where I came from."

"I can't believe they made you sleep outside."

"It wasn't so bad."

"Wasn't so bad? There's a lot more to life than just being *not so bad*. How about being *happy*?"

"Happiness is nothing but good health and a poor memory."

His brow furrowed. "What?"

"Albert Schweitzer said it."

He rolled his eyes. "You're too smart for your own good."

"Thank you," she said genuinely. "No one has ever called me smart before."

"*Prego.*"

She stared at him. "*Prego*? The spaghetti sauce?"

He chuckled. "It means *you're welcome* in Italian."

"Oh." She turned her attention back to the photo. "Why don't you have a picture of your mama?"

"I do, but they're hard to look at."

Haven smiled softly. "I bet she's beautiful."

"Of course she is," he said playfully. "She made me."

———

Vincent sat in the silent office for a moment before opening his top desk drawer again. He pushed a few things around and grabbed the small photograph from the bottom. It had been there for years, the edges worn and image faded although it rarely saw the light of day.

He gazed at the picture of his wife, his chest aching. He desperately wished she were there because, out of everyone, she'd be able to tell him what to do. She would know what to say, how to make it right again. Maura always had the answers, even if they were ones Vincent hadn't liked to hear.

Reaching into his shirt, he pulled out the chain that hung around his neck and absentmindedly fiddled with the small gold band. It matched the one he still wore on his finger. He never had the nerve to take it off.

Carmine pulled out a chair for Haven in the dining room and sat across from her. Tess and Dia stayed for dinner, sitting on the side with Haven, while Dominic and Celia sat near Carmine. Vincent took the chair at the head of the table and bowed his head, saying his usual prayer.

They told stories about past holidays, and Haven listened intently, absorbing every word. Her eyes twinkled, a smile on her lips. It was an odd moment, but as Carmine glanced around the table, it felt right, like they were supposed to be there. That she belonged with him, with all of them, and some twist of fate had led her there.

He didn't care what she said—happiness was more than good health and a poor memory. Happiness was *this*. It was her, and him, and that moment. Fuck Albert Schweitzer. He could kiss his ass. Happiness was *real*.

After dinner, Haven and Carmine headed upstairs to his room. She wrapped her arms around his neck, her fingers lacing through his hair as she pulled him to her, kissing him passionately. He resisted at first, caught off guard, but caved and walked her back to the bed. Pulling off his shirt, he tossed it to the floor before lying down on top of her. She rocked her hips, pressing into him. Carmine hissed as the unexpected friction sent shivers through him.

He wanted her more than he had ever wanted anything. He wanted to consume her, to taste her flesh and explore her body. And he wanted to fuck her, but he couldn't. She wasn't a girl to be fucked. She was a girl to be made love to, and as much as he wished he could, he didn't know how.

He pulled from her lips, his strong voice contradicting the yearn in his body. "We need to stop."

"Stop?"

"Yes, stop." He hesitated—when the hell had he become the voice of abstinence? "We just, you know . . ."

He didn't know, but she nodded. "Okay, Romeo."

"Romeo?"

"Like in *Romeo and Juliet*. They come from different sides but meet in the middle. We have the forbidden love part, right?"

"Yeah, but we're not killing ourselves, Haven, so that's about as similar as it gets. Besides, Romeo's an idiot. Pick someone else."

"How about Shrek?"

His brow furrowed. "Shrek? Really? He's an ogre."

"Shrek and Fiona thought they were different when they weren't."

He contemplated that until he realized he was comparing his life to a cartoon. "Pick another."

"*Titanic*? Rose and Jack weren't supposed to be together."

"Seriously? He dies. I'm not gonna jinx myself here."

She was quiet, running her fingers across his abs and tracing his scar with her fingertips. "How about we just be Haven and Carmine? We don't know the ending, but we can always hope for the best."

"I like that," he said. "Besides, there's a reason we don't know how the story ends."

"Why?"

"Because it doesn't."

25

Haven opened the dryer door and flung the wet clothes into it, listening as everyone chatted in the foyer. Celia had a flight to Chicago in a few hours, and Dr. DeMarco was going with her for a few days. They were saying good-bye, so she'd slipped away and secluded herself in the laundry room, feeling like she was unfairly imposing on family time.

There was a light tap from the doorway after a moment, and she turned to see Celia. Haven stiffened when she wrapped her arms around her in a hug. "It's been great getting to know you."

"You too, ma'am."

"Call me Celia, dear," she said. "I have to go before Vincent complains, but I couldn't leave without saying good-bye to you."

Haven was touched she cared so much. "Good-bye, Celia."

Celia smoothed Haven's hair before walking away. Haven turned back to the dryer, and Carmine strolled in after they left. "Dia wants to know what time we're going tonight."

"Do you think I should go?"

"Of course. Why wouldn't you?"

"Well, your friends will be there. I'll probably just be a complication."

Truth was, it was New Year's Eve, and she didn't want to watch Carmine from afar all night.

"Don't ever call yourself a complication," he said. "And yeah, I want you to come."

"Okay," she said softly.

He ran his hands down his face with frustration. "Okay? We're back to that again? If you don't wanna go, say so. I'll stay home too. I just thought it would be nice to get out tonight. And honestly, everyone knows about us already because of Lisa's big mouth. Damn *schifosa*."

"What's a *schifosa*?

He tugged at his hair. "An ugly girl."

"Do you really think she's ugly, or are you saying that because you're angry with her?"

"She's all right, I guess."

She smiled to herself. "I'll go tonight. I just don't want to embarrass my boyfriend in front of the *schifosa*s he goes to school with."

He stared at her like he was dissecting her words. "That's the first time you've called me that."

"Called you what?"

"Your boyfriend."

She hesitated. "Isn't that what you are?"

"Yeah," he said. "You've just never acknowledged it before. I was starting to wonder if *you* were embarrassed."

The New Year's Eve party was being held in a vacant field on the outskirts of Durante, a cotton farm that had been abandoned years before. The barn still stood, empty and collapsing, the ground overgrown from lack of use.

Haven eyed the place peculiarly as Carmine parked, dozens of cars surrounding them. It was already late, everything shrouded in darkness, but Haven could see a large bonfire in the distance. Carmine took her hand as they strolled through the field. A few people greeted him, but Carmine seemed distracted. He diverted them to the left, taking her to where Dia stood by herself along the side. "I'll be back, okay? Stay here."

He looked torn as he let go of her hand before walking away.

This was the reason she had considered not coming in the first place. "I'll be fine on my own. You can go have fun, Dia."

Dia laughed. "Fun? I think not. This is so not my scene. I'd rather hang out with you."

Her response surprised Haven, but she was relieved when the words sank in.

The two of them chatted for a bit, and people walked past as if they weren't there. Haven heard familiar laughter eventually and turned around in enough time to see Dominic before he draped his arm over her shoulder. Tess paused in front of them as Dominic thrust a cup at Haven. "Here, got you a drink. Don't take anything from any of these other fuckers around here."

She took it from him, sniffing the liquid. "Uh, thank you."

"Sure thing. I didn't know what you'd want, so I just got you some beer from the keg. I figured you wouldn't like it, but none of us do and we drink it anyway." He raised his own cup and hit hers with it. "Welcome to the club."

He tipped back his drink, chugging, as Haven took a sip and grimaced at the bitterness. She drank the beer despite its taste and loosened up as they joked around. She laughed along with them, almost feeling like she fit in.

"Hey, Dom."

The voice rang out behind them. Dominic turned, swinging Haven around with him. She tripped over her own feet when she saw Nicholas.

Dominic and Nicholas bumped fists. "What's up?"

"Not much." Nicholas nodded his head toward Haven. "You decide to trade Tess in?"

Dominic laughed. "No, I'm just watching over this one so the vultures don't circle."

"Yeah, I heard Lisa running her mouth earlier." Nicholas turned to her. "Nice to see you again, Haven."

She was surprised he was being nice after what happened during their last meeting. "You, too."

He smiled. "So, what did one snowman say to the other?"

She shrugged. "I don't know, what?"

"Smells like carrots."

She didn't get it, but Dominic laughed.

"Anyway, I just wanted to say hi," Nicholas said. "I'll catch you guys later."

He walked away, and Haven looked at Dominic curiously. "You still like him after he said something bad about your mama?"

Dominic nodded. "Nicholas shouldn't have said what he said, but he just wanted to hurt Carmine. And before you came along, Twinkle Toes, the only way to hurt him was through Mom."

Dominic swung her back around to join the others, and they chatted as she drank the rest of her beer. A little later, she heard a chuckle nearby, so close it made her skin prickle. Carmine leaned down, his lips beside her ear. "Hey, hummingbird."

Carmine's breath hit her neck, the smell of mint and alcohol intoxicating her senses. She couldn't focus on what was going on, the electricity sparking off him sending currents through her. She felt lightweight, buzzing, on top of the world.

She worried she was going to fall over.

He pulled her to him from behind, resting his chin on her head as he held his drink to her lips. She took a sip, his warm beer as bitter as hers had been.

Dominic groaned. "Didn't I tell you not to take cups from people?"

"It's just Carmine," she said.

"So? He could drug you."

"I could," Carmine joked. "I did once, remember? Actually, no, *twice*. I forgot I got you high that time, too. Not to mention the time I got you drunk. Christ, I'm horrible. I've corrupted you."

She wanted to disagree but could only grasp on to his forearms as he kissed her neck. The feel of his mouth against her skin ripped all coherent thought right from her head.

"You're trembling," he said. "Let's take a walk."

Carmine grabbed her hand, linking their fingers together as he wordlessly led her through the parked cars. He kissed her, and she parted her lips, deepening it as he walked her backward to the Mazda. Breaking the kiss briefly, he grabbed her, and she yelped with surprise as he set her down on the hood. He settled between her legs, and she laced her fingers through his hair as their lips met once more.

Her heart raced at the closeness. His body was flush against hers, the heat radiating from him warming every inch of her. He pulled away slightly to take a breath, their foreheads touching with a light sheen of sweat on his. Her nose brushed against his as she stared into his eyes, the green radiant. Looking into them, she could see the emotion inside him, hints of all those things flourishing in her. To Carmine, she wasn't a possession. She wasn't a title. She was just a girl.

A girl who suddenly felt like she was floating.

"I love you." The words tumbled from her lips easily, like they had rolled from her tongue hundreds of times. But they hadn't. She had never said them before, but as she heard them in her own voice, every cell in her body knew they were true. She hadn't known what love was, but she knew it now. Love was the fluttering in her tummy whenever Carmine was near, the twinkle in his eyes when he laughed, the heat in her body from his words. Love was happy. Love was safe. Love was green.

Love was him—the beautifully flawed boy who made her glow.

He stared at her, those words hanging in the air between them.

"And I love you," he said, his voice a whisper, but Haven felt it powerfully, deep down in her soul. "*Per sempre.*"

"*Sempre?*" she asked.

Cracking a smile, he brushed his pointer finger softly across her lips. "Always and forever."

A loud whistling sounded out at that moment, followed by a thunderous bang. Haven ducked and covered her ears as Carmine continued to stare at her. "It's fireworks."

He helped her down and leaned against the car door with her to his chest, his arms around her. There was another loud whistle, and she looked in the direction of it as the bang rang out with a burst of color. She gaped at the vibrant lights in the sky, and Carmine chuckled. "See, just fireworks, *tesoro*. Nothing to be afraid of. They won't hurt you."

They watched them quietly before the crowd by the bonfire counted down. Carmine swung her around to face him, more fireworks going off in the distance. He leaned down and kissed her deeply when the countdown reached one.

"Do you have any idea how important you are to me?" he asked, pulling from her lips. "I'm finding myself again because of you. I never thought it would happen. My mom used to talk about fate, and I think you're it . . . you're my fate. You were brought to me for a reason, for us to save each other. Because you weren't the only one needing to be saved, Haven. I was drowning, and you rescued me." He paused. "Happy new year, hummingbird."

She laughed. "You said all of that without cursing."

He blinked a few times. "I guess I did. Well, then . . . fuck."

Carmine held Haven tightly, the two of them enjoying the new-found silence. The fireworks had stopped and the crowd quieted, so all that was left was the two of them in the darkness. He could smell her shampoo, feminine and sweet, and all he could think about was how sexy she looked. Those other girls, with their and miniskirts and makeup, weren't sexy to him anymore. *La mia bella ragazza,* with her chewed-up fingernails and flushed cheeks, was sexy. Because sexiness wasn't manufactured—the shit was real.

She was real.

"I never hoped for a future until I met you," she said after a while, "but I want us to have one."

"You don't know how much I love hearing you say that." He brushed her hair aside and ran his tongue up her neck, circling her earlobe. "Can I keep you?" he whispered, laughing and pulling away from her as soon as the words came out. "What's wrong with me? I'm quoting *Casper*."

She glanced back at him. "*Casper*?"

"Yeah, Casper the friendly ghost." He hoped she knew what he was talking about, but she just stared at him. "It doesn't matter. It's some stupid movie. You'd probably like it."

A hard edge laced her voice. "What are you saying?"

He blanched. "I didn't mean it like that. I wasn't suggesting you'd like it because it was stupid or because you're stupid." He groaned. "Not that you're stupid, because you aren't. That didn't come out right. You know I don't think that. You'd have to be fucking stupid not to see you're smart." He paused. "I should probably shut up now."

The corner of her lips turned up as she leaned back against him. "Thank you."

"For knowing when to shut up?"

She laughed. "No, for always thinking about my feelings. I know that's not something you're used to doing. I've never had someone look out for me before."

"I'll always do what's best for you, Haven," he said. "I've thought about it a lot, you know. After I turn eighteen and can access my trust fund, we could disappear together and get away from all of this bullshit. Probably couldn't take the Mazda, though, since it has a GPS chip in it."

"A GPS chip," she whispered.

"Yeah." Carmine looked at his watch. "You wanna head home?"

She nodded. They climbed into the car, and he put it in gear, driving down the small road toward the highway as Haven looked out the side window at the trees lining the road.

"What's wrong?" She was being too silent.

"I thought you knew."

"Knew what?"

"That I was chipped, too."

He looked at her with confusion, turning down the music in the car. "What do you mean?"

"Like your car—a GPS chip."

Carmine slammed the brakes as soon as the words registered, the car skidding to a stop with a loud squeal. Haven braced her hands against the dash, eyes wide with shock.

"There's a tracking chip on you? Where?"

"It's in me," she said. "Under my skin."

"You've gotta be kidding. Your father chipped you like a dog?"

She shook her head. "My father didn't do it. Yours did."

He blinked a few times. "Are you sure?"

"I'm sure. He stuck the needle into my back. He also scraped my cheek with some kind of cotton swab. I don't know why, but he did it. He said I can never escape. It's impossible."

Carmine's stomach sank. He was going to be sick.

Vincent stepped off the elevator on the fifth floor of the Belden Stratford Hotel and strolled toward his room at the end of the hall. The dim lighting was easy on his tired eyes. He couldn't recall the last time he'd gotten a good night's sleep, his hectic schedule taking a toll on him.

Jet-lagged, he was looking forward to having some down time. The next ten hours of his schedule were uncharacteristically clear, and he had no intention of doing anything but lying in bed. He was sick of traveling. Sick of working. Sick of talking. Sick of thinking. He wanted, for once, to savor a bit of peace.

The moment he stepped into his hotel room, the phone in his pocket rang. He looked at the clock—six in the morning.

He pulled out his phone, too exhausted to deal with business, and was surprised to see it was Carmine. Vincent sat down on the edge of the bed. "Isn't it a bit early for you to be up, son?"

Carmine sighed. "It's called insomnia, remember? I never sleep."

Vincent knew the feeling well. "What's wrong?"

"Nothing's wrong," he said. "Can't I call my father to wish him a happy new year?"

Vincent was surprised. Carmine had certainly never called for casual conversation before. "Happy new year to you, too. Did you all have a nice night?"

"It was okay, I guess."

"No fighting?"

"No, I didn't send anyone to the hospital."

"Good," he said, yawning. The sky outside was starting to lighten as dawn approached. "What are you guys going to do today?"

"I don't know," Carmine said, "but I guess you'll be able to tell later. You know, because of the tracking chip in Haven."

The words went straight over Vincent's head. It took a minute for them to sink in. "She told you about that?"

"She may have mentioned it," he said. "She also may have said you swabbed her cheek. She isn't, like, our cousin or something, is she? Illegitimate child? Were you fucking around on Mom?"

Vincent sighed. "Of course not. There's no blood relation."

"Okay, whatever. I was just curious."

Vincent closed his eyes. His son was on to him.

Peace was fleeting once again.

26

The first week of January swiftly passed as the boys headed back to school. Haven lay in bed for a while that Friday morning before strolling into the library. Glancing toward the stairs, she gasped and grabbed her chest. Dr. DeMarco stood in front of her with his arms crossed.

He had been in Chicago all week, so he was the last person she expected to see. She stared at him, wondering when he'd gotten home, but more curious as to what he was doing on the third floor. There was a part of her—the part that would never forget what he did—that screamed something wasn't right. She searched for some hidden emotion and saw a flicker of aggravation in his eyes.

The monster lurked today. "Good morning, Dr. DeMarco."

"Good morning." His voice was cold and detached. "Grab your coat and meet me downstairs."

Fear consumed her, but she tried to keep her outward composure. He continued to stare at her, waiting for acknowledgment. She didn't know why—it wasn't as if she could say no. If he told her to be somewhere, she'd be there if she wanted to or not.

"Yes, sir."

She exhaled sharply once he was gone, shaking her head as she grabbed her coat. She stuck her hands into her pockets as she descended the stairs, her palms sweaty. Was this the end of her time here? Was he tired of her? What would he do to her? Would he sell her? What if she never saw Carmine again?

In the middle of her near-breakdown, a hand gripped her shoulder. She recoiled from Dr. DeMarco behind her. "You're awfully jumpy today."

"Sorry."

He glanced at his watch. "Come on. I don't want to be late."

Dr. DeMarco opened the front door, and she kept her head down as she stepped outside. He set the alarm and locked up, brushing past her to the car as if she weren't there.

Haven stared in the side mirror as he drove down the driveway, watching the house disappear behind the rows of dense trees. Sighing, she glanced at Dr. DeMarco, wishing she knew what bothered him. She kept her gaze on him for too long, and he glanced over at her. "It's rude to stare, child. If you have a question, ask it. Otherwise, mind your manners. I'm not in the mood for insolence today."

She had no idea what insolence was, but she had no intention of giving it to him. "I was wondering where we were going, sir."

"The hospital," he said, the same time Haven spotted the building in the distance. He pulled into a front parking spot and turned off the car. "Just like the football game, I expect you to be on your best behavior."

She sat still, staring out the windshield at the sign with DR. VINCENT DEMARCO written on it in blue. "I'll be good, sir."

Haven followed him into the building, keeping his pace so as not to lag behind. They headed straight for the elevator and despite the fact that it only took thirty seconds, her anxiety tripled during the ride to the third floor. Logically she knew Dr. DeMarco wouldn't hurt her in public, but it wasn't easy being rational when confined in a small box with a man capable of harm.

She breathed a sigh of relief as the doors opened, and she followed Dr. DeMarco down a long corridor. Watching her feet, she didn't notice he'd stopped until she ran into him. Gasping, she took a few steps back and held her hands up to shield herself. Dr. DeMarco stood in place, his hand twitching at his side. He balled it into a fist, fighting to keep his temper in check.

Pulling out a set of keys, he unlocked a door and flicked on a light inside the room. "Sit down. I'll be back."

As soon as she stepped into the room, his footsteps receded down the hallway. She stood in one spot, reading his nameplate on the desk, before surveying the rest of the office. It was orderly, books lining a shelf and folders neatly stacked on his desk. There weren't any personal items, no family pictures or WORLD'S GREATEST DAD coffee mugs. The walls were white and plain, everything wooden except for the black leather chairs.

It looked like the house—sterilized.

She sat in one of the chairs and folded her hands in her lap, picking at her fingernails. Dr. DeMarco returned eventually and sat down behind his desk, putting on his glasses. She risked a peek at him and saw he was reading a file. He sensed her eyes again and sighed dramatically. "Ask."

"I was wondering why we were here, sir."

"I needed to get back to work, and you need a shot." He pulled a book off a shelf and handed it to her. "A nurse will be around in a while, but other than that, you're going to be sitting here most of the day. May as well entertain yourself, since you apparently know how to read now."

Dr. DeMarco's office was silent, except for the sound of the occasional turning page. Haven fidgeted as the minutes slowly passed. After a while there was a knock at the door, and Dr. DeMarco stood up to answer it. "Good afternoon."

A young blonde-haired woman walked in, smiling sweetly at Dr. DeMarco. "Happy birthday!"

Haven froze. No one had told her it was his birthday.

"Thanks," he said, not sounding enthusiastic as he turned to Haven. "I'll grab some lunch."

He narrowed his eyes in a silent warning before walking out.

"I'm Jen," the woman said once he was gone. "It's nice to meet the girl who whipped Carmine into shape. How did you manage that, anyway?"

Her heart rate spiked as Jen pulled out a needle. "I don't know . . ."

"It's unexplainable, huh? That boy used to land himself or someone else in the ER every week with all the fighting he did. It's been months since it's happened. Dr. DeMarco has to be happy." She paused, smiling widely. "Turn around and unbutton your jeans. This has to go in the rear."

Haven did as she was told, wincing as the needle penetrated her skin.

"It's hard to believe the worst medical attention Carmine causes anyone these days is for his girlfriend to get birth control."

Birth control? She pulled her pants back up as the door opened and Dr. DeMarco walked in. He set two food containers on his desk, pushing one toward Haven as she retook her seat. Haven opened her container and poked at the food.

"You two enjoy your lunch," Jen said. "Once again, it's nice to meet you, Haven. Don't let those DeMarco men give you too much trouble. Sometimes you have to show them who's boss."

Dr. DeMarco let out a laugh at those words.

Jen started to walk out but paused in the doorway. "Plus, I've heard Carmine likes kinky girls."

The amusement died in Dr. DeMarco's eyes, his expression twisting again to aggravation. As the door shut, Haven's hand trembled and shook the fork.

"Eat," Dr. DeMarco said forcefully. She flinched from his harsh tone and took a bite, so nauseated she had a hard time swallowing. After about ten minutes of thick tension and forcing down half of her food, she set her fork aside, hoping that would satisfy him.

He grabbed her container and dropped it into the trash can with a thud. She watched as he picked up his office phone and dialed a number, putting it on speakerphone as it rang. Dread rocked her when the familiar voice answered the line.

"Yeah?" Carmine said. "Why are you calling me at lunch?"

"I need to see you at the hospital as soon as you get out of school."

There was a pause. "I didn't do it."

Dr. DeMarco sighed. "Didn't do what?"

"Whatever you think I did."

"Just come to my office," Dr. DeMarco said. "I'm not in the mood for your antics today."

He hung up before Carmine could respond, his attention shifting to Haven. "It's my birthday."

"Happy birthday, sir," she said. "No one told me."

"That's because there's nothing to celebrate. It may be the day I was given life, but it's also the day my life was taken from me. I may be able to hop into the car and drive to the store, but it doesn't mean anything. Anything I'm told to do, I have to do it or face death. Were you aware of that aspect of my life?"

She shook her head. She wasn't aware of much. Carmine alluded to the things his father did, but he never elaborated. Nobody did.

Dr. DeMarco continued after a moment. "I've watched it happen too many times. Men ordered to murder their own family, and they either do it or die themselves. The man who visited the house? He's my master, just as—no matter what I do—you'll continue to see me as your master. Because I hold the key to your survival, just as Sal holds the key to mine. I wasn't much older than Carmine when I got involved, and I was as stupid then as he is now. He has no idea what it is he's getting himself into—neither of you do."

Haven was too stunned to speak. She waited for him to say something else, but instead he picked up his pen. She figured the conversation was over and reached for the book to pass the time when Dr. DeMarco's voice rang out, paralyzing her. "Are you in love with him?"

The book slipped and hit the floor. "Who?"

"You know who," he said. "Don't pretend to be dumb with me."

Bile rose up at his demanding tone. "Yes."

He grabbed a black case, and Haven's heart raced as he moved to sit in the chair beside her. He pulled out his laptop and set it on the desk so they both could see. "Carmine asked if you had a tracking chip inside you. I wasn't happy he inquired about it."

"I, uh . . . I didn't know I wasn't supposed to tell."

"That's not why I was unhappy. It doesn't matter to me whether or not he knows. What matters to me—what worries me—is that he's so interested. The only reason I can come up with as to why Carmine would confront me is if he's contemplating doing something that would be affected by your chip. And the only scenario that makes sense is my son taking you on the run."

She froze as Dr. DeMarco opened a program on his laptop. "I'm not going to run away, sir."

He held his hand up to silence her before punching a few numbers into the program. A map popped up, a red dot flashing in the center of it. "The problem is you've been around some of the most dangerous men in the country. Because of that, you're desensitized to moderately harmful situations. I love my son, but he's volatile. I was the same way at his age, and I know what results from that. I'm not a horrible man. I have a heart, and I've been trying to let nature take its course, hoping everything would fix itself, but Carmine's growing impatient. He's digging in deep."

He pointed at the dot on the screen. "That's you. No matter where you go, all I have to do is open this program, punch in the code, and it'll give me your location. Running is only going to get someone hurt, and I can't let that happen. I'd try to explain it to Carmine, but he'd want answers I can't give him—answers he's better off never hearing. So instead, I'm telling you. If you go on the lam with my son, I'll track you down and kill you. I don't want to, but I can't sacrifice him. And if you two are stupid enough to try to disappear, Carmine will end up hurt at the end."

She stared at him, frightened. The last thing she wanted was for Carmine to suffer.

"I don't like keeping secrets from my son, but his safety comes first. Because these secrets? They revolve around you."

He turned off the laptop and returned it to the bag before sitting back down in his chair. Haven remained quiet, trying to absorb what he'd said. Too many people had been hurt because of her. Carmine couldn't be one of them. She couldn't let that happen.

"I know it's a lot to take in," Dr. DeMarco said. "I'm walking a fine line trying to distance my son from this lifestyle. When I vowed my life to the organization, I swore they would always come first. Little did I know, years later, they'd expect me to hand over my son. Sal views Carmine as the *Principe*, a Mafia prince, and if he discovers I spoke out against them, he'll see me as a traitor. Do you know what the punishment for treachery is in my world? What happens to people when they forget their place?"

She flinched at his choice of words. "Death."

"So you see the predicament I'm in. You're helping my son in ways I've failed him, but you need to realize I'm trying to help him, too. I'm saving him from something he doesn't realize he needs to be saved from. I just haven't found a way out of this without somebody getting hurt, a way where someone doesn't have to be sacrificed."

He grabbed his pen again and sorted through papers, subject closed. Haven watched him for a moment before picking up the book from the floor.

Before Haven knew it, the door behind her flew open, and Dr. DeMarco groaned. "How many times do we have to go through this, Carmine Marcello, before you stop entering rooms without permission?"

Haven sat still, staring straight ahead at the desk, her skin prickling as Carmine plopped down in the chair beside her. "I had permission. You told me to be here."

Dr. DeMarco shook his head. "Give me your car keys."

Carmine tensed. "Excuse me?"

"What is it with you kids acting ignorant? Give me your keys."

"This shit again?"

"Son . . ."

Carmine pulled out his keys and threw them on his father's desk. They landed on a pile of papers, and Dr. DeMarco picked them up before tossing a different set to Carmine.

Carmine looked at him with confusion. "Why are you giving me the keys to the Mercedes?"

"Because it's not yours."

"What does that have to do with anything?"

"I figured you'd prefer to use someone else's," Dr. DeMarco said, "but if you'd rather her start with the Mazda, by all means take your keys back."

Carmine shook his head. "You aren't making any fucking sense."

"Watch your mouth," Dr. DeMarco said. "If you'd stop being defensive, you'd see I was telling you to teach the girl how to drive."

Carmine's eyes widened. "You're fucking kidding me?"

Dr. DeMarco groaned. "Sometimes I want to knock the shit out of you, son."

"You realize you're cursing at me for cursing, right? What kinda role model are you?"

"Not the type of role model you need. Do what I say, not what I do. You're too good to follow in my footsteps."

"Too good to be a doctor?"

"You know what I'm talking about."

There was a subtle sadness in Dr. DeMarco's expression that struck Haven hard. Up until then, she hadn't been able to sympathize with him. She could understand him now, could see his fears, and the most startling part was they wanted the same thing.

How was that possible? She couldn't wrap her mind around it.

"Doesn't seem so bad," Carmine said. "Look what it's gotten you."

"Looks are deceiving."

"You're telling me," he said. "So, why are we at the hospital? Implanting shit? Running more tests? Or let me guess—it's a secret?"

Dr. DeMarco's expression flickered with the same aggravation Haven had seen earlier in the day. "You kids get going. I have patients to see."

He walked out, leaving Carmine and Haven alone. They sat quietly for a moment after the door closed before Carmine stood up. "It scared the hell out of me when I saw you sitting here. I thought I was gonna have to sucker punch him, grab you, and run."

His words brought back everything Dr. DeMarco had said. Last week, Carmine told her he'd put her safety above his desires, and now she needed to do the same. She didn't want him to get hurt, and if that meant giving Dr. DeMarco her loyalty, she'd do it for Carmine.

Because she'd rather sacrifice herself than him suffer a single moment because of her existence.

———

Haven stepped off the curb and paused beside the passenger door to the car. She and Carmine stood there silently for a second before he cleared his throat. "Why are you over here? You're driving."

"Now?"

He jingled the keys in front of her face. "Yeah, why not?"

She took them. "But I don't know what I'm doing."

"I'll walk you through it. See the black thing with the big-ass red button on it? Push—"

Before he could tell her what to push, she hit the red button. The lights flashed as the horn blared. He hit the button to stop it as she smiled sheepishly. This was about to be a disaster if they couldn't get the doors open without a mistake. "You see the button with the picture of the opened lock?"

"Yes."

"Press that motherfucker." She pressed it, her face lighting up when the car unlocked. He smiled at her expression of pride. "Good. Now get into the car, but don't touch anything."

Haven climbed into the driver's side as he got in beside her, and Carmine laughed at how far back the seat was. He used the controls to adjust it so she could see over the dash and reach the pedals.

She put on her seatbelt and raised her eyebrows. "Aren't you going to wear yours?"

"Do I ever wear it?"

"No, but I don't know what I'm doing."

"Driving is a piece of cake," he said. "You can't be that bad at it."

"Whatever you say."

"That's right—whatever I say. And I say put the key in." She stuck it in the ignition. He waited for her to turn it but she didn't. "Are you going to start the car or what?"

She glanced at him nervously. "You didn't tell me to."

Haven turned the key and the engine roared to life, but she continued to hold it so it kept grinding. "Christ, let go before you burn the starter up or something!"

She pulled her hand away. "Sorry."

"It's fine," he said. "I should've told you, but I figured you'd know that much."

"I can count the number of times I've been in a car on one hand. I know nothing about them."

"I didn't think about that," he said. "Look—gas to go, brake to stop. R is reverse to go backward, D is drive to go forward, and P is park . . . to fucking park. Side mirrors, rearview mirror—you look into them to see what's around. Got it?"

"I think so," she said. "What about all of the signs?"

"Stop at the big-ass red octagons that say STOP. The rest aren't really important. And if the stoplight is red, you stop. If it's green, you keep going. It's common sense."

"What if it's yellow?"

"Uh, if the light's yellow, speed up to get through it before it turns red. I hate waiting."

"Okay."

"All right then, baby. Put this bitch in reverse and back up."

She grabbed the gearshift, putting it in reverse, and took a deep breath before hitting the gas. The car jolted backward as she whipped it around, running up on the sidewalk. She slammed the brake hard, and they stopped abruptly. Carmine clutched his seat. "Christ, I said hit the gas, not floor it. Just press lightly."

She put the car in drive and pressed the gas. They drove through the parking lot to the STOP sign, and she hit the brake hard, jolting them again. She stayed there, and he grew impatient, wondering why she wasn't going anywhere. "If there's nothing coming, you can go."

She sighed. "And where am I going, Carmine?"

"Oh, that way," he said, pointing left.

She looked both ways before turning out onto the road, and Carmine wondered why she hadn't signaled until he realized he forgot to explain that part. She got into her lane, her hands trembling against the steering wheel. They neared a yellow light, and he expected her to brake. Instead, she slammed the gas and ran straight through it after it turned red.

"You ran a fucking red light, Haven! Red means stop!"

She cut her eyes at him. "But you said I should hit the gas when it was yellow."

"Yeah, if you can make it through, which you couldn't."

"How was I supposed to know?"

He had no answer. How was she supposed to know when he hadn't told her? He felt bad for snapping and glanced through the windshield in enough time to see her heading for a mailbox. "Oh, fuck!"

He grabbed the steering wheel and turned it sharply, the side mirror clipping the mailbox. Haven slammed the brakes, the car skidding to a stop on the side of the road.

He let go of the wheel. "Let's see if we can try this again. I'll shut up and quit distracting you, and you just pay attention to the road."

He was going about it wrong, but he didn't know how to teach something that came naturally to him. He grabbed his seatbelt and put it on, waving his hand and silently telling her to go.

Haven pulled back into the lane and hadn't driven more than a hundred feet when she came to a YIELD sign. It struck him that he hadn't told her what it meant, but he was too late. She blew right through it without slowing down.

Tires screeched, and Haven screamed as she slammed the brakes in a panic, the wrong thing to do if she cut off a car. He told her to hit the gas again, and she clutched the steering wheel tightly as her eyes welled up with tears.

"Pull into the parking lot to the right," he said as they neared the grocery store. Haven turned, and the car skidded to a crooked stop across some parking spots. A tear slid down Haven's cheek. Carmine undid his seatbelt and pulled her into his arms. "I made that a lot harder than it should've been. I think someone else would be better at teaching you this."

"Why do I have to learn?"

"So you can get around on your own," he said. "Besides, it's a nice skill to have, and one you'll appreciate when we start over."

She pulled from his embrace, a curious expression on her face. "Start over?"

"Yes, a clean slate. No matter what it takes."

"You really think . . . ?"

"I know."

"Then I don't want anyone else to teach me to drive. I want it to be you."

He chuckled. "Your short-term memory must be fucked if you forgot about the disaster of a teaching job I just did."

"We're learning everything together, remember? Driving should be no different."

"Okay, then," he conceded. "Let's try one more time. First and foremost, when you come to a yellow light, slow the fuck down and stop."

27

Haven stood in the kitchen, surveying the refrigerator as she contemplated what to cook. Dr. DeMarco's words infiltrated her thoughts, echoing like a song on repeat. She wanted a life with Carmine, but they would need to find a way that didn't involve running. Was that possible? She wasn't sure. But against her better judgment, she desperately hoped so.

Haven yelped when an arm slipped around her waist, so lost in thought she hadn't heard Carmine approach. "Let's get drunk tonight, *tesoro*."

"Why?"

"Because it's Friday? Does one need a reason to get drunk? I promise to be a perfect gentleman." He leaned down, nipping at the nape of her neck with his teeth. "Well, maybe not a *perfect* gentleman."

She laughed but didn't bother with a response.

"You know, we do have air-conditioning," he said. "You've had that fridge door open for so long I thought maybe you were trying to cool the kitchen or something."

"I'm thinking about dinner."

"Awesome, because I'm starving." He grabbed a glass from the cabinet. She took it from him, and he looked at her before just shrugging. She grabbed a jar of cherries and a bottle of Coke, making him a drink. He took a sip. "You're entirely too good to me."

"You can make it up to me later," she said playfully.

"If you wanna go upstairs, I'll make it up to you right now."

"Dinner's supposed to be ready at seven, which means I only have thirty minutes to throw something together," she said, pulling some sausage out of the freezer. She stuck it into the microwave to defrost, but Carmine grabbed the sausage and tossed it back into the freezer. "What are you doing? You're going to get me in trouble!"

He didn't answer, instead pulling out his phone and scrolling through it to make a call. As soon as the line was picked up, he asked them to grab some pizza before coming home. He ended the call with a cocky smirk.

Haven rolled her eyes. "We're still not going upstairs."

"Fair enough, but I do wanna get drunk tonight."

Haven heard a car approaching and watched the Mazda pull up outside. Dr. DeMarco stepped out with some boxes of pizza. "He's home."

The front door opened, and Carmine sighed exasperatedly as he let go of her. Dr. DeMarco walked into the kitchen and laid dinner on the counter before glancing at Carmine, a light groan escaping his throat. It was barely audible, and Haven looked at Carmine with uncertainty as he sipped from his cherry Coke.

The two of them exchanged keys, and Dr. DeMarco headed for the door again before any of them could react. He walked to his car, pausing at the passenger mirror. A long scratch dug into it, noticeable against the shiny black paint. He turned slowly toward the house, his eyes coming to rest on Haven at the window. She worried he would come back inside to somehow punish her, but he climbed into the car and drove away instead.

Haven turned to Carmine once he was gone. "I think I want to go upstairs now."

"We can do that," he said, snatching the top box of pizza. "I can still get fucked up, right?"

She smiled at his expression, his lips turned down in a childish pout. "Of course you can."

"And you're gonna drink with me, aren't you?"

"If that's what you want."

"I wanna do everything with you," he said. "Even shit we'd be better off not doing together."

"Like driving?"

He laughed. "Yes, so let's get smashed and forget you nearly killed me today trying."

———

Haven brought her cup to her lips and took a sip of the sweet fruity drink. The alcohol taste lingered in the background, not so bad that it hindered the taste. "This is good. What is it?"

"Sweet-Tart. You know—orange soda, Kool-Aid, and Everclear." Haven didn't know, but she liked it anyway. She took another sip as Carmine grabbed his bottle of liquor and took a drink. He was shirtless, and Haven was captivated by the way his stomach muscles grew taut as his body quivered. His calloused hand scratched the scar on his side, his long fingers transfixing Haven.

He crouched down to look under the bed and dug out the shoeboxes, glancing inside before shoving them back under. He found what he was looking for and pulled out a gray game console and a controller, wordlessly hooking it up to his television.

"What is it?" she asked.

"Classic Nintendo," he said.

"And you're going to play it?"

"We are," he corrected her, blowing into a game before sliding it in the console. "Or we're certainly going to try."

He turned it on. The game started right away as he sat on the floor, stretching out his legs and patting the space between them. She sat down between his legs, and he held the controller in front of her to explain the buttons. She watched as he navigated the first board.

"Mario's a rite of passage. You're nobody until you've conquered it." His tone was serious, yet youthful and innocent. It made her smile. "Here, finish this part."

She took the controller. "But what if I kill him? He can die, right?"

"He comes back to life. It's not like we'll have to plan a funeral."

It took her three tries to get the coordination to jump him over things. Carmine grabbed their drinks and sat back down, pulling her body against his chest.

The next few hours passed as they fell into a cycle. She'd kill the character, and Carmine would complete a level so she could try the next one. Haven could feel the alcohol in her system, her limbs tingly and head foggy. She found it nice, the two of them doing something so childish and carefree. He was giving her parts of a life she'd missed out on.

She was playing a board with a bunch of turtles when Carmine nuzzled into her neck. Distracted, she ran the character right off a ledge and tossed the controller down in frustration.

"Does my drinking bother you?" Carmine asked, taking a swig from the bottle of vodka.

"You don't drink enough for it to," she said. "You aren't a mean drunk like Master Michael."

"I'd like to kill that guy," Carmine said. "You don't know how bad I want him to suffer."

She shook her head. "You can't do that."

"Why not? You can't seriously care about him."

"No, but I do care about you. I don't want you to hurt people. I don't want you to be a killer."

Carmine pulled her back to him tighter, kissing the top of her head. "You know, I never knew what I wanted out of life. Going to Chicago always made the most sense, but now that I have you in my life, I'm starting to see it differently. What you want matters, so if you don't want me to do that shit, then I have to really think about it. It'll be your life, too, and you mean a lot more to me than any of them."

She smiled as his words washed through her.

Carmine took the game apart and put it back into the box.

"I wondered what was in those," she said. "I worried it was just more porn."

He laughed. "It's where I keep the old me."

She sat down on his bed with her drink as he pulled out a small box, digging through it briefly before pulling out a black picture frame. She took it from him carefully, her gaze resting upon a photo of a woman with bright red hair and eyes the same color as Carmine's.

Haven couldn't breathe. It was the face she had seen repeatedly in her dreams, the angel in white that glowed in the sunlight. Emotion ripped through her, her voice a broken whisper. "She's an angel."

Carmine took the frame from her, but instead of placing it back into the box, he set it on his desk. "She is," he said quietly. "Now, anyway."

———

Dreams filtered into Haven's sleep that night. It was a dark, cloudless night, the glow of the moon illuminating the scene in her mind. She was back in Blackburn again, a fresh-faced little girl with nappy hair, trying to squeeze by to see out of the stables. "What's going on, Mama?"

"Nothing that concerns you, baby girl," her mama said quietly as she tried to shoo Haven away. "Go lie down."

"But I'm not tired," Haven argued. "Please, Mama? I want to see."

"Nothing's happening," she said. "It's all over."

Haven gave up on trying to go around, instead getting on the ground and scurrying between her legs. She could faintly make out the outline of a car with the trunk open. On the ground beside it, motionless, lay a person. "It's Miss Martha!"

"Hush," her mama said. "You don't want them to hear."

"Sorry, Mama." Haven tried to whisper, but she couldn't help herself. She watched as Miss Martha was placed into the trunk, her eyes closed like she was sleeping. "Where's Miss Martha going?"

"Away from here," her mama answered.

"What's away from here?"

"A lot," she said. "There's a whole world out there."

"Is Miss Martha going out there to the world?"

"No, Miss Martha's gone to Heaven."

"What's Heaven?"

Her mama sighed. "Heaven's the greatest place you can imagine. People don't hurt anymore when they go to Heaven. There's peace there. It's beautiful. Everyone's beautiful."

Haven smiled excitedly. "Will I get to go to Heaven?"

She nodded. "Someday an angel will come to take you away."

Suddenly the darkness erupted in blinding light. Haven shielded her eyes. She could feel the sun burning her as she ran, air fanning her sweaty skin. She pretended to fly, like Miss Martha did to Heaven the night before, and slammed into something in her path.

Falling to the ground, she could barely make out the form in the blinding light. She was confused until a soft voice shattered the silence. "You're awfully dirty, little one."

The blindness cleared as the form knelt down to look at her. Sheer beauty, love, and compassion. Up until then, Haven hadn't seen an angel, but she was sure one had come.

28

The room was encased in bright light when Carmine woke up. His head pounded, his eyes burned. He blinked a few times as he sat up, realizing he was alone.

Stretching, he popped two Tylenol to squelch the hangover before strolling out of the room. As soon as he reached the second floor, his footsteps wavered when Haven stepped into the hallway with his father. Her eyes met his the same time Vincent noticed him. "Do you need laundry done again?" he asked.

"No. Why?"

"Two days in a row you've walked around with barely any clothes on."

He looked down at himself. "My, uh . . . goods are covered."

"Well, I'm glad at least that much sank in over the years."

He chuckled. "What, you think you're too young to be a grandfather?"

"As a matter of fact, yes," he said. "I'm only forty-one. But frankly, I'm just as worried about you picking up something as I am about you impregnating someone. For a while, every time you said the words, 'what's this?' I feared you would expose yourself to show me something suspicious."

Carmine laughed. "Well, thanks for the concern, but I assure you my dick's in fantastic shape."

Vincent shook his head as he glanced at Haven. "You're excused, child. I'm sure you have things to attend to."

She practically bolted for the steps as Vincent turned back to Carmine. "Go get dressed."

"Why? It's not like I'm indecent."

"I didn't say you were indecent, but I have a free day, so I thought we'd go shooting like old times."

He gaped at him. "Vincent DeMarco cleared his schedule to spend time with little ol' me?"

Vincent sighed. "Go before I change my mind."

Chuckling, Carmine headed upstairs and threw on some clothes. He was in the bathroom brushing his teeth when Haven walked in. "Are you and Dr. DeMarco going away?"

He nodded, rinsing out his mouth. "We're gonna go play with our guns."

"You'll be safe, won't you?"

"Yeah, he's not going to shoot me or anything," he said. "I tested him a few times, and he even pointed a gun at me once, but he couldn't pull the trigger."

Instead of making her feel better, her panicked expression only grew. "He pointed a gun at you?"

"Relax, he's probably pointed a gun at everyone at some point," he said as he finished getting ready. "You gonna miss me, *tesoro*?"

"I always miss you when you aren't here."

He put on his coat. "Give it a few more months and you'll be tired of my ass."

"Never."

"Great to hear, but what's that shit they say? Absence makes the heart grow fonder? Me leaving means you'll love me more when I get back."

───────────

The outdoor firing range was a few miles outside of town in the Swannanoa Valley. The field, about four hundred yards in length, had a covered pavilion with various-sized targets. They'd visited it a few times during the years but hadn't been back since the incident with Nicholas . . . since Carmine went away.

Carmine had been a decent shot since he was a kid, but Vincent's aim was impeccable, his hand as steady as a professional marksman's. His bullet ripped straight through the bull's-eye effortlessly.

Vincent reloaded his M1 Garand after expelling all the rounds and held it out to Carmine. "Do you want to try the rifle?"

Carmine took it and hesitated before handing his pistol to his father. Aiming, Carmine fired once and smirked when it hit the target.

"That was luck," Vincent said, loading the pistol and firing it. He hit the farthest target, unloading the rounds into it.

"Fucking show-off," Carmine said, taking another shot and hitting the target again. "See, that wasn't luck. That was skill."

"You're not so bad," Vincent conceded. "Nicholas can attest to that."

Carmine rolled his eyes as his father exchanged weapons with him again. He shot at the target, the atmosphere thick with unspoken words. Vincent unceremoniously fired off a few more rounds before lowering his weapon and staring off into space. Carmine realized it then . . . this wasn't just a casual shooting trip. This wasn't just father/son bonding time. There was something on Vincent's mind, something that would be talked about before Carmine would be allowed to go back home.

If Carmine would be allowed to go back home.

"Is that what you wanna talk about?" Carmine said, knowing he'd have to crack first. "Nicholas?"

"No," Vincent said. "Unless he's the reason you've been in a good mood lately."

Carmine stared at his father as those words sank in. He knew.

"I couldn't help it," Carmine said, the stress making his voice quiver. "It's not like I set out for this to happen. It just . . . did."

Vincent remained silent, his lack of response grating on Carmine's nerves. "Come on, I know you have an opinion—no need to hold back. I can take it. Tell me how fucking disgusted you are that your son would go as low as to fall for a damn sla—" He faltered, unable to finish the word.

"Whether or not you say it doesn't change anything," Vincent said. "It doesn't make the girl more or less of one."

Carmine waited for something more. "Is that all you have to say? I said I can take it. Tell me it's wrong, that it'll never work because people like us don't belong together. Tell me she's not good enough for me. Tell me she could never love me."

"Is that what you want to hear?"

He narrowed his eyes. "No."

Vincent casually glanced at his watch like he was unaffected by the conversation. "Why don't we get some lunch?"

Carmine cocked an eyebrow. "It would be easier to kill me here."

"Kill you? What kind of person do you take me for?"

"Well, fuck. I thought you might be the kinda person to hurt an innocent girl. Good to know I was wrong about that shit."

"I'm a man who makes mistakes, a man who doesn't expect to be forgiven for them, but a man who *does* expect his children to be respectful," he said sharply. "If you want to talk this out using our anger, we can, but I hoped we could discuss it like adults."

Carmine hesitated. "Fine."

"Now, are you going to apologize for throwing that in my face?"

Carmine scoffed. "I'll apologize for saying it when you apologize for doing it."

Vincent and Carmine were seated as soon as they reached the restaurant and both ordered the first thing on the menu. After the waiter brought their food, Vincent turned to his son. "I want you to listen carefully, Carmine. What the two of you have is harmless right now, but I don't want to hear about it. You may care for the girl, but she isn't yours. You're probably going to hate me for saying this, but I'm in control. The first time she neglects what I tell her, I'll put a stop to it all."

Carmine clenched his jaw as his anger boiled over, and Vincent held his hand up to stop the impending explosion. "I'm not going to harm her, but I'll send her away if you force my hand. I'm not giving you my blessing, but I'm not forbidding it either. I'm smart enough to pick and choose my battles, and I have more important ones to fight right now."

He stared at his father. "Fair enough."

Vincent turned his attention to his food. "I just wonder if you know what you're getting into."

"Well, I'm kinda sorta hoping the asshole who owns her won't own her forever."

Vincent's eyes snapped in his direction. "That's a nice piece of information to have, but it wasn't what I was talking about. Why do you think I asked you to teach her to drive, Carmine? Why I asked you to take her grocery shopping?"

"To try to break us apart."

The answer irritated Vincent, and he dropped his fork. "Have you not been listening? You think I get off on toying with others? Do you honestly think your mother would've married me had I been that horrible?"

"I don't know. I have no idea what was going on in Mom's head, but I'm sure she wouldn't be happy about what you're doing with Haven."

"You were young when she died, and frankly, your view is skewed. I've done a lot over the years that would disappoint your mother, but buying the girl isn't one of them."

"Buying her? You think my mom would be okay with that? You're sick!"

Vincent slammed his fist against the table. "Who are you to talk to me like that? Look how you treat everyone!"

"And whose fucking fault is that, huh?" Carmine pushed his chair back as he stood. "Whose fault is it I'm fucked up? Whose fault is it I had to watch her die?"

Vincent glared at him. "Not mine."

A voice cleared beside them as the manager approached. Others stared, disturbed by the commotion. Vincent pulled some cash from his wallet, throwing it down on the table before walking out.

Not a word was spoken during the drive. When they reached the house, Carmine tried to get out, but Vincent stopped him.

"I had you do it so you'd see what you were getting into. She's been cut off from everything, Carmine. In the confines of the house, maybe things are great, but that's not the real world. On the off chance you get to be together, I figured it was better if you had experience dealing with that part of her. It's going to be there every step of the way, because when you're raised like she was, you don't have the know-how to live any other way. I tried to help you, not hurt you."

Carmine opened his mouth to speak, but his father continued before he could. "You think your mother would be disappointed I brought her into this house? I think you're wrong. Would she like it? No. *I* don't even like it. But I think your mother would've been disappointed had I thrown the child into the world blindly. Society would've eaten her alive. Probably still will."

Carmine had been focused on everything his father was doing wrong and never considered what might be helping Haven.

"She needs a semblance of her normal before she can be introduced to ours," Vincent continued. "You love her? Fine, love her. But don't contradict me. This isn't fun, Carmine. I'm not enjoying this, but I'm doing it and that should be enough to earn your respect. You have to stop acting like you're powerful and wise, because you're neither. You need to grasp that, son, or I'm going to lose you like I lost your mother."

Vincent got out, slamming the door so hard the windows vibrated.

Haven lay in the middle of Carmine's bed, sprawled out on her back when he entered. He took off his coat and shoes before lying down beside her. Haven's eyes fluttered open. She blinked a few times, smiling when they made eye contact.

"*La mia bella ragazza,*" he said. "Napping in the afternoon?"

"I ran out of stuff to do," she said. "Everything's clean."

He sighed. "A nap actually sounds good right now."

She eyed him curiously. "Bad day?"

"It was confusing, but I wouldn't call it bad," he said. "Any day that includes lying in bed with you, *tesoro,* can't be bad."

She ran her fingertips across his lips. "I missed you."

"*Mi sei mancata,*" he said. "That's 'I missed you' in Italian."

"Well, *mi sei mancata,* too."

He laughed. "I'm a guy, so you say, *mancato.* You know, with an *o* and not an *a.*"

"*Mi sei mancato,*" she repeated.

"There you go! Watch out, look at my girl getting bilingual."

————

Haven sat back on her knees, humming to herself as she surveyed the sparkling kitchen floor. She'd been scrubbing it for more than an hour, removing the black scuff marks from the marble tile. Dr. DeMarco never spoke to her about cleaning. The rare occasions she forgot to do something, he overlooked it. Sometimes she felt like she was living in another universe with how drastically her life had changed. She never imagined living an existence where she could throw down the broom and put the laundry on hold to catch a television program in the middle of the afternoon.

A lot of it happened without her realizing it. Before she had come to the DeMarco house, she was constantly focused on tasks to stay out of trouble, but now she thought about herself more.

And that was something she had never been allowed to do before.

She stood, catching a glimpse of something when she turned around. Dr. DeMarco stood in the doorway, watching her silently.

It was noon, and she hadn't realized someone was home. "Are you hungry, sir?"

He nodded. "You can make some lunch, *dolcezza*. We'll watch TV while we eat."

She blinked a few times after he walked out. *We?*

After making some chicken salad sandwiches and distractedly throwing together two cherry Cokes, Haven headed into the family room. Dr. DeMarco lounged in a chair with his legs stretched out in front of him, his smile falling when he took his lunch.

She sat down on the couch and picked at her sandwich as he took a sip of his drink. "Can I ask you something, child?"

"Yes, sir."

He pulled a cherry out of his soda. "Did you make these on your own, or did my son ask you to?"

"I made it on my own. I wanted to be nice."

"Interesting."

"Is something wrong with that?" she asked.

"No, I was just curious," he said. "I'm curious about a lot, actually."

"Like?"

"Like, how did you know to use the special cleaner on my windows?"

Her brow furrowed. "It was written on the bottle."

"So you're admitting you could read back then?"

Her blatant mistake stunned her. She nodded, afraid to speak.

"I already knew it at the time, but I was surprised you'd slip up on your first day. You aren't as slick as you think you are."

Queasiness overtook her. She set her sandwich down. "How did you know I could read?"

"I discovered it years ago on a trip to Blackburn. You had a book. Had I not known, though, you would've given yourself away anyway. The moment your illiteracy was mentioned, you looked left. That's your tell. When you're hiding something, you look to the left."

Haven said nothing, forcing herself to look straight ahead.

29

Carmine paced the foyer, the sound of his feet against the wooden floor echoing through the downstairs. The sun hadn't risen and he already couldn't stand still.

After what seemed like another hour, although only a few minutes had passed, a car pulled up outside. He swung open the front door so forcefully he was surprised he didn't rip it from the hinges. "You're late."

Dia pushed him out of the way to step in the house. "You told me six. It's five forty-five."

His brow furrowed. "It's not six yet?"

"No, it's not." She handed him a piece of paper. "Relax, it's going to go fine."

"You're sure? I mean, it's enough, isn't it?" Dia raised her eyebrows, her expression causing his foolish panic to surge. "Christ, it's too much. I'm going overboard."

"She's going to love it, Carmine."

"I've never done any of this before," he said. "I don't know what I'm doing."

"I know. It's sweet of you. I'm more than happy to help."

"Thank you," he said. "I'll get some cash in town and pay you for your freelancing."

She laughed. "No need to. This one's on me. I'm looking forward to hanging out with her."

"No shit? You actually wanna socialize with a girl in my life?"

Dia rolled her eyes. "It's not my fault you used to only bring Moanin' Lisa around."

———

Haven picked at her cheese and mushroom omelet, listening as Dia ranted about school as they sat in a booth at Crossroads Diner, a small restaurant in the center of town. Dia had woken her up an hour before and asked Haven to have breakfast with her. She had resisted, afraid to leave the house without permission, but Dominic called Dr. DeMarco to ensure it was okay. She didn't know why she was there, but she was grateful someone wanted to spend time with her.

Even if that person was still a mystery to Haven.

After Dia finished her pancakes, she excused herself to the restroom. Haven grew nervous as she disappeared. Being in public by herself, surrounded by strangers, put her on edge.

"What's a beauty like you doing eating alone?"

She grew rigid as Nicholas slid into the booth across from her. "I'm with Dia. She went . . . somewhere."

"Cool, it'll be nice to see her," he said. "So, I have a question for you."

She gazed at him apprehensively. "What?"

He reached into his coat pocket and pulled out a small pink box of candy hearts, dumping a few of them in his hand. "What do you call a vampire's sweetheart?"

She smiled. Another joke. "I don't know."

He popped a piece of candy in his mouth. "A ghoulfriend. Get it? Like girlfriend but a ghoul?"

She stared at him, not seeing what was funny about that.

Dia returned and slid into the booth beside Nicholas. "What are you doing here?"

He shrugged. "Stopped by for some breakfast on my way to the station. I have community service with the police chief."

Dia's brow furrowed. "Shouldn't you be in school, though?"

"Looks who's talking—shouldn't you?"

"I took the day off," she said. "Haven and I are getting her ready for her date."

Date? The word caught Haven off guard. Nicholas looked just as surprised. "Date? With who?"

"With her boyfriend," Dia said when Haven remained quiet. "You know—Carmine."

Nicholas's expression fell. "DeMarco?"

"What other Carmine is there?" Dia asked. "And don't be so shocked. He's not the same person you knew."

"Carmine will never change." Nicholas's voice was scathing. "He might pull the wool over your eyes, but I'm not charmed by him like everyone else. Everyone in this ridiculous town still thinks the sun rises and sets on that guy, that he can do no wrong. It's bizarre." He paused, fiddling with his candy. "I have to go."

Dia scooted out of the booth to let him pass. He put a piece of candy down on the table in front of Haven before stalking away, shoving the door open and leaving the diner without eating.

Haven glanced down at the orange candy heart in front of her, reading the words TALK 2 ME faintly written on it in pink.

Carmine paced the foyer again, dressed in a black suit and nervously twirling a red rose. Ever since he had told Dia about his plans, she had been calling it Operation Cinderella, although he thought it was more like Operation Please-Don't-Fuck-This-One-Up. The closest he got to being Prince Charming was being a *Principe della Mafia*, but there was nothing remotely romantic about that.

His mind ran through all the potential catastrophes as he waited, already preparing for the worst. He might say something wrong and offend her. She might be disappointed or overwhelmed by it all. The picnic would be a disaster, with food poisoning or invading ants. If none of that happened, it would storm, even though the weatherman assured a clear night.

Earthquake. Tornado. Tsunami. Monsoon. Hurricane. Flood. Hail. Blizzard. He didn't know if half were possible, but he imagined them all happening at once.

Eventually the clunky hunk of junk Dia called a car pulled up outside. His heart pounded hard. It was only Haven, he reminded himself. It was the girl who, somehow, saw him at his worst and still managed to love him.

The door opened and Haven stepped in. She fidgeted in a white dress, a tiny bit of makeup on her face, her wavy hair tamed and pulled back. *"Buon San Valentino,"* he said, holding out the flower. "Happy Valentine's Day."

Smiling sheepishly, she took the flower from him.

––––––––––

Carmine turned off the highway when they made it to Black Mountain, driving straight to the art center on Cherry Street. The sign above the main entrance of the gray building announced what it was, but as Carmine helped Haven out of the car, all he saw in her expression was confusion.

"It's a gallery," he explained, not knowing if she'd understand.

"Like a museum?"

"Yes, like that."

Excitement flared in her eyes, and he knew then he had made the right choice. He took her hand to lead her inside. The place was dim, only a subtle glow of light throughout the building, shining above the scattered exhibits. "Come on, *tesoro.*"

She didn't move. "Don't you have to pay?"

"No." He hadn't expected her to ask that. "You don't have to pay to look at the art."

He stood there, apprehensive about what she thought. Now he started to feel bad bringing her somewhere that didn't cost him a dime.

"This place is really free?"

"Yes."

"Why?"

He never thought about it before. "Educational reasons, I guess. Artists are kinda like musicians and work more for pleasure than money."

He had no idea if he was right or not, but it sounded good.

They walked around, pausing every few feet to check out exhibits—carvings and pottery, sculptures and paintings, drawings and photography. It wasn't the usual thing he would find interesting, but anything was enjoyable with Haven around. She glowed the entire time, and he just stood back, listening with amazement as she analyzed and dissected the art.

"You need to go to college," he said. "You're too damn smart not to."

She narrowed her eyes. "Is it appropriate to curse in a gallery?"

He laughed. "Fuck if I know."

She shook her head. "Do you really think I could go to school?"

"Yeah, I do. And you know I could help you, right?"

"I know you could try," she said playfully. "Whether or not it works is another matter."

They went through the rest of the gallery, chatting casually and holding hands. Toward the end of their tour, Haven paused in front of a pencil drawing, a figure of a woman from the back with a vibrantly colored sphere hovering in the air beside her. Haven was transfixed by it, a smile gracing her lips as she reached out to trace the outline of the drawing. "I like this one. It reminds me of myself."

"How so?"

"Well, the girl . . . she's stuck in a life where everything's bland and hopeless, but then this beautiful thing comes along and brings color into her world. Color she never expected to see."

He stared at her, stunned, before turning back to the drawing. He had no idea how she had gotten something so deep from a pencil sketch. "You know, maybe we'll see your work in a place like this someday."

"You think I'm that good?"

"Of course I do."

———

Carmine turned on a side road that weaved through the mountain, driving until the small cabin came into view. It was just one room, a bed and a fireplace, with a small bathroom built in. He parked the car in front as the sun peeked out from behind the clouds, casting light along the meadow surrounding it. Tucked in among the trees were some deer, and Carmine stared at them as one took a few steps in his direction, feeling like he'd been sucked into a Disney movie.

If one started talking, he was fucking running.

"What is this place?" Haven asked as they climbed out of the car.

He pulled the key from his pocket. "Home for the next twenty-four hours. I rented it."

She eyed him skeptically. "No wonder you took me to a free gallery. This must've cost a fortune."

He laughed as he grabbed a basket of food from the car and spread a blanket out on the grass. "Come on, let's eat. I think I can still afford to feed you."

Haven looked at it with surprise. "A picnic?"

She sat on the blanket, spreading her legs out in front of her. He sat beside her and pulled out the containers of food. Haven grabbed a grape from one and popped it into her mouth as he took the top off of the tall green bottle. Haven watched him warily as he poured the bubbly drink.

She took a glass carefully. "Is this alcohol?"

"I'm afraid not, *tesoro*. Sparkling grape juice. We're going sober tonight."

She looked surprised as she took a sip.

They munched on the food for a while, chatting and laughing. She kicked off her shoes as they talked about trivial things, like TV and weather, before delving into more serious topics. She told him stories from her fucked-up equivalent of a childhood, and in turn, he talked about his mom.

Carmine reached inside the basket and pulled out two Toblerone bars. "Dia said you're supposed to give chocolate to your sweetheart on Valentine's Day."

Haven opened hers and pulled off a triangle. "I thought Saint Valentine's Day was just a massacre."

He choked. "How do you know about that?"

"*Jeopardy!*"

Saint Valentine's Day massacre, when *La Cosa Nostra* in Chicago killed seven Irish associates. Carmine was curious if she realized the connection between his family and those things, but he thought better than to bring it up. The last thing he wanted was to have their night tainted by reminders of the world they'd have to go back to.

They watched the sunset quietly. It was one of the things he loved about her—she never felt like she had to fill the silence. He gazed at the sky when something wet splat on the center of his forehead. Closing his eyes instinctively, he reached up and prayed he hadn't been shit on by a bird. He felt another drop after a second and groaned at the same time Haven laughed. "It's raining."

He sighed. Of course the weatherman wouldn't know what he was talking about.

———

They settled onto the cabin porch as the rain steadily fell, a curtain of water cutting them off from the world. Haven watched it quietly, while Carmine strummed his guitar.

"Will you play something for me?" she asked. He started to reply, to tell her he was playing something, when she spoke again. "Something happy, please."

He sighed. No more *Moonlight Sonata*. "Uh, sure. I'll play a song that reminds me of us."

"Really?"

"Yeah. It's a real song," he said. "I mean, like one you hear on the radio or whatever."

"Will you sing it too?"

He stared at her. He could probably rupture eardrums and break sanities with his voice, but he couldn't deny her. Not when she looked at him that way. "Okay, but this might not be pretty."

Her smile grew. Carmine strummed the first few chords of Blue October's "18th Floor Balcony" before softly singing the lyrics. He could feel her gaze on him, his fingers wavering, but he tried to keep focused so not to mess up. He could tell her all day long that he loved her, but this was cracking his chest open and stepping out of himself fully for her to see.

He glanced at Haven toward the end of the song, his fingers stilling when he saw tears streaming down her cheeks. Reaching over, he brushed some of them away.

She let out a shaky breath as she placed her hand on top of his. "Can we go inside?"

He led her into the cabin for the first time, and she paused right inside the door, surveying the dozens of roses faintly visible in the glow of the room. He scooted around her and turned on some music, scanning through songs when Haven brushed against him. She pulled off her coat and draped it over a chair before grabbing a rose. Bringing it to her nose, she inhaled its sweet scent as she sat on the bed, her bottom lip clamped between her teeth.

Carmine tossed his suit coat onto the table and lit the fireplace before walking over to her. Her expression made his steps falter. "You okay, hummingbird?"

Her voice cracked. "Perfect."

"Perfect, indeed."

He cupped her cheek and kissed her as she ran her hands

through his hair. She moaned as he pushed her onto her back and leaned over her with his hands on both sides of the bed. He pulled from her mouth to take a breath and nudged her head to the side to kiss her neck.

"Carmine," she whispered as he kissed toward her collarbones. "Make love to me."

Strong emotions swirled through him—shock and elation, with a ton of fear—as his eyes met hers. He wanted to . . . Christ, did he want to . . . but there was no turning back from that. "Haven . . ."

"It feels right," she said. "We're right."

He felt it, too. There in that moment, it was just him and her, no one and nothing else. They were all that mattered—two people, desperately in love and wanting to show each other. No master and slave, no class divides. No *Principe della Mafia* and his sweet forbidden fruit.

They never really felt that way, but it was hard to ignore the labels. There were reminders everywhere of the people they were supposed to be, the ones they didn't want to be, but it was different here. Here, they were away from everything threatening to tear them apart. Here, there were no complications, no need to hide or pretend.

Carmine didn't respond. No words were necessary. That bitch of a voice inside his head, doubting and nagging, had finally been silenced.

He gazed at her, absorbing all the love, before leaning down and softly capturing her lips with his. He kissed her tenderly as he placed his hand on her knee, slowly running it up her inner thigh. She squirmed under his touch, a whimper escaping her throat as she ran her hands under his shirt, tingles swimming through him as she caressed his bare skin.

Pulling away, he crouched down beside the bed and pushed up her dress, watching for any sign of distress. "You can change your mind at any time, hummingbird."

"I won't," she said, her voice trembling as she raised her arms, letting him pull her dress over her head. He was in a stupor as he gazed at her, the contrast between her scarred skin and the dark undergarments striking. The strong, feisty girl suddenly seemed fragile, and he could never live with himself if he somehow broke her.

She reached over and unbuttoned his top button, but he grabbed her hands. "Relax, okay? Let me worship you."

Her lips curved at his words. He unclasped her bra, tossing it on the floor, and gazed at her as he grazed his hand across her breasts. A blush started on her cheeks and trickled the whole way down her body.

She lay on the bed when he finished undressing her, fisting the comforter. Loud moans bounced off the cabin walls as he caressed every inch of her flesh with his tongue. Her body writhed, her legs vibrating as she melted for him. She smelled sweet like nectar he was desperate to consume. A starving man, craving her like nothing before.

She cried out when her body exploded in pleasure, the sight of her pushing Carmine over the edge. He shrugged off his shirt, discarding it with Haven's clothes, before kissing her deeply. She wrapped her arms around him, her breathing erratic as he unbuckled his pants and dropped them to the floor. "We can stop—"

Her voice was a ball of fire. "I don't want to stop."

Relieved, his excitement outshined his fear. Hovering over her, he kissed her jaw and nipped at her neck, his heart thumping hard in his chest at the warmth radiating from her. Her hands on his skin were electric as she ran her fingers lightly over the scar on his side. She tilted her head as he kissed the dip in her throat, his lips moving along her collarbones.

His nerves flared as he reached between them to grasp himself. "I'll go slow, okay?"

She clung to him, her brittle fingernails digging into his back, her body rigid when he pushed inside of her. A whimper escaped her throat as he stilled his movements to give her time to adjust. *"Tanto gentile e tanto onesta pare la donna mia,"* he whispered, the words from Dante's *La Vita Nuova* flooding from his lips. *"Quand'ella altrui saluta, ch'ogne lingua deven tremando muta, e li occhi no l'ardiscon di guardare."*

His voice was breathy from anticipation as he tried to soothe her, her body relaxing more with each word. He moved again and sparks flew through his body at the sensation.

"That was beautiful," she said.

"The poem or the penetration?" he asked, not thinking before saying the words. "Shit, I shouldn't have said that."

"I meant the poem, but the other part's nice so far too," she said shyly. "And you should've said that, because that's who you are."

"Yeah, well, I'm trying to be tender," he said. "You deserve to be romanced."

"I don't need romance. I need you."

Her eyes fluttered closed. Electricity coursed through him from where they were connected, goose bumps popping up as shivers ripped down his spine. As he made love to her, he finally felt what that meant. They were experiencing something together, an intensity he'd never felt before. It was all of her, every inch of her body, inside and out, merging with his.

"Only you," she whispered, as if she could read his mind. "It'll only ever be you, Carmine."

Her words ignited a fire inside of him, stirring up the possessiveness that demanded they belong together, forever, just like this. They moved together deliberately, falling into a perfect rhythm. Her noises grew louder, and he grabbed one of her hands, linking their fingers together as he pressed it into the mattress.

"I love you," she said breathlessly.

A noise escaped his throat involuntarily in response, a rumbling growl as hunger swirled through him. *"Ti amo.* Christ, I love you, Haven."

There was an ache in his chest, originating in his heart, the pain of all-consuming, overflowing love, so powerful it took his breath away. He continued to fill her and took her other hand, placing it above her head on the bed. His body weight rested against her as he hitched her knees up. Nuzzling into her neck, he tasted the saltiness of sweat as their bodies slid together smoothly.

Afterward, when the feelings subsided, she snuggled against him, her hand on his chest over his wildly thumping heart. They lay together, legs entangled, as they relished in the postcoital glow. He wanted to ask if she could feel his heart beating, but he kept his mouth shut, choosing instead to enjoy the silence.

Just two kids, together and in love. There was still nothing that needed to be said.

30

The weeks that followed their stay in the cabin flew by, half a year having elapsed since Haven had been forced to leave her mama behind. She adapted to the world outside the desert, little things that once intimidated her now a regular part of her life. She still kept up with her work, cooking and cleaning every day, but there was always time left over. She had never had time to do things leisurely, and the more she indulged, the more she couldn't imagine ever going back.

Free time, Carmine called it. His choice of words made her laugh.

Drawing and painting, reading and crafts—her days were a flurry of unrestrained creativity. She had taken some notebooks from Carmine and filled pages with words, scribbling down everything on her mind. It was disjointed, riddled with errors, but it wasn't meant for others' eyes. She found it liberating, like a valve had been turned, the pressure inside her releasing. The nightmares came less often after that, like she had chased away the monsters with the power of her words.

She grew more comfortable being outside the house too. Carmine took her wherever he went, giving her cash so she could count it out and pay. She ordered her own food, picked out her own things, and spoke for herself whenever the opportunity arose.

Life hadn't only changed for Haven—it shifted for all of them. Dr. DeMarco spent every weekend in Chicago while Dominic prepared for college, since he would graduate in a few months and head across the country with Tess. Even Dia was graduating, but she was staying close by in Charlotte.

Haven was in the kitchen early the morning before Easter Sunday, cleaning up breakfast as Carmine leaned against the counter, watching her as usual. "What do you wanna do today?"

She shrugged. "Whatever you want to do."

"If I knew what I wanted to do, do you think I'd bother asking?"

"Yes." She laughed. "You always ask my opinion."

"Well, do you have an opinion this time?"

"We can hang out here."

"We spend too much time in this shithole." He paused, his expression brightening. "So, what do you wanna do today?"

"Whatever you want to do, Carmine."

"I hoped you'd say that."

Grabbing her hand, he pulled her to the downstairs office and punched in the code to unlock the door. He stepped inside, but she dug her heels in, refusing to follow. "I'm not supposed to go in there. Dr. DeMarco said some doors stay locked for a reason."

"It is locked for a reason, just like I have a code for a reason."

"Why's that?"

"Because my father isn't always home and sometimes we need shit in here."

She stared at him, contemplating his words, before hesitantly stepping inside the room. Carmine placed his hand on her hip, kissing the nape of her neck. "See, that wasn't scary."

"It's not the room I'm afraid of," she muttered. "Why are we in here, anyway?"

"I'm gonna teach you how to use my gun."

She gaped at him. "You're joking."

"Do I look like I'm joking? There's nothing else to do, and I feel like blowing off some steam. Besides, do you know how sexy you're gonna be shooting something?"

She wasn't sure. "I don't think your father would want me to touch a gun after I touched his."

"You touched Nunzio's," Carmine said, matter-of-factly. "He didn't get mad about that, did he?"

"I was protecting myself."

"This is the same thing. You never know when you might need to shoot to protect yourself."

She sighed. *So persistent.* "Okay, but why are we in here?"

Carmine pulled the rug out of the way and opened a trapdoor in the floor. "Targets. Ammunition. Safety shit. Depending on your mood, maybe a bulletproof vest for me."

She gaped at him. "I'd never shoot you."

"I know. Not intentionally, anyway."

She cautiously walked over to the entrance to the basement, and Carmine held her hand as they headed down the narrow steps. *"Terra di contrabbando,"* he said when they reached the bottom. "Welcome to the land of contraband."

Her eyes swept across the concrete room, taking in the massive crates. "Everything down here is illegal?"

"No, but it's all pretty fucking unsavory," he said. "The front ones are mainly alcohol."

"What about the ones in the back?"

"Come on, I'll show you. Just don't touch anything."

She followed behind him, coming to a halt when the guns came into view. Dozens of them hung on the wall in neat rows, arranged meticulously by size. "Whoa."

Carmine covered his hand with his shirt as he dug through a box behind her. He tried to hand supplies to Haven, but she wasn't paying attention as she gaped at the weapons.

"What can I say? My father loves his guns." Carmine opened a cabinet and pulled out a box of bullets. "But you already knew that."

She tore her eyes away from them. "Yeah."

"You don't have to be afraid of guns, though," he said. "It's the dumbasses with their fingers on the triggers that you have to worry about. As long as you stay away from them, no problem."

She glanced at the weapons again. "What else is down here?"

"More guns, a shitload of casino chips, the dungeon . . ."

Her eyes widened. *Dungeon?*

––––––––

It took the two of them an hour to reach a wide-open space tucked into the woods, the ground covered in an array of wildflowers, a line of tall pine trees surrounding it like nature had deliberately built a fence. Carmine dropped his backpack to the ground as Haven scanned the clearing, a look of awe on her face.

After setting up a target near the tree line, he positioned Haven's body and grabbed his gun, explaining the safety and number of rounds. He told her to keep it steady and use her foresight to focus on the target, blocking out everything else.

Once she got it, he handed her the earmuffs and safety glasses. Taking a step away, he watched her aim, her hands shaking as she squeezed the trigger. He flinched as she popped off her first round, the recoil and expelled cartridge startling her. She screamed and nearly dropped the gun while he stared at the target—she hadn't come close.

He put his arms around her again, holding the pistol with her hands on top of his. They fired off the rest of the rounds that way and she relaxed. After reloading, he handed her the gun and gave her some room. The first shot breezed by the target, closer that time, but her hands still shook.

He ended up reloading twice, not a single bullet hitting its intended spot. She came close, though, her eyes twinkling with excitement every time she squeezed the trigger. He tried to imagine how she felt wielding something so powerful, imagining the adrenaline surging through her veins.

Hitting the target after the third reload, Haven shouted and turned to Carmine, forgetting to lower the gun in her excitement.

Carmine ducked, throwing his hands up protectively as she aimed at his forehead. "Watch what you're fucking doing!"

She lowered the gun. "I'm sorry!"

He dropped his hands. "Never aim a gun at someone unless you're willing to shoot that motherfucker."

She nodded in understanding and turned away, firing a round that grazed the target. She smiled, trying to hold in her excitement. Sighing, Carmine walked up behind her and placed his hands on her hips. He pulled off the earmuffs and tossed them on the ground before lining her back up to the target. "You're doing really good."

She aimed with a look of determination on her face. He could feel her body tense in anticipation, her muscles firm and arms vibrating. He placed a light kiss on her earlobe without thinking, and she whimpered. Losing focus, she squeezed the trigger, a round echoing through the trees.

"Oops," she said as birds squawked in the distance.

He laughed and nuzzled into her neck. "Better the birds than me."

The walk home was a lot harder than Carmine remembered the walk to the clearing being. By the time the house came into view, the sun had set and he was utterly exhausted. The two of them headed for the stairs, but hadn't made it to the second floor when there was a knock at the door. Haven continued upstairs as Carmine disabled the alarm, finding Max on the porch. "What's up?"

"Is your dad home?"

"No. He's in Chicago."

"Shit, I need to give something to him," Max said, reaching into his pocket for an envelope.

"I'll take it for you," Carmine said, holding out his hand, not questioning him. He didn't want to know what type of business Max had with his father. Max dealt drugs to save money for school, which alleviated some of Carmine's guilt when he bought from him. He felt like he was doing it for a good cause, like participating in a coke-a-thon to send a deserving kid to the Ivy League.

La Cosa Nostra, though, avoided the drug trade.

"Thanks, man. I told him I'd have it to him, and, well, I don't want to be late with your father."

Carmine took the envelope and said good-bye to Max before closing the door. He went into the office under the stairs again and took the large painting off the wall, exposing the safe underneath. He pulled out his keys and stuck the small golden one into the lock, punching in the code as he turned it. The safe unlocked, and a folder slipped out as soon as he opened it, papers spilling onto the floor. Bending down to pick them up, the word *Antonelli* caught Carmine's eye on one of the papers. He froze, a coldness washing through him when he read *genetic testing* across the top.

His mind worked fast as he debated what to do, time ticking away, his opportunity dwindling. Curiosity overrode his logic as he grabbed the test results.

Besides Haven's, there were no names, but it indicated a conclusive mtDNA match from somewhere. Written along the side, in his father's messy scrawl, were the words *CODIS partial match confirmed*. Carmine kicked himself for not paying more attention in science class.

He shoved the papers back into the folder and placed the envelope in the safe, locking it all up before heading upstairs.

———

Loud noises woke them later that night, doors slamming on the floor below. The bed shifted as Haven sat up, wide-eyed. "What was that?"

"I have no fucking clue," Carmine said, glancing at the clock. Three in the morning. He climbed out of bed when he heard heavy footsteps in the library, heading right for them. Dread hit him when the door flung open, Vincent appearing in the doorway.

Even in the darkness, his rage was obvious.

"Go to your room, girl," he barked, not taking his eyes off Carmine as Haven bolted out of the room. "What's wrong with you? Do you have a death wish?"

No matter what answer Carmine gave, he'd be wrong.

"I thought you were smarter than this. Did you honestly think today was a good idea? You can't be that dense! And I know you're up to something, son. I know you, by God, but I'm telling you right now—whatever it is won't work."

Carmine said not a word.

"I don't want you stepping foot in my office or the basement again. You have no business in there anymore. And I know what you saw, too. What you *read*. I can't imagine what ideas are floating around in that head of yours, but don't dare act on it. Whatever it is, don't do it." Vincent paced, muttering to himself. "If you weren't turning eighteen soon, I'd send you back to the academy tomorrow. I already have half a mind to get rid of the girl."

"You aren't gonna do a goddamn thing to her," Carmine said. "You're gonna leave her alone."

"I'll do anything I want with her! Have you not been listening to me? You're going to get yourself killed! You may not care about your life, but I can't let you throw it away. I'll do whatever I have to do to make sure that doesn't happen, even if it means her being collateral damage."

Carmine clenched his hands into fists, those words driving him to the brink. "Fuck you! I'll kill you if you hurt her again!"

"Maybe you will," Vincent said. "In fact, I don't doubt it, but at least your mother's *sole* will still have his light. She would've never wanted you involved in this."

"Don't use Mom as an excuse to justify your bullshit! I love Haven! Accept it!"

"I can't!" Vincent stepped toward him. "You're just a child, Carmine."

"I may be seventeen, but I'm not a kid. I haven't been a kid since I got shot because of you!"

"You don't know what you're saying. You don't know the devastation that girl has inflicted on my life! Just look at us! Look what she's causing!"

"She's not causing it, you are! You're the one who brought us into this life! You paid money for her—for a fucking child—and you wanna blame her for this?"

Vincent shook his head. "I tried to help her! I've done everything I could for that girl, and none of it's enough. Nothing's ever enough! It's impossible! Worthless! You don't know how much I've suffered because of that little bitch!"

The moment the word escaped his lips, Carmine's composure slipped. Red flashed before his eyes as he struck, his fist connecting with his father's mouth. "Don't call her that!"

Before Carmine even realized his father had moved, Vincent was on him. He slammed him into the wall, the force of the blow knocking the wind out of Carmine. He gasped for air as his father pinned him against the desk, knocking things on the floor as the two of them scuffled.

Dominic burst into the room, hearing the commotion, and grabbed his father's shoulder. It registered with Vincent what he was doing, and he quickly pulled his hands away. Backing up, he swiped his fingers across his bloody mouth. "Why couldn't you trust me, Carmine? Why couldn't you let me handle this?"

"Why couldn't you give me a reason to?"

"Keeping you safe isn't a good reason?"

Carmine didn't hesitate. "My safety means nothing compared to hers."

———

Standing in the doorway of the bedroom, Haven surveyed the damage from the fight as Carmine grumbled, opening his desk drawer and grabbing a bottle of liquor. He grimaced as he took a drink and kicked the desk drawer closed before plopping down in the chair and staring at the floor in the darkened room.

Unable to take the tension, Haven busied herself by picking up things that had been knocked over. She plugged in the alarm clock and tried to set it, but she gave up with the numbers still flashing twelve. Grabbing the picture frame from the floor, she winced as a small shard of broken glass stabbed her thumb. Blood oozed from the cut as she set it down on the desk.

"Christ, you're bleeding."

Carmine tried to grab her hand, but she pulled away. "You broke the picture frame."

He groaned. "So? Just stop cleaning. None of that shit is important!"

"It is important." She fought back tears. "It's your mama."

She continued picking up the rest of the stuff, having no idea what else to do. Frustrated, Carmine snatched the bottle of liquor from the desk and flung it at the wall. It shattered, glass and alcohol spraying everywhere. Haven flinched, closing her eyes as her tears slipped through, flashes of memory striking her as hard as fists. Michael's anger, the shattered glass, and the revolting stench of spilled liquor.

"You're worthless," he had screamed, spitting the words at her. "You can't do anything right, girl! You're the worst thing I ever did!"

She reopened her eyes, watching the annoyance fade from Carmine's face. "I shouldn't be yelling at you. None of this is your fault."

"It is," she said quietly. "I'm tearing your family apart."

Carmine knelt beside her, grabbing a notebook and tossing it on his desk. "This family was torn apart when my mom was killed, so unless you wanna take credit for that, you can drop that bullshit."

Haven lay in bed with Carmine later, brushing her fingers along his swollen knuckles as guilt ran rampant through her. No matter what he said, she believed she had caused it.

She didn't sleep much, the peace she had found over the weeks tainted as Carmine slipped in and out of consciousness, thrashing around with nightmares.

In the morning, she headed downstairs in a daze and pulled things out for Easter dinner. The Mercedes wasn't parked in its spot in the driveway. She wondered if there was even a point in cooking with Dr. DeMarco gone.

The morning flew by, morphing into afternoon, before eventually shifting into early evening. The boys made their way downstairs, tension lingering in the house, but she was too exhausted to deal with what it meant. She stood in front of the stove, going through the motions like she'd been taught to do, while Carmine sat on the counter, staring at her. Dominic bounded into the room, grabbing one of the deviled eggs she'd made. "You feeling all right today, Haven?"

"She's on autopilot," Carmine said, answering for her. "Happy Easter to us all."

She said nothing, a faint sound outside drawing her attention. Glancing out the window, she stared at Dr. DeMarco's car as it came to a stop. Carmine leaped down from the counter and wrapped his arms around her protectively, when the front door opened and Dr. DeMarco headed their way. He paused a foot from them, his voice strained. "Let me see your hand, Carmine."

"Excuse me?"

"You put too much stress on your fourth and fifth fingers when you hit me. I'll be surprised if you didn't fracture them."

"Fuck you."

Dominic sighed exasperatedly. "Just let him look at your hand and get it over with, bro."

Carmine stayed still for a moment before pulling his hand from Haven's hip. Dr. DeMarco's expression remained blank as he eyed his son's hand, and Carmine winced a few times as he pressed on his knuckles. "You'll be fine."

"Like I said . . ." Carmine pulled his hand away. "Fuck you."

Haven carried the food to the table once it was done and planned to go to her room, but Carmine stopped her, pulling out a chair and motioning for her to sit. The tension mounted through dinner. No one wanted to be there, none of them wanting to deal with it, but it couldn't be avoided anymore. The wheels had been set into motion.

A fork clanged as Dominic cracked first. "We have to clear the air. We need to have a sit-down."

Dr. DeMarco scoffed. "You know nothing about sit-downs."

"You're right, but we're going to have our own version," Dominic said. "No one leaves the table until we get some answers."

"There are some questions I can't answer," Dr. DeMarco said.

"That's fine," Dominic said. "If you can't answer something, tell us. Plead the fifth—it'll be good practice. But things can't keep going like they are, Dad. We used to feel like a family—a dysfunctional-as-hell one, but still a family. And now it's every man for themselves."

Dr. DeMarco stared at his plate. "Fine. Family meeting."

The word *family* struck Haven. She jumped to her feet. "May I be excused, sir?"

Dr. DeMarco waved her away, while Carmine slammed his hands down on the table. "Sit down, Haven. This involves you, too."

She froze, having no idea what to do until Dr. DeMarco pointed at her chair. "Take your seat."

She sat down, folding her hands in her lap, but wished she had left anyway when Dominic started the conversation. "First of all, Dad, what's your problem with Haven?"

"Why do you think I have a problem with her?" Dr. DeMarco asked.

Carmine scoffed. "Maybe because you fucking threaten her?"

"Calm the hell down," Dominic said, pointing at his brother. "There's no yelling in my sit-downs. Let me handle this."

Carmine grumbled under his breath and crossed his arms over his chest.

"That's better." Dominic turned to their father. "Maybe because you fucking threaten her?"

Dr. DeMarco shook his head. "I have nothing against the child."

"But you said . . ." she started before she realized what she was doing. She shut her mouth, nervous she had spoken out.

"I said what?" Dr. DeMarco raised his eyebrows. "Be out with it."

"You told those men I wasn't worth it."

"You're right, and I won't take it back. Doesn't mean I have a problem with you, though."

Carmine fidgeted, fighting to remain silent, while Dominic continued with his questions. "So if you don't hate her, what's the big deal about her and Carmine being together?"

"Because there are complications they don't understand," he said. "I've told them they can be together for the time being."

Carmine couldn't restrain himself any longer. "Can't you see how unfair that is? We can be together 'for the time being'? What the hell does that mean?"

"It means until I figure things out, I can't give you any guarantees on the future."

"What things?" Carmine asked. Dr. DeMarco didn't answer. "Fine, I'll figure it out myself. Just tell me who she's related to."

"I can't. If they find out you know, you're going to get hurt. I need you to understand that."

"What's the big deal?" Dominic asked. "She has family . . . isn't that good?"

"No, it's not. He'll expect her to be handed over, and she wouldn't be safe with him."

Haven's mind furiously tried to work through what he'd said.

"No one's taking her," Carmine said. "I won't let it happen."

"You think I don't know that? You'll follow right behind, and I can't have you both being taken down. I'm trying to find a way out where you walk away from this, but you're making it difficult."

"Do I know him?" Carmine asked.

"I can't answer that."

He laughed dryly. "I'll take that as a yes."

"Mind your own business!" Dr. DeMarco said. "You have to forget all about the DNA test!"

"Why can't you?" Dominic asked. "Forget about it. Let the information die."

"Because three can keep a secret if two of them are dead. That's why. People know. You have no idea the dilemma this has put me in, how hard it has made helping her. Carmine has no regard for his own life. He made that clear again last night. Threatening him won't affect him, but threatening her will. And it's not an idle threat. If it comes down to it, I'll choose my blood."

Haven's heart thumped hard in her chest as Carmine snapped. "You're stupid if you think I'd just move on with my life if something happened to her."

"I know you think that—"

Carmine growled. "Don't pretend to know my feelings! Stop treating me like a child!"

Dr. DeMarco slammed his hands down on the table. "Then grow up! I know how you're feeling, because I felt the same way when I was your age! I know what you'd risk for her, but I can't let you. I have to at least try for your mother!"

Carmine's eyes narrowed. "Mom has nothing to do with this."

"Your mother has everything to do with it! She loved her!"

Carmine blanched at that, his eyes darting to Haven before going right back to his father. His mouth flew open, like words were trying to force themselves out, but there was nothing but silence.

"Your mother was too naïve," Dr. DeMarco continued, his voice somber. "She'd insist there was a way out of this where no one got hurt, but she'd be wrong. Someone's going to get hurt. I just hope it's neither of you."

The tension returned after the turn in conversation. Carmine's voice shook when he spoke. "Who did it?"

"Who did what?" Dr. DeMarco asked, not bothering to look up from his plate.

"You know what. Who killed her? We're clearing the air here. I wanna know who shot me."

"Their names don't matter."

"Then why did they do it?" he asked. "The least you can do is tell me what caused it all."

"There's no point, Carmine. What's done is done."

Carmine laughed dryly. "Don't give me that. I have a right to know whose fault it is."

"I don't know."

"What the fuck do you mean you don't know?"

"I mean I don't know who to blame!" Dr. DeMarco said. "Your mother—God, I loved your mother, but she went behind my back and did things she knew she shouldn't have done."

"What things?" Carmine asked. "Why did she do them?"

"Why did your mother do anything? She wanted to help."

"Help who?"

"It doesn't matter, Carmine."

"Yes, it does," he said. "I wanna know who was so important she'd risk everything for them. I wanna know who she'd throw her life away for!"

His anger frightened Haven. Dr. DeMarco stared at his son, his expression blank but gaze intense. Carmine's enraged expression softened as his brow furrowed, and he broke eye contact. Dropping his head down, he ran both hands through his hair and blinked a few times.

"You're too much like your mother, Carmine," Dr. DeMarco said quietly. "I can't let history repeat itself. Not anymore."

Carmine pushed his chair back, throwing his napkin down on the table and bolting from the room without waiting to be excused.

"Is this sit-down adjourned?" Dr. DeMarco asked. "I'd hate to walk out in the middle of it."

"Yeah, it's over," Dominic said. "It was a failure, anyway."

Dr. DeMarco stood, patting his son on the back. "We're walking away from it with our lives intact. We're not always that lucky in real sit-downs."

A flood of emotion rushed through Carmine as he locked himself in his bedroom. Horror. Shock. Love. Longing. Gratitude. Anger. Remorse. He kicked the bed frame as he walked by it, tugging his hair so hard his scalp throbbed. A ton of weight pressed against his chest, crushing him with the force of the truth.

It was Haven. She was the reason his life had been shattered.

He tossed things around, trying to release some pressure, his thoughts convoluted as he shifted blame, trying to find logic where none could be found. Everything was supposed to be easy for him, so why did it feel so fucking complicated?

He snatched the picture frame from his desk and stared at the photograph of his mom, a streak of Haven's blood smeared on the broken glass. Tears of resentment stung his eyes. Nothing had changed, but everything seemed different.

He threw the frame down and stepped into the bathroom, his gaze falling on his muddled reflection in the mirror. His bloodshot, sorrowful eyes reminded him of her, and the last thread of control he'd been holding on to snapped.

His fist connected with the mirror. It cracked, shards of glass flying as he pounded on it in a rage, not slowing down until it was obliterated, his reflection gone from sight. Emotion swirled through him again as he slid down to the floor, drawing his knees up to his chest. His anger gave way to despair as the tears started to fall. He surrendered to it, not having the willpower to fight anymore.

The anguish took over as he put his head down. He let himself slip under and wallow in the misery of what he'd lost.

Darkness cloaked the bathroom when Carmine resurfaced. He walked to the sink, glass crunching under his shoes. The cuts on his hand stung as he washed away the blood.

Grabbing a bottle of vodka from his stash, he went down the stairs, seeing the light on in his father's office. He didn't bother to knock before stepping inside, kicking the door closed behind him. Plopping down in the leather chair, Carmine took a drink of the liquor.

"I never wanted to tell you," Vincent said. "I thought it would be cruel. Your mother asked me to save her, but Frankie Antonelli wouldn't let the girl go. So I told her to drop it, but she didn't. She couldn't. I realized what she was doing too late. I was too late."

It all hit Carmine hard, and he blinked rapidly to ward off the tears. "Did she figure out the secret? Is that why they killed her?"

"She was on the right track, had even hired a private investigator, but I don't think she had enough time to put the pieces together. She would have, though. It was only a matter of time."

"And you blame Haven for it."

"It's not her fault," Vincent said. "She was just a child."

Carmine laughed bitterly. "You think I don't fucking know that? Of course it's not her fault. Doesn't mean you don't blame her anyway."

Vincent sighed. "Sometimes we suffer a loss and try to blame a single cause. Disproportionate responsibility is what they call it. Makes it easier to cope when you can channel your grief somewhere tangible so—"

"Cut the medical bullshit. It's a scapegoat."

"Scapegoat," Vincent repeated. "You're right. I've come to grips with it for the most part, which is why I felt it was safe to bring her here. But yes, I do still have moments where I slip back into that mind-set and wish she didn't exist."

Carmine could hear the disgust in his voice. "Was it Frankie who had her killed?"

Vincent nodded. "A few years ago, Sal told me Frankie panicked about your mother asking questions, said it was because the Antonellis' son fathered the girl. He didn't want his family's dirty little secret to come out. It's kill or be killed in our world, son."

Carmine could feel the vodka burning through his veins. He ran his hand through his hair, cringing at the pain. His father frowned. "You must've been pounding on something hard."

"Just had a small mishap with a mirror."

"You should go to the hospital for an X-ray."

Carmine held up his bottle of vodka. "I have all the medicine I need right here."

He took another swig of it as his father muttered. "I pity your liver, heading straight for cirrhosis at seventeen. It'll kill you if you keep it up."

"We all gotta die at some point, Dad," he said. "May as well go out for something I love."

He brought the bottle to his lips for a drink, and as the liquid flowed, it struck him what he'd said. That was exactly what his mom had done.

31

The sound of the bell rang through the brightly lit room. There was a collective shuffling as the students gathered their things. Carmine closed his science book awkwardly with his left hand, his right wrist in a bandage, sprained from the incident with the mirror in his bathroom.

"Don't forget to study, folks!" the biology teacher, Mr. Landon, called out. "Quiz tomorrow!"

Carmine grabbed his backpack before strolling to the teacher's desk. Mr. Landon erased the board and turned, caught off guard to see him. "Is there something I can help you with?"

"I wondered if you could explain mtDNA."

Mr. Landon pursed his lips. "We covered that at the beginning of the semester."

"I know, but I'm a bit confused."

Truthfully, he hadn't paid a damn bit of attention. Carmine always relied on luck and common sense to pass his classes, and most of the time he had just enough of both to get by.

"Well, unlike nuclear DNA, mtDNA isn't unique to us. We share it with our mothers."

"So my mtDNA would be the same as my mom's?"

"Yes, just as it's the same as her mother, and her mother's mother, and so on."

"But can men be traced through it? I mean, say mine was tested. Who would it match?"

"People related to your mother. Whatever your mtDNA, it came directly from the maternal side."

Carmine was stunned. He'd naturally assumed the test had something to do with Haven's father and his connections to the mob, never considering it could deal with Haven's mom.

"Is that all you needed?" Mr. Landon asked.

"Yeah." He hesitated. "Actually, no. Do you know anything about GPS?"

"What specifically do you want to know?"

"Is there a way to disable a signal?"

"Well, there are ways to block them," he said. "GPS chips need a line of sight to the satellite tracking them, so any big obstruction will keep the signal from getting out. Also, reflective materials like water or metal can cause the signal to bounce back."

"Is it the same for tracking chips in people?"

Mr. Landon snickered. "That's science fiction. Human tracking chips don't exist."

Bullshit. Just because the FDA hadn't approved them didn't mean they weren't out there. "Hypothetically speaking. If a person had one implanted under their skin, is there a way they could keep from being found?"

"They could stay in a windowless room or learn to breathe underwater. Otherwise, it would connect to the satellite as soon as they stepped into the open."

"So basically becoming a prisoner or drowning is the only way to disrupt it."

"I'd think so, yes. There's no way to say for certain, though, since it's completely hypothetical."

"Thanks."

He turned to leave when Mr. Landon called his name. "Your inquisitiveness gives me hope for you, so keep it up."

Carmine smiled to himself as he walked out. While his teacher was proud, his father would flip if he knew he'd asked those questions.

Vincent slowed the car as he neared the tall brick house, swinging a sharp right into the driveway. He parked behind the red convertible and climbed out, locking it and setting an alarm.

The neighborhood was decent, not too much crime in that part of town. He wasn't worried about any of the locals, as they'd have to be foolish to step foot onto the property uninvited. Everyone around there was well aware *la famiglia* controlled the streets, just as they knew Vincent's position of authority and the power he held. They respected him for it. Most of them didn't like him, but he didn't care about their personal feelings.

For the moment Vincent stepped into the streets, his emotions didn't exist anymore. He had no compassion, no sympathy, no empathy, and no remorse. He couldn't. And the longer he spent in Chicago, the colder he grew.

It was one of those warm spring nights that Maura had always enjoyed, where she could open all the windows and let the breeze blow through. He used to complain about how hot she let the house get. He'd been temperamental then, and many times he wished he could go back and erase his scathing words.

Del senno di poi son piene le fosse. Hindsight is 20/20.

He strolled to the front door and rang the doorbell before rolling up the sleeves of his light blue button-up shirt. The sound of high heels echoed inside before the door opened. The woman stood before him, a smile on her shiny red lips. "Hello, Vincent. It's been a while."

She moved out of the way to let him pass. He wordlessly made his way to the front room and took a seat on her black leather couch. She joined him, holding a glass of red wine. He took it, bringing the glass to his nose and inhaling, taking in the aroma. Maura always liked red wine.

"So, how long are you in town for this time?" she asked, taking a sip of her drink, while he just held his. He didn't drink anymore, hadn't for a long time.

"Until I'm dismissed."

She wasn't naïve to the lifestyle. She'd been born into it, a *Principessa della Mafia*. She knew he couldn't talk about what he did, so conversation between them was kept to a minimum—no misleading and certainly no misconceptions.

"Are you hungry?" she asked. He gazed at her, his eyes roaming her body, admiring her snug black dress and thigh highs. Her skin was tanned, her hair dark brown, her eyes an odd shade of hazel with tiny flecks of green in them. The green reminded him of the eyes he had gazed into every night for years.

He looked away from her. "Sure."

They ate dinner while she talked and finished off the bottle of wine. Vincent just listened and nodded at the right times. Afterward, he strolled to the window and gazed out as she cleaned up, the stars and moon shining brightly above her enclosed backyard.

The clicking of heels approached, the sound stopping right behind him as her reflection greeted him in the window. She smiled mischievously, running her hands up his back. She rubbed his shoulders, massaging them firmly. "You're always tense, Vincent."

He let out a soft sigh. "That's why I come to you. You know what I need."

She hummed in response as she ran her hands under his shirt, her manicured fingernails lightly scraping his skin. Maura never had fingernails, always chewed them down to little stubs—sometimes so much her fingers bled.

She undid his buttons, her lips pressing lightly against the nape of his neck. Her breath was warm, her kiss sticky from the color on her lips. "I think I know what you need now."

Vincent said nothing as he redressed an hour later.

It was moments like these, when Vincent should feel at ease, that he often felt the full weight of the world he lived in pressing against his chest. If he could go back, he would change so much, but all he could do was go forward and make sure that what had happened to him didn't happen to Carmine. He could make sure that twenty years from now, his son wasn't the one fucking nameless women who meant nothing, trying to keep a grip when all he really wanted was to let go.

The clock on the car's dash read midnight when Vincent backed out of the driveway and started toward Highway 290. He drove for thirty minutes before he pulled onto the long winding path that cut through the hillside, driving through the front gate: Mount Carmel Cemetery.

He turned off the car and climbed out, walking through the grass, past the graves of some of those who had lived his life and died. The Capones were buried in this section, dozens of other *Mafiosi* scattered throughout the cemetery. He'd be there someday too, buried in the plot beside his wife.

His steps faltered as he spotted the gravestone, his chest constricting. Kneeling in front of it, he ran his hand along the name on the cold marble marker.

Maura DeMarco

April 1965–October 1996

"Ama, ridi, sogna—e vai dormire"

"My sweet Maura," he said. "I know it has been months, but I haven't felt like I deserved to visit you. How disappointed you must be."

He sat down in the grass, eyeing the sentence that aligned the bottom. "*Ama, ridi, sogna—e vai dormire,*" he said, his voice a strangled whisper in the darkness. "'Love, laugh, dream, and go to sleep.' That was how you lived your life, and I'm trying to follow your lead. I got her, you know. I finally got her for you, and you're not here for it."

He laughed cynically as tears slipped from the corner of his eyes. "You were probably angry at me when I locked her in her room, as upset as you must've been that day all those years ago when I . . . I . . ." He trailed off. "You know what I almost did, what I tried to do that night . . . the night I killed them. I know you were watching, and you were the one who stopped me. Even dead, you're still saving her. I could imagine you standing there with your forehead wrinkled—how you used to look when you got mad. I hated disappointing you, but what I wouldn't give to see that face again."

He paused, shaking his head. "The girl's okay, I guess. We all are for now. I'm trying to figure out how to keep us that way. She's growing and coming into her own. It reminds me of you, and that's harder than you could imagine."

He wiped his eyes with the back of his hand, brushing away the tears as he sat quietly, savoring the silence. Seeing her name, something tangible to remind him she had been real, soothed his frazzled nerves, and for the moment, he almost felt at peace.

After a few minutes, he stood and brushed the grass off of his pants. "I won't stay gone so long next time. I love you."

He walked away, heading across the cemetery to his car. The tears came to a stop, his heart growing numb on the drive back to Chicago.

By the time he crossed into the city limits, he felt cold again.

32

Haven stood in the doorway to the bedroom, quietly watching Carmine as he did his homework. He sat at his desk with his head in the palm of his left hand, staring intently at a laptop. He hadn't sensed her presence, or if he did, he chose not to acknowledge her.

Carmine groaned. "What does the Greek alphabet have to do with math?"

She blurted out the answer. "Pi?"

He jumped at the sound of her voice and swung around. "Did you just ask if I wanted pie?"

"No, Pi is a part of the Greek alphabet, and it's also a math, uh, thingy."

He stared at her for a moment before what she said registered. "Well, thank Alex Trebek for that. You could probably do my damn work and save me a lot of aggravation, you know."

She blushed. "But if I did it, how would you learn?"

"I don't see myself ever needing to know this shit," he said, shaking his head. "Anyway, is there something you needed?"

"I'm supposed to go to Dia's, remember?"

She wasn't sure how he'd forgotten, since it was his idea in the first place. "Oh, yeah, right." He grabbed his keys off his desk. She expected him to stand so they could leave, but instead he held them out to her.

She stared at the keys. "Aren't you going to drive me?"

"You know how to drive," he said, jingling them. "I don't have time to play taxi, *tesoro*. I have a ton of homework to get done and errands to run."

Her brow furrowed. "How will you run errands if you don't have your car?"

"I'm going with Dom," he said. "You remember how to get to Dia's, right? It's a straight shot. I dropped you off there when you got your dress."

"Uh, yes, but . . ."

"And stop by the store on your way home and grab some Coke for me, will you? It's just the next street over. There should be some cash in the glove box."

She gaped at him. "But . . . your car. I can't drive it."

He sighed exasperatedly. "Why not?"

"Because I've only ever driven Dr. DeMarco's, and that's when you were with me."

"Mine drives like his does. And if it makes it easier, pretend I'm in the passenger seat. Just curse a few times. It'll feel like I'm there."

He turned around, subject closed.

It was the middle of May, and today was Durante High School's prom. Three weeks before Carmine had sprung it on her, casually telling her she needed to pick out a dress. Dia offered to take her shopping a few days later, and Haven got a blue one with dark golden trim.

The past few weeks had been a confusing time for Haven. There were highs and lows, the changes sometimes so abrupt that it was impossible to brace for it. The anticipation and excitement was always there, brewing underneath the surface, but there was also fear—a fear of the unknown, a fear of the plunges.

It wasn't always bad. Carmine lost his temper quite a bit, but there were also moments, such as that one in his bedroom, when he did something uncharacteristic of the boy she'd come to know. He was protective of his car, yet he had handed her the keys without a thought even though she didn't have a license.

————

The Harper family lived in a one-story tan house in the center of town, modest but big enough for the four of them. Dia and Tess shared a bedroom, the close quarters often reason for their sisterly bickering. Haven saw proof of it as soon as she arrived, a piece of duct tape on the carpet running straight down the center of the room, cutting it in half. The left was clean and decorated with shades of pink and posters of movie stars, while the right half was in disarray, hundreds of photographs covering the wall.

"Have a seat," Dia said, motioning toward a chair in front of a desk. Haven sat on the edge of it and glanced around at the mess, fighting off the urge to clean for her. "So, are you excited?"

"Of course I am," Haven said, although her anxiety overshadowed her excitement.

Dia eyed Haven peculiarly as she fiddled with her hair, running her fingers through the wild locks. "Nervous, huh? Your answer sounded way too rehearsed."

"I am excited," she said. "I've just never been to a dance before."

"Me, either," Dia said. "The only reason I'm going to this one is because I have to cover it for the yearbook. Otherwise, I'd stay home."

"You don't have a date?"

She shook her head. "The administration would have an aneurysm if I brought someone."

"Why?"

Dia looked at her with surprise. "Not everyone is accepting."

"Why wouldn't they accept you?"

"I'm not into boys," Dia said, treading carefully with her words. "No one's told you that?"

"Well, Carmine said he didn't have the right equipment for you." Haven turned bright red when what he'd meant sank in. "Oh, he means—"

"No dick for Dia!"

Haven glanced at the doorway as the voice interrupted. Tess strolled into the room, tossing a garment bag on her bed and unzipping it to expose a bloodred dress.

Dia rolled her eyes. "Classy."

"I'm just speaking the truth," Tess said, pulling off her shirt. Haven gaped at her as she stripped out of her clothes. Tess noticed her expression and laughed, standing in front of her in a bra and panties. "I'm not ashamed."

Dia laughed. "She's not modest, either."

Tess shrugged, not arguing against that. She shimmied into her dress before grabbing a pair of high heels from the closet and slipping them on. Strolling over to her dresser, she gazed at her reflection in the vanity mirror and smoothed her hair before applying some red lipstick. She did it so casually, so quickly, so fluidly. Haven watched with admiration.

Dia continued to play around with her hair, yanking and tugging it every which way, but Haven had no idea what she was trying to do. The same thought ran through Tess's mind because she turned around, groaning. "Dia, what are you doing to the poor girl's head?"

"I'm trying to French braid it."

"French braid? What is she, twelve?"

Tess grabbed a flat iron and bumped her sister out of the way as she plugged it in. Shrugging, Dia plopped down on the bed as Tess undid the sloppy braid. Once the flat iron was warm, she straightened Haven's hair, smoothing the waves that had never before been so tame. Tess pulled the top half back, securing it with a clip, before unplugging the flat iron and going back to her side of the room.

Dia showed Haven to the bathroom to put on her dress. Haven slipped into it and glanced in the mirror, not recognizing the girl staring back. Her hair was bone straight and shiny under the glow of the light. The dress hugged her in all the right places, accentuating her newfound curves.

Curves. She pinched her hips with awe, wondering where they had come from and how she hadn't noticed them before.

She headed to the bedroom, pausing near the doorway. Tess gazed in her mirror again, applying another coat of lipstick, while Dia slipped on a pair of black combat boots.

"Don't you have to get dressed?" Haven asked Dia as she dropped a pair of gold flats in front of her.

"I am dressed."

Haven put on the shoes as she surveyed Dia's clothes. She had on a black skirt and a vibrant blue tank top with rainbow-striped tights. "You are?"

"She is," Tess said. "To Dia, that's dressed up."

The hairs on the back of Haven's neck stood on end the moment she stepped into the grocery store alone, the feeling of being watched overwhelming. Self-consciously, she put her head down and walked swiftly to the soda aisle. Bending down to grab a twelve-pack of Coke, her skin prickled as a presence approached.

"What do you call cheese that doesn't belong to you?"

"I'm not sure, Nicholas." She picked up the soda and turned to face him, stunned to see him wearing a black suit. It was the first time she had seen him without his flip-flops and baseball cap.

"Nacho cheese." He grinned. "Get it, nacho, not yo'? Not yo' cheese, since it isn't yours?"

The moment it clicked, she shook her head. "That's cheesy."

He laughed at her attempt at humor. "Funny. My kind of girl."

She blushed. "Thank you. I see you're dressed up."

"Of course I am. It's prom."

"You're going to the dance? You don't go to school here, do you?"

"Neither do you."

"But I have someone to go with."

He sighed dramatically. "Yeah, well, so do I. I may not be a pretty boy like Carmine, but I can still pull my fair share of ladies. Speaking of your boyfriend . . ."

"Don't start."

He held his hands up defensively. "Hey, I was just going to say I'm surprised he's letting you in public by yourself."

"Why wouldn't he? I can go to a store alone."

"Can you?" The seriousness to his voice sent her nerves flaring. Could she? Considering this was her first time doing it, she had a hard time answering yes.

"Sure," she said, eyeing him suspiciously. Her heart pounded furiously in her chest. He couldn't know the truth. Carmine would have warned her.

"That's nice," he said. "You know, you have a fascinating accent."

She was taken aback by the shift in conversation. "I have an accent? I think you do."

He laughed. "I sound like everyone else around here, but I've never heard an accent like yours. Where did you grow up?"

"California."

"What parts?"

She hesitated. "The desert."

He nodded. "No wonder I've never heard it. You're the first native Californian I've met. You were born there, right?"

She nodded, his line of questioning baffling her.

"Well, Haven, since I was wrong and you can go out by yourself, you should come visit me sometime."

Her eyes narrowed at the invitation. "Why are you interested?"

"You seem like a nice girl," he said. "There's no harm in us being friends."

"Do you want to be friends because you want to get to know me, or do you want to be friends because it'll upset Carmine? Because I can't be friends with someone who wants to hurt him."

She spouted off the words, not comprehending what she was saying until it was already past her lips and lingering in the air between them.

"I'm not that petty of a person," he said.

"How am I supposed to know?"

"You'd have to trust me."

"I can't," she said. "I don't trust people."

"But you trust him?"

"I do," she said, "and nothing you say will change that."

"Fine, but that doesn't mean you can't trust me, too."

She stared at him. Could she trust him? "I should go."

She walked away, pausing briefly when he called out to her. "Haven? You look beautiful. Carmine may be an asshole, but he's a lucky asshole."

She smiled. "Thank you, but I think I'm the lucky one."

After paying for the soda, Haven drove back to the DeMarcos' house to find a new shiny sports car parked out front. As she opened the front door, she was about to call out for Carmine when there was a bang in the kitchen. "What fucking took you so long?"

She sighed, not bothering with an answer. If he was in a bad mood, nothing would change it.

She paused in the doorway to the kitchen, stunned at the sight of him. He had on a black suit with a blue tie and a pair of black Nikes. Carmine turned to her, his eyes instantly raking down her body as she set the soda on the counter and handed one of the cans of Coke to him. He took it carefully, his eyes never leaving her.

She turned to leave the room, her nerves getting the best of her, but Carmine grabbed her arm to stop her. "You're breathtaking."

His eyes flickered to her mouth, and he kissed her sweetly. She parted her lips, welcoming him to deepen it, but instead he pulled away. It had become a common occurrence the past few weeks, a consequence of his recent temperament.

He turned his back to her to fill a glass with ice as she headed for the family room, sitting on the couch and folding her hands in her lap to wait. Carmine strolled in after a minute and set his glass down on the table, a plastic container in his other hand. He pulled a blue and gold flower out of it and slipped it on her wrist. "It's a corsage."

"It's beautiful," she said, gazing at it.

The front door to the house opened, and Dr. DeMarco walked in. "That's a nice car outside," he said right away, forgoing any type of greeting.

Carmine sighed. "Don't worry—I rented it. It'll go back to-morrow."

Dominic and Tess showed up a few minutes later, followed by a disgruntled Dia. They huddled outside to take some pictures. After a few minutes of cameras flashing, Carmine grabbed Haven's hand and pulled her away. He hesitated at his car, scanning it for damage, before heading toward the rental. "I've always wanted a Vanquish. I feel like James Bond driving this motherfucker."

"James Bond?"

"Yeah, you know—007, the secret agent?" She shook her head, and he sighed. "It's a movie."

"Sorry," she said. "I've never seen it."

"It doesn't matter," he said, motioning for her to get in. She wanted to believe him, but his frustrated expression told a differ-ent story.

The drive to the restaurant was quiet as Haven's nerves ran amuck. After about thirty minutes, she couldn't take the silence anymore and attempted conversation. "This is a pretty car. You couldn't get one of these instead of yours?"

He laughed dryly. "This costs six times more than my Mazda. There's no way my father would fork over a quarter-million dollars for a car. The only thing he'd spend that much on is a house." He paused. "Or you, maybe. Don't know how much he paid for you."

His words stung. She blinked a few times, willing herself not to let her hurt show as she turned to stare out the window.

"And I guess it's pretty, if you can call a car pretty."

Haven didn't speak the rest of the drive.

They arrived at the restaurant, and Carmine led her inside to join the others. He occasionally said something that rubbed her the wrong way while they ate, but someone would diffuse the situation before it spiraled. Haven wasn't fond of this side of Carmine. It was a part of him she wasn't well acquainted with . . . a part of him she didn't want to know.

The waitress came by to make sure they had everything they needed, her eyes lingering on Carmine longer than necessary. He ignored her like he usually did, but Tess didn't let it slide. "She could see your girlfriend sitting right beside you. Doesn't she have any self-respect?"

Carmine shrugged. "Bitches can't help it."

Tess glared at him, his response not what she wanted to hear. "What the hell's got into you?"

Carmine's brow furrowed. "What are you talking about?"

"Your attitude, that's what. It's a damn shame, too. I almost liked you for a while."

"Yeah, well, I never fucking liked you."

Haven tensed at the hostility as Dominic hit the table with his fist. "Enough! I don't know what your problem is, Carmine, but you need to figure it out. I'm *this* close to laying your ass out."

Carmine glared at his brother. "What have I done?"

"Do you not hear yourself? You're acting more and more like the old you."

"I am not," Carmine said.

"Yes, you are," Dominic said. "And I'm telling you now—fix it. Haven deserves better than the way you've been treating her."

Haven watched Carmine warily as he stared at his brother. The tension at the table was thick, and she started to panic. "I, uh . . . I need to go to the restroom."

She stood, and Dia jumped to her feet to show her where it was. She breathed a sigh of relief once she was alone and stayed there until she calmed down. There was a tap on the door, and she expected to see Dia still waiting, but instead came face-to-face with Carmine.

"Can we talk, *tesoro*?" She nodded and followed him outside to the car. Carmine put the key into the ignition. "I didn't realize I was being such an asshole. I've had a lot on my mind."

"Do you want to talk about it?"

He sighed, drumming his fingers against the steering wheel. "Not really. That probably makes me a bigger asshole, but I just . . . can we start over? You finally get a chance to experience teenage shit, and I'm fucking it up. I should be groveling at your feet, thanking you for giving me this chance. You shouldn't love me, but you do, and you don't know how thankful I am for that, how much I appreciate having you in my life."

She gazed at him with surprise. It was the nicest thing he had said in a while . . . possibly ever. "I'm glad I have you, too."

"Good," he said, starting the car as Haven put on her seatbelt. "And I'm sorry about the Nikes."

"What about them?"

"Tess said they give the impression I don't care, but I do. I just really like my Nikes."

"I like them, too."

He looked at her with the first genuine smile she'd seen grace his lips all evening.

The school gymnasium was decorated in white and gold, sparkling lights strung up all over the ceiling. A balloon archway greeted them inside, streamers and glitter covering everything. Carmine grimaced at the cheap decorations, while Haven was completely mesmerized. "It's pretty," she said, her words barely audible above the thumping bass of the song.

He chuckled at her enthusiasm. "Do you wanna dance?"

"I, uh . . ." She surveyed the crowd on the dance floor. "I've never danced."

"Not true," he said, pulling her in front of him with his hands on her hips. "We danced on Halloween."

"That's different," she said. "You kind of just swung me in circles, and nobody was watching."

"No one's watching now." He was lying. Eyes focused on them from all over the gym. "Besides, the only way to learn how to dance is by dancing, and I think I'm getting better at this teaching gig."

They stopped along the edge of the crowd, and he pulled her against him, swaying them to the music. He leaned down with his lips beside her ear and sang along, his voice relaxing her.

Carmine moved her hips to the beat until she was able to keep rhythm on her own. She saw the curious onlookers watching, but Carmine's warmth made her feel safe. They danced for a few songs before he led her over toward a table, grabbing two plastic cups and pouring punch in them.

They mingled with his classmates for a bit. Haven caught sight of Nicholas after a while with Lisa clinging to his arm. She avoided eye contact with him, focusing her attention on Carmine, but she could feel his gaze from across the room.

The punch eventually caught up to her, and she excused herself to use the restroom. She was washing her hands when the door opened, hostility filling the confined space as Lisa walked in. There was no way to leave without walking past her, so Haven shut off the water and took a deep breath. After drying her hands, she took a few steps in her direction.

"Excuse me," she said, hoping she would let her go without trouble, but Lisa didn't move an inch. "I'd like to leave."

"I'd like you to leave too," Lisa said. "Leave town, and leave Carmine alone."

The way Lisa leered, getting pleasure from her pain, reminded Haven of Katrina and all the times she had kicked her when she was already down. There hadn't been anything she could do about it then, but she didn't have to take it anymore. Not here, not now.

She wasn't going to hand over control to people who wanted nothing more than for her to hurt.

"I said excuse me." Haven took another step forward. Lisa didn't move, so Haven bumped into her and grabbed the door. She swung it open and stepped out as Lisa gripped her shoulder. Haven turned around in enough time to see her make a fist.

Before Lisa could attack, arms jerked Haven away, and Nicholas absorbed the force of the punch in his chest. "Whoa, Laila Ali, watch where you're swinging!"

Lisa sneered at him. "What did you call me?"

"She's a boxer," Haven said. "Muhammad Ali's daughter."

"Why are you talking?" Lisa asked, taking a step toward her. "Nobody asked you."

"Hey now." Nicholas tried to come between them, but he wasn't quick enough. Lisa gripped Haven's arm, tearing her corsage off and hurling it onto the floor. Nicholas intervened again, and Lisa stomped away as he picked up Haven's flower.

She took it carefully as he smiled, but something was off about his expression, something that spiked Haven's anxiety. "Is something wrong?"

"I've known the DeMarcos for a long time, you know," he said. "We used to be close, and when you spend a lot of time with people, you learn things about them. Like . . . some of the stuff their family does."

Her brow furrowed. "I don't know what you're talking about."

"I'm not an idiot, Haven," he said, his voice low. "I have no intention of dying any time soon, that's for sure. I know how to keep my mouth shut, but I can't hold it in anymore. You told me you were from California, when not long ago Carmine said you were from Chicago. And they don't just invite people to live with them. They don't let anyone get close unless they can control them some way, and it freaks me out what that means for you."

She felt queasy. "What do you mean?"

"I mean you aren't some friend of the family. I think you had no choice whether you came here."

"I had a choice," she said, remembering Dr. DeMarco's words that first day. "We always have a choice."

"Look, it's not like I can do anything. I'm just a kid, and I don't know your situation. For all I know, you could've been kidnapped and are being held for ransom, or, hell, maybe you're in hiding. I don't know, but that doesn't mean I don't feel bad knowing you might be trapped."

She was nervous to talk about it in public. "They're nice to me."

"I'm sure they are, but that doesn't make it right, and it makes me sick that Carmine's taking advantage of you."

Her fingernails dug into her palms as she tried to keep from reacting. "Carmine loves me."

"I have a hard time believing he loves anyone."

"I love him."

"Let me guess, he's the first person to treat you that way? He smiles at you and whispers sweet nothings in your ear? He speaks Italian and makes you swoon? Yeah, he did that to every girl in this building at some point. That's who he is."

"Nothing's going to change my mind."

"Fine, but like I said, that doesn't mean we can't be friends. If you need to talk, I'm around."

"Why do you care so much?"

"Because somebody should."

She opened her mouth to tell him Carmine cared, but before she could, Carmine's seething voice rang out behind them. "Leave her alone!"

"Nicholas helped me," Haven said right away, not wanting him to get the wrong idea.

Carmine wrapped his arm around her waist as he glared at Nicholas. "Helped you with what?"

"Lisa cornered her, so I did what any man would do," Nicholas said. "Actually, most would've watched two chicks going at it, but

I didn't want Lisa to get her ass whipped at prom. I'm hoping for a little action tonight."

Carmine looked at her. "Lisa tried to fight with you? Again?"

"I see it's not a one-time occurrence," Nicholas said.

Haven held up her corsage. "She broke my flower."

He took it from her and cursed under his breath, pulling her away when Nicholas's voice called out. "Knock, knock."

Feeling guilty, she looked at him once more. "Who's there?"

Carmine stopped moving, not amused.

"Tank," Nicholas said.

"Tank who?" She got it the moment the words rolled from her lips. Tank who . . . Thank you.

Nicholas smiled. "You're welcome, Haven."

Soft music played and people paired up to dance as Carmine put his hands on Haven's hips, drawing her closer. "You okay, *tesoro*? She didn't hurt you, did she?"

Wrapping her arms around his neck, she gazed at him. "No, Nicholas stopped her."

"Nicholas," Carmine sneered under his breath, his eyes darting across the room to where Haven knew he still stood. "He's always involving himself in shit."

"I'm grateful for it," Haven said. "Lisa punched him instead of me."

Those words sparked a smile on Carmine's face. "Good."

Haven rolled her eyes as Carmine licked his lips, kissing her slowly as they swayed to the music. Love swelled inside of her. This was her Carmine, the one who wasn't afraid to let his guard down and let her inside. In the middle of a crowded room, no one existed but them. He was all she saw, all she was aware of—his face, his smell, his warmth, his love.

The emotion took control of her as tears threatened to spill over. The song wound down, and the two of them stood in the center of the dance floor, staring at each other. "Can we . . . ?"

"Yeah, let's go home."

Carmine was all over Haven the moment they stepped foot onto the third floor of the house. His lips captured hers in a fiery kiss as he pulled her tightly against him. It had been a while since he had kissed her this way, as if he needed to siphon the air from her lungs to breathe.

"Carmine, we should . . ." She shivered when his lips moved to her neck. ". . . I think we really should . . ." She let out a whimper as he nipped at her skin with his teeth. ". . . It's just that . . ."

She didn't know what she was saying, what she meant, why she was even trying to talk. She couldn't think straight. Every cell in her body yearned for him, wildly rejoicing at the feel of his hands on her again, yet the words kept spilling out on their own.

"Maybe we should just, you know . . ."

Carmine groaned, a mixture of desire and frustration. "I need you."

That was all she had to hear. His declaration took every hesitant word that was on the tip of her tongue and replaced them with much different ones. "I need you, too."

"It's been too long," he whispered as they stumbled through the library, toward the bedroom. "I need to feel you again. I need to be with you, on top of you. Fuck, I need to be inside of you."

A feral groan vibrated her chest at those words, a sound she never realized she was capable of making. They barely had time to get inside the bedroom and shut the door before they were tearing at each other's clothes. She dropped her dress to the floor, stepping out of it, as Carmine kicked off his shoes. They flung fabric across the room, the glow of the moon filtering through the window the only light they had to see. Carmine slapped at the wall, looking for the light switch, but gave up with a resigned grunt in a matter of seconds.

Haven let out a yelp of surprise when he clutched her thighs and quickly pulled her up. Her legs wrapped around his waist as he pressed into her, sending a shiver through the core of her body, seizing her muscles. She clung to his neck, kissing him feverishly as he stumbled a few steps, tripping over her discarded shoes.

She pulled back from his lips. "Don't drop me."

"Never," he said breathlessly the same moment his grip slipped. He dropped her onto the mattress and she laughed as she bounced. "Never, huh?"

"I did that shit on purpose, *tesoro*," he said playfully, chuckling as he climbed over her.

Their bodies fit together easily, perfectly, like they had always belonged that way. It was lightning, and thunder, and electricity, as the two souls merged as one. All was forgotten as they gave in to their raw needs, each stroke longer, deeper, harder, their moans and grunts and cries louder and louder.

They stilled their movements when they had nothing more to give, covered in sweat and breathing heavily. Haven lay on top of him, her head on his bare chest as she tried to calm her wildly beating heart. She could feel Carmine's beneath her, his pulse racing twice its normal speed.

He caressed her side and thigh, drawing patterns on her skin with his fingertips. She wondered what he was thinking, what he was drawing, but part of her was afraid to ask.

"I'm sorry," he said eventually. "I've been holding back, and that's not fair to you. I know I'm a pain in the ass, but you're the only good thing I have."

"You shouldn't apologize," she said. He asked her to forgive him for something she had been doing, too. He gave her everything, had taken her to his prom, and she had gotten to wear a pretty dress and dance with a devastatingly handsome boy. It was her dream, a dream she had never thought possible. She felt inadequate sometimes, and she knew it was her insecurities eating away at her. But now . . . now she truly felt she didn't. "Carmine, I have to tell you something."

His fingertips stilled midpattern on her stomach. "Huh?"

"I think Nicholas knows about me."

Carmine sat up quickly. "What are you talking about?"

"He knows I'm a . . . slave."

His eyes darkened. "Did he fucking call you that?"

"No, he just knows—or he suspects—I'm not here willingly."

"How?"

"I don't know. He said he wanted to be friends, because he thought I could use one."

"He wants to be friends? Yeah, right. That motherfucker wants what I have. He wants to take everything from me! Don't you see that?"

She shrugged. Honestly, she wasn't sure anymore.

———

The past month had been one of the most complicated of Carmine's life, his love and anger at odds with each other. An epic battle brewed inside him, different sides fighting for control of his heart and mind. Everything pushed him over the edge, and what Haven had told him wasn't helping him remain calm.

After she was asleep, he threw on some clothes and headed downstairs. The light was on in his father's office so he tentatively knocked on the door, waiting a moment before opening it. Vincent looked at him from behind his desk. "You're the last person I expected to see."

"Why?" he asked, sitting in the chair across from him.

"Because you knocked. That's not like you."

"Yeah, well, I don't know myself anymore, so I guess I'm capable of anything at this point."

He nodded. "Are you dealing okay?"

"I'm over that shit."

"I don't believe that for a second," Vincent said. "It took me years to come to grips with it."

"Well, I don't have years. I don't even wanna think about it, much less talk about it."

"Okay, then." Vincent eyed him peculiarly. "Is there another reason you came down here?"

"Yeah, it's about tonight—"

"How was prom? Did you have a good time?"

Carmine groaned, irritated he cut him off. "It was fucking peachy, Dad. Now can I finish?"

Vincent waved him on.

"We ran into Nicholas, and he said something. He said he knew the truth about Haven."

Carmine watched as his father's expression shifted, a blank mask overcoming his face. Each second of silence grated on his nerves. Why was he just sitting there?

"It's possible he knows more than he should."

Carmine sat forward. "My enemy knows the truth, and you didn't think to tell me?"

"He's not your enemy, Carmine. I know what enemies are. I know the threats they pose. Nicholas knows no more than Dia or Tess. I can't kill him any more than I could kill those girls. Or is that what you're suggesting—wiping out everyone who might know? That's not how you get a clean slate with her, son. You can't run from the truth."

"But how can he be trusted when he's betrayed me before?"

"Because if he was going to tell, he would've by now," Vincent said. "I'm not going to murder a seventeen-year-old kid because you think it'll make you feel better. You'll deal with the guilt of his death for the rest of your life, and I have enough people to worry about right now."

Carmine stared at his father. "Like *him*?"

"Yes. *Him*."

"So you haven't figured out how to deal with *him*?"

"I'm just delaying the inevitable, hoping when the time comes I do the right thing . . . whatever that may be."

"You know, I could probably guess who—"

"Don't even go down that path, Carmine Marcello," he said. "I'm not going to tell you again."

Carmine nodded, but there was no way he could stop thinking about it. "There are only so many people you'd be afraid of, though."

Vincent lost his cool and stood, shoving his chair back and pointing at the door. "Get out."

Carmine begrudgingly headed to the third floor and collided with Haven at the top of the stairs. "Whoa! Where are you going?"

"I didn't know where you went," she said.

"Where I've been doesn't matter. All that matters is where I am now." He scanned her. She had on a pair of his flannel pants, rolled up to stay on, and his football shirt—the same thing she'd worn that first day in the kitchen. "You know, you look good in my clothes, but how about we go take them back off?"

She gasped as he pulled her to his room. "Well, good morning."

"Yeah, it's definitely about to be a good morning," he said playfully. "And a good afternoon. And a good evening, if I'm lucky."

They made love quietly on and off all afternoon, careful not to be overheard. She sprawled out on the bed beside him after a while, sleeping peacefully on her stomach. The blanket barely covered her bottom half, leaving her back exposed. He stared at her skin, wishing she'd never gotten any of those marks. He wished she'd never had to experience pain, and he hated those fucking scars. But on the other hand, they were a part of her, and to him, there was nothing ugly about her.

She deserved more than she had, and Carmine couldn't wait to give it to her. To give her a real life where she was free. Free of her imaginary chains, free of heartache, free of danger. Just . . . free.

He traced the word with his finger over her scarred back. *Free.* It was all that mattered to him.

33

"You're going to die."

Those four words cracked the silence that had enveloped the room. Vincent fought the urge to balk, instead keeping his calm disposition. It wasn't like it was something he hadn't already thought to himself dozens of times, but hearing it verbalized in that cold, emotionless voice made it real.

He looked in the direction the words had come from and met Corrado's piercing eyes, so dark Vincent couldn't differentiate between the pupil and the iris. They were the same eyes dozens had looked into during their last moments on earth, eyes that could break the hardest of men. They were the eyes of a murderer, a man who could reach inside his coat, pull out his .22-caliber Ruger Mark II pistol, and put a bullet in Vincent before he knew what was happening. More importantly, they were the eyes of a man who wouldn't hesitate to do it if necessary.

"I know," Vincent said, keeping his voice even despite his anxiety.

It was the first of June, and tomorrow Dominic would graduate from high school. Out of everything Vincent had done in life, Dominic felt like his greatest accomplishment. Just the fact that he had survived intact and was setting off on a path that didn't resemble the one he had walked down at his age made Vincent feel as if he had done something right. Here was something he hadn't destroyed, someone's life he hadn't ruined.

But his pride was overshadowed by another event, one that had forced him to break his silence. In two short days, Carmine would turn eighteen. His youngest son would be emancipated in the eyes of the law and outside forces were threatening to take his life away. The Don wanted the *Principe*, a puppet he could mold into a brutal, calculating soldier. Sal wasn't above manipulation, and Vincent was afraid of what he would do to get his hands on Carmine.

Corrado and Celia had flown in for Dominic's graduation and to celebrate Carmine's birthday. The kids had gotten up before dawn to head to Asheville for the afternoon, and Celia was upstairs, purposely giving the two men some space.

"She doesn't look like a *Principessa*," Corrado said.

"I had the same thought."

"But you're positive of it."

"Absolutely."

"I always suspected there was more to that girl," Corrado said. "It never made sense that Frankie would put a hit out on your wife because she was interested in his granddaughter. Sure, he treated the girl horribly, but it wasn't worth going to extreme measures to cover up. But this . . . this is worth killing over."

Vincent cringed. Corrado noticed his reaction and clarified. "Not saying she should've died. I still, to this day, wish I would've done more, but I never thought Antonelli could be so heinous."

"None of us did."

Corrado looked away from him. "It's hard to believe she's one of our own. It's surreal to discover, after all of these years, the little slave girl is Joseph and Federica's granddaughter. Their baby survived and ended up in Antonelli's care. What are the odds they'd be related to . . . ?"

"Salvatore," Vincent said.

"He has surviving family, after all."

So many people had been lost in the chaos of the '70s, a lot of bodies never recovered. It started with one man making a spectacle of the lifestyle and escalated to a clash that spread throughout the country. It became about revenge and bloodshed, men going against everything the organizations stood for in the name of vengeance. The same families that had sworn to protect women and children were so blinded by hatred they took it out on the innocent.

Joseph Russo had been discovered buried in a cornfield years later. Antonio sent men out looking for Federica, hoping she had gone undercover with their baby. But a bundle had been dropped off on his doorstep one night, human bones wrapped in a pink baby blanket. There were no DNA tests in those days, but everyone believed it then—Federica and the baby were dead.

But they'd been wrong. The baby had survived, going by the name Miranda, living right under their noses their entire time.

"I knew you were hiding something, but I never imagined it would be this," Corrado said. "The odds of that woman turning out to be Sal's dead niece are about as likely as Jimmy Hoffa showing up tomorrow on the corner of Lincoln Avenue and Orchard Street."

"I'm inclined to believe anything's possible now."

"True," Corrado said. "They disappeared around the same time. I'll be on the lookout for Hoffa whenever I'm in the neighborhood."

His tone was so serious Vincent couldn't be sure if he was joking or not. He usually couldn't with Corrado and didn't dare laugh either way.

"So whoever killed them gave the baby to the Antonellis, and Frankie took the child knowing who she was. He ordered the wife of a fellow *Mafioso* murdered to retain his secret, because he knew what he'd done would be an automatic death sentence," Corrado said, summing up in a few seconds what had taken Vincent an hour to stumble through.

"As it would be for me."

"Yes."

"You understand why I've done what I've done, right?" Vincent asked. "You understand why I couldn't turn the girl over to him?"

"We wouldn't still be sitting here if some part of me didn't," Corrado said. "The fallout would be disastrous. Not only would you be killed on principle, but her life would also be in danger. Squint's set upon inheriting the dynasty, banking on the fact that he's the closest thing the Don has left to a relative. Carmine's in enough danger because of Sal's interest in him. Adding the girl to the equation would jeopardize them both."

"Not to mention what it would mean for the organization," Vincent said. "They never determined who killed Joseph and Federica, or what they did with her body. Sal would go on a rampage, and we have enough problems right now."

"He'd start another war," Corrado said. "We'd all be in danger."

"I know. And I'm not worried about myself. I just don't want the kids to be taken down by this."

"So you want the *Principe* and the *Principessa* to ride off into the sunset and live happily ever after? That's not asking for too much, right?" he asked, his voice mocking. "I hate to break it to you, but this is the real world, Vincent. I have a greater chance of getting you out of this than I do of keeping them unscathed. I honestly don't know what you expect of me."

"I'm not asking you to do anything. I just—"

Corrado cut him off. "You're getting soft. I don't know what happened to you, but I don't like it. You claim you aren't trying to involve me, but you've done so from day one by involving my wife."

"I didn't intend—"

"No, I'm sure you didn't intend it, but I would've thought you, of all people, would understand. You lost your wife to this, and now you're putting me in the same situation! For someone who grieved so wholly, you surely didn't hesitate to set me up to endure the same. I want nothing more than to refuse your request right now, but I can't. I have to help you, even though it goes against everything I've sworn myself to, because it's the only way to protect Celia." He stared at him pointedly. "This girl better be worth it."

"She was to Maura."

Corrado rubbed his face with frustration. "The things we do for women. What possessed you to run her DNA in the first place? You know who her parents are."

Vincent sighed. "I wanted to get her a green card."

"A green card?" he asked incredulously.

"I knew it was too risky to try to get her a birth certificate, so I thought I could get a green card to legally establish her here. With her father being a citizen, she'd be approved as long as the relationship could be established. I knew Michael wouldn't agree willingly, so I thought a DNA test could strong-arm him."

"And you couldn't just ask me?"

"I told you—I didn't want to involve you."

Corrado shook his head. "Do you think Antonelli knows?"

"I doubt it. He wouldn't have given up the girl so easily if he knew. He would've bartered for more. And I'm sure he didn't know anything when . . . *it* happened."

Corrado watched him intently. "It's been five years now, huh?"

"Today," he said. "Today makes five years."

June first, the anniversary of the day Vincent hit rock bottom. Most would assume bottom was when his wife died, or the year after when he'd been unable to face his children, but rock bottom came years later . . .

Closing his eyes, he could still feel the hot air blowing in his face as he sped down the desolate highway. His hands shook, his body desperate for rest, but there was no way he could have stopped. He'd gone too far to give in.

His cell phone chimed loudly from the passenger seat, the harsh green light illuminating the darkness. His heart pounded vigorously at the sound, adrenaline surging through him. He ignored it like he had the last dozen times it rang.

For twenty-six hours he'd been driving, blatantly disregarding the code, but he wasn't thinking of the future. He wanted vengeance. He had walked inside that house in Lincoln Park the day before and stood in front of the man who controlled his life, hearing the four words that pushed him forward. "Frankie Antonelli did it."

Frankie Antonelli did it.

The closer Vincent got to the secluded ranch, the more frenzied he grew. A few miles from the turnoff to the property, the headlights of a car flashed his way. Vincent slowed down, watching as the familiar car whizzed by. Rage consumed him.

Frankie Antonelli did it.

Vincent made a U-turn and accelerated rapidly to catch up. Red lights flared in front of him as they hit the brakes, noticing Vincent's approach. Frankie could have outrun him, but by the time he realized what was happening, it was too late. Vincent rammed into him, turning the wheel and clipping the back corner of the car. His chest slammed into the steering wheel on impact, his vision blurring as he painfully gasped for air.

Tires squealed, followed by a loud crash as Frankie's car flew into some large boulders jutting out of the desert. Vincent swerved before coming to a stop in the opposite direction on the highway, the car still intact and on all four wheels. Smoke and dust lingered from the collision, making Vincent's eyes water. He rubbed his face, his vision blurring, and he took a deep breath as he grabbed his pistol from the floorboard. Stepping out, his weak legs shook as he put weight on them.

Frankie Antonelli did it.

Frankie's car was totaled, the front end demolished from the impact. As Vincent approached, he heard wheezing from the driver's side. The window was shattered, glass crunching under his feet. Frankie's legs were crushed under the front of the car, while his wife, Monica, slumped over in the passenger seat. Blood poured from her ears. Glancing back at Frankie, Vincent could see tears streaming down his face. "Frankie Antonelli did it," he said, his voice oddly calm.

Frankie tried to shield himself as Vincent brought up the gun, slamming it in the man's face as he blacked out in rage. By the time he resurfaced, the body in the driver's seat was unrecognizable and Vincent's hands were coated in blood.

He took a few deep breaths, trying to ignore the pain in his chest as he stepped back from the wreckage. Gas pooled underneath the car, the odor of it strong. Vincent scoured through his pockets and pulled out the beat-up pack of Marlboros. There was one cigarette left. He lit it, feeling the burn as the smoke scorched his lungs. The nicotine soothed his nerves.

After a few drags of the cigarette, he flicked it toward the car, igniting the puddle of gas.

Vincent climbed in his car and drove to the Antonellis' ranch, pulling down the driveway. The place appeared uninhabited, but that wasn't true. People were there, and he knew where to find them.

Without thinking it through, Vincent stepped inside the stables. He'd take the girl. He'd do it for Maura. He'd make it all better. He'd rescue her from filth.

He paused when he saw her asleep on a tattered old mattress in the corner stall, the stench of manure thick and stifling. He took a few steps toward her to get a better look and saw her clutching a book in her arms. So small and frail, she looked helpless, but Vincent wasn't fooled.

The bloodlust rose back up, desperation hitting him. He raised the gun and pointed it at her head, no hesitation as he pulled the trigger. Confusion hit him when nothing happened—no loud bang, no piercing scream, no blood.

His Smith & Wesson had never failed him before.

The sound of Corrado's voice pulled him from the vicious memory. "Is that the last time you killed?"

Vincent sighed. "Yes."

"As long as you realize you'll have to kill again, we shouldn't have a problem."

"Thank you," Vincent said as Corrado stood to walk out.

"Don't thank me. You still might die."

34

Carmine spotted his uncle the moment they stepped through the front door. Corrado surveyed them, assessing like he always did, and Haven's head went down, her gaze focusing on the wood floor. Carmine reached for her instinctively, pulling her to him.

"Corrado," Carmine said, nodding at him.

He returned the greeting. "Carmine."

Carmine could feel Haven trembling, every exhale coming out as a shudder. Sighing, he leaned toward her and frantically searched for the right words to say. What could destroy the fear built up from being tortured for so many years and having the man in front of them refuse to help?

"He's a decent guy," Carmine said. "Minus the whole murdering thing."

Yeah, that wasn't it.

Haven gripped Carmine's arm that was around her, her nails digging into his skin.

"This is my girlfriend, Haven," Carmine said. "I don't know if you've actually met her before."

Everyone stared at him, but Carmine felt Haven relax in his arms. Her grip on him loosened as Corrado turned to her. "No, I haven't had the pleasure."

Haven remained silent for a moment before she spoke, her voice restrained. "Nice to meet you, sir."

She held out her hand to Corrado. Carmine stared at it,

stunned, as she extended her hand to the man she knew had never considered extending his to her.

Corrado looked just as surprised as he shook it lightly. "As it is you. If you'll excuse me, I'm going to settle in."

He headed upstairs, and Carmine smirked as Haven turned to look at him. There was curiosity in her eyes. "Your girlfriend? It's not like he doesn't know what I am."

He shook his head. "What you are, Haven, is my girlfriend."

"But—"

"No buts. Quit thinking about yourself that way. They're just technicalities." She cracked a smile as he used the word. "They're titles other people give us. They don't make us who we are. If you're a slave, than I'm nothing more than *Principe*. Is that all I am? A Mafia prince?"

"Of course not."

"That's what I thought," he said. "Just because some people see us that way doesn't mean it's what we are. We'll overcome our labels together. They don't matter; they don't make us who we are. We make us who we are. Fuck those motherfuckers."

She laughed. "When did you get so smart?"

"Baby, I've always been smart," he said playfully. "I'm just lazy as hell and rarely show it."

The atmosphere was awkward at the dinner table that night. Haven didn't appear comfortable, so Carmine placed his hand in her lap and soothingly rubbed her thigh.

Everyone disbursed after dinner, and Haven headed into the kitchen to clean up. Celia followed her, and Carmine lingered in the doorway for a bit, trying to stay out of the way. He was leaning against the doorframe while she loaded the dishwasher when a voice cleared behind him in the foyer.

"I need to see you in my office," Vincent said.

Carmine scanned his head to make sure he hadn't done anything his father clearly had said "don't fucking do," but he came up blank for once. "I'll be there in a minute."

After making sure Haven was fine, he went upstairs and stepped into the office the second he reached it. He hesitated in the doorway, noticing his uncle standing off to the side.

"Does he ever knock?" Corrado asked.

"He's getting better at it," Vincent said.

Carmine groaned as he sat down. "Did you call me here for a lesson on manners?"

"No, but they're important to have," Corrado said. "Reminds me of how my mother used to ask if we were raised in a barn when we forgot our place."

"Yeah, well, your mom's a bitch." The words flew out before Carmine even registered them. "Shit, I mean, some people *are* raised in barns, so that's not nice manners in itself, you know?"

Corrado stared at him, his gaze so severe Carmine started sweating. Vincent simply smirked, amused about the situation. Carmine wanted to tell him there was nothing funny about this, but he didn't dare open his mouth. It was clear he was capable of saying things he shouldn't say.

"I believe that's the point I was trying to make before you interrupted with commentary on my mother," Corrado said. "Correct me if I'm wrong, but your girlfriend's one of those people, and she has a lot better manners than you do."

"You learn to fake respect for people when they threaten your life, whether you want to be polite or not," Carmine said. "I'd venture to guess half the time Haven says, 'yes, sir,' she's really screaming inside, 'fuck you, asshole.'"

"Do you want to initiate someday, Carmine?" Corrado asked.

The sudden shift in topic caught him off guard. "Excuse me?"

"Stalling is unnecessary. You react impulsively, so just answer. Do you want to be initiated?"

"I don't think—"

Corrado cut him off, his voice sharp. "That's right, you don't think. And you're in for a rude awakening if you intend to join the life, because all that you said about respecting those you'd rather not because of the hold they have on your life? That applies to all of us. If we forget our place, we get a bullet. So if the answer to my question is yes, I advise you to take a few pointers from that girl who was raised in the barn and learn to at least act respectfully toward those you may not respect."

"No," Carmine said. Corrado's eyes narrowed at his response, and he realized it sounded like he was trying to be difficult. "I mean the answer is no."

Corrado motioned toward Vincent. "Continue then."

Vincent took a deep breath. "We need to talk about what you saw in my safe."

Carmine wasn't sure if he wanted to hear the truth spoken out loud, but he motioned for his father to continue. For the next twenty minutes, Vincent rattled on about underground wars and all of the lives that had been destroyed, the devastation evident once the smoke cleared. Although Carmine wasn't surprised, the words still managed to make his hair stand on end. "She's Mafia royalty?"

Vincent nodded.

"Do you understand the seriousness of the situation?" Corrado asked. "Although your father means well, he's doing the same thing Frankie did—he's knowingly holding *Mafiosi* blood in his possession. I'm going to do everything I can to contain this, but there's a chance it'll be exposed. And when that happens, we're all going to be in danger . . . especially you and her."

"Why us especially?"

"Because your father and I would be killed, Carmine," Corrado said. "You'd become pawns."

He was quiet, letting it all sink in. "Something doesn't make sense to me. Why would Frankie risk his life keeping the kid? Why not sell Haven? He didn't care about her."

"We can't know for certain," Corrado said, "but Monica Antonelli wasn't stable. She was, uh . . ." He waved his hand as if to think of a word. ". . . *fuori come un balcone.* It was the reason they moved to the desert. Rest, they called it. Rehabilitation from a mental breakdown, but she never recovered. I think Frankie took advantage of an unfortunate situation to try to help his wife. No one would ever suspect it, and he lived so far away she wouldn't be seen by anyone who could recognize her."

"Plus, no one keeps small children for labor," Vincent added. "You can't have a toddler washing dishes or cooking meals. No one would've considered she had been sold and not killed because of that. Child slaves end up one place, and they may have broken conduct and murdered innocents, but some things were still off limits to us all."

Carmine sighed. He had a lot to think about. "Is that all? Can I go?"

Corrado snickered. "He may barge in, but at least he has enough sense to wait to be dismissed."

"Not always," Vincent said. "Sometimes he just walks out."

The next morning, Haven made breakfast while Carmine sat off to the side, watching her. She'd have moments where she was herself, laughing and being playful, but as soon as Corrado came near, it slipped away. She moved around him like there was magnetic polarity, always keeping a certain amount of distance from him.

It reminded Carmine of his mom, that fact not helping to brighten his mood. Nostalgic, the sorrow and longing crept in, bringing him down. It wasn't his graduation and he felt cheated.

Carmine filled a flask with vodka before they set off for the school. He pulled the Mazda into the parking lot and got out as Haven nervously looked around. "Relax, hummingbird. We're only here to help my brother bid high school farewell."

"I just don't want to embarrass you."

He put his arm around her. "You'll never embarrass me."

"What if I fall down the stairs in front of everyone?"

"You won't be walking down any stairs."

"Well, I don't need stairs. What if I just fall?"

"You won't. I'll hold you up."

"What if I take you down with me?"

"You think you can take me down?" he asked playfully. "I guess I fall, then. Hate to break it to you, but that won't embarrass me."

She huffed. "What if I get hiccups and interrupt graduation?"

"If that happens, I'll probably laugh, but whatever. You still aren't gonna embarrass me."

"But what if . . ."

By the time Haven was done asking her questions, they were safely seated in the back of the auditorium. Everyone settled and the ceremony started, the graduating class making their way in. Haven watched with wide eyes. As ridiculous as it all was to him, it was significant to her. She'd never gotten to experience high school.

Carmine didn't know what to say, so he just sat quietly and watched as Principal Rutledge blabbed about how proud he was. Usually Carmine blocked out the inspirational bullshit they spewed, but Haven listened with so much passion it made him want to know what she was hearing.

"Take a second to imagine your future," the valedictorian said when she stepped to the podium. "Imagine your life—your job, your spouse, your kids—but don't imagine the future you think you're heading for. Forget all the expectations and concentrate on what you truly want. Visualize the road that will take you there. That's your path. That's where you belong."

Carmine pulled Haven to him, kissing her hair as she laid her head on his shoulder.

"None of the truly great in this world became that way by doing what they felt they had to do. If Isaac Newton had become a farmer like his mother wanted him to, or if Elvis would've listened when he was told to stick to truck driving, we'd know neither man today. We know them because they had the courage to follow the path they envisioned."

The speech wound down, and Haven drank in every word of it.

The graduating class threw their caps into the air and everyone filtered out. Haven stood off to the side on the plaza with Tess and Dia as Carmine sat down on the brick wall lining the school. He watched her quietly, absorbing every smile.

Dominic sat beside him, still wearing his blue gown.

"Congrats," Carmine said, pulling out his flask and taking a swig before handing it to his brother.

"Thanks." Dominic took a drink and shuddered. "You know, Haven looks happy."

Carmine nodded, glancing at her. She was laughing at something. "Yeah, she does."

"She's changed a lot these past nine months. She's not the same frightened girl who showed up the first day. She's smart, too. I'm graduating, and she corrected my vocabulary the other day. I said I felt nauseous, and she said the word I wanted was nauseated. Fucked me up, bro. Didn't know there was a difference."

He smirked. "Sounds like something she'd do."

"She doesn't flinch anymore, either."

"I hated the flinching."

They passed the flask back and forth before Dominic spoke again. "It was her, wasn't it?" Carmine nodded and Dominic sighed, handing the flask back. "I figured. You got this look on your face at the family meeting, like she wrecked your car or something. It was the only thing that made sense."

Carmine took a deep breath, feeling guilty he had blamed her. He still sometimes had moments where knowing the truth was hard. It would always hurt, but it was a pain he'd learn to live with.

"I think Mom would be happy to see her," Dominic said. "To see how much she's changed. I guess that's what she wanted, and you did that for her."

"I didn't do anything."

Dominic laughed. "The hell you didn't. You think that's Dad's doing? He brought her here, but you made the difference. Mom always said you'd do great things in life, and I see it now, because no matter what you do tomorrow, Carmine, what matters is you did that today."

Carmine gazed at Haven as he mulled over his brother's words. She seemed so relaxed, so at ease, so much like a regular girl. Just looking at her, laughing and chatting, it was hard to imagine she'd been through the things she'd endured. "All I did was love her."

"Ever think maybe that's what she needed? Sometimes we don't have to really do anything. We have to just be."

They sat there until the flask was empty. Carmine slipped it into his pocket as Dominic stood. "You know what's kind of funny? Well, not funny, but ironic, maybe? She's been here nine months now, and it takes nine months to create life. It's like she's been reborn."

Dominic walked away but paused after a few steps, his brow furrowed. "Actually, I don't think that's irony. Haven would probably correct me again and say I was being symbolic."

Carmine chuckled. "Or metaphoric."

35

A shiver ran the length of Carmine's body, causing his muscles to grow taut. Haven stared at his sleeping form for a while, watching the rise and fall of his chest as he breathed. There was a stirring inside of her, warmth starting deep inside her chest. It frightened her, yet it made her feel like she was floating on air.

It was *hope*.

Haven grabbed the blanket and covered Carmine before climbing out of bed. She dressed, giving him one last look before heading downstairs to the kitchen. She pulled out the ingredients for an Italian cream cake and had the batter together when subtle footsteps echoed behind her. They were restrained, the steps of someone trying to go undetected.

But Haven noticed.

Her hands shook as she scooped the batter into pans, attempting to ignore the presence. She put the cake into the oven and set the timer. A cold chill ran the length of Haven's spine when Corrado finally spoke, his voice quiet and flat. "Good morning."

"Good morning, Mr. Moretti," she said, turning to look at him. He was dressed in a black suit, his jacket open and hands in his pockets. "Can I get you something?"

He didn't move, his stance so statuesque she wondered if he was even breathing. "No," he said finally, the word echoing in the tense silence.

She resumed making the frosting as he moved toward her. Instinctively, she took a step away. If Katrina had taught her anything, it was to stay out of the way whenever possible.

Corrado grabbed a bottle of water and stood off to the side, watching some more. Dr. DeMarco walked in after a few minutes and gave Corrado a curious look before his eyes found their way to her. "Good morning, *dolcezza.*"

She breathed a sigh of relief at the kindness in his voice. "Good morning, sir."

"I'm surprised to see you awake so early today," he said. "I take it Carmine's still asleep?"

"Yes, sir."

The timer for the oven went off. Haven pulled out the cake layers as Dr. DeMarco stood near her, gazing out the window with a wistful expression. The sun was rising, lighting up the driveway and the thick forest surrounding the property.

"They'll be here soon," he said, his attention shifting to the cake. "Italian cream cake."

"I made it for Carmine's birthday."

Irritation flashed across his face.

"Fascinating, isn't it?" Corrado asked from across the room. "I've never felt such a strong sense of déjà vu before."

Dr. DeMarco clenched his teeth, turning his gaze outside. "When you finish, child, I need you to make sure Carmine's awake. I'd go myself, but something tells me he's probably not decent."

He stressed the word *decent.* Haven's cheeks flushed. "Yes, sir."

Corrado laughed. "I'm quite sure this is one of those times Carmine was referring to, Vincent."

Dr. DeMarco shook his head and left the kitchen, while Corrado lingered. "When you wake Carmine, tell him his godfather is coming." He walked out, muttering, *"Tale il padre, tale il figlio,"* under his breath.

Teresa Capozzi enjoyed the finer things in life—the fastest foreign cars, the thickest mink furs, and the best vintage Dom Perignon wines. An air of superiority oozed from her pores, her demeanor shaped by her greed. It was well known that Mrs. Capozzi thought of nothing but herself and her next drink. Nobody liked her, not even her husband of forty years, but she didn't care. Teresa Capozzi didn't want to be liked; she wanted to be envied.

Haven watched out the window in the kitchen as the woman stepped out from the passenger seat of the rented Porsche and smoothed her tight black dress. She sauntered toward the house in her high heels, ignoring Salvatore when he tried to take her arm.

The closer Teresa got, the better Haven could make out her features. The woman looked as if she were made out of plastic, her face expressionless and coated in heavy makeup. Her body was disproportionate, every part of her tucked and tweaked.

Dr. DeMarco greeted the couple as Celia made drinks, ignoring Haven again when she told her she could handle it. Haven threw together a cherry Coke for Carmine, spiking it with a little vodka. They carried the glasses into the family room, and Haven's anxiety grew as she approached their guests. She handed a glass of scotch to Salvatore, her hand shaking from nerves.

"It's nice to see you again," he said.

"You too, sir," she said, avoiding his gaze. Haven handed a glass of some orange liqueur to his wife. "Here you go, ma'am."

Teresa took it, bringing it to her nose and inhaling. "This isn't made right," she said, thrusting it toward her and spilling some on the floor. The room went instantly silent.

"I'm sorry," Haven said as she took the drink back.

She turned around and nearly collided with Celia, who grabbed the glass from her hand. "I must be losing my touch. I thought I made it perfectly."

Teresa glanced between Celia and Haven. "I must've been mistaken," she conceded, reaching for the glass again and taking a sip. "Perfect as usual, Celia."

"I thought so," she said, a hint of amusement in her voice. "We all make mistakes."

The expression on Teresa's face said she didn't agree.

Celia took a seat across the room, and Corrado sat down on the arm beside her. Haven handed the cherry Coke to Carmine and started to move away, but he pulled her into his lap and wrapped a protective arm around her. Teresa coughed as she choked on her drink, her eyes shifting to Dr. DeMarco as she let out a bitter laugh.

"Teresa," Salvatore warned, but she simply smiled as he turned his attention to Carmine. "I'm afraid we won't be able to stay long, *Principe*. We have a flight for a vacation in Florida, but I had to take a detour to wish you a happy birthday."

"I appreciate it," Carmine said. "I wasn't expecting to see you."

"It's not every day my godson turns eighteen. This is a big deal."

"Doesn't seem that way."

Salvatore laughed. "Oh, but it is. Do you have any plans this summer?"

Carmine's grip on Haven tightened, but his voice showed no sign of distress. "Football camp. Other than that, we'll probably just hang out before my brother leaves."

"And after summer's over?"

"I'm sure senior year will be kicking my ass for a while."

Salvatore raised his eyebrows. "And after you graduate?"

Carmine remained silent for a moment. "College, I guess."

Salvatore's smile diminished. He glanced at Dr. DeMarco as if he expected him to speak up, but he didn't say a word. "And the girl?" Salvatore asked, his gaze shifting to Haven. "I'm curious what your family intends to do with her. Given the situation, I gather you don't plan to let her be sold."

Carmine's eyes narrowed. "Of course not."

"Of course not," Salvatore echoed. "And after you're gone for college, your father won't want to live here alone with her. Just think of the gossip. I'm sure the rumors are already aplenty."

Dr. DeMarco cleared his throat. "I've been weaning her to the world, so she can join it."

"That's noble of you, Vincent, but I'm not sure that's wise," Salvatore said. "She must know quite a bit. How can we be sure anything she's seen or heard won't be disclosed to anyone?"

Dr. DeMarco glanced at her. "I'll vouch for her."

His words were met with a vicious laugh from Salvatore. "After what happened when . . . well, you know . . . I don't think your opinion can be taken at face value on this."

"It's not the same," Dr. DeMarco said.

"Yes, it is, Vincent. You know the dangers and risks. You can't let her loose without someone taking responsibility for her, and you're in no frame of mind to do it."

It sickened Haven to have her fate being discussed as if she weren't there, but equally as shocked that Dr. DeMarco intended to let her go. She couldn't fathom why the man would go through the trouble of paying for her if he planned to let her walk away.

"Maybe she should come with me," Salvatore said. "She'd be taken care of in my home."

"No way," Carmine said. "If you need someone to take responsibility for her, I will."

Salvatore shook his head. "You can't do that when you're not a part of this. Besides, I'm not positive that's the right course of action."

They were at an impasse when another voice chimed in, quiet but forceful. "I'll do it."

Everyone's attention turned to Corrado.

"What?" Salvatore asked.

"I'll vouch for the girl," he said again.

Salvatore looked as if he'd been struck. "Are you sure you want to?"

"It's not a matter of want," Corrado said. "If it's necessary, I'll do it. I trust Vincent when he says she won't talk, and if she does, I'll handle her. Simple enough."

The guests departed around six in the evening, and Carmine opened presents from his family. Feeling bad for having nothing to give him, Haven watched longingly as others bombarded him with an array of gifts. Afterward, they put on a movie, but Haven couldn't focus on what was happening.

About halfway through, she told Carmine she was going upstairs, wanting a moment alone. She headed to her bedroom and climbed into the cold bed. Pulling the blanket over her, she snuggled into a pillow and drifted off to sleep. She was awoken later when the bed shifted, and she blinked a few times as she adjusted to the darkness.

Carmine slid in beside her. "Hey."

"Hey." Her voice was thick with sleep. "What time is it?"

"Midnight," he said as she snuggled up to him. He was warm and smelled like a mixture of cologne and smoke. "We watched *Scarface*. Go figure."

"That's nice," she said, although *Scarface* sounded like a horror movie to her. It reminded her of monsters, and a flicker of hers flashed in her mind. She squeezed her eyes shut tightly to ward off the image of mangled skin. "I'm sorry I couldn't get you anything for your birthday."

"I have all I need, Haven. We can be together now."

"Did they really mean that stuff about me?"

Carmine buried his face in her hair. "Yes."

The confirmation sent her emotions surging. "It's that easy?"

He sighed. "I wouldn't call it easy. The hard part is ahead of us. But you'll be able to do whatever now: go to school, marry me, make a houseful of babies if that's what you want. Could leave my ass, too, if you wanna do that."

She was stunned he'd think that. "I'll never leave you."

"That's good to hear, *colibri*. I'm just saying you could."

"What does it mean when someone vouches for you, anyway?"

He said nothing. Sleep nearly took Haven under as she figured he wasn't coherent enough to answer. He finally spoke, though, his voice barely loud enough for her to hear. "It means they guarantee your loyalty. Slaves aren't the only ones who pay for others' mistakes, Haven. Corrado just swore if you made one, he'd pay for it with his life."

She blanched. "But I don't want anyone to get hurt because of me."

"Corrado knows what he's doing," he said. "You may not trust them, but you gotta trust me when I say this is the only way, baby. It's the only way you can be free."

Free. She once looked up the word in the thesaurus Carmine had given her and memorized the words on the page: unrestrained, emancipated, independent, individualistic, liberated, self-directing, self-governing, self-ruling; antonym: bound, enslaved. That had been her—enslaved—but not anymore. Now, because of Carmine, she knew what the word *free* meant, and soon, she realized, she could know how it felt.

36

Carmine was in a fog as he dragged himself out of bed the next day. After washing the sweat and grime from his body, he gazed at his reflection in the mirror. He desperately needed a haircut and a shave, but otherwise he looked like the same Carmine DeMarco. Same person he had seen every day for years, but he didn't feel the same anymore. It wasn't because he was older or wiser—far from it. It was because of her.

He smiled when he saw Haven in the library, her fingertips grazing the spines of a row of books. She pulled one off a shelf, her brow furrowing as she studied the front cover. He chuckled at her expression, and her eyes snapped in his direction. "I didn't hear you come out of your room."

"You aren't the only one who knows how to be quiet, Ninja."

She replaced the book on the shelf. "Hmm, well, maybe we should get you a bell."

"Hey, at least I don't almost give you heart attacks. You used to startle the hell out of me. I thought for sure you'd need to give me CPR a few times."

She raised her eyebrows. "Don't be so sure. You make my heart race every time you come near me."

He strolled over to where she stood and leaned down to kiss her. He nipped at her bottom lip as he pulled back, pressing his palm against her chest. "How's the heart?"

"Feels like it's going to explode."

"It won't," he said. "It's strong; it's not gonna break."

Her smile fell. "Promise?"

Carmine stared at her, confused by her sudden shift in demeanor, when it struck him what he'd said. "Promise. I'll do whatever it takes to make sure it continues to beat."

"Good."

"So what are you doing in the library?"

She turned around, scanning the books again. "I was looking for something to read. I feel like I should learn something."

"I get out of school for the summer, and you decide it's time to learn? That's kinda backward."

"I know, but if I'm going to be free, I shouldn't be stupid."

"You aren't stupid, but there's nothing wrong with learning. If you wanna learn, I'm all for it. Actually, you know what? I have an idea."

Grabbing her hand, she offered no resistance as he pulled her toward the steps. Once they reached Vincent's office on the second floor, Carmine grabbed the knob but hesitated. He knocked instead, and Corrado opened it, stepping to the side so they could enter. Haven stiffened as she took a seat, looking at Carmine nervously as Corrado walked to the other side of the room.

"Do you need something?" Vincent asked from behind his desk, his fingers stilled on the keys of his laptop.

"I wondered how hard it would be to get Haven a GED."

Vincent sat back and pushed his glasses up on his nose. "Now?"

"Well, not right this damn minute, but soon."

"Depends on what you want it for," Vincent said. "We could have one made for her, but it might not pass a strict vetting process."

What was the point if she didn't learn anything? "I'm talking about her earning one."

"Oh. I suppose it wouldn't be too difficult. She'll need some documents and a driver's license for proof of identity, but I can pull some strings and get her the stuff. All you have to do is make sure she's ready to test."

"Seriously?" That simple? "I wish I would've known sooner."

"Don't get any ideas," Vincent said. "You made it this far; you can finish high school. She wasn't afforded the opportunity, but there's no reason she can't test for a GED if she wants one."

Haven glanced between them. "GED?"

"Stands for General Education Diploma," Carmine said. "Or General Equivalency Diploma. I don't know."

Corrado shook his head. "General Education Development."

"Whatever, it could stand for Goddamn Endocrine Disorder for all I care," Carmine said. "It means the same thing."

Vincent laughed loudly. "You just wished a hormone deficiency on the girl."

"Oh, we don't want that," Carmine said. "I mean a diploma."

Haven stared straight ahead. "Diploma?"

"Yeah," Carmine said. "It's just a piece of paper, but it means you know enough to complete high school. You can get into some colleges with it."

Her eyes widened. "I can get one of those? A GED?"

"Yes," Carmine said.

"If you want one," Vincent said. "It's up to you."

Haven blinked back tears. The man who controlled her life—her master—just told her something was up to her. She tried to speak, but no sound came out when she opened her mouth, so she nodded instead.

"It's settled, then," Vincent said. "I'm sure you can find some practice work online. Anything more and you'll have to wait for the documents."

Vincent turned his attention to his laptop, the conversation over.

The moment they stepped into the hallway, Haven flung herself at him. Carmine stumbled a few steps but managed to keep his balance as she leaped up and wrapped her legs around his waist. He clung to her tightly so she didn't fall.

Haven buried her face in his neck, her hands finding their way into his hair. Carmine was stunned into silence, unable to do anything but stand there and hold her.

———

Carmine pulled the cake out of the fridge when they made it to the kitchen, and Haven watched as he cut a slice for himself. "So you like the cake?"

He grabbed a fork. "Italian cream cake's my favorite."

"Is it really?"

He smirked, taking a bite. "It is now."

Haven laughed as Dominic strolled into the room. "Whoa, I can't believe you're eating without me. That's foul."

Shrugging, Carmine hopped up on the counter as Dominic cut a massive piece for himself. Soon the rest of the family joined them, Corrado and Celia getting pieces and standing off to the side while Dr. DeMarco grabbed a bottle of water. He closed the fridge door and turned to look at them, his gaze shifting toward the cake.

"Have you tried some, Dad?" Dominic asked.

"No."

Dominic cut another slice and slapped it on a plate, holding it out to his father. "You should."

"I'd rather not," Vincent said, eyeing the plate with distaste.

Dominic shrugged. "Your loss, but I tell you—this is the best cake I've ever had. She's a great cook."

"Yeah," Carmine said. "Probably all the Italian in her."

He tensed when he realized what he'd said and noticed his father had the same reaction. Vincent opened his water and took a drink as Carmine tried to think of something to say to shift the conversation elsewhere. Before he could, Dominic laughed. "Must be. You know damn well she has Carmine's *full-blooded* Italian in her all the time."

Vincent coughed as he choked on his drink. Celia snorted, trying to hold back her amusement, but Dominic didn't bother containing himself. The laughter died down as Vincent caught his breath, looking at him with disapproval. Carmine waited for him to say something, but he just walked out.

After he was gone, they burst into another round of laughter. Haven looked at Carmine with confusion. "I thought you were half-Irish."

Carmine opened his mouth to answer but closed it again, shaking his head. There was no way to explain it without embarrassing her.

———

Night fell, the house as still as a graveyard. Vincent sat in his office, glaring at the plate on his desk. The small sliver of cake was just enough to taste, but the thought of taking a bite made his stomach churn.

Maura always made Italian cream cake. It had been her favorite.

He fingered the small gold band around his neck, his pinky finger barely fitting halfway through it. The metal was startlingly cold against his skin but not as cold as Vincent felt inside.

After another minute of staring at the cake, he picked up the plate and tossed it into the trash. It hit the bottom of the empty wastebasket with a loud clank, and Vincent didn't give it another thought. He slipped the necklace under the neckline of his shirt again, concealing it, and picked up a stack of papers on his desk.

X-rays, consultations, broken bones, stitches. Diseases, rashes, infections, viruses. One awful diagnosis after another, but Vincent preferred it to the morose thoughts swimming in his head.

For as many lives as he'd destroyed, as many people as he'd watched die, there were countless others he'd saved. And as exhausted as he was, somewhere in the mound of files in front of him had to be another patient who could take the sting of death away.

If only for a little while.

37

The warm June weather gave way to a sprawling Carolina heat as July dawned. Triple-digit temperatures seeped into the region, stirring up thunderstorms and intermittent showers every day. Fireflies emerged again, flickering in the night sky, as a sense of contentment settled over Haven.

She ventured outside with Carmine every day, strolling through the backyard in her bare feet. She climbed trees and chased bugs, picked flowers and ran through sprinklers, and all the while Carmine urged her on. His support became invaluable to her, and Haven couldn't imagine going a single day without him.

She'd have to, though. They both knew it.

"Aren't you gonna be late, bro?" Dominic asked as he walked into the family room, where the two of them sat. Haven sighed exasperatedly, having asked that same question a moment ago. She had been trying to get Carmine to leave for the past thirty minutes, but he wouldn't budge.

Carmine slouched down. "I'm not going."

Dominic laughed. "Scared you'll get hurt?"

"I'm not afraid," Carmine said.

"Then quit whining and go."

Carmine grumbled incoherently, still not appearing like he had any intention of moving. He was scheduled to attend football camp for a week in Chapel Hill. He'd been fine with going away and talked incessantly about what he would do when he was there,

and she had listened, although she didn't know what encroach-
ment or interference or any of that other stuff meant. She was just
grateful he was sharing something with her.

But this morning, when Haven opened her eyes, there was no
smile on Carmine's lips. None of the excitement was present anymore. All she saw was her own anxiety reflecting back to her.

"You have to go," she said at the same time he uttered the words
he had been repeating all morning: "I'm not going."

He pretended to be interested in the television, but she could
see his eyes drifting to the clock. Time was running out. He was
supposed to be at the University of North Carolina by five to
check in and it was already past one.

"I'll still be here when you get back."

His eyes snapped in her direction. "Of course you will. Where
else would you be?"

She sighed—that was the wrong thing to say.

"Don't worry about her, man," Dominic said, walking up behind them. "I have plans for her this week. I'm going to keep her
so busy she won't even realize you're gone."

Haven smiled but didn't believe his words.

"You'll get her in more trouble than she could ever find on her
own," Carmine said. "Maybe that's why I'm not going."

Dominic laughed. "If you aren't going, you must not trust her."

Anger flashed across his face. "You don't know what you're
talking about."

"Afraid she can't hack it without you?"

"I know she can."

"So why aren't you going?"

Carmine glared at him but didn't respond.

The front door opened, and Dr. DeMarco paused in the entrance to the family room. "I thought you'd be gone by now," he said,
focusing his attention on Carmine. "Aren't you going to be late?"

Carmine's expression softened into a pout. "Would you people
get off my nuts? I'll go in a minute."

Dr. DeMarco walked away while Dominic punched Carmine on the shoulder. "That's it, be a man! The sooner you leave, the sooner Haven and I can start having fun."

Carmine rubbed his arm but once again didn't respond to his brother. Dominic walked out, and Carmine pulled Haven to him. "I'd hide you in my suitcase and take you with me if I could."

"Don't worry. Go do some field goals and play some runs."

"I'm the quarterback, *tesoro*. I don't kick field goals. And it's running plays, not playing runs."

"Oh. Well, go quarterback."

He laughed and let go of her. "Don't let that *cafone* make you do anything you don't wanna do."

"Okay. It's only a week, so I'll be fine." She wasn't sure who she was reassuring more with her words, him or herself.

He ran his fingertips across her cheek, and kissed her one final time before standing. "I'll see you later."

"Good-bye, Carmine," she said, the words making his steps falter as his shoulders tensed. She thought he was going to turn around and say something to her, but he simply walked out, shaking his head.

She sat quietly in the family room as he grabbed his stuff and headed for the front door. "You're definitely going to be late," his father said from the foyer.

"I'm going. Isn't that enough?"

Carmine's bedroom was quiet that night without his presence. Haven tiptoed inside and snatched his favorite pillow off his bed before running to her room. She crawled into bed and snuggled with it. His familiar scent lingered, surrounding her like a warm shroud.

Haven closed her eyes and pleaded for sleep to come quickly.

The next morning, a loud banging ricocheted through the room, and Haven jumped out of bed as Dominic's voice carried through the door. "Rise and shine!"

She glanced at the clock—a few minutes past seven. She pulled open the door when Dominic knocked again, and he grinned brightly, raising his eyebrows. "Too tired to get changed last night?"

She glanced down and realized she still had her clothes on from the day before. "I didn't think about it. Why are you up early?"

"Because I'm starving! Breakfast is in order."

"Did you want me to make you something?"

He laughed. "Of course not. Damn, girl, are you awake yet? Do you really think I'd drag you out of bed so you could cook? We're going out for breakfast . . . just you and me."

———————

Crossroads Diner was packed when they arrived, and much to the dismay of some waiting patrons, Dominic got a table right away. Looking through the menu, Haven ordered French toast while Dominic rattled off a list of eggs, bacon, sausage, pancakes, fruit, and toast. She wasn't surprised because she was used to feeding him, but he smiled sheepishly anyway. "What can I say? I'm a growing boy."

"I think you're done growing, Dom."

He laughed, pushing up his shirtsleeve and flexing his weak muscle. "I need fuel, though. These guns are the only ones I carry and they don't come naturally, little sis."

"Little sis," she said, echoing his words.

"Yeah," he said. "Someday you might make it official by marrying my shithead little brother."

She smiled at the thought.

The waitress returned with their food, and the two of them ate. Despite the fact that the place was noisy, a comfortable silence surrounded their table.

"Did you ever think it would be this way?" Dominic asked after a few minutes.

"What way?"

He waved his fork in the air, motioning all around them. "This way. Coming here, having a life, getting a family, meeting Carmine. All of it, really. Did you ever think this would happen?"

She contemplated his question as he took a bite of food. "My mama said I'd end up somewhere like this, but I figured I was given the life I had so the most I could do was get used to it."

"I can relate," Dominic said. "Did you know I was adopted?"

She was caught off guard. "No."

"I am. My real mom . . . well, no, Maura was my real mom in every way that counted. The woman who birthed me was raped, and out I popped."

Haven's mouth dropped open. "I was made the same way."

"I figured," he said. "See, you and I aren't that different. None of us are when it comes down to it. The only difference is my mom stumbled upon me at the right time and saved me from what could've been a disaster. I wonder all the time where I'd be if they hadn't taken me in."

"You got lucky."

"I did," he said. "You and Carmine aren't that different, either. My brother's a spoiled little shit—that's why he's picky. Everyone always catered to him. Not saying I was neglected, because I wasn't, but Carmine received the kind of attention I never had to deal with."

"What kind of attention?"

"Attention from, uh . . . Dad's friends." He glanced around to see if anyone was listening. "At my christening when I was a kid, there were about two dozen people. It was relaxed, a potluck at the house. Carmine's christening was a few months after mine, and hundreds of people came to show their respect. It had to be catered and held in a reception hall."

Haven frowned. "That's horrible."

"Not really," he said. "I'm sure I was jealous then, but I don't envy my brother. Before he could walk or talk, people were making plans for his future. I'm grateful I never had that kind of pressure."

"Why him?" she asked. "Why not you?"

"Because he's Dad's son, a DeMarco, and that's what they care about—the Italian blood." He paused. "Or what they used to care about. I don't know anymore. But anyway, to what I was saying. Carmine's spoiled, but deep down he's still a terrified little boy, trying to figure out where he belongs, just like you're that girl looking for her place in the world. You two were searching for the same thing."

"You think?"

"I know," he said. "And my mom would've called that fate."

———

After leaving the diner, Dominic stopped by the Harper residence to pick up Tess. She threw a duffel bag into the back of the car and crossed her arms over her chest, her usual scowl on her face as she sat in the backseat in total silence.

Once they reached the house, Tess thrust a shopping bag at Haven. "It's a swimsuit."

She was taken aback. *A gift?* "Thank you, but I don't need one."

Tess looked amused. "If you're going to the lake with me, honey, you do need one."

"Lake?" Haven asked. "What lake?"

"We're heading down to Aurora Lake for the day," Dominic said. "It'll be a blast."

Haven glanced at the bag. "And I'm supposed to wear this?"

Tess nodded. "Yes."

Haven went straight upstairs to her room and stripped out of her clothes, leaving them in a pile on the floor. The swimsuit was a black one-piece that tied around the neck, the bottom cut like shorts. Haven put it on and tied it the best she could, tugging at it to make sure she was covered.

———

Aurora Lake was located in a valley ten minutes south of the Durante city limits. The community of Aurora surrounded it, a few hundred residents living along the twenty-seven miles of shoreline. Although the lake was man-made, much of the land beyond the homes remained untouched.

Haven climbed out of the car and spotted the water in the distance. It went as far as she could see, wildly tall trees bordering it on all sides. Despite its enormity, something about the place put her at ease. Beyond the grassy lot they had parked on was tan sand, reminding her of the desert ground she'd been used to all her life.

"Welcome to paradise . . . or as close as we get around here," Dominic said, juggling some lounge chairs under his right arm. They headed toward the water, setting up on the sand in an area partially encased in shade. There wasn't a cloud in sight, and the warm summer breeze felt nice on Haven's skin.

Dominic set out into the water while Tess stripped out of her clothes. Haven pulled hers off carefully and sat down, watching the few people who were already playing out on the lake. Someone started a game of volleyball after a few minutes, and Dominic and Tess joined the game while Haven relaxed under the sun's rays.

It didn't take long for the temperature to rise, sweat trickling down Haven's face. She grabbed a bottle of water from the cooler and took a drink when a familiar voice rang out. She coughed, gasping for air as the liquid went down her windpipe.

"Excuse me?" she sputtered, coming face-to-face with Nicholas. She took a deep breath that burned her chest. "What did you say?"

He stared at her as he plopped down in Tess's lounge chair, kicking out his feet and getting comfortable. "I said I didn't think Carmine would let you come down here."

Her eyes narrowed. "We've been through this. He doesn't tell me what to do."

"Okay," he said. "Then I'm surprised you would come here when he can't. You know, because of trying to kill me and all."

That hadn't crossed her mind. "This is where you live?"

Nicholas pointed behind them at a white two-story house about a hundred yards away. It stuck out among the others, the paint fresher. "That would be my place, so technically speaking, you're sitting in my yard right now."

"Oh, well, he didn't try to kill you," she said. "It was a misunderstanding."

He laughed dryly. "A misunderstanding? He's seriously clouded your judgment."

"No, your judgment's clouded. Carmine made mistakes, but he's a good person. You shouldn't sit there and pretend you're innocent. It's stupid! I wasn't there and I know you're both being ridiculous about this . . . this . . . rivalry thing. So get over yourself, because you can't talk about him like that to me. I love him."

She stood and stomped away.

"Haven, wait," Nicholas called out as she walked to the edge of the water. She heard him behind her but didn't acknowledge him. "Look, I just have a hard time believing he cares about anyone. I don't like the idea of him taking advantage of your situation."

She glared at him when he stopped beside her. "You know nothing about my situation! Carmine's supportive of me, so how dare you judge him when he's braver than you'll ever be!"

Nicholas stared out at the lake. "So, uh . . ."

"I don't want to talk about it," she said. "No more about Carmine."

"I wasn't going to say anything about him," he said. "I was going to ask if you were getting in the water."

"Oh. No."

"Why not?"

"I can't swim."

"You don't have to swim to get your feet wet." Nicholas pulled off his shirt and tossed it onto the sand. He took a few steps into the water, stopping to look at her when it reached his knees. "What are you waiting for?"

"I don't think so."

"Trust me." She let out a sharp, cynical laugh the moment the words came from his lips, and he immediately backtracked. "Okay, don't trust me. But do you really think I'm stupid enough to let you get hurt? I told you before—you're nice and all, but I don't plan to die over you. And I guarantee, if you drown, they'll kill me."

Haven stood there for a moment longer before taking a few steps into the lake, her bare feet sinking into the soft earth. She stopped before the water reached her waist.

"So why is six afraid of seven?" Nicholas asked, breaking the tension with a joke.

She held her hands on the surface of the water. "I don't know. Why?"

"Because seven, eight, nine." He smirked. "Get it? Seven *ate* nine."

She nodded. "I get it."

"But you didn't laugh. You never laugh."

"It wasn't funny."

He let out a heavy sigh. "Why did the boy throw his toast out the window?" She shrugged. "He wanted to see the butter fly."

"See the butter fly?" The joke dawned on her when the words came out. "Oh, like a butterfly."

"Yes, a butterfly. Why did the guy get fired from the orange juice factory?" Another shrug. "He couldn't concentrate."

"Like the orange juice that's made from concentrate?"

He ran his hands down his face. "You're hard to crack, you know. I've never failed at making someone laugh before. I may as well have asked why the chicken crossed the road."

"Why did the chicken cross the road?"

"To get to the other side, of course." She smiled at that one, and he threw up his hands. "Well, damn. You've never heard that before?"

"No."

"You need more comedy in your life. Carmine drained you of a sense of humor."

Before she could say anything, he disappeared under the water, and a splash flew in her direction. He resurfaced, and she groaned. "That wasn't funny."

Nicholas stepped out of the lake and grabbed his shirt. "Apparently nothing I say or do is."

Haven hesitated but followed behind, not wanting to loiter in the water alone. They strolled over to the lounge chairs. She grabbed a towel while he plopped his wet body down.

"So, you guys really are in love? It's not bullshit?"

"We are."

Nicholas grabbed Tess's purse. Haven watched in shock as he rooted around in it. He pulled out a pen and an old receipt, scribbling something on the back of it.

"Here's my number," he said, holding it out to her. "You call me if you ever need anything. I promise to say nothing bad about your boyfriend . . . not a lot, anyway."

She took it and read the number. *555–0121*. "Uh, okay."

"It's not a crime to have people to talk to," he added, standing. "I'll catch you later, Haven."

Once again, at seven in the morning, Haven awoke to Dominic's insistent pounding. She pulled herself out of bed and trudged over to the door, finding him in the hallway with a grin. "Hey, Twinkle Toes. I'm proud you remembered your pajamas this time."

The week passed in a repetitious haze, mornings at the diner and afternoons with Dominic and Tess. Dia would occasionally stop by to play a game or watch television, and evenings were Haven's to do as she pleased. She spent them in the library, reading under the moonlight. She studied relentlessly for the GED, doing practice tests Carmine had printed out for her.

Little cooking or cleaning got done, except for the occasional sandwich at dinner or a load of dishes. She felt bad slacking off on her duties, but whenever she attempted to clean, Dominic pulled her away. She was afraid of what Dr. DeMarco would think, but he didn't seem to notice.

It was the afternoon of the sixth day when Haven sat in the

family room with Dominic, staring at the clock on the wall. She counted the seconds as they ticked by, each one bringing her closer to Carmine's return.

———————

"Fuck!"

Pain shot through Carmine's wrist as his fingers numbed. He shook his hand, trying to get rid of the tingling, as the coach bellowed, "Shake it off, DeMarco!"

Carmine groaned, flexing his fingers. What did it look like he was doing?

To say he had had a bad week would have been the understatement of the century. Carmine was out of shape, his wrist was sore, and half the team harbored resentment for him for one reason or another. All he wanted to do was play football and go back home, but karma had finally caught up with him.

And karma was a bigger bitch than Tess Harper.

The last day of camp had arrived, and Coach Woods had been railing on him since he stepped onto the field that morning. Carmine was close to giving them all the middle finger and strutting away, his irritation to the point of no return.

The whistle blew, and Carmine lined up to grab the ball. Taking a few steps back, he looked for the wide receiver and snapped the ball, grinning at the perfect spiral as it soared through the air.

"Wipe that smirk off your face, DeMarco," Coach Woods said. "There's no room for your ego on the field."

Mistake after mistake was made in their scrimmage, balls fumbled and throws missed more times than Carmine could count. He got sacked more than once, pain radiating through his back as Coach Woods berated them for their incompetence. After the final whistle blew, signifying the end of camp, the coach called Carmine's name and clapped him on the shoulder. "You played well today."

Carmine just stood there. He hadn't expected to hear those words.

"I'm hard on you because you have potential," the coach said.

"It might not be appropriate for me to say this, but the UNC coaches were watching and expressed some interest in you."

His mouth dropped open. "No shit?"

Instead of chastising him for cursing, the coach laughed. "Yes, but they don't like hotheads, DeMarco. No one does."

———

It was late evening when Carmine reached Durante. He pulled up in front of the house and climbed out, stretching his sore back when the front door swung open. Haven came toward him, leaping off the porch. Their bodies collided, and Carmine stumbled as she buried her face in his chest. He wrapped his arms around her as she looked at him adoringly, a hint of worry in her eyes.

"Your face," she said, running her fingers gently across a bruise on his cheek. "What happened?"

He smirked. "I fell."

Rolling her eyes, she reached up on her tiptoes and pressed her lips to his, her hands passionately locking in his hair. When she pulled away for air, Carmine laughed. "If I'm gonna be greeted like that, maybe I should go away more often."

"No way! You're not allowed!"

"Okay, then." He pulled her to him tightly. "I fucking missed you, hummingbird."

"I missed you, too."

Haven grabbed his arm and tugged, pulling him inside. Carmine bypassed his father's office and his brother's bedroom, foregoing greetings for the time being. "Did you do anything exciting while I was gone?" he asked as they settled into his room.

She shrugged. "Mostly just normal stuff."

Normal stuff. Never in his wildest dreams did he think he'd hear those words from her.

Sitting on the bed, Carmine rubbed his aching back as Haven eyed him suspiciously. She pushed his hand out of the way to massage him, and he moaned involuntarily at her touch. "You're too good to me, *tesoro*."

"You always say that, but it's not like it's agonizing to touch you," she said. "So did you get sackled or something?"

He laughed. "Sackled?"

"Isn't that what it's called when you get knocked down?"

"When everyone else gets knocked down, it's a tackle. When I do, it's a sack. Two different things." He let out a moan as she rubbed his sore muscles. "I had my ass kicked out there this week, but I impressed some of the coaches. They mentioned me playing after high school. I don't know if I wanna go to school here, but it's nice to know the option's there."

She continued working on his back. "Where *do* you want to go?"

"Wherever you wanna go," he said. "I'm gonna leave that up to you."

38

Haven stood off to the side and fought back the tears welling in her eyes. Everyone gathered in the foyer and chatted animatedly, the excitement palpable as Dominic's booming laughter rang out above it all, infiltrating Haven's ears and causing her grip to falter.

It was a Sunday afternoon at the end of August. Summer was coming to an end when, to Haven, it felt like it had just begun. The past month and a half had been filled with activity: art galleries, museums, aquariums, and zoos. She drove and read, laughed and played, loved and learned, and in the bustle of life, everything else faded away.

Carmine occasionally had football practice and took her along. There were others there—family, friends, and girlfriends—gathered in groups, but Haven sat off to the side on the bleachers, watching Carmine by herself. He was confident and aggressive on the field, and she told him he made her proud, but he shrugged it off as if it weren't a big deal. It was, though, because it was his future . . . *their* future.

A future that suddenly seemed a bit more real.

Dominic's bags were packed and stuffed into the Mercedes out front. He and Tess were boarding a plane in a few hours, and Dr. DeMarco was flying out to help them settle in. They were excited about the changes their lives were undertaking, but Haven dreaded saying good-bye. She had looked up the University of Notre Dame on a map with Carmine's help, and while only a few inches separated Indiana from Durante, she knew those inches might as well be a lifetime.

"Let's get this show on the road," Dr. DeMarco said. "We don't want to miss our flight."

Haven's feet left the ground before Dr. DeMarco finished speaking. Dominic lifted her into the air and twirled her around. "I'll miss you, girl."

She laughed and hugged him. "Thank you for everything . . . especially that sandwich."

He set her on her feet. Reaching into his pocket, he pulled out his keys and carefully took one off. He slipped it into her palm, squeezing her hand tightly around it. "Keep my car safe for me."

She gaped at him. "What?"

"I can't take it, so you may as well drive it."

Final good-byes were exchanged, and Haven felt the tears slipping down her cheeks as they disappeared out the door. Only a few seconds passed before the door flew back open, Dominic peeking his head in again. "Oh yeah, Twinkle Toes? Good luck on your test tomorrow."

———

The trip to the city the next morning took an hour. Carmine talked nonstop the entire drive, but Haven heard nothing except her heartbeat thrashing in her ears. They made it to the local community college with time to spare, and Haven headed inside alone, black spots infiltrating her vision as she fought to keep herself together.

The bright fluorescent lights hanging from the ceiling irritated her eyes. Haven stood in the doorway, taking in the small wooden desks and hard blue plastic chairs. She'd never been inside of a classroom before. People pushed past her, not bothering to apologize, as she hesitantly walked to the big desk at the front. She smiled politely at the instructor, although she felt like she'd be sick. "I'm Haven Antonelli."

He checked her name off a list and collected her paperwork before pointing her to a seat. The testing started at eight o'clock on the dot. Haven breezed through the fifty questions on grammar and punctuation, but the second part of the writing test stalled her.

She'd practiced a lot by filling her notebooks, but she had never written anything for someone else to read before.

The instructor announced they had forty-five minutes as Haven read her essay prompt:

What does it take to be a good parent?
In your essay, describe the characteristics of a good parent. Use your personal observations, experience, and knowledge.

Students huffed and pencils scratched against paper as Haven stared at her topic. What *did* it take? Her father, abusive and malicious, refused to acknowledge he had created her. She suffered years of torture under his care before he had sold her with no regard. If Dr. DeMarco hadn't come along, she would have ended up at an auction, sold as a sex slave for money to buy whiskey and Cuban cigars.

Haven's anger grew as she bit down on her lip. Her mama had the best intentions, even though she was helpless. She hid her for protection and never failed to keep the one thing even Haven had lost over the years—hope.

Haven blinked away tears as memories assaulted her. Twenty minutes had gone by, so she took a deep breath and started writing. She wrote whatever came to her mind as she thought of her mama, how a good parent never gave up and always encouraged their children to dream.

The instructor called time as Haven put a period on the end of the final sentence. The rest of testing flew by, and they were dismissed at three in the afternoon. The Mazda was waiting in the fire lane with the music blaring, and Haven quietly slipped into the passenger seat.

Carmine turned his music down as he pulled from the curb. "How did you do?"

She smiled softly as he offered her his hand. "Okay."

Neither spoke on the drive back to Durante. When they arrived at the house she went right to the kitchen to make something to eat. Carmine sat on the counter beside the stove and watched her as she cooked. "Are you making enchiladas?"

She nodded. "They were, uh . . . my mama liked them."

"Looks good," Carmine said.

"Thanks."

"We can eat and watch a movie or something."

"Okay."

"Or maybe we'll play a game."

"Okay."

"Actually, I'm tired, so maybe we'll go straight to bed."

"Okay."

"Probably won't even fucking eat."

"Uh, okay."

The room grew silent as Carmine glared at Haven. His shift in demeanor startled her. "Are you okay?"

"I'm fine," he said. "You, I'm not sure about. Since I picked you up, you've barely said a dozen words and half of them were *okay*. Did something happen?"

"No."

"Did you fail?" He raised his eyebrows. "Did you freak out or something?"

"No, I think I did okay." She cringed as she said that word again.

"Then what's wrong?"

"I'm just thinking about my mama."

"You wanna talk about her?" he asked, his voice quiet and genuine, all traces of frustration melted away. "You don't have to keep it to yourself."

"I know, but I don't know what to say. I miss her, and I'll probably never see her again. I never got to tell her good-bye or that I love her. It hurts to think about, because I used to wonder if we even loved each other, but I realized today Mama did love me. And I love her, but I never told her that."

"Never?"

"Never," she whispered as Carmine hopped down from the

counter to hug her. "I shouldn't be crying about this to you because you have more reason to grieve. My mama's alive, and yours is . . ."

He flinched before she could speak the word. She pulled from his arms and tried to apologize, but he pressed his pointer finger to her lips. "My mom lived, Haven. She was free to make her choices, and she did just that. She made fucking stupid decisions, and she died because of it. Your mom has never been able to make a decision, so I think you have more to grieve than I do."

Sunny Oaks Manor was anything but sunny today. A storm waged outside, rain steadily falling as gusts of wind bent the flimsy trees around the property. Thunder rumbled as lightning lit up the darkened afternoon sky, making it feel like the middle of the night.

Vincent stood in his mother's apartment, watching the ambulance parked outside. The EMTs, in their vivid yellow raincoats, loaded the black body bag into the back. Quietly, he made the sign of the cross and whispered a short prayer.

"Don't pray for that old hag," Gia said, somehow overhearing him without her hearing aides. "It's her own fault she's dead."

"How?" The staff said Gertrude died peacefully in her sleep.

"She left her window open last week. I tried to warn her, but she wouldn't listen. That black bird flew in like it owned the place."

Vincent sighed. "I don't think it was the bird, Ma."

Gia waved him off. "What do you know?"

"Well, I am a doctor."

"Oh, you quacks never know what you're talking about," she said. "You always want to give people pills and take their blood from them when it's unnecessary. God doesn't make mistakes, Vincenzo. People die when they deserve to. You know that."

Vincent clenched his hand into a fist at the subtle dig about Maura. "What about Dad? Did he deserve it?"

"As many *goomah*s as your father had? I'm surprised his heart lasted as long as it did."

Vincent would never understand his mother's callousness. Sometimes he wondered why he bothered visiting when she obviously didn't appreciate his company.

The ambulance pulled away from Sunny Oaks, and Vincent's eyes followed it to the corner in the storm. His gaze lingered there, his stomach dropping as he took in the dark SUV parked less than a block away. He hoped he imagined things, but his instincts told him it was no coincidence. He'd only been joking when he suggested they were watching him, but he realized he'd been right. He was being followed.

"Are you listening to me?"

"No," Vincent admitted, turning to his mother. "What did you say?"

"I'm not repeating myself for you," Gia said. "It'll suck the breath from my lungs and take time off my life. That's probably what you want, isn't it? For me to die? Then I wouldn't be a burden anymore. Your own mother . . . you treat me like garbage."

Vincent sighed exasperatedly. "What do you want from me, Ma?"

"Nothing, Vincenzo. I want nothing."

He glanced at his watch, fresh out of patience. "I should go. Dominic and Tess are waiting."

Gia narrowed her eyes. "Who are they?"

"You know who Dominic is," he said, trying to keep calm, but he had had about as much of her as he could take. "He's your grandson, and Tess is his girlfriend."

"Is she Italian?"

"No, she's American. Scottish heritage."

"Scottish? At least that's better than the Irish. What about that other boy of yours? Does he have an Italian girl?"

Vincent walked over to his mother and kissed her forehead, heading toward the door without answering.

The week flew by in a blur as Haven and Carmine were left alone. It was easy for them to forget during those days, when it was just the two of them, that barriers stood in their way. It seemed so simple, their lives merging fluidly within the confines of the house; but the outside world was closing in on them fast. A black cloud hovered in the distance, threatening to burst, but the problem was they didn't know when, where, or how it would come down. It could be an inconvenient drizzle or a flood that washed everything away. There was no way to prepare for the storm when they couldn't predict what would happen when it struck.

It was Friday afternoon, and they were in the family room watching a movie, their bodies pressed together on the couch, legs entwined as she lay in his arms. His lips wandered down her jaw, his mouth vigorously sucking on the flesh of her neck.

The sound of Haven's light moans was cut off abruptly when the alarm beeped and the front door slammed. Panicked, Carmine sat up as his father stormed into the room. Instinctively, he shifted his body protectively in front of Haven's as Vincent clenched his hands into fists. "My office. *Now.*"

"Who?" Carmine asked tentatively as his father walked away.

"You."

Carmine stood and pulled Haven to her feet. "Go to my room and stay there while I find out what's happening."

Haven followed him upstairs, but his legs were longer and she couldn't keep up with his stride. Carmine went straight for his father's office, thrusting the door open without bothering to knock. Vincent was hunched over his laptop, typing furiously away at the keys. "They're coming."

Carmine's brow furrowed at the vague statement. "Who?"

"Ed McMahon and the prize patrol. Who do you think is coming?"

The mocking tone caught him off guard. "Feds?"

"I wish." Vincent shook his head. "It's probably only a matter of time before they come knocking, but no . . . we're not that lucky today.

I got a call a few minutes ago that Sal hopped a plane to come here with no warning. I don't know why, and I have no idea what they want."

"What does that mean?"

"I don't know." Vincent opened desk drawers and rifled through files. "I'm hoping it's unexpected business, but it could be one of you they're after, so I need you out of here in case. Corrado doesn't think you should be anywhere without protection."

"I have a gun," Carmine said.

Vincent's head shot up. "A lot of good one gun does you as a *nobody*. They could kill you and no one would know unless you had one of us by your side."

Vincent's phone vibrated against the desk, and he held his hand up to silence Carmine. He answered it formally, his voice as even as possible. "DeMarco speaking . . . Yes, sir . . . I'll be here."

He hung up, tossing the phone down as he eyed his son peculiarly. "Pack some bags. We need to get the ball rolling on things."

Haven paced the floor in Carmine's bedroom, listening attentively for noises from below, but her ears were met with silence. No yelling. No screaming. No commotion at all.

The stillness only served to fuel her imagination as she conjured up wild scenarios—none of them remotely good. Her hands shook, fear coursing through her as a door slammed on the floor below. Footsteps hurried up the stairs as her heart thumped harder, so frenzied she could feel the blood rushing through her.

The door flung open, slamming the wall with a bang, and Carmine hurried in. He headed straight for his closet and threw things around, tossing two duffel bags onto the bed. "Pack some shit."

She didn't move. "What?"

"We need to get out of here, Haven."

Haven felt woozy. She wanted to ask what was happening, desperately wanted him to explain, but she knew the answer would terrify her. She staggered to the bed and sat down as Carmine ran to her room, Dr. DeMarco's words echoing through her mind. She had promised she would never run again. She swore she wouldn't follow Carmine blindly.

"Why are you sitting there?" Carmine asked when he returned, his arms full of clothes. Thoughts swirled madly around her mind as he filled both bags and held his hand out to her. "Let's go."

The moment the words rolled from his tongue, her mind was made up. No matter the consequences, she had to go with him.

They hurried downstairs and Carmine pulled her onto the porch, not bothering to close the front door in his haste. Unlocking the car doors, he tossed the bags into the back and motioned for her to get in. As soon as they were settled, Carmine started the car and thrust it into gear. The tires spun and gravel sprayed as he sped away from the house.

"What's going on?" Haven asked once they got on the highway, her voice cracking and stomach bubbling. "Why are we running? Did something happen?"

"We needed to get out of there before they showed up."

She gaped at him as they pulled up to a red light in town. "Before who showed up, Carmine?"

He stared straight ahead. "Them."

Not understanding, Haven followed the trail of his gaze, her eyes falling on four sleek black sedans sitting at the same red light, facing the opposite direction. "Are they . . . ?" she started, unable to finish the question. She'd seen those cars before.

"*La Cosa Nostra*," Carmine said, the Italian words flowing beautifully, but the knowledge of what they meant sent a chill down Haven's spine. Monsters.

The light turned green, and Carmine drove through the intersection. "You might wanna get comfortable, because it's a long drive to California."

Intense emotion hit her, stealing the breath from her lungs. "California?"

He nodded. "We're needed in Blackburn."

39

Carmine glanced at Haven in the passenger seat, frowning at the angle of her neck. She curled up the best she could with the seatbelt on. Reaching over, he brushed some hair out of Haven's face and tucked it behind her ear. He ran the back of his hand across her cheek, feeling the roughness of the red blotches from crying. She hadn't said anything about where they were going, but her tears spoke volumes about how she felt.

They had been on the road for three days, stopping occasionally to catch some sleep, but the majority of the time had been spent in the cramped car. The sky was overcast, the weather growing worse every mile, the constant drizzle turning into a downpour. Carmine slowly navigated the heavy traffic, his nerves on edge as he firmly gripped the steering wheel.

Haven sensed his unstable mood when she awoke and waited for him to attempt conversation first. "We're almost to the state line," he said quietly.

She stared out her foggy window. "Have you ever been to California?"

"Not that I remember," he said. "I always wanted to, though."

"Do they have colleges here?"

"Of course."

"Any I could go to?"

"Sure," he said. "What kinda classes do you wanna take?"

"Art, maybe," she said. "I don't know if I'm good enough to—"

He cut her off. "You are good enough. And yeah, there are plenty of art schools out here."

For the first time in days, something other than trepidation shined from her eyes. "Really?"

He chuckled. "Yes, really, but why California?"

She shrugged. "I like the palm trees."

Her serious tone as she answered caught him off guard. Most people overanalyzed where to go to school, choosing places based on student-teacher ratios, reputations, and sports teams, but she chose a place because of the scenery. He found it amusing, but he wasn't at all surprised. The little things in life mattered once again.

"Do they have them in New York?"

"Palm trees?"

She laughed. "No, art schools."

"Oh. Yeah, of course. Art schools are everywhere."

"Have you ever been there?"

"A few times when I was a kid. My father used to go to New York on business."

"I saw on *Jeopardy!* it's the city that never sleeps."

He smiled. "Some people call it the city of dreams, too."

She gazed at him. "Maybe we could go there to follow our dreams."

"Maybe." He laughed. "But I'm pretty sure they don't have palm trees."

The Blackburn city-limit sign was worn and faded, the green paint sandblasted to a dirty gray. The white writing on it was barely legible. Carmine did a double take as they passed by. "Did that say population *seventeen?*"

"I didn't think it was that many," Haven said. "I ran for hours."

Nothing but uninhabited land surrounded the barren highway. "I believe it. We haven't passed anything for miles."

They drove for a few minutes before he spotted something in

the distance. He slowed the car, hoping to find a gas station since the gauge hovered near empty. A hotel would be nice too, since his eyes burned from fatigue, but as he neared the structures, his hope diminished. The abandoned shells of buildings looked as though a small gust of wind could knock them down. His hair stood on end as they drove through, an eerie feeling overcoming the car.

"This is a ghost town," he said. "Where the hell are the people?"

"Maybe they moved."

He laughed dryly. "Or they all died."

"Some did," she said.

Her strangled voice told him a story existed behind those words, but it wasn't the time to ask questions. She looked to be teetering on the brink of a breakdown, and he couldn't risk pushing her over the edge.

Carmine continued to drive, passing another city-limit sign. They'd gone from one side of Blackburn to the other without seeing a living soul. The town was an enormous prison cell. There were no bars or chains, no physical restraints, but it was a mass of oblivion cut off from the world. There were no people, no cars, no stores, no houses . . . there wasn't even any color.

It was like it didn't exist.

Suddenly, so much made sense to Carmine. He knew she had grown up isolated, but knowing and seeing were vastly different things. He wanted nothing more in that moment than to pull over and hug her. She communicated, and drove, and took GED tests. She opened herself up to everything when she had literally come from nothing.

Nothing.

In the next town, they came upon a tiny motel. Carmine paid the old man at the front desk in cash and grabbed the key from him with little conversation. He grimaced at the shabby conditions while Haven shrugged. "I've stayed worse places."

She had. He understood now.

Carmine was startled awake by a ringing the next morning, the shrill noise causing his heart to violently pound. Sitting up, he rubbed his eyes and grabbed his phone off the stand beside the bed.

He answered without looking, hoping it was his father calling with some news. "Yeah?"

"Have you arrived?" *Corrado.*

"Yeah," Carmine said, yawning halfway through the word.

"I'll be at the Antonellis' today," Corrado said. "We have some business to attend to. Can you bring the girl to me?"

Glancing in the bed beside him, Carmine met Haven's apprehensive eyes. "Yeah."

"Yeah?" Corrado sighed. "Is that the only word you know?"

The sarcastic ass in Carmine wanted to say, "Yeah," but he knew it wasn't wise to fuck with a poisonous snake, so to speak. "No, sir."

Corrado rattled off the Antonellis' address as Carmine scoured the room for something to write with. He found a short, dull pencil in a drawer and snatched the Bible out of the nightstand, opening it and tearing out the first page. Haven gasped and sat up as he scribbled down the address. "I can't believe you tore out that page. It's the Bible, Carmine!"

He rolled his eyes. "Do you really think anyone who comes here would be reading this?" he asked, holding up the Bible. "People who stay here are far from holy."

"We stayed here."

"Like I said, far from holy." He chuckled. "But whatever, I didn't tear out anything with the story on it. The page says *Holy Bible.*"

"It's still wrong," Haven said.

"Maybe, but I needed to write down the Antonellis' address."

She froze, her expression panicked. "Why?"

Sitting down, he brushed some wayward curls out of her face. She looked so vulnerable, and he wanted nothing more than to right every wrong and make the world better for her sake. "You wanna see your mom, don't you?"

She blinked rapidly. "Can I?"

He ran his fingertips along her cheek. "I'll make sure of it."

Her eyes glassed over with tears as she threw herself at him, knocking him back onto the bed.

––––––––––

Carmine punched the address into the car's navigation system, and it led them back down the same remote highway from the night before. After a few miles, it alerted them to a path cutting through the desert, and Haven tensed a fraction of a second before the navigation system announced they'd arrived. She recognized it, he realized. She could sense it in the middle of nowhere.

Haven trembled as he crept down the path, her fear so powerful he could feel it. The ranch came into view, and she inhaled sharply as Carmine parked behind Corrado's rented sedan.

"I don't think I can do this," Haven said, shaking her head so frantically it made him dizzy.

Carmine grabbed her hands. "Listen and listen good, *tesoro*. You may wanna run as far away from this place as possible, but you can't. Not anymore. You can't let them control you. You can't let them win. You're strong, Haven. These motherfuckers tried to tear you down, but it didn't work because you built yourself up. You're a force to be reckoned with. You're tough and passionate, and you can't let these people get to you. That's what they want."

The anxiety in her expression was replaced with something else, a look Carmine could recognize anywhere: *determination*.

"So we're gonna get out of this car, and we're gonna go in this house, and we're gonna tell these people to kiss our asses, because they can't touch us. And you're gonna go out there and tell your mom you love her, because you deserve that chance."

Having said everything he could say, Carmine got out of the

car. He groaned at the heat, the bright sun blinding him. Grabbing his sunglasses, he put them on and unbuttoned his long-sleeved green shirt. "Fuck, it's hot."

Haven stepped out timidly. "I remember it being hotter."

"Well, I'm about to burn up," he said. "It's hot as Hell."

"It *is* Hell."

He gaped at her. "You cursed."

"*Hell* isn't a curse word."

"Yes, it is."

She shook her head. "It's in the Bible, Carmine. If you spent more time reading it and less time tearing pages out of it, maybe you'd know that."

He laughed, but a slamming door interrupted the moment. Haven went rigid as Carmine glanced at the man standing on the porch, his eyes a familiar deep brown shade Carmine knew well.

"If this is Hell," Carmine said, "does that make him the devil?"

40

Michael Antonelli stood on his front porch, a glass of whiskey in his left hand and a lit cigar in his right. He wasn't speaking. He wasn't blinking. He didn't even appear to be breathing.

Haven stared at him, stunned by how utterly unchanged he looked. It had nearly been a year, but seeing her old master in his khaki pants and polo shirt, too tight around his bulging gut, made it feel like no time had passed.

The tense silence shattered when the door behind Michael opened, jolting him back alive. Blinking rapidly, he moved out of the way as Corrado stepped onto the porch. "Carmine, Haven . . . nice to see you. Are you enjoying your trip?"

The nonchalance of the question surprised Haven, but Carmine didn't appear to be put off as he answered. "It's been fine, except for the fact that I feel like I'm being boiled alive."

Haven smiled involuntarily at his complaining as Corrado's gaze turned to Michael. "Are you going to invite the kids in, Antonelli, or do you intend to let my nephew burst into flames? I was under the impression you remembered how to be hospitable."

"Oh, yeah!" Michael stuck his cigar into his mouth and opened the screen door. "Come inside."

Carmine took Haven's hand and led her into the house, the two of them following Corrado down the hallway to a cramped office in the back. Haven hesitated, scanning the cluttered walls. For years she had lived on the property, trapped and forced to work in servitude, but never in that time had she been in that room. Michael said it was private, his sanctuary.

Michael walked in behind them and took a seat in front of a shiny mahogany desk as Corrado stood off to the side with his arms crossed over his chest. "We're waiting for one more."

Haven looked to Carmine, but he offered no explanation if he had one.

After a few minutes there was a knock on the front door of the ranch. Corrado walked out to answer it, returning with another man carrying a briefcase. Michael tensed as he eyed him, blinking rapidly. "What are we—? Why's the lawyer here?"

"Let's get this done," Corrado said, ignoring the question. Haven sat down, slinking into a chair in the corner so not to make a scene. Michael glared at her from across the room, uncomfortable silence enveloping the space between them, an invisible wall of pressure separating their chairs.

The lawyer talked about naturalization and citizenship, but none of it made sense to her. He filled out paperwork as he spoke but hesitated on a document, glancing at Haven. "Miss, what's your birthday?"

Her heart thumped wildly. "I'm not sure. Mama said it was in the fall."

The man's forehead creased as his eyes shifted to Michael. "Mr. Antonelli? Her date of birth?"

Michael grumbled but said nothing coherent as Corrado sighed exaggeratedly. "September tenth, 1988."

The lawyer wrote it down, while Haven stared at Corrado. She wondered how he knew, the date running through her mind. September 10 . . . it was two weeks away.

When finished, the lawyer handed the paperwork to Corrado, who set it on the desk in front of Michael. "Sign it," he demanded.

Michael begrudgingly signed before shifting the stack of papers in Haven's direction. She could feel his eyes on her as he held out the pen. She took it without looking at him. Glancing through the papers, she spotted the blank lines beside where he'd signed. Her hand trembled as she scribbled her name beside his.

She wondered if he was surprised she could write. *Take that, buddy.*

"That's it," Corrado said. "It's done."

What was done? Haven wasn't sure, but Michael didn't appear happy about it.

———

Haven stepped onto the porch of the house, taking a deep breath of the scalding desert air. Her stomach felt queasy, her nerves running amuck. She needed space. She needed to be away from those people. She needed Carmine.

She called for him, but a loud commotion stopped her before she could step back inside. Startled by the disruption, Haven turned, her breath hitching when she saw her mama standing at the corner of the house, a bunch of metal tools laying in a pile at her feet.

Unlike Michael, she looked different. Her dark hair was streaked with gray, and wrinkles lined her weary face. A dirty shirt swallowed her skeletal frame, a pair of shorts exposing startlingly thin legs. Her mama had always been skinny, but now she was a shell of her former self.

"Haven?"

The sound of her voice was like blistering iron striking Haven's chest. Her feet frantically carried her to her mama, their bodies colliding as they both fell to the ground. Her mama's embrace was strong despite her frail body, her hands traveling Haven's back and hair as she clung to her. "My baby girl! You're here!"

"Yes," she choked out. "I'm here."

Her mama pulled from the embrace. "Why are you here? You have to get away!"

"It's okay," Haven said. "No one's going to hurt me."

"You can't be sure! You know how they are!"

Haven tried to smile through her tears. "I'm here to see you."

Her hands explored Haven's face. "I don't understand. It doesn't make sense."

"Carmine brought me. He's, uh . . . he's my master's son. I love him, Mama."

"You love him?" She stared at her, blinking rapidly. "This is bad. You can never let him know!"

"Stop!" Her mama's panic caused her anxiety to flare. "He already knows. He loves me, too."

"How?" She shook her head. "Haven, he's—"

"Wonderful, Mama," she interrupted, knowing whatever she said would be wrong. "He treats me like a treasure, and he's giving me a life . . . the kind of life you always wanted me to have."

They sat on the ground for a few minutes, neither speaking after that was verbalized. Her mama's panic lessened, the look Haven had seen growing up creeping back in.

Hope.

Eventually, Haven stood and helped her mama to her feet. "These are nice clothes," her mama said, giving her a once-over. "I hope they don't get mad you got them dirty."

Haven blocked her mama's hands as she tried to brush the dirt away. "It doesn't matter. They're different."

Tears welled in her mama's eyes at the statement, but the banging screen door stopped her from saying anything. Michael stepped onto the porch and looked at them. "Miranda."

No good ever came from being singled out. Frenzied, her mama gathered the things she had dropped. "I'm sorry, sir. I'm supposed to be in the garden."

Michael put his hand up to stop her, and Haven and her mama both flinched at his sudden movement. "Don't interrupt me. The girl's here with, uh . . . she's our guest, so work can wait for now."

Her mama gaped at her after Michael walked away. "Guest?"

Haven smiled. "I guess I should start at the beginning, huh?"

They spent the next few hours walking around the property as Haven told her mama about life in North Carolina, telling stories about celebrating Christmas, watching fireworks, and going to a dance. The more Haven spoke, the more her mama lit up. The life came back into her, little by little easing Haven's guilt.

They were standing at the edge of the garden as her mama kicked around some dirt in her bare feet, pulling a few stray weeds. She couldn't refrain from working even when told she didn't have to. "The DeMarco family. That name sounds familiar."

"They've been here before," Haven said. "I used to think the woman was an angel."

Her mama looked at her. "Your angel?"

Haven nodded. "I thought I made her up, but I guess she was real."

Her mama's eyes drifted past her shoulder at something, and Haven swung around to see Carmine approach. "Speak of the devil."

"I thought we said the asshole in the house was the devil," Carmine said, shaking his head. "Christ, he's a dickhead. I thought Corrado was going to kick my ass for saying shit to him."

She sighed, knowing he had no filter to stop things from springing from his lips. "What did you say?"

"I don't know. I said a lot. He's kind of a punk, you know? He'll fuck with those lesser than him but can't stand up to his equals." His eyes widened. "I'm not saying you're less than him or anything, or that I'm better than you, because I'm not. You're better than him. Hell, you're better than me, and I tell—"

Haven covered his mouth so he'd stop rambling, and her mama gasped. Turning to look at her, Haven pulled her hand from Carmine's mouth as a reflex, but he wrapped his arms around her before she could move away. "You should introduce me, *tesoro*."

She smiled. "Mama, this is Carmine. Carmine, this is my mama."

"Nice to finally meet you," he said politely, holding out his hand.

Her mama hesitantly took it, staring at him.

Corrado's voice interrupted then as he stepped out of the house. "The food's ready. I thought you'd like to know, since Carmine complained earlier he was going to die of starvation."

Haven rolled her eyes as Carmine chuckled. "What? I haven't eaten anything today."

"Go eat if you're hungry," she said.

"Are you coming? You haven't eaten, either."

Haven stubbornly shook her head. "I'm not eating when she can't."

Her mama sighed. "Eat if they'll let you, Haven. I'll be here when you're done."

"No."

Carmine's brow furrowed. "Why can't she eat?"

"Master feeds us at night, but never during the day . . . and definitely not with them."

"I forgot about that," Carmine said. "That's bullshit. You should eat when you wanna eat."

"It's fine."

Carmine let go of Haven and went for the house. "No, it's not. Wait here. I'll fix this shit."

———

A few minutes later, the screen door slammed as Carmine stepped outside, heading toward them with two plates. Haven smiled when he approached. "You're so good to me."

"Hey, that's my line," he said playfully, handing Haven a plate. "Quit stealing my shit."

He held the other one out to her mama, who made no attempt to take it, so Haven did. She eyed the sandwiches, the bread smashed down with a handprint in the center of it. "Did you make this?"

"Yes," Carmine said. "I can make a sandwich, you know."

Smiling proudly, Haven thrust the second plate at her mama. "Eat."

She took it, her hands shaking. "Thank you."

"You're welcome," Carmine said. "You two sit down somewhere and eat." Haven went to sit right where she was, but Carmine grabbed her arm. "You can't sit somewhere less dirty?"

Ignoring him, she plopped down. "I'm already dirty."

Carmine shook his head as a small dust cloud rose into the air. "Now you got *me* dirty."

"Unless you plan to do your own laundry, I don't see why you're complaining."

He laughed. "Because it wouldn't be me if I didn't complain. Enjoy your sandwiches. It's the best I could do. You know I can't cook, but I do love you."

He kissed her before heading to the house as her mama finally sat down beside Haven. The frailty and exhaustion was still evident in her face, but she appeared at peace.

Carmine stood at the window, watching Haven out in the yard as time wound down, the sun dipping below the horizon and turning the sky the color of glowing coal.

He could feel Michael's eyes boring into him from where he sat across the room, puffing on his third cigar. The stench of smoke made Carmine's stomach turn. Michael wheezed when he breathed, like he was constantly struggling to speak, but not a word had come from him in more than two hours. *Fucking coward.*

Corrado strolled over to Carmine, both of them taking in the scene outside.

"You have to help her," Carmine said, the thought of separating them tearing him up inside.

Corrado continued to stare straight ahead. "Do you remember when your grandfather died?"

"Vaguely," he said. "I was only six."

"I was outside your grandparents' house after the funeral, and your mother sat down beside me. Your mother . . . she never liked to come near me, so for her to do it was a big deal." He paused. "When she gathered the courage to speak, she said those exact words: You have to help her."

Carmine gaped at him. "Haven?"

Corrado nodded. "I told your mother it wasn't my place, but I should've tried. I owed her that much."

"You owed her?"

"Yes, I did, but why is irrelevant. The only thing that matters is I never made it up to her."

"Does that mean you're gonna help?"

He cut his eyes at him. "I vouched for her, didn't I?"

"Yeah, you did, but . . ." Carmine trailed off, glancing out at Haven in the yard. "What about her mom? Can't you help her?"

"I can't help everyone. There will always be someone, somewhere, who needs something."

"I know, but this isn't just someone," Carmine said. "This is her family, like we're family."

Corrado's stare was hard. "You're playing the family card?"

"I, uh . . ." Carmine hesitated, but there was no point denying it. "Yes."

"You're certain you want to do that?"

Corrado's tone made Carmine question it momentarily. *Did he?* "Sure."

Turning to the window, Corrado shook his head. "The most I can do is let her live in my home. It's a risk, but frankly, after vouching for your girlfriend, I doubt it's possible to dig myself in any deeper. If I die, that'll be what kills me. Everything else is extra." Corrado turned to Michael, who still sat quietly in his chair. "Any objections, Antonelli?"

Michael stammered. He hadn't heard a word of what they'd said. "Uh, I . . . well, I don't know."

Corrado raised an eyebrow, the look on his face enough to make Carmine balk. "What do you mean you don't know?"

"I mean . . ." He shook his head. "Sure, it's fine with me."

Corrado turned around. "We'll handle it all tonight, then. Drop Haven off at the hotel and come back. It should be settled by then."

———

Carmine finally made his way outside. As soon as Haven spotted him, a cold sense of dread settled deep within her. He paused a few feet away. "I'll give you a minute."

Her mama pulled her into a hug, tears streaming from her eyes, but a radiant smile shined from her lips. "You don't know how much it means to me to see you like this. My baby girl, with the world at her fingertips."

Haven squeezed her tightly. "I love you, Mama."

"I love you too. I always have. I want you to go out there and live your life."

Her chest ached at having to leave her again. "I miss you."

"I miss you too, but the world is a better place with you in it," her mama said, pulling from the hug. "Now get away from this place. I'm happy to see you again, but I'll be happier knowing you're out there living."

"But I can't leave you here, Mama. Not again."

"Hush," she said sternly. "Don't worry about me."

Haven tried to speak, wanting to object, but her mama didn't give her a chance.

"Go," she said again. "You found your place in the world. Don't let me hold you back from it."

Haven covered her mouth as tears blurred her vision. Taking a few steps back, she gave her mama one last look before running for the car.

41

It was pitch black when Carmine made it back to the ranch that night, the dry desert air still scorching. He started toward the house, irritable and uncomfortable, but froze when the front door opened. Miranda walked out, her eyes darting around wildly. Even in the darkness, Carmine could make out a faint hand-shaped mark on her throat.

"Who did this to you?" Carmine asked. "I'll fucking kill them."

Panic flashed in Miranda's expression. "Please don't make a scene."

He fought to keep a grip on his temper. "It's wrong."

"I know, but . . . please." She stepped into the yard, nervousness in her expression. She worried she was being watched. "I remember when your mama visited. She used to talk about a world outside of this place for my daughter. She said Haven was special."

Hearing those words made Carmine's chest ache with longing. "She is."

"It means a lot to hear you say that. I hardly recognize my daughter, you know. She's still that sweet baby girl I raised, but she's happy. She's better off away from all of this." She walked away but paused after a few steps. "I heard someone talking about safe houses once and how they helped people get free. They called them *havens*. I named her that because she was my haven. She was my safe place in this ugly world. When she was born, I had a reason to live. My baby girl, my Haven, needed to be protected.

I've done all I can, so I'm asking you to look out for her out there. Keep her away from people like these. Can you do that?"

Carmine was stunned at the trust she placed in him. "Yes."

"Thank you," she said. "I can rest easy now."

The front door opened and Miranda bolted for the stables before he could say another word. Carmine glanced at the porch as Corrado stepped out, his eyebrows raised. "Did you tell her?"

"No, you scared her away before I could."

A loud screeching ricocheted from the house. Footsteps pounded across the floor as a woman's voice echoed out to them. "My brother vouched for that little bitch?"

Carmine went up the steps, but Corrado grabbed his shirt to stop him. "Don't say anything."

The front door thrust open, and Katrina stepped out. Her steps faltered when she saw Carmine, but she regained her composure and turned to her brother. "I can't believe you, Corrado! What did you make my husband sign this morning?"

"He signed what was necessary," he said, his outward appearance not reflecting the anger brewing on the inside.

Katrina laughed bitterly. "Necessary? None of this is necessary! You're freeing that damn girl and taking her mother? What's gotten into you? Is it because of *her*? Is that what this is about?"

Fire flared in Corrado's eyes as he lost his composure. "Enough!"

Carmine's heart thumped frantically, but Katrina wasn't fazed. "It is, isn't it? Trying to make up for the past? It can't be fixed!"

"I'm not going to tell you again, Katrina."

"I'm not afraid of you," she said, closing the distance between them. "You're screwing up my life over this! Why do these people matter? Just because these stupid DeMarcos fall—"

Corrado's arms shot out, his hands grasping her by the throat and cutting off her words midsentence. She choked, her manicured fingernails digging into his flesh as she tried to pry his hands off. Even as she drew blood, Corrado didn't waver.

"Are you done now?" he asked, the eerie calmness returning.

Katrina gurgled as she fought for oxygen and words. "Burns, doesn't it? Imagine how they feel when you torture them. Imagine how *she* felt that day, Kat, when those men were choking her, when they were violating her, and you did nothing to stop it."

Corrado continued to stare at his sister, giving no indication he was going to let go. Michael bounded out the front door of the house and gasped. "Stop! You'll kill her!"

Corrado's eyes snapped to Michael. There was no emotion in his expression, nothing but darkness. This was the Corrado Carmine feared.

Before he could dwell, a commotion rang out from the stables as the horses reared up, spooked by something. Corrado let go of Katrina, his eyes meeting Carmine's as he hurried down the steps. Carmine leaped off the porch after him.

"She's not her," Katrina screamed. "Just because he's doing the same thing as his father doesn't mean they're the same!"

Those words caught Carmine off guard. He swung around to look at Katrina, not paying attention to where he was going. He ran straight into Corrado's back as his uncle stopped in the doorway to the stables. Corrado shoved Carmine inside, and sickness rocked through him as the air left his lungs. He dry heaved, trying to breathe through the bile that flooded his chest. It burned, suffocating, and his vision blurred as he nearly blacked out.

Flashes of memory hit him, buckling his knees. The gunshot, the blood, the terror, the hooded figure pointing the gun at him. And there was his mom, lying dead in the darkened alleyway after the shrill screams rang out in the night.

Corrado yanked him upright by his shirt and shoved him again, forcing him back to reality. "Get a grip, Carmine."

A small wooden stool lay on the ground in front of him, tipped over in a pile of hay, while a pair of dirty bare feet swung a few inches above it. The frail, familiar form hung limp like a rag doll, affixed to a low rafter by a piece of thick rope.

Carmine lunged forward and grabbed Miranda's legs as he

yelled for help. Corrado yanked a pair of garden shears from the wall and snipped the rope. The body fell on Carmine, and he staggered a few steps, nearly losing his footing. Laying her on the ground, he checked for a pulse but couldn't find one.

Katrina and Michael rushed in as Carmine did CPR, pounding on her chest and desperately forcing air into her lungs. Her body was still warm like she was asleep, but her wide eyes and ashen face told another story. Carmine could hear Katrina shouting and Michael's rushed voice, but the sound of his blood pumping through his body drowned out their words.

Panic. All he could feel was panic.

Nothing Carmine did helped. Ribs cracked sickeningly under the force of his compressions, her body not absorbing any of his air. Miranda lay still on the ground, her heart no longer beating.

Corrado grabbed his shoulder. "She's dead."

Carmine shrugged him off. "No, she's not! We have to save her!"

"It's too late."

"It's not!" He hysterically pushed on her chest some more. "Why are you just standing there?"

"There's nothing we can do."

"Help her! You told me you would, you fucking liar!"

Corrado grabbed his arm, pulling him away from Miranda's lifeless body and shoving him back onto the ground. "She's too far gone."

"How the hell do you know?"

His expression was cold. "I know a dead body when I see one."

Carmine sat in the dirt, his eyes stinging with tears. He looked around frantically, hoping it was a vicious nightmare he would soon wake up from, and spotted a smug smile on Katrina's lips.

The sight of it made him lose control. "This is your fault!" He looked between Katrina and Michael. "You killed her! You made her do this!"

"Who cares?" Katrina snapped. "She's a slave!"

The moment those words met his ears, all logic fizzled away. "No, she wasn't a slave!"

"Carmine!" Corrado warned.

"She was a *Principessa*!" he said, ignoring his uncle. "Salvatore's gonna kill you when he finds out!"

Grabbing the garden shears from the ground by his leg, Carmine flung them at Katrina and struck her in the side when she tried to move away. Deranged, she grabbed a shovel and ran toward him. He scurried backward and tried to get to his feet as she raised the shovel above her head. Corrado reacted swiftly, pulling his gun from his coat and aiming it at his sister with no hesitation. The sound of the gunshot ricocheted off the walls in the small enclosure, and Carmine recoiled at the deafening noise. The horses reared up again, spooked by the gunshot.

Katrina gasped as the bullet ripped through her chest, her footsteps halting as she swung the shovel in reaction. It slammed into Carmine's shoulder blade, sharp pain running through his left side. Katrina sputtered and dropped the shovel to clutch her chest. Another shot rang out, hitting dead center between her eyes, and she dropped to the ground.

A frantic Michael screamed, lunging for him, and Corrado reacted once more. Ducking, Carmine covered his head when the gunshot rang out, blood splattering in his direction as the bullet ripped through Michael's skull. He fell forward with a thud beside his wife, limp on impact.

Carmine dry heaved again as Corrado fired a few more shots into their bodies, his finger casually pulling the trigger as if it meant nothing. As if they weren't people. As if they weren't his *family*.

Glaring, Corrado yanked Carmine off the ground. He staggered a few steps as he gained his footing, his legs trying to buckle under his weight. He swayed, trying to hold everything in, but the annihilation sent shockwaves through him.

Corrado returned his gun to his coat and pulled out his cell phone as Carmine sat on the small stool. Putting his head between his legs, he covered his face with his hands and took deep breaths. He counted to ten, trying to calm down, but his ears rang and head pounded as Corrado spoke calmly into the phone.

One.

"There's been an incident."

Two.

"I burned two, sir."

Three.

"A confrontation escalated."

Four.

"I had to act."

Five.

"My sister and her husband."

Six.

"I take full responsibility."

Seven.

"I'll get a place ready."

Eight.

"And I'll accept any consequences . . ."

Nine.

" . . . even if it means rescinding my vouch for the girl."

Ten.

Carmine stared at his uncle when he hung up. "Rescind your vouch?"

Corrado slipped his phone into his pocket. "Yes. You better hope Sal feels forgiving, because I just broke our code of conduct."

"I, uh . . ."

"There's nothing else to say, Carmine. What's done is done."

"But, uh . . ." Corrado's nonchalance scared him. "Your sister. You always protect your family."

"Well, you're my nephew, correct?" Carmine nodded. "And Katrina attacked you, correct?" Another nod. "That means I protected my family. My sister and her husband made their beds, and it's nobody's fault but their own they now lie in them."

Carmine didn't speak, afraid he'd get sick if he tried. He never imagined things would happen like this—never imagined the day would end with him splattered in blood, the same blood that coursed through Haven's veins, while both of the people who brought her into existence were dead.

"It's over now," Corrado said, looking at the bodies. "This isn't yours to deal with . . . it's mine. But I hope this teaches you a lesson, and you finally realize you don't know everything."

Haven jolted awake, a sinking feeling in the pit of her stomach as she sat upright in the dark motel room. The black-and-white static on the television screen faintly illuminated Carmine standing by the doorway. A strange sensation trickled through her, a coldness starting in her chest. "Carmine?"

He stared at her, and in the glow of the television, she could see his panic. His eyes shined with tears of desperation, and she knew something had gone wrong.

"What happened?" she asked. "Is everything okay?"

Carmine took a step forward and ever so slightly shook his head. The subtle movement rocked her foundation. When he stepped farther into the light, she could see the red on his shirt, the splatter of blood. She had seen it before, streaking her blue dress as she stared down at the body of the fallen teenage girl. It was the mark of desolation. It was the mark of death. "Oh God, are you okay? Are you hurt?"

"It's not me," he whispered, his face twisting in agony. "She's gone."

She's gone. Haven knew those words. He'd said them about his own mama.

Haven's chest constricted as it felt like her lungs had collapsed, her insides bursting into vicious flames. "No!"

Carmine's raspy voice echoed with distress as he reached for her, but she pushed him as hard as she could. "Stop! You're wrong! Where is she, Carmine? What happened to my mama?"

Despite her attempts to get away, Carmine grabbed her and squeezed her tightly. She tried to push out of his arms but he held on, never wavering. "Let go! Tell me where she is!"

He shushed her, and she could hear his voice tremble as he started to cry. "I'm sorry, hummingbird, but she isn't coming back."

His tears shattered what was left of her resolve. Uncontrollable sobs ripped from her as she wailed on him, screaming that he didn't know anything. Balling her hands into fists, she repeatedly hit him in the back. He took every blow in stride, never once loosening his grip.

"I'm sorry," he said. "I did everything I could, but she's fucking gone."

Her panic surged. She chanted the word *no* and screamed incoherently, telling him he needed to go make it right. She blamed him, because he wasn't giving her an explanation, his reassuring words only stinging more. He ignored his ringing phone, not moving an inch as he took everything she threw at him, every harsh word and painful scream.

Every "I hate you" echoing from her chest was followed by an "I love you" from his lips. Every time she begged him to let go, he told her he would be there forever. His hold was strong, his arms familiar, but it did nothing to take away her pain.

"She didn't suffer," he whispered. "It was her choice."

Haven barely said a thing for days. Carmine explained to her what happened, told her what he knew, but she didn't react. She said nothing. They stayed in the motel in California for the rest of the week, but by the time the weekend rolled around, they had to go. The Mafia had departed and his father was still alive, having diffused another situation. They had only come to clean out the basement, worried about the police attention centered on Vincent.

The drive was strained without conversation. Carmine stopped frequently during the day to take breaks. By the time the weekend came to a close, they were pulling back into the city limits of Durante. He parked beside his father's Mercedes when they reached the house, and he climbed out, stretching. Haven went straight inside, not bothering to wait for him. He followed her, running into his father the moment he stepped into the foyer.

Vincent eyed them cautiously. "Hey, kids."

"Hey," Carmine said.

"Dr. DeMarco," Haven said. "May I be excused, sir?"

"Of course, *dolcezza*. You don't have to ask."

Carmine frowned, watching as she disappeared up the stairs. "I guess I'm going to bed."

His father sighed. "Take it one day at a time, Carmine."

42

Bookcases towered above Haven like skyscrapers. Strolling among the stacks, she occasionally pulled out a book and surveyed the front cover before skimming the description on the back.

They'd been back in Durante for a few days, just in time for Carmine's senior year of school. He immersed himself in class and football, leaving Haven with days to fill on her own. She cooked and cleaned, but she still had hours left over with nothing to do and no one to talk to.

Needing something to distract her, she turned to the library, hoping to get lost in a different world, to be absorbed in a fictional time and place, the life of someone else. She wanted to forget about everything so she wasn't constantly plagued with thoughts of her mama's last moments. She found herself wondering what she'd been thinking: Had she been scared? Had she been in pain? Was there ever a moment that she second-guessed her decision?

The feeling of failure nagged Haven. She ran that day in Blackburn because she had been desperate to save her mama, and she hadn't forgotten that. But now it was too late. Her mama was gone.

Haven ran her fingers along the spines of some books, and came across one without a name. She pulled out the leather-bound book and a piece of paper tumbled to the floor. She picked it up and unfolded it, her brow furrowing when she saw it was a letter.

Walking to the chair by the window, she sat with the book in her lap as she scanned the withering note.

10/08/97

Mrs. DeMarco,

   After careful consideration, I've decided I can no longer be
a part of this investigation. I took the case without knowing
the details, and had I known them at the time, I would have
declined. For all intents and purposes, Haven Antonelli does
not exist, and I implore you to forget you ever encountered
her. Enclosed you'll find a full refund of my fees. Consider
our contract severed, and I request you no longer contact me
concerning this.

Arthur L. Brannigan

Private Investigator

   Stunned, Haven scanned the paper a second time, certain she
had to have misread, as pieces of the puzzle filled in to expose a
hidden picture that left her speechless. Eyes brimming with tears,
her stomach dropped when she realized the date on the top of the
paper.

   October 8, 1997—a few days before Maura DeMarco had been
killed.

———

Vincent tapped his pen against his desk, surrounded by mounds of
files. Work piled up, but he couldn't focus on it. His attention kept
wandering, his thoughts and eyes drifting toward the live feed
playing on the screen beside him.

   It had been two weeks since the kids had returned from Blackburn, and the days had proven to be some of the longest of Vincent's life. The atmosphere in the house was tense, the silence that
followed both of them unsettling. He sat behind his desk every
night and watched his son pace the hallway just feet from the
office door, his hands assaulting his hair as he berated himself.
Vincent couldn't hear him, but he knew where his thoughts were.

   Vincent pressed a few buttons on the computer and the screen changed to a view of the library. He spotted the girl, curled up in the chair by the window with a book on her lap. It was the same place she had been every night while his son paced—sitting in the darkness and staring out into the yard. She withdrew further and further as time went on, but Vincent was too exhausted to mediate.

He was in deep with *la famiglia*. He lied, cheated, plundered, and slaughtered for them, but one thing he had prided himself on was his loyalty. He may have been a criminal, but at least he could think himself an honorable one. That had fallen to the wayside as of late, and they weren't ignorant to his behavior. They made that obvious during their recent visit. Every one of them was trained to spot deception . . . and Vincent was weary of being dishonest.

Maura had once told him that while not everyone lived, everyone did die, and with death came release. Death meant freedom—freedom from the things that hold us back. Vincent used to tease her when she said such things, but he understood now. He understood what it was like to wish you could find peace, but you couldn't because your work wasn't done. You hadn't served your purpose, and until you did, you were damned to keep going. Vincent envied those who could rest in peace. What he wouldn't give to have the weight of the world lifted from his shoulders.

He switched cameras once more and went back to the hallway. Carmine still paced, his eyes darting between the office and the stairs to the third floor. Vincent glanced at the time: after eleven in the evening. Carmine usually made his decision before now and stomped up the stairs. The girl would scurry out of the library, darting to her bedroom before he made it there.

Tonight things changed, though. When Carmine headed toward the office door, Vincent felt nothing but relief. Judgment Day had come. One step closer to peace.

The knob turned and Carmine stepped inside, slamming the door behind him. Vincent refrained from chastising him for not knocking, thankful he had actually made it inside. "Sit down," he said, switching the view back to the library.

Carmine flopped down in the chair with a huff. Vincent met his gaze, seeing the curiosity and confusion. Resentment lurked underneath, but Vincent couldn't blame him.

"You look like you haven't fucking slept in years," Carmine said. "And Christ, have you eaten?"

Vincent leaned back in his chair. "You want to discuss my health, Carmine?"

His expression was sober. "Yeah, you look fucked up."

"Well, thanks for the compliment, but something tells me you haven't spent the past week loitering outside my office gathering the courage to hold an intervention."

"How . . . ?" Carmine paused. "You've been watching the cameras."

"Yes," he said, "and I was beginning to wonder if you ever planned to come in."

Carmine sighed. "I didn't know what to say. No sense barging in just to look at you, since you look like shit and all."

"Considering you're here now, does that mean you've figured it out?"

"No, I just got tired of standing in the hall."

"Ah, I'm better to look at than the white walls, at least?"

Carmine cracked a smile. "No, but it's nice to know I'm not the only one around here who remembers how to joke."

"*Tale il padre, tale il figlio,*" Vincent said, regretting his choice of words the moment they escaped his lips. Carmine's smile fell, and Vincent knew exactly what he wanted to know. He'd been dreading this day for years.

"When we were in Blackburn, Katrina said something," Carmine started. "She said just because we were doing the same thing didn't mean we were the same . . . that Haven wasn't *her*. And it's not only that—there's other shit, too. So I'm wondering, you know . . ."

"You want to know how I met your mother."

"The truth."

The truth. Vincent couldn't avoid it anymore.

It had been a scorching afternoon as he stood in the yard of the Moretti mansion in Las Vegas. He brought his hand up to block out the blinding sun as he walked around the side of the house, searching for shade. As soon as he turned the corner, he crashed into someone there. Dropping his hand, he blinked rapidly at the girl in front of him. Pale skin glowed in the sunshine, a stark contrast from her fiery red hair. Deep green eyes watched him cautiously as he stared into them in a trance. Her mouth moved, but the words were lost on him. His stomach twisted, his heart unexpectedly gripped in a vice.

Colpo di fulmine. He was done for.

"Is there a problem?" she asked when he pulled her into the shade.

"The only problem is I don't know your name."

She smiled. "I'm Maura."

Maura. Her hair flowed past her shoulders and freckles dotted her nose. She wasn't Italian—not even close. No Italian he had ever met had eyes that color.

Those eyes . . . Vincent could never get enough of them. And as he looked across the desk at his youngest child, he saw the same eyes watching him suspiciously.

"We met at Celia's engagement party," he said, looking away. Sometimes it was still hard for Vincent to take.

"And what was an Irish girl doing at a party for two Italians?"

Vincent wondered the same thing that day.

He and Maura had sat against the side of the house, his legs spread out in front of him as he fanned his sweaty skin. Maura's knees were pulled up to her chest as she plucked the dry grass around them.

"You're not hot?" he asked. They had been sitting there for at least an hour.

"No, but you can go inside. The cool air will make you feel better."

"Will you go with me?"

"No way," she said. "That wouldn't be good at all."

He laughed. "Then I'm not going, either. They haven't noticed I'm gone, and until they do, I'm staying right where I am."

"Will they notice you're gone?"

"No, I doubt they remember I'm alive," he said. "What about you?"

Before she could answer, her eyes darted past him. Vincent turned around and groaned when he saw Katrina at the corner of the house, watching them.

"Go away, loon," Vincent said. "I'm not in the mood for you."

"What the hell are you doing?" Katrina spat.

Maura jumped to her feet, looking away as she trembled. "Sorry, Mistress."

Mistress. The moment she said it, he knew the truth.

"Well?" Carmine asked impatiently, pulling Vincent from his thoughts. "Why was she there?"

"She was the help."

"The help?" Carmine's tone was clipped. "Like a maid? Was she a waitress? Because the two of you were fifteen, and that's not old enough to be employed. Not like you people follow laws or anything . . ."

Vincent sighed. "She wasn't paid."

Carmine sprung forward, raising his voice. "It's true? Seriously?"

"Yes."

Carmine shoved the front of the desk as he stood, thrusting it into Vincent. He grabbed the laptop before it hit the floor as his son rambled. "How could I have been so fucking stupid? Never would I have imagined she had been . . . you'd have . . . Christ!"

Vincent shifted his desk back into place. "You can say the word."

"I know," he snapped, "but can you?"

"Of course. It's just a word."

"Then say it. Drop the 'she was the help' bullshit and say it."

"Slave," Vincent said. "Trafficking victim. Call it what you will, it's all the same."

Carmine's anger flared. "And the Morettis had her? Is that why Corrado says he owes her?"

"You'd have to ask him. That's not my story to tell."

"Of course it's not your story to tell," Carmine said, slamming his hands down on the desk. "The cop-out answer of the year. Nobody wants to tell me anything, so they pawn it off on everyone else. I can't believe you kept this from me! After everything, how could you not tell me?"

Vincent pushed Carmine's hands away. "It's in your best interest to settle down. If you want an explanation, take a seat. If not, get out of my office. The choice is yours, but I'm not going to sit here and let you scold me like a child."

Carmine glowered at him, clenching his jaw. Vincent could tell his son wanted to say something, but Carmine was smart enough to know that to get answers, he'd have to do things Vincent's way.

Sighing, Carmine flopped down in the chair. Vincent straightened some papers that had been disturbed, giving the computer a quick glance before addressing his son. "When do you suppose I should've told you? When you were two and didn't know what slavery was? When you were eight and thought your mother was infallible? After she was gone, when you were already hurting? The time was never right."

"But don't you think I had a right to know who my mother really was?"

The question sent Vincent's temper flaring. "That's not who your mother was! How many times have I overheard you telling the girl that that doesn't define her? How many times, Carmine? And yet you have the audacity to turn it around and use it against me, against your mother?"

"I didn't mean—"

"It doesn't matter what you meant," Vincent said. "This is why I never wanted you to know. Maura wanted people to see a wife and a mother—a woman—not a victim. I let her leave the past behind, and maybe it was unfair to you, but it was her life. It was her decision. I loved your mother, and we went through hell fighting to be together. I've tried to make it as easy as possible on you, so maybe you'd learn from my mistakes. I had to learn through trial and error. I lost my patience with her so many times because I didn't understand."

Carmine covered his face with his hands as he attempted to rein in his emotions. "She always seemed well adjusted."

"That was our intention," he said. "We didn't want to taint your perception of the things she did. If you knew the truth, you'd question everything."

Tears pooled in his eyes. "And this is why she was desperate to help Haven?"

Vincent was rocking Carmine's foundation, so he purposely treaded carefully. "Maura wasn't born into it, but she knew what the child had to look forward to. Your mother wanted to save her before reality hit. The older they are when you pull them out, the less likely they are to adapt."

"Is this why we don't see Grandma? Were you afraid she'd tell us the truth?"

A bark of laughter sounded through the room, and it took Vincent a second to realize it had come from him. "Uh, my mother . . ." He laughed again. "Let's just say she has her beliefs. A slave was bad enough. An Irish slave was worthy of disownment."

"So she was Irish? That part's true?"

"Yes. Her father fell into some trouble with the Irish mob. They snatched Maura as collateral when she was six."

"She was kidnapped? Didn't people look for her?"

"Of course they looked for her, but more than two thousand kids go missing in this country every day. Your mother disappeared before the Internet or any agencies for missing children existed, and certainly before there were things like Amber Alerts. All they had was word of mouth, and once everyone stopped talking about her, it was like she'd never existed."

"But what about her parents?"

"They were killed," he said. "Maura was sold a few times and ended up with Erika Moretti."

"Who freed Mom? Who vouched for her?"

"I suppose you could say I did. Your grandfather said if I wanted something in life, it was my responsibility to earn it. So I initiated, and I'm still paying for it today." He paused. "Is that all you want to know? Because I'm exhausted and don't have the energy for this conversation anymore."

Carmine nodded, although Vincent could tell he wanted to know much more.

"I'll talk to your brother, but whether or not you tell the girl is up to you."

"I don't think so," he said. "She has enough on her mind."

"I imagine she does," Vincent said, glancing at the computer to see she still hadn't moved. "Her mother's life ended as hers began. Speaking of which . . ." Opening the right bottom desk drawer, he grabbed some files and held them out to Carmine. "Here's the girl's paperwork. It'll take a while before the estate is settled, but no one will contest her inheritance. Technically it all goes to Corrado, anyway, but he'll hand it over to her once it comes through . . . along with her freedom, of course."

"That's the best gift anyone could give her."

"It's not a gift, Carmine. It's what she's been entitled to all along."

Rain splattered the window as it fell from the clouds hovering above. There was no sign of the moon or any stars tonight, nothing but blackness. Ominous, but fitting . . . it was how Haven felt on the inside.

Empty.

She might have been taking oxygen into her lungs as her heart pushed blood through her body, but a part of her had stopped existing. It had been a slow, torturous death, agonizingly painful as she withered away from the knowledge it had been her fault.

Glancing at the clock on the wall, Haven strained her eyes to make out the numbers. There was enough light for her to see the little hand past midnight, another day having begun.

September 10.

She watched the rain for a while longer before a shadow moved. Carmine stood a few feet away, watching her. "I think we should go to bed."

Grabbing the book in her lap, she set it on the table and hurried to the room before he could say anything else. Carmine followed her and shut the door, pulling her body close to his when he climbed into bed.

"Buon compleanno, mia bella ragazza," he said. "Happy birthday."

43

Haven gazed across the room with blurry, tired eyes, seeing Carmine near the doorway, holding a small plate with a cinnamon bun on it. A single blue candle stuck out from the top. Haven could smell the fresh pastry, the subtle scent of something burned told her who had made them.

"You baked?" she asked, stunned.

Carmine looked sheepish. "I wasn't gonna attempt a cake. These damn things were hard enough. It took me forever to figure out how to open the canister. I had to call Dia and ask."

Haven smiled as he approached, her chest swelling with love to the point it was painful. Despite everything, he was still her world, her one and only. Part of her may have felt dead, but there was still another part of her that lived for Carmine.

"That's sweet," she said, taking the plate. "You didn't have to. I told you—"

"I know what you told me," he said, "but I can't ignore your birthday. You've never had one before. It's special, so no arguing, because it's rude to argue when people wanna do shit for you. It's like, punching a gift horse or something."

She laughed. "Looking a gift horse in the mouth?"

Rolling his eyes, he reached into his pocket for a lighter and lit the candle. "Yes. *A caval donato non si guarda in bocca*. Just take it with a smile, and it'll be over before you know it." The moment he pulled his hand away, Haven blew out the flame. "Eager, are we? Did you make a wish?"

Her brow furrowed as he pulled the candle from the pastry. "A wish?"

"You make a wish before you blow out the candle," he said. "It's the whole point. But you'll get another chance later with Dia."

She tensed. "What?"

"We're gonna spend the night in Charlotte with Dia for your birthday. Come on, did you seriously think you'd get out of dealing with her? We're pretty much her only friends."

He looked at her imploringly, pleading for her not to argue.

Haven tore the cinnamon bun in half, sharing it with him. The bottom was black and hard to chew, but she said not a word about it as she choked down her piece. Once Carmine finished his, he grabbed a stack of papers and handed them to her.

"What is this?" she asked.

"That, *tesoro,* is your life."

Haven scanned the top paper, a certificate of citizenship, and tears formed when she saw her name. She flipped through the others as her emotions ran rampant, but the papers did nothing but confuse her. Wills, codicils, executors, beneficiary distribution, uniform transfers, custodians, residuary estate, fiduciary . . . "What does all this mean?"

"That's your inheritance. It'll take a few months before you see anything from it. Actually, it should've taken months for the rest of it, too, but Corrado somehow got it pushed through within a few days. I don't know how he does it. Extortion, probably."

She stared at him. "Inheritance?"

"Yeah, property and money and shit. I mean, I understand you're not gonna wanna keep the house, but you can sell it or—"

"What?" she asked. "What house?"

He stopped speaking and looked at her with surprise. "Uh, the house in Blackburn."

"Are you saying that house belongs to me?" He nodded, and she blinked a few times as she tried to absorb the information. "I don't want it. I don't want anything that belonged to those people."

Frowning, Carmine grabbed her hand. "Look, don't think of it as them giving you anything, but after what you've been through, you kinda deserve this. It's like atonement. And I'm not saying any amount of money will make up for it, because it won't. But after all of the torture and everything you lost, you're at least entitled to this. Does that make sense?"

"Yes."

"And money will help with these things," he said, grabbing the papers and shifting them around so the citizenship certificate was back on top.

"What happens to me now? I'm still here . . ."

"My father said you can stay here as long as you want, but you don't have to."

"But where else would I go?"

"Wherever you want," he said. "I told you that. California, New York, Timbuktu, Bum Fuck Egypt . . . You name it, we'll go. Or you can go alone. Whatever you want."

Tears streamed from her eyes, and she clutched the papers as her hands shook. Carmine pulled her down onto the bed as emotion took control and rocked her body in his embrace. Overwhelmed, she didn't know what to think. "I don't want to go anywhere without you, Carmine."

They stared at each other, his green eyes a flurry of emotion. He wiped the tears from her cheeks before his fingertips brushed across her lips. She let out a shaky breath as he kissed her, finally let go of the papers. They dropped to the bed as she ran her fingers through his unruly hair.

"*Ti amo,*" he whispered against her mouth. "*La mia bella ragazza.* I want you to marry me."

She gasped. "*Marry* you?"

"I don't mean today or tomorrow. It doesn't have to be this year or, fuck, next year. But someday, when you're ready, promise you'll spend your life with me?" His words made her stomach flutter. "Look, I know I'm doing this shit all wrong, but—"

"Okay." Her voice cracked. "Yes."

He stalled. "Yes?"

"Of course I will, Carmine!"

His face lit up as he smashed his lips to hers feverishly, and she laughed into his mouth, kissing him back. The outside world melted away as his hands roamed her body, his fingertips causing sparks to ignite across her skin. Knowing she was free and had a life of her own, and that despite everything she'd been in the past, he still wanted her for the future, made her insides burst into flames of passion.

————

It was early evening when Carmine pulled into a parking lot across from the dingy brick apartment building in the city. The old elevator vibrated as it took them to the sixth floor, and they headed down a narrow hallway to apartment sixty-seven.

Carmine reached up to knock, but the door opened before he could. Dia stood before them, wearing a pair of ripped jeans and a blue top, her hair a mixture of black and purple streaks. "Happy birthday!"

She ushered them inside, and Haven froze the moment she stepped into the front room. The walls were a cream color, the paint barely visible due to the hundreds of photographs wallpapering every inch. The apartment was decorated in colors so vibrant the large bunch of birthday balloons blended in. There were presents next to them and a small, round cake.

Gratitude and guilt battled for control. "You shouldn't have."

"Don't be a buzzkill," Dia said, pulling her over to the table. Haven sat down as Carmine leaned against the wall and gazed at her.

Dia stuck candles into the cake and lit them, stepping off to the side to belt out the birthday song. Haven stared at the flickering flames, remembering to make a wish this time.

Please, she silently pleaded. *Bring my mama back to me.*

Taking a deep breath, Haven blew out the candles and watched the puffs of smoke rise from the smoldering wicks. Dia pulled them out before thrusting a present at her, making her flinch.

"Sorry," Dia said quickly. "I'm just excited for you to see it."

Haven opened the package and pulled out a small copper box with a glass window on the top of it. Inside the window was a four-leaf clover, along with red hearts and shiny silver beading.

"It's a reliquary box," Dia said. "You're supposed to store your favorite things in it."

She smiled. "I don't think Carmine will fit."

"I don't think so either," Carmine said, chuckling. "Not even my dick would fit in that thing."

————

There were more presents to open, and afterward they ate the cake. The three of them watched movies and listened to music all night, the evening feeling more like a regular day than a celebration. Haven felt ridiculous for her anxiety over it all, grateful to be able to relax with friends.

Friends. It was still surreal to her that she had people in her life she could call friends.

"So, have the two of you thought about what you're doing next year?" Dia asked eventually. "I'm guessing you're not going to be staying in Durante much longer."

Haven glanced at Carmine, who just shrugged. "It doesn't matter to me. If she marries me, I'll follow her to the gates of Hell."

Dia had been taking a drink but choked, spraying soda all over herself. Coughing, she threw her hands into the air. "Did you say *marry* you?"

"Yes."

"You proposed?" Dia jumped up and grabbed Haven's hand. "Where's the ring?"

Carmine groaned. "I didn't have one."

"Did you at least get down on one knee?" she asked. Carmine shook his head, and she smacked him on the arm. "What kind of freaking proposal is that?"

"Not a real one," he said. "I asked if she'd marry me someday."

"That's even worse!" Dia tried to hit him again, but he was prepared and dodged the blow.

"Shit, stop hitting me. It's not like I planned it. It just came out."

She shook her head. "All the planning you put into Valentine's Day, and you completely blow the proposal."

He opened his mouth to respond, but Haven chimed in before he could. "I don't need any of that stuff."

Carmine smirked. "See, Warhol? I didn't fuck up."

"You still could've gotten down on one knee."

Carmine chuckled. "Well, I may have gotten between her knees, if you know what I mean."

Rolling her eyes, Dia sat down. "So you banged. I'm sure that was romantic."

"We didn't *bang*," Carmine said. "We made love."

Carmine's presence was scarce the next two weeks, even more so than before. He would slip out of the house for school while Haven was still asleep and wouldn't get home from football practice until dinnertime. After they ate, the two of them would head upstairs, where Carmine did his homework before going straight to bed.

They didn't even sleep in the same room most nights anymore.

Haven's shame grew as the days passed, and Carmine's demeanor shifted along with hers. Falling back into old patterns, he would lose his temper and lash out, and Haven would brush it off, despite that his words often hurt.

It was Friday evening, and Carmine's first game of the year.

Haven's palms were sweaty when she climbed in the driver's seat of Dominic's car at around seven o'clock. *It's for Carmine,* she told herself. No amount of people would get in her way of supporting him.

When she reached the school, the noise from the stadium could be heard from the parking lot, the announcer on the loudspeaker screeching above them all. She stood by the car, trying to gather the courage to move, when someone grabbed her shoulder. Her heart pounded furiously as she swung around, her hands protectively covering her face.

"Whoa," Nicholas said. "It's just me."

She dropped her hands. "What do you want?"

"Do I have to want something? I figured I'd walk you inside."

"If you're hoping to hurt Carmine by having him see us together, you can just leave."

"Honestly, that hadn't crossed my mind, but now that you mention it . . ."

"Good-bye, Nicholas." Her frustration was enough to make her legs finally move. She made it a few feet when she noticed a group of girls blocking the entrance, with Lisa in the center.

"I thought you might like an escort past the firing squad," Nicholas said, walking up behind her. "But if you'd rather go alone—"

"No."

Sighing, he pressed his hand against her back. "Come on, then."

She walked again, staring at the ground, and heard laughter as they approached the stadium.

"Picking up Carmine's leftovers?" Lisa asked. "I didn't realize you were that desperate."

Nicholas shook his head. "Do you even hear yourself? You used to be his main course. If I were desperate, I'd be with you instead."

He pulled Haven toward the ticket booth and paid for his ticket, but she just stood there, frantic. She hadn't considered that she would need money. "I, uh . . . I didn't think . . ."

His brow furrowed as he reached for his wallet again. Tossing a few dollars at the lady working, he grabbed a second ticket and handed it to her. She tried to object, not wanting him to pay for her, but she had no other way to get in the game.

He led her to the bleachers, his walk more of a strut as he shoved his hands in the pockets of his cargo pants. His shoulders slumped, his dingy ball cap concealing his gaze as Haven scanned the crowd, spotting Dia in a center section.

Before she could thank Nicholas, he'd already slipped away.

Haven headed up the bleachers, her nervousness waning as she took a seat beside Dia. Haven waved at Carmine on the sidelines, but he just stared at her from the field, expressionless. She wasn't surprised—another one of his moods, she guessed. It was certainly nothing new these days.

The coach called his name, drawing his attention away, and he headed onto the field without another glance in her direction.

The spectators were as rowdy as Haven remembered from the year before, but this time she was more at ease in the crowd. Her body buzzed with excitement by the time the game came to a close, and Carmine ran straight for the locker rooms as the crowd descended upon the field.

Haven and Dia headed over to the grassy knoll to wait. She stood near the chain-link fence as Dia strolled around taking pictures.

A throat cleared as Nicholas leaned against the fence beside her. "I know—me again. I forgot to tell you a joke."

"Go ahead."

"Did you hear—?"

Before he could finish, Carmine's harsh voice rang out, shouting Nicholas's name as he hastily approached. A chill shot down Haven's spine, her stomach dropping when she saw his hands clenched into fists. Nicholas took a step away. "Look, I don't want any trouble."

Carmine laughed bitterly, shoving him. "If you didn't want any trouble, you wouldn't be here."

"I was just talking to her, man."

"And what right do you have to do that, huh? Stop using her to get to me!"

Nicholas glared at him. "If anyone's using her, it's you! It's sick what you're doing! You have her fooled into believing you care!"

Carmine's fist connected with Nicholas's jaw at those words. His head snapped to the side from the blow, blood spurting from his mouth. He wiped it away, stunned, as Carmine shouted, "Stay the fuck away! She's mine, and I'll be damned if I'll let you take her from me!"

"You possessive bastard! If you loved her, you wouldn't say things like that!"

That set Carmine off. Pouncing, he knocked Nicholas to the ground as Haven clutched the fence and yelled for help. A group of boys intervened at the sound of the commotion, hauling them off the ground and separating the two. Dia forced her way through the crowd as she frantically looked around. "What happened?"

Carmine ignored the question as he turned to glare at Haven. "Out of everybody, why does it have to be him? Are you trying to hurt me? Is that what this shit is about?"

She blinked a few times, stunned by his anger. "What?"

"You heard me. I give you space, thinking that's what you want. And I get it, Haven. I fucking get it. You're hurt. But you can talk to *him*? You can smile at *him*? Is it *me*? If you don't want to be with me, tell me."

"I do!" His words stung. "I love you!"

"You have a fucking funny way of showing it," he spat. "I've changed my life for you. I'd kill for you. Fuck, I'd die for you! Just tell me what's wrong. Tell me what to do."

"I don't know." She shook her head. "I can't."

"You can't?" he asked with disbelief. "You don't get it, do you?

You don't know what I've given up for you. You don't know what I've lost because of you!"

Those words hit her hard. She gasped, everything clouding over as her hand shot out, striking him across the face. He cupped his cheek, the shock from the blow melting his anger. Haven covered her mouth before running for the exit, needing to think, needing to be away from him so she could make sense of what she'd done.

She had hit him. *Him.* She was going to be sick.

Shoving past people, she hurried out of the stadium, fumbling in her pocket for the keys. A horn blared as she nearly backed into another car, and she slammed the brakes to let them pass, her hands violently shaking. Tears obstructed her vision as she pulled out onto the road and sped through the busy town.

She drove toward the house but was too scared to stop. Too scared to face it. Too scared to lose him. She passed the driveway, continuing down the highway in the dark. It took a few minutes for it to dawn on her where the road led, her shame reaching an all-time high when she drove past the sign that read WELCOME TO AURORA LAKE.

Haven pulled into the small lot and sat in silence for a moment, struggling to breathe. She felt like she had been sucked into a twister, the world spinning as her body shook. She climbed out of the car, thinking she'd be sick, and forced the fresh air in her lungs as she stumbled toward the sand.

She ended up at a dock and strolled down it, glancing out at the lake. Moonlight reflected off the dark water, and she stared into the blackness, soothed by it.

Casual footsteps approached eventually. "Please don't jump. I really don't want to go in after you. It's probably cold."

She smiled at Nicholas's nonchalance. "I'm not going to jump."

"Good," he said as he stopped beside her, his lip busted, bruises already forming on his skin.

Haven frowned as she peeked at him. "I'm sorry he hit you for talking to me."

He waved her off. "He'd never apologize, so don't do it for him."

She said nothing, staring back out at the water.

Nicholas sighed. "I'm surprised to see you here."

"I shouldn't have come."

"But you did."

"I did." She was quiet for a moment, debating what to say. "It was my birthday."

"Really? Well, happy birthday."

She smiled sadly before saying the words she had longed to say for days, ones she swallowed back whenever Carmine was near. "There's nothing happy about the day I was born."

44

Carmine stared at the darkened house, clutching his phone to his ear. He'd assumed Haven would go straight home, but he had clearly been wrong. "She's not here."

Dia sighed on the line. "She's probably scared."

"You think I don't know that? She's afraid of me, Dia. Of *me*."

He couldn't get the image out of his mind, the fear in her eyes as she ran from him.

"Doesn't she know I understand how she feels?" he asked. "I lost my mom, too."

"Yes, but you're irrational when it comes to talking about your mother's death."

Her words made his temper flare. "*Vaffanculo*."

"You're proving my point," Dia said. "Look, I'll call you back. I want to check something."

She hung up without awaiting his response.

Carmine just stood there until Dia called him back. "Any luck?"

"She's safe."

Relief washed through him so fast he nearly collapsed. "Where did you find her?"

"She's down at the lake."

He froze, grabbing the hood of his car as his legs went weak. Yeah, he was going to fucking collapse. "What do you mean she's at the lake?" Dia didn't respond, her silence all he needed for the truth to register. "Nicholas."

"Calm down," she said before he had a chance to get worked up. She knew him well, which meant she also knew her words wouldn't work.

Carmine's anger spiraled out of control. "Calm down? I'm tired of this bullshit. If this is how she wants to be, they can have each other."

"Carmine . . ."

"This is why I never wanted to fall in love."

"You don't mean that."

"Don't fucking tell me what I mean!" Betrayal fueled his rage, and he threw his phone at the car, cursing as a lump formed in his throat. His vision clouded over as his hand clenched into a fist. He slammed it against the windshield, the glass on the passenger side cracking from the force of the blow. Desolation coursed through him as he did it again, the windshield caving as his fist broke through. Pain stung his knuckles, the jagged glass ripping the skin.

He took a deep breath as he went inside, his father greeting him in the foyer. The smile on Vincent's face fell when he took in Carmine's expression, his eyes drifting to his bloody hand. "What happened?"

"Nicholas happened."

Vincent groaned. "How many times do we have to go through this?"

"Whatever. The Mazda took a worse beating than Nicholas did."

"Your car? What happened tonight? Where's the girl?"

"I already told you—Nicholas happened," he spat. "And her fucking name is Haven. *Haven.* Use it sometime."

Vincent stared at him, taken aback.

"And if you wanna know where Haven is, find Nicholas. They're down at the lake somewhere." An idea hit him the moment he said that. "You're gonna go get her, aren't you?"

Vincent pinched the bridge of his nose. "Her life is her own, Carmine. She can have friends, and you should respect that."

"After what he did to me, you expect me to respect him? I'm supposed to like this?"

"I didn't say you had to like it, nor did I say you should respect him, but you ought to respect her right to make her own choices, whether you like them or not."

"I do," he said. "I'm not that big of an asshole. I tell her all the time to make her own decisions."

"Well, you should see this as her doing that."

Groaning, Carmine pushed past his father and headed for the stairs. "How come no one's taking my side on this?"

Vincent laughed, the sound hitting a nerve. "This isn't about choosing sides. I told you someday the real world would creep up on you."

"Oh, I know it," he said. "I knew it the moment she slapped me."

Vincent grinned. "She hit you?"

"What's so fucking amusing?"

"I'm pleasantly surprised," he said. "Not saying she should've hit you, but I'm shocked she'd let go like that. She may make it out there in the world, after all."

"Ever heard of Stockholm syndrome?"

Haven eyed Nicholas warily at those words. His legs dangled over the end of the dock, his pants rolled up and feet skimming the surface of the water. She sat cross-legged beside him, their discarded shoes scattered on the deck. "No, what is it?"

"It's when someone gets mushy feelings for their kidnapper."

She sighed when she realized where he was going with it. "I wasn't kidnapped."

"So the good doctor didn't cut out letters from a magazine and glue them together to make a colorful ransom note for you?"

"No."

"Interesting," he said. "It doesn't have to be a kidnapping, though. It's when someone being held hostage gets feelings for their captor."

"That's the same thing you said the first time. Besides, Carmine isn't holding me hostage."

"But you are being held, right?"

"I didn't say that."

"You didn't not say it, either," he said. "And sometimes people in that situation end up brainwashed."

"I'm not brainwashed."

"How do you know? Because 'I'm not brainwashed' sounds suspiciously like something a brainwashed person would say."

She shook her head. "You just don't want to believe Carmine's different now, do you?"

"Nope," he said, "but stop changing the subject. We're talking about you being kidnapped."

"I told you—I wasn't kidnapped."

"I know. I thought for sure you were, though. I was banking on you having parents out there searching for you."

Her chest tightened at his words. "My parents are dead."

She could feel his eyes on her, his stare intense, but she didn't dare look at him. After a moment he turned away and kicked the water again. "My mom's dead, too. She died when I was young. I still have my dad, but we don't get along. He always expects the worst from me, so I figure, why try to do right when he'll never see it? But I'm eighteen now, so I may as well move out. Start over somewhere new, where people don't hear the name *Nicholas Barlow* and automatically think 'degenerate asshole.'"

"You think people look at you that way?"

"I know they do," he said. "It's worse now that Carmine's . . ."

"Now that Carmine's what?" she asked when he didn't finish. "Now that he's different?"

He didn't respond, and that was answer enough for her. A smile tugged her lips. Maybe there was hope for a friendship, after all.

It was quiet, the only sounds being water splashing and crickets chirping in the night. Nicholas cleared his throat after a few minutes. "Did I tell you the joke about the butter?"

"The butterfly one?"

"No, the butter one."

"What butter one?"

He groaned. "You're screwing up my punch line. Let's try it again—did I tell you the joke about the butter?"

"Uh, no. I don't think so."

"Then I butter not tell you," he said. "You might spread it."

He cut his eyes at her, grinning, but she just stared at him. "Spread what?"

Shaking his head, he looked away. "If it's the last thing I do, I'll get you to laugh at one of my jokes someday."

————

Carmine stood in the library by the window and stared out into the backyard. He wondered what Haven thought about as she sat there at night, or if her mind was as vacant as the blackness. He could faintly recall those months after his mom's death, so in the grips of heartbreak that attempting to hold a conversation took too much effort. It was like the life had been sucked out of him, his insides a bottomless pit of grief.

He spotted the book lying on the small table and grabbed it, surveying the blank cover before flipping it open. Sloppy handwriting covered the withered paper; confusion hit him when he realized it was a diary. Sickness brewed in his stomach when he opened it to the front, seeing *Maura DeMarco* written inside the cover. Closing the book again, he lost his breath. After everything he had done to shield Haven from the truth, she had stumbled upon it anyway.

He sprinted out of the library, pulling his keys from his pocket as he flew down the steps two at a time. Once he hit the second floor, his father stepped out of his office, the sound of frantic footsteps drawing his attention.

"Carmine, wait!" Vincent took a step toward him, but Carmine didn't stop. He went out the front door to his car, unlocking it as his father stepped onto the porch. "Don't go there!"

Carmine hesitated before starting the car. Haven had been gone for more than an hour, and there was no way he could let it go another minute.

Speeding down the highway in the darkness, he held his breath as he flew past the Aurora Lake sign, knowing he had reached the point of no return. He swung around a curve and slammed the brakes when he caught a glimpse of the Audi. The Mazda skidded to a stop beside it, and he jumped out, heading down toward the water. He jogged along the shore, searching for some sign of her, before spotting them sitting on the dock.

Nicholas's eyes fell on Carmine as he approached. Haven must have sensed him too, because her head snapped in his direction. She jumped up and recklessly took a step away, nearing the edge of the dock. Her foot skidded, but Nicholas grabbed her before she fell. "Whoa, what did I tell you? I'm not going in the water after you."

Carmine held up his hands. "I'm not here for a fight."

Nicholas looked at him suspiciously. "What are you doing here? You know you aren't allowed."

"I know," he said. "You can press charges if you want. I just need to talk to her."

"If she wanted to talk to you, she would've gone to you. Can't you give her some space?"

Carmine ran his hands down his face in frustration. "It's important. I'll leave, I will, but I need to talk to her first." He focused his attention on Haven. "Please, hummingbird?"

She nodded. "Okay."

"You don't have to," Nicholas said. "You don't have to do anything you don't want to do."

Carmine glared at him but kept his mouth shut as Haven replied. "I know."

Nicholas glanced between them before gently rubbing Haven's arm. "Take care. You know how to reach me if you need me."

Her eyes nervously flitted to Carmine as she said good-bye. He started toward Haven after Nicholas walked away. "I know what you found."

A horrified expression flashed across her face. "Oh God."

She looked like she wanted to run from him again, so he reached out to stop her. "I already knew it was you. I've known for a few months."

"And you didn't tell me?"

"I was trying to protect you. I didn't see the point in telling you."

"Your mama died because of me, and you didn't see the point? I destroyed your life, Carmine!"

"Christ, you were just a little girl. You didn't do anything wrong."

Tears streamed down her cheeks. "I took your mama from you."

"No, you didn't. The person who pulled the trigger took her."

"You're wrong." She wiped her tears away. "How can you look at me? How could you love me after that?"

"How can I not? I'd die for you, so how could I blame you for my mom feeling the same way?"

"It shouldn't have happened," she said. "I'm not worth it."

"Don't say shit like that. You can't shut down and pull away from everything."

"But you said—"

He cut her off before she could repeat the things he had said. "I was angry. We all do shit when we're upset we don't mean. I've lost too much as it is. I don't want to lose you too." She choked back a sob as he pulled her into a hug. "Fuck, *tesoro*. I don't know how we're gonna get over this, but we need to find a way. I'm miserable without you."

He held her, comforted by having her in his arms again. She pulled from his embrace as her crying slowed and peered at him.

"I'm sorry if I hurt you by talking to Nicholas. It's just . . . no matter his reasons, he went out of his way to try to make me laugh."

While Carmine questioned Nicholas's motives, he realized, as he stood there, that everyone had been right. He needed to respect her decisions; he had to let her make mistakes. "You know he fucking hates me."

"He's angry, but he doesn't hate you. I think he misses you."

He laughed bitterly. "He says bad shit about me."

"He does, but like you said—we say things we don't mean when we're hurt. The two of you used to be close, and now you have me, but who does Nicholas have? I understand why he doesn't want to accept you've changed, because he hasn't. He doesn't want to believe you're not the same, because that means he really is alone. He lost his only friend."

Heaps of paperwork surrounded Vincent. He'd been sitting there for hours trying to get it knocked down, but he couldn't focus. He was exhausted, and everything was falling apart.

The office door thrust open as Vincent read the same paragraph for the fifth time, his son strolling into the room. "You're making my night hell, Carmine. You're lucky you didn't get arrested."

"I have something that'll make it all better . . . or it's just gonna make your life worse."

Carmine dropped a book on top of the paperwork, knocking the pen right out of his hand. Vincent sighed. "What's this?"

"You don't recognize my mom's diary?" he asked. "Haven found it in the library."

He slumped into his chair, staring at the book in a daze. "I suspected your mother kept one, but it never struck me it might've been with the other books when Celia packed everything up in Chicago for me. I must've stuck it on the shelf without realizing what it was."

"Well, that's where it was, so there you go."

After Carmine walked out, Vincent ran his hand over the worn cover before opening the book, his curiosity fueling him as he flipped to the last page. The familiar handwriting made him feel like someone had plunged a hand into his chest and gripped his heart, squeezing it.

He scanned the passage, seeing the date. October 12, 1997. She'd written it the day she died.

The closet door in Carmine's room was stuck this morning. I had to break the knob to open the door. Another thing to add to the list . . . the bottom step is loose, the kitchen window won't budge most days, the tire swing fell down, and the front door is in desperate need of new paint. Such small things, one after another, all easily fixed but it doesn't feel that way. It feels like everything is falling apart around me, the world crumbling as I stand here, still. I think time has run out—not for her, but for me. I've hit a wall and it's too late to turn back. Not that I would, even if I could. Vincent doesn't understand right now, but someday he'll see what I see. Someday he'll realize why I couldn't give up on her. Maybe when that happens, he'll hang the tire swing again. Maybe the window will be replaced, the step nailed down, and maybe the door will be repainted. Blue this time, instead of red. I'm tired of seeing so much red. Maybe then it'll be our time to have peace. And maybe then she'll finally be free. I think when that happens the world will stop crumbling.

Vincent closed the book. His world was still crumbling.

Haven stood by the kitchen window and gazed out into the driveway, her eyes fixated on the Mazda, the passenger side windshield buckled from Carmine's fist. Even from where she stood she could see the streak of blood from his knuckles.

"I woke up alone."

The gritty voice rang out behind Haven, drawing her from her thoughts. She turned to see Carmine in the doorway. "You looked peaceful," she said. "I didn't want to disturb you."

She glanced at his hand, the bruising on his knuckles dark this morning.

"It's fine," he said, noticing the attention. He flexed his fingers to prove his point, his jaw rigid as he fought back a grimace. His hand was clearly not fine, but she didn't argue with him.

They stared at each other in silence. There was so much that needed to be said, but Haven had no idea where to start. All of it was overwhelming. Her eyes filled with tears as she blurted out, "I'm sorry," the same time Carmine spoke, echoing her words and distress.

He frowned. "Why are you sorry?"

"You're hurt," she said.

"I told you, Haven. My hand's fine."

"Not your hand," she said. "*You.* I hurt you, and I didn't mean to."

"You did," he said, "but I did the same thing. I'd be a hypocrite to blame you. I could've stopped this before it started, and that's why I'm sorry."

She turned around, his apology making her feel worse. He was trying to reassure her when he was the one who needed to be comforted. He deserved to have the burden lifted from his shoulders, but she selfishly stood in silence, unable to find the words to ease his pain.

His bare feet slapped against the cold, hard floor as he shuffled over to her, pausing at the window. "Christ, look at my car."

"I'm sorry," she said again.

"You have to stop apologizing," he said, startling her as he grabbed her hips. "It happened, it was fucked up, but it's over now. Dwelling on who hurt who isn't gonna make the shit go away. You can't hold grudges and expect anything to get better, because it won't."

"Is that what you've done?"

"I've been doing it for years, all the while wondering why my life was shitty. I'm tired of repeating the same mistakes over and over again. It's time to accept what happened and forgive."

She was amazed by his sudden burst of maturity when less than twelve hours before he had been volatile. It was as if he'd been completely crushed, defeated to the point that he had no will left to fight.

"Does that mean forgiving Nicholas too?"

He went rigid. "What does he have to do with this?"

"You said nothing would get better holding grudges so I figured—"

"You figured wrong. That's different."

"How?" she asked. "You said dwelling on stuff wouldn't help anything. It happened, but it's over, so it's time to move on. Right?"

He stared at her. "He's an asshole, Haven. He hurts everything he touches."

"That's the same thing he says about you. He's wrong, and I've told him, but maybe you are, too."

"I'm not."

"Okay. I'm just saying maybe the two of you aren't that different, and maybe if you can put everything aside, you guys can—"

"I know what you're saying, and that's a lot of fucking maybes. It's not gonna happen, so there's no point talking about it. In fact, I don't wanna talk about him at all, ever."

She stopped talking, his tone telling her the subject was closed. The tension in the room mounted again, and she fought the urge to apologize for irritating him.

"*Il tempo guarisce tutti i mali,*" Carmine said, rubbing his chest where those words were inked on his flesh. "When I first got the tattoo, I didn't believe it, but I do now. You can get over anything with enough time. I'm not sure how much it's gonna take to work through this shit we have going on, but I have all the time in the world for you."

He wrapped his arms around her, and she closed her eyes as she hugged him. "If you didn't believe it, why'd you get the tattoo?"

"It's something my mom used to say." He let out a curious laugh. "Reminds me of you and your random trivia. I don't know why it took me so long to see the similarities. It should've been obvious that my mom had grown up like you."

Haven pulled away from him. "What did you say?"

He cut his eyes to her. "Which part?"

"Your mama was like me? You mean a slave?"

He cringed at the word but nodded. "I thought you knew. You saw the diary."

She shook her head. "I only read the piece of paper that fell out of it, Carmine."

His eyes widened. "I thought you read the whole thing. Hell, I would've read it. I gave it to my father so I wouldn't be tempted."

"Dr. DeMarco knows?"

"Of course," he said. "He's known for years. It's no coincidence you ended up here."

All of a sudden, as she stood there in the kitchen, the fog lifted and everything became clear. The reason he bought her, the reason he was freeing her. Masters were supposed to take life away, yet he had done everything in his power to give her one instead . . . and he had done it all for the woman he loved.

That knowledge made it feel like the ground was moving.

Haven was in her room that afternoon when Carmine came in, clutching a large white envelope. "You have mail, *tesoro*."

She eyed him warily as he sat on the edge of the bed, handing the mail to her. The return address was from North Carolina Community Colleges. "Is this . . . ?"

"Your test results."

She stared at the envelope as she ran her finger along the seal.

"Are you gonna open it or what?"

The enthusiasm in Carmine's voice frazzled her. It was the first time she had put herself out there, and the thought of failing scared her. "Can you do it for me?"

He shook his head. "You should do it."

She carefully tore the flap and pulled out the paper. The actual scores meant nothing to her as she stared at the certificate attached to the transcript, the words HIGH SCHOOL EQUIVALENCY DIPLOMA etched along the top with a golden seal.

"I passed?" she asked, trying to hold back the excitement threatening to burst forth, but it was stronger than her. She threw herself at Carmine before he could get out a word, knocking him over. "I passed!"

"You did," he said. "Can't say I'm surprised. I knew you would."

He kissed her slowly, softly, pure passion emanating from him. It was an innocent kiss, yet so much more. It was a kiss of redemption, of forgiveness and pride. It was a kiss that said no matter what may have happened in the past, there was still hope for the future.

Hope. It was a feeling she reveled in now, instead of cowering from as before. "Thank you for believing in me," she whispered against his mouth.

"You don't have to thank me," he said, pulling back with a smile. "And don't worry, because everything will work out. We're one step closer. You can go to college now."

"What about you? When are you going to test for college?"

"Soon," he said. "I signed up before we went to California."

"Are you excited?"

He chuckled. "I wouldn't call the SATs thrilling, *tesoro*. I'm just ready to get it over with. I need to fill out applications, so we need to figure out where we're going . . . especially if I'm gonna try to play football. California? New York? Camelot? Emerald City? Take your pick."

She had no idea where half of those places were. "I don't know."

"Well, think about it, okay? But not today. Today's for celebrating, not thinking. Look at where you were a year ago and look at you now. You're free, you have a degree, and we're in love and gonna make it through this shit even if it kills us." He paused, his brow furrowing as she laughed. "Yeah, that didn't make sense, but you get what I'm saying. We haven't had a reason to celebrate in a while, so come on, get up, put on some decent clothes, and let's forget about all of this for a while and *be*. We don't get to just *be* enough."

She glanced down at the black pants and Durante High School football shirt she wore. "What's wrong with my clothes?"

"Everything I said and all you got from that is me telling you to change?" he asked with amusement, pulling her to her feet. "Change. Clothes, not you. I don't want you to ever change, but I'm kinda tired of looking at that fucking shirt."

"I like this shirt," she said defensively, his laughter filtering back in as he left the room.

45

Haven stayed busy during the days when Carmine was at school, but it was difficult for her not to dwell on things when alone. Guilt continued to gnaw away at her.

She awoke the third Saturday in September as Carmine got out of the shower. She lay still in bed and watched him as he tried his best not to disturb her. He stood in front of the closet, and even in the semidarkened room, she could make out the definition of his back muscles and the lines of his tattoos. His skin glowed in the faint light filtering in from the open bathroom door, mesmerizing her. Even his scar shimmied as he absentmindedly rubbed it.

If there was one image of Carmine DeMarco she never wanted to forget, it was this one—him exposed and vulnerable, sneaking around his own bedroom in the dark. It was something few would ever see, but it was an image she couldn't bear to lose. Most people knew the selfish young boy, spoiled and irresponsible, but she was lucky enough to see Carmine for who he truly was. Completely stripped down to the core, a gentle soul despite his scarred exterior.

The quiet contentment he oozed when he thought no one was watching took her breath away. She loved him with every fiber of her being, and just the fact that, after everything, he could still stand in front of her as he was spoke volumes.

He sighed and slipped on some clothes before grabbing a pair of Nikes from his closet. He kicked the corner of the bed as he walked by and cursed profusely under his breath. Haven tried to stifle her laughter but failed, his head snapping in her direction when he heard her.

"How long have you been awake?" he asked, sitting down to slip on the shoes.

"A few minutes."

"And you were what, watching me get dressed?" He playfully nudged her with his elbow. She blushed, hoping he couldn't see it in the darkness, but nothing escaped his notice. "Yeah, you were."

"I couldn't help it. You're too beautiful not to watch."

"And you're half-asleep and don't know what the fuck you're saying." He kissed her as he stood. "I have to go or I'm gonna be late for this fucking test."

"Good luck."

"Thanks, *tesoro*. I'll see you in a few hours."

She listened as his footsteps descended the stairs, an odd feeling overcoming her. It felt like all the happiness had been sucked from the room.

––––––––

Haven had made her way down to the kitchen and poured a glass of juice when a door closed somewhere on the first floor. She tensed instinctively as footsteps started in her direction. *Relax*, she told herself. *It's only Dr. DeMarco.*

"Good morning," he said when he walked in.

It was the most he had spoken to her in days. "Morning, sir."

He appeared disheveled, dark circles under his eyes. He was worn down by life, and Haven wondered, as she gazed at him, how much of that she'd caused.

"I'm leaving for Chicago. Do you need anything before I go?"

The Mazda was in the body shop getting fixed, so Carmine had been driving the Audi around. "I'm fine, thank you."

Dr. DeMarco departed a few minutes later, while Haven spent the morning dusting the same things she dusted every other day that week. It was sometime after eleven, and she was cleaning out the pantry when a vehicle pulled up outside. Walking to the window, Haven gazed out at the unfamiliar blue car in the driveway.

The driver's side door opened, and Jen, the nurse from the hospital, stepped out. Haven headed for the foyer, but the sound of the doorbell ringing stopped her dead in her tracks. Something about it sent a chill down her spine, coldness radiating through her so quickly she thought she would be sick.

Something wasn't right. She could feel it.

She grabbed the phone from the family room, hesitating before pressing the speed dial for Dr. DeMarco's cell phone. Leaning against the wall, she waited while it rang.

"Is everything okay?" Dr. DeMarco asked. She had never called him before. She never thought she would have to. "What's going on?"

The doorbell rang again, making her flinch. "I'm not sure, sir."

"Is that the door? Is someone there?"

"It's the nurse you work with. I was going to answer, but—"

"No," he said sharply, his tone frightening her into immediate silence. The doorbell rang a few times in succession before Jen knocked on the door. "Don't answer it, child. Get a hold of Carmine. I don't want you alone right now."

Something was definitely wrong if Dr. DeMarco sensed it.

"Set the alarm. The code's 62373."

She already knew it, but Haven wasn't going to say anything.

Hanging up, Haven clutched the phone as she tiptoed to the door, punching in the code and pressing the button to activate the alarm. Jen stopped knocking after a moment, her muffled voice carrying through the door as Haven pressed her ear to it to listen. "What do you want me to do? She isn't answering . . . Yes, I'm sure she's there . . . Doc left this morning like he was supposed to."

There was a pause as Haven's heart pounded furiously. They wanted *her*?

"No, she's not with him. He's taking that test, remember?" Jen continued, the distress in her voice alarming. "I know, but please don't be mad! I promise I'll make this work. I know what it means to you."

Haven's knees nearly gave out as Jen pounded again. "Hello? Are you in there?"

Haven scampered over to the side, huddling in the corner as she dialed Carmine's number on speed dial. It went straight to voice mail, and Haven let out a shaky breath.

"I'm going to break in if you don't answer this door!" Jen yelled, her demeanor turning from eagerness to anger. "I'll be damned if I'm going to let you ruin this for me!"

Jen beat on the windows as Haven looked back down at the phone. Without hesitation, her fingers dialed the number that popped into her head: *555–0121.*

She had stared at the paper with the phone number so much it had been burned into her mind. It rang as she curled into herself, fighting to keep her composure.

The phone was picked up after the fourth ring, the voice tentative. "Uh, hello?"

"Nicholas." She spoke as quietly as she could. "It's Haven."

"Haven? Are you okay?"

"Yes. Well, at least, I think I am, but I need help and I don't know who else to ask. Dr. DeMarco told me to get ahold of Carmine, but his phone isn't on. He broke it, I think."

"So . . . you're calling me instead?"

"Yes," she said, "to find him."

"Wait, you want me to track down your boyfriend?"

She sighed. "Yes, I need him to come home."

"And you think this is a good idea? No offense, but I'm not in the mood for another fight."

"I know, but it's important. Please? He's taking a test at the high school. The SAT thing."

"Jesus, you not only want me to tell Carmine what to do, but you want me to trespass on school property and drag him out of the SAT? He's going to kill me. I'm going to die today."

"He'll understand," she said as Jen wiggled the knob of the front door.

———

Glaring at the paper on his desk, Carmine read the last question for the twentieth time, but he was no closer to an answer than he had been five minutes ago.

He groaned as he slouched in the hard plastic chair, shifting position to get comfortable. The girl beside him shot him an annoyed look, and he cocked an eyebrow at her, daring her to say something. She huffed dramatically before focusing back on her test. He stared at her, unable to place her name.

Michelle? Mandy? Monique? He couldn't fucking remember.

She cut her eyes at him again and mouthed, "What do you want?"

"Nothing," he said, turning to his paper. He didn't care about her. He barely noticed anyone anymore. They were all the same, and there wasn't a single thing any of them could do for him. Haven was everything he wanted, the reason he sat in this room, stressing over this ridiculous test, so he could take her away and start a new life somewhere.

The administrator announced there were five minutes left, and Carmine sighed loudly as he read the question once more. He tried to wrap his brain around the analogies, but he didn't know what half the words meant. He gave up and dropped the pencil, not bothering to answer. The only analogy that mattered was *weed is to smoke, as pussy is to fuck*, because that was the only thing that would ease his nerves today.

After the tests were collected, Carmine headed for the exit, rolling his neck to get the tension out of it. He strolled out to the parking lot with the rest of his classmates, where the sound of squealing tires stopped him in his tracks. He looked up, his brow furrowing in confusion when the old pickup truck pulled into the parking lot.

"Isn't that Nicholas?"

Carmine cringed as Lisa spoke behind him. Nicholas parked his truck and climbed out, glancing around in a rush. He looked in Carmine's direction, muttering to himself as he approached. "Carmine, I need to talk to you about Haven. She—"

He didn't have time to finish before Carmine swung. Nicholas's head snapped to the side when the fist connected. Staggering backward, Nicholas glared at him. "There's something wrong with you! I told her you'd go psycho if I came here!"

"Excuse me?" Carmine grabbed Nicholas's shirt. "When did you talk to her?"

Nicholas pried his hands off, shoving Carmine away. "Twenty minutes ago when she called me."

The words stung. "What do you mean she called you?"

"I mean—*ring, ring*—she called my phone," he said. "What else would 'she called me' mean?"

Carmine lunged at him, but Nicholas was prepared this time. He barely stumbled before striking back, jabbing Carmine hard in the ribs. He gasped at the unexpected shot. Before he could recover, Nicholas struck him in the nose. Carmine's vision blurred as sharp pain shot through his face, blood flowing instantly. Someone grabbed his arm before he could get his wits about him, and he turned to see that a crowd had formed.

Carmine wiped his face with the back of his hand, smearing blood all over himself. He grabbed the bottom of his shirt and pinched his nose with it, trying to stop the bleeding.

"You know, you'd think you'd show some damn gratitude," Nicholas said. "I didn't have to come here."

"Why did you? You're wasting your time."

"Maybe I am, but I came here because Haven asked me to. She didn't have anyone else, and she needed you to come home. I try to do her a favor, and instead of listening, you'd rather fight for no reason."

"Why did she ask you to get me?"

"I think someone was there or something."

Carmine tensed. "How do you know?"

"I don't know. I heard a doorbell."

Carmine pushed past Nicholas and sprinted for the car. His father was leaving town, so no one should have been at the house. He sped through the streets of Durante, trying to figure out who it could be. Salvatore? Had *La Cosa Nostra* come again?

Fresh skid marks aligned the driveway when he arrived home, ruts dug into the path, but there weren't any cars in the yard, the house as quiet as he'd left it hours before.

Parking near the porch, Carmine climbed out and looked around, nothing raising any red flags. He unlocked the door and disabled the alarm when it beeped, his blood running cold when he saw the phone lying on the floor in the foyer. Glancing around suspiciously, he tried to remain calm as he made his way upstairs. He didn't find Haven on the third floor, so he slipped into his bedroom and pulled his gun from the top of his closet. He had hidden it there before he dropped the Mazda off to be fixed, not wanting to carry it in his brother's car. After checking to make sure it was loaded, he slipped the pistol into his waistband and went back down to the first floor.

His footsteps echoed in the house as he headed toward the kitchen, stopping in the doorway. Haven stood behind the island, her arm drawn back as she clutched a rolling pin. Carmine could see her trembling from where he stood.

If he hadn't been confused, he might have found it amusing. "Are you okay, *tesoro*?"

She nodded. "Are you?"

"Yeah, why wouldn't I be?"

She blinked a few times and continued to gaze at him. "What happened?"

"Shouldn't I be asking that?"

"Yes, but your nose . . ."

Carmine grabbed his nose, wincing. He'd forgotten about his injury. "Had a little scuffle with Nicholas."

She gasped. "You didn't hurt him, did you?"

"No, he got me this time." He cringed, not wanting to admit that. "Why did you call him?"

"Jen was here. Dr. DeMarco told me to call you. You didn't answer, and she was upset I wouldn't open the door, so I called him."

His phone hadn't worked since he had thrown it at his car. "So, did Jen give up?"

"I don't know. She threatened me and said—"

"She threatened you?"

"Yeah, but she left, and—"

"What the fuck did she want?"

"I don't know. I looked outside and—"

Her words faltered as the roar of an engine approached. Carmine stepped over to the window, seeing the truck pulling up out front. "It's Nicholas."

Nicholas headed for the house as Carmine went into the foyer and opened the door.

"Everything cool?" Nicholas asked, stopping a few feet away.

"It's fine," Carmine said. "You're not needed here."

"Carmine," Haven scolded as she stepped past him. Her eyes darted around as she stepped off the porch and loosely wrapped her arms around Nicholas in a hug. "Thank you. Not many people would've done that for me."

Nicholas stood frozen before halfheartedly patting her back. "Ah, no big deal," he said, but it was a big deal. Carmine almost felt bad for hitting him, but the throbbing in his nose counteracted any guilt. "So, crisis averted and all that jazz?"

"It was Jen," Carmine said. "My father must've kicked her to the curb. You know how scorned bitches are."

"I don't think—"

"She always was shady," Nicholas said. "I never understood why he'd stoop that low. Even I wouldn't touch her."

"Bullshit," Carmine said. "You slept with her."

"No, I didn't."

"Yes, you did. We were at the hospital last year, and I dared you to do it."

"Are you forgetting you tried to kill me that weekend? I never had a chance to try!"

"I didn't try to kill you. If I wanted to kill you, I'd kill you. I only snapped because you stabbed me in the back."

Nicholas glared at him. When he finally spoke, he said the last thing Carmine expected to hear. "You're right."

He raised his eyebrows. "Excuse me?"

"I said you're right. I shouldn't have said what I said, and I'm sorry about that, but you screwed up too, Carmine."

It was the first time Nicholas had ever acknowledged he had wronged him, and it caught Carmine off guard. "Yeah, I probably shouldn't have gotten with your sister. I'm so—uh, shit, whatever."

Haven eyed the two of them in shock. "Wow, are you—?"

"Anyway." Carmine cut her off before she could make a big deal out of it. "Everything's fine. Haven could've handled it. She had the rolling pin ready to whoop some ass."

The phone in the house rang, and Carmine ran to the foyer to grab it off the floor. He answered it as he stepped out onto the porch. "Hello?"

"Carmine?" Vincent's voice cracked a bit. "Can you hear me?"

"Uh, yeah."

"So, I have a joke for you," Nicholas said, turning to Haven. Carmine rolled his eyes as his father said something about the airport, but the reception grew worse and Nicholas's voice drowned him out. "What's black, white, and red all over?"

"I don't know," Haven said. "What?"

A loud bang rang out in the distance. Carmine accidentally dropped the phone and cursed, reaching down to pick it up, when a piercing scream cut through the air. The hair on Carmine's arms bristled as he spun around in time to see Nicholas drop to his knees, red seeping onto his white shirt. Clutching his chest, he opened his mouth to speak, but no sound came out. He dropped forward to the ground within a matter of seconds.

Haven screamed again, so loudly Carmine's ears rang.

Everything felt like it happened in slow motion. He jumped off the porch and landed on top of Haven as another bang shattered the air. He knocked her to the ground behind the car, his body weight forcing the air from her lungs.

"Listen to me," he said, pinning her trembling body there as she struggled to breathe. "I'm gonna count to three and start shooting back. I need you to get in the damn car. Got it?"

She was unresponsive as another shot rang out. Carmine winced as it collided with metal, the bullet striking the car. "Christ, Haven, you need to fucking listen to me. I need you to do this, so can you?"

Her voice shook as hard as her body. "I think so."

Carmine reached up and opened the passenger door a crack. "It's gonna be fine."

Yet another gunshot cut through the stifling air. He flinched at the sound and took a deep breath. They were taunting them, he realized. Whoever it was could have easily killed them both by now.

He started counting, and Haven's eyes widened as she clutched him. "Wait!"

"Christ, we don't have time to fuck around here!"

"I love you." The words caught in her throat and escaped as a sob. The sound of it burned, like she had taken a knife and plunged it straight into his chest, twisting it.

"Don't act like we won't see each other again in thirty seconds," he said, grabbing his gun from his waistband. "Get in the god-damn car, baby. *Three*."

He stood and aimed at nothing in particular, firing off rounds in the direction the shots had come from. Running to the driver's side, he cursed when he tripped over Nicholas. Shame overwhelmed him as tears stung his eyes, but he fought to hold himself together for Haven's sake.

Bullets whizzed by him as he ducked inside the car. Haven curled into a ball in the passenger seat, sobbing. He fumbled with the keys as he laid the gun down between them.

He threw the car in gear and swung it around, slamming the gas to get away from the house. He reached over and brushed Haven's hair aside to get a good look at her as he flew down the driveway. "Are you okay, *tesoro*? Talk to me, please."

She flinched when he touched her. "Nicholas! We can't leave Nicholas!"

"We have to," Carmine said. "It's too late for him."

She shook her head hysterically. "But he was just helping!"

"I know, hummingbird." He swung the car onto the main road. He wasn't sure what else to say. "I know."

He tried to focus on the road, but something caught his eye in the rearview mirror. A black car sped straight for them. "Fuck."

Haven glanced behind them. "Oh God."

"Put on your fucking seatbelt," he said. She froze for a split second before snapping it on. Carmine wanted to say something to comfort her, but he wasn't sure those words even existed. The vehicle rapidly approached as gunshots cut through the air again, bullets hitting the back of the car. The right rear tire blew out as it was struck, the car jolting, but Carmine managed to keep it on the road. A moment later the left tire shredded, the screech of metal rim against the highway drowning out the sound of gunfire. Sparks flew, and Carmine's panic deepened when he realized they couldn't outrun them now. He grasped the steering wheel to brace himself and looked at Haven, unparalleled devastation reflecting in her eyes.

"Carmine," she said. The sound of his name on her lips made his chest swell with love despite the fear. Nothing would ever overpower it. He stared into her deep brown eyes, and it seemed as if time stopped. It always would, he realized. Carmine's world wouldn't go on without her.

"I love you, too," he said, struggling to fight back the emotion so as not to scare her. "*Sempre.*"

The moment he said the word, the black sedan rammed the back of their car. They skidded off the side of the road toward some trees. Carmine threw his hands out instinctively to protect Haven, knowing it was too late to stop it. He thrust forward and hit the steering wheel, pain ripping through his chest as the air left his body.

Blackness stole him instantly.

46

The airbag deployed with a loud pop, silencing Haven's screams as her seatbelt locked into place. Slamming into it, she gasped for air, unable to take a breath until it deflated. She glanced at the driver's side, her chest on fire as she tore off her seatbelt. Carmine was slumped forward, his airbag splattered with blood from his face. Haven screamed his name, pawing at him, trying to find some sign of life, and she cried out with relief as he took a shaky breath.

The slam of a car door nearby alarmed Haven. The black sedan was parked alongside the road, everything hitting Haven at once as four men approached, all of them shrouded in black masks.

They were a blur in her panicked state, their rapid approach severing any grip she might have had on herself. She considered trying to run, but she wouldn't leave Carmine when he couldn't fend for himself. "Carmine, I need you! Please!"

Her distress skyrocketed as the men neared, their voices muffled to her ears. Glancing around the front seat, she spotted Carmine's gun on the floorboard. Her heart pounded vigorously. She hesitated for a split second before grasping it with trembling hands.

Someone appeared at the driver's side, and Haven pulled the trigger as a reflex. It sounded like an explosion in the confined space, and she yelped, remembering to keep a grip on the gun so it didn't slip out of her hand. The bullet shattered the driver's side window and grazed the man's face. He grasped his cheek and turned as someone screamed, the man behind him dropping to the ground a few feet away.

The first man ripped off his mask as he spun back around, and Haven shrieked when she recognized Nunzio. He whipped out his pistol and reached into the window, grabbing Carmine by the hair. Yanking his head back, Nunzio pointed the gun to his temple the same time the passenger door opened and a gun pressed to the back of her head.

The person behind her spoke, his voice heavily accented. "Drop the fucking gun, sweetheart."

She let go of it instantly as the man grabbed her arm and dragged her out of the car. He threw her to the ground and picked up the weapon, checking it as Nunzio slammed Carmine's head against the steering wheel.

"Please," she screamed, feeling sick as the word rolled from her lips. "Please don't hurt him!"

"Shut up," Nunzio said as the man tossed him Carmine's gun. "Did your boyfriend teach you how to use this thing? I never understood what Sal saw in him. *Principe della Mafia*, the future of the organization. He doesn't have the brains for this."

He glared at her, an eerie silence surrounding them as Nunzio slipped Carmine's gun into his coat. "Get her up. We don't have time to dick around."

The man yanked Haven to her feet and pulled her toward their car. She hyperventilated, frantically looking for some way to escape.

"What about him?" a third man asked, glancing at their partner on the ground. His voice also carried an accent.

"Leave him," Nunzio said. "I would've killed him, anyway."

"And the kid? DeMarco?"

Haven's heart felt like it stopped in that instant, pain radiating out through every inch of her body. She screamed and tried to pull away, fear making her knees buckle. The man's grasp slipped, and she collapsed, sobbing. "Please don't kill him! I'll go with you, I will! I won't fight! Just don't hurt him!"

Devastation consumed her when the man drew his gun and pointed it at Carmine. She let out a shriek, the sound originating somewhere down inside of her soul and resonating so loudly her own ears rang. Both men in front of her recoiled from the sound as something hard slammed into the back of her head, the force silencing her.

"Shut the fuck up," the man with the thick accent said, followed by another strong blow that knocked her forward.

"Please!" she screamed again through the pain, not caring what happened to her as long as they didn't touch Carmine. He was still alive, and she needed him to stay that way. "I'll do anything! Don't shoot him!"

A foot slammed into her side, and she whimpered, trying to catch her breath.

"That's enough," Nunzio said. "We need her in one piece. Just leave DeMarco before she gives me a headache."

The guy lowered his gun as Nunzio pulled her to her feet, eyeing her so intently her skin crawled. He pulled her close to him and leaned down, his nose grazing her cheek. She could smell the blood on his face as he smeared it against her. "He'll die soon, anyway."

She held her breath, revolted, and collapsed to the ground when he let her go.

"Put her in the car," Nunzio said, walking away. Arms wrapped around her waist and dragged her toward the road. She could faintly make out Carmine's body slumped over in the car, the sight of him crippling the last of her resolve. She screamed his name, desperately hoping he would hear her and wake up.

The man covered her mouth to silence her, and she panicked, biting down on his hand. Her teeth tore his flesh, repulsive blood filling her mouth. He pulled away enough to give her a chance to slip from his grasp. She spat and ran for the car but was grabbed as soon as she made it to the driver's side.

"I thought you were going to play nice?" Nunzio asked, dragging her back to their vehicle. He forced her into the backseat as the others climbed in, tires squealing as they drove away.

Nunzio grabbed a small pouch and unzipped it, pulling out a needle full of clear liquid. "It's a shame I have to do this."

She gasped as his hand grasped her around the throat. She struggled, slamming her fists into him as hard as she could, trying to knock the needle out of his hand. He jabbed it into her thigh and held her tightly for a minute longer as she faded, slipping into unconsciousness.

"Carmine?"

The sound of his name registered in Carmine's ears, but the voice was muddled and sounded far away. It was familiar, though, and he strained to hear.

"Carmine, open your eyes."

Everything was black but oddly hazy, like he was submerged under water or in a thick fog.

"Come on," the voice said, clearer than before. He recognized his father and tried to respond, but he couldn't get words to form, strangled moans vibrating his chest.

"Wake up, son," Vincent said. "This is important."

Carmine forced his eyes open but winced at the pain radiating from his head. He groaned as he moved, the stabbing feeling spreading with each attempt. His distorted vision blurred everything.

He was still in the car, the front end wedged against some trees. Smoke and heat still filtered from under the hood, so he couldn't have been unconscious too long. He saw his father standing beside the driver's side door and made a move to get out, but Vincent stopped him. "You shouldn't move. You're injured."

"I'm fine," Carmine said, unsure if that was true. He climbed out and grasped the side of the car to stabilize himself, his legs wobbly. He felt sick right away and hunched over, vomiting.

"You have a serious concussion," Vincent said. "Probably some fractured ribs. Looks like a broken nose and—"

"Quit fucking diagnosing me," he said. "Where's Haven?"

"I hoped you could tell me. I was on my way back to the house and saw the car here."

Carmine's panic flared. "I, uh . . . She was with me. We were at the house and someone started shooting. Nicholas got hit."

"Nicholas? Where is he?"

"Still at the house. I had to leave him and get the fuck out of there." He fought back his guilt, unsure of which hurt worse—the emotional anguish or the physical pain. "We were trying to get away, but a car ran up on us, and here we are. Or, fuck, here I am. Where is she?"

"We'll find her," Vincent said. Carmine wondered how he could be calm, and froze when something a few yards behind him caught his attention. His heart pounded forcefully when he realized it was a person.

His father glanced in that direction. "Johnny."

"Johnny? Who the fuck is Johnny?"

"Nobody important. I'm not even certain that's his name. He's part of Giovanni's street crew."

"One of your own?"

"He has a gunshot wound to the abdomen, but it's not necessarily fatal," Vincent said. "Missed his major organs, but I'm venturing a guess it hit his spinal cord."

"A gut shot? I thought you shot to kill?"

"I didn't shoot him," he said, shaking his head. "I hoped you could tell me who did."

"You found him there?" Carmine stared at his father, bewildered, before turning to the car. The passenger side door was open and the seatbelt was unlatched, so he didn't think Haven could have been too hurt in the accident. There wasn't any blood on her side.

"Maybe she went for help," he said, tossing things around. "Where's my gun?"

The moment he said it, he spotted the single .45-caliber cartridge on the passenger side floorboard. He picked it up and got back out of the car, eyeing it as his father sighed. "I had a feeling something like this would happen—even before I knew she was related to Sal. After everything I lost, I knew saving her wouldn't be easy. They all knew how important it was to me. I was afraid someone would take her for leverage. I should've known it would be him."

Carmine's legs wobbled. "Nunzio?"

Vincent nodded. "No one has heard from him in days. He was called in for a sit-down and didn't show. It was the reason I was going to Chicago this weekend."

Carmine felt the bile rising up. The thought of her being somewhere with Nunzio sickened him. He couldn't begin to imagine what she was going through.

"I'll kill him," Carmine said. "He'll pay for this."

"He will," Vincent said. "But right now, we need to be more concerned with finding her."

It turned out to be a brisk night, a storm rolling in from the west making the waters of Aurora Lake more turbulent than usual. Vincent stood at the end of a long pier a few miles from the Barlow residence, huddled up in his coat as he tried to shield himself from the harsh winds.

Vincent could easily recall the first time he met Nicholas, a warm fall day at the local elementary school. Carmine had just turned ten, and it was the first time Vincent had made it to one of his football games. Between juggling his job at the hospital and managing his work with *la famiglia*, he had little time left over for his children.

But that day, he had snuck out of work early to watch. Toward the middle of the game, a scrawny boy with tanned skin took a nasty spill, and someone's cleat gashed his cheek. It was a superficial wound, so Vincent grabbed a first-aid kit from the car, sparing the boy a trip to the emergency room. "Thanks, Doc," he'd said. "Oh, what did the doctor say when the invisible man asked for an appointment?"

"I'm not sure."

"Sorry, but I can't see you today." He laughed hysterically at his joke. "Get it? Can't see you? You know, because he's invisible!"

Vincent smiled. "I get it."

Halftime began as he finished fixing the boy's wound, and Carmine ran over. "Dad! You came!"

Intense guilt hit him. "I did."

Carmine threw his arm around the boy's shoulder. "This is my best friend, Nicholas."

Those words caught Vincent off guard. Carmine's teachers all reported the same thing—he was closed off and shut down, so much so that it was as if he weren't there.

Vincent's pager went off as he stood there, the moment lost in that split second as the beeps rang out. The sparkle in Carmine's eye dissipated, the child Vincent had grown accustomed to returning without a single word spoken.

But all hope was not lost, Vincent realized, because Carmine had someone. Someone he could be *Carmine* around—the young, innocent boy, haunted by demons others couldn't see.

After their fallout, he watched his son spiral out of control. He was walking down the one path Vincent wanted him to stay far away from—the path leading straight to Chicago. But then she happened. The girl who had never been able to call her life her own taught a boy who had the world at his fingertips exactly what it meant to live. He wasn't alone anymore.

Nicholas, however, was.

Vincent never forgot the joke he had told him that first day, because Nicholas was a lot like the invisible man. Drifting his way through life, unnoticed by most. Vincent saw him, though, even if he couldn't fix him. And as he stood on that pier under the cloak of darkness, he wished he would have done something more to help.

He gazed down at the water, fixated on the spot where Nicholas's body had disappeared moments before, and felt nothing but disgust. He had watched the boy grow up and had now sent him to a watery tomb like many of his adversaries.

"Oggi uccidiamo, domani moriremo," he said, his gloved hand making the sign of the cross. Today we kill, tomorrow we die.

Vincent headed to his car hidden in the trees, and he drove away from Aurora Lake without looking back. He had already cleaned up the house, having hosed down the driveway and redistributed the gravel to hide all signs of the incident, but he had bigger issues he needed to deal with.

———

As soon as Vincent made it home, he slipped inside the room under the stairs and headed down into the basement. The place was cleaned out, the crates relocated elsewhere, so he had no problem navigating the room. He reached the large bookcase along the back and opened a metal electrical box on the wall beside it. He slid a section of panel down, revealing a small keypad, and punched in the numbers 62373.

There was a loud click. He slid the panel up, closing the electrical box as the bookshelf shifted a few inches. The door led into a safe room, or what his youngest referred to as *the dungeon*. The room, not much larger than a prison cell, had steel reinforced walls layered with bulletproof Kevlar.

It was the kind of room few men went into and even fewer came back out of alive.

He flicked a switch along the side, and fluorescent lights lit up the small space. He squinted and blocked out the blinding glare with his hand. Groans rang out from the corner where Johnny lay shackled to a table on the concrete floor.

"Vincent." The voice was barely audible. "Help me."

"I will," Vincent said, "but first you're going to help me."

"I can't move. I can't feel my legs."

"I know. The bullet hit your spinal cord."

"A bullet? I'm paralyzed! Oh God, my legs!"

Vincent sighed with annoyance. "Toughen up."

"What happened?" Johnny struggled to move. "My fucking legs!"

"What happened is I got a call that someone was at my house, so I came home to investigate and found my son unconscious, his girlfriend missing, an innocent kid dead in my front yard, and you injured. You, at the scene of an attack on my family. So how about you tell me what happened."

"I, uh, I don't know . . . I got shot, and I don't know how or who . . ."

Vincent said, leaning against the table and crossing his arms over his chest. "I understand how this life is. We get drawn into things that get out of control, but it's not too late to fix it. I need you to tell me what Nunzio wants with the girl."

"I can't!"

Vincent could sense his panic and fought to keep his expression calm so as not to alarm him further. "You have to be in pain, and you need your wound cleaned before infection takes hold. It's your only option."

"I can't tell you anything," he said. "I don't know anything."

"You're lying," Vincent said. "You wouldn't go along with something unless you knew why. Where did he take her?"

"You have to believe me, Vincent. I can't tell you!"

"You can tell me, you just won't! There's a difference, and that difference is as vast as life and death."

"Please!"

He shook his head. "Don't beg! It's unbecoming of you."

"You have to understand—"

"No, you have to understand. They've taken something important from me, and I'm not going to stop until I find her. If you want even the slightest chance of making it out of this room alive, you'll tell me what I need to know."

"If I tell you anything, they'll kill me."

"If you don't tell me, I'll kill you," he said. "And I won't take mercy on you. Every minute she's out there, you're going to be right here, and I'm not going to end your suffering until she's back where she belongs."

———————

The tension was so thick you could cut it with a knife. Carmine had heard the phrase so many times, but it wasn't until that moment, sitting in that immaculately clean car and fighting back nausea at the stench of fresh leather, that he finally understood what it meant. It was stifling, the hostility rolling from the man beside him too much to take.

Carmine had a fractured rib, a broken nose, and a mildly sprained wrist on top of the concussion. Vincent had called in a favor, and one of his colleagues agreed to see him off the record. Despite Carmine's insistence he didn't need any doctors, Vincent demanded he go, and when Vincent DeMarco demanded something, even Carmine couldn't say no. So when Corrado arrived in town, the two of them had set out for a clinic while his father stayed back to deal with the devastation.

"You're not gonna kill that doctor I saw, are you?" Carmine asked, the heavy dose of morphine in his system clouding his thoughts.

Corrado said nothing, and Carmine wasn't sure whether that was good or bad.

"I don't think you should," he said. "He's just a doctor."

"Carmine?"

"Yeah?"

"Shut up."

Carmine decided then he *should* probably shut up.

Disoriented, he glanced at the clock on the dashboard and saw it was midnight. Haven had been gone for twelve hours, and the clock kept ticking as if the seconds didn't matter.

He sighed, the strain in the car growing.

Carmine felt like he could breathe again when they reached the house and put some space between them. He headed inside and paused in the foyer as his father stepped out of the room under the stairs. Corrado shuffled in and closed the front door. "Has he talked?"

"No," Vincent said. "He's given me nothing."

Corrado brushed past Carmine, giving Vincent a peculiar look before disappearing into the room. Vincent muttered something under his breath, refusing to look at Carmine as he strode away. Carmine sat down on the steps, putting his head down and rocking back and forth for a while, before pacing the hallway. As the morphine faded from his system, so did his patience.

Eventually, he heard footsteps on the stairs as Vincent approached at the same time Corrado stepped out, both men stopping in the foyer. Carmine looked between them, his last bit of control slipping. "Why are you just standing there? Can't you do something? *Anything?* Christ!"

Before the last word was verbalized, Carmine was jerked by the back of his collar and slammed into the wall. He lost his breath as Corrado shoved a gun to his fractured rib. "Have you still not learned your lesson? Is one of us going to have to die before you realize this isn't a game? These are our lives you're messing with, and I, for one, will not tolerate you endangering me more than you already have! I don't care whose child you are."

Carmine's heart pounded rapidly. He didn't doubt for a second that his uncle would shoot him.

"Corrado," Vincent said. "Let him go."

Corrado released Carmine and swung around, turning the

weapon on Vincent. Carmine inhaled sharply as he watched it play out. Vincent stood as still as a statue, not blinking as he stared down the barrel of Corrado's gun.

"You keep pulling me in deeper and deeper, Vincent," Corrado said, lowering his pistol.

"I know," Vincent said.

Corrado turned to Carmine. "That mouth of yours is going to get every single one of us killed. If you can't close it yourself, I'll close it for you."

———

The next day dawned when Carmine made his way up to the third floor, his chest constricting as he pushed open his bedroom door. He sat on the edge of the bed and grabbed a pillow, clutching it to his chest as tears formed in his eyes.

Every bit of composure he had was ripped away as he inhaled Haven's scent, which lingered there. The grief swallowed him, refusing to let go until his father interrupted in the middle of the afternoon. "We're leaving for Chicago soon," Vincent said.

Carmine set the pillow down and wiped his tears, cringing at his torn, blood-splattered clothes. "I should change."

"I prefer you stay here in case she shows back up."

Carmine laughed bitterly as he stood. "She's not a lost dog. She didn't wander out of the backyard and get lost in the woods somewhere."

"I understand, but you should reconsider. It's dangerous and—"

"I'm going," Carmine said, cutting him off. "If you don't want me to go with you, I won't, but I'll be on the next goddamn plane whether you like it or not."

"Fine, but you need to watch yourself, son. You can't run off on a vigilante mission. I can't focus on getting her back if you're out there wreaking havoc and counteracting everything I'm doing."

"I know. I'll keep my mouth shut and let you do what you do.

I'm not fucking naïve. I know what might be happening to her, but I need to be there, no matter what."

Vincent pinched the bridge of his nose. "Fine. We'll tie up some loose ends then leave."

Carmine gazed at him. "Loose ends? Is it, uh . . . you know, that guy, and . . ."

He couldn't finish his thought, but he didn't have to. Vincent understood. "We have Johnny in the basement. He hasn't said much, but I injected him with sodium thiopental a few minutes ago."

"Sodium what?"

"Sodium thiopental. It's a barbiturate. It suppresses the higher cortical functions of the brain, and since lying is such a complex process and it's easier to—"

"English, please."

"Truth serum," Vincent said. "Hypothetically, anyway."

Carmine nodded. "And Nicholas?"

Vincent stared at him, the look on his face the only answer Carmine needed. Even across the room, he could see the sorrow. "There wasn't anything I could do."

———

Dawn broke as Vincent stood in the safe room, once again interrogating a suffering Johnny. "Tell me where she is and this will end."

"I can't," he said for what had to be the hundredth time, even proclaiming ignorance with the truth serum coursing through his veins.

Corrado approached, his dark eyes filled with rage. It wasn't something Vincent saw often. It was a look that said someone was about to die.

Violently.

Vincent stepped out of the way as Corrado strode over to the cabinet along the wall. He rifled through it, pulling out knives and pliers, methodically laying the tools on the steel worktable in the safe room. "While you're still alive, we're going to play a game of eeny, meeny, miny, moe."

Unable to stomach what was about to happen, Vincent walked away. A loud scream of agony echoed through the basement before he made it to the steps.

Johnny would be leaving the room soon . . . in pieces.

Corrado resurfaced an hour later, drenched from the rain outside and splattered with blood. His face was unreadable once more. "Russians."

The lone word nearly stopped Vincent's heart. "She's with the Russians? Why?"

"Because she's one of ours. Isn't that reason enough?"

"They know?"

"They may have known before we did," Corrado said. "This is spiraling out of control. Up until now, you've taken a backseat, but that can't happen anymore. This isn't going away."

Vincent knew that, even if he didn't want to admit it. "Where are the Russians keeping her?"

"Joey didn't know."

Vincent's brow furrowed. "I thought his name was Johnny."

"Joey, Johnny . . . what's the difference?" Corrado started walking away. "I took care of the body. You can clean up the mess."

Vincent headed back down to the basement, cautiously making his way to the safe room. The concrete floor was soaked in red, splatters of it on the ceiling. He wasn't sure how Corrado managed to do that, but he didn't plan to ask.

He'd learned long ago never to ask for details.

The rain outside was so heavy Carmine couldn't see the tree line a few hundred yards away. He gazed out the family room window in such a trance that he didn't hear footsteps approaching. He caught a glimpse of Corrado's reflection in the glass and grabbed his chest, wincing as he turned around. "You scared me."

Corrado unbuttoned his soiled shirt. "You aren't very observant."

"You're just stealthy, like a fucking ninja."

Ninja. The moment he said it, he felt like he had been slapped. Tears tried to force their way from his eyes, but he held them back in front of his uncle.

"You watch too much television," Corrado said. "The mark of a successful assassin is the target never knowing what hit him."

Carmine stared at him. "I'm not a target, though . . . at least I hope not."

The corner of Corrado's lips tugged into a small smile as he lit the fireplace. After the fire waged, he tossed his shirt into it and watched it burn. "I remember when you and your mother went missing. A few of us were at your house, and you were late. Vincent sent a car, but it came back empty. Driver said you were already gone. Despite your father's fear that night, he did what he had to do. He learned to wear that calm mask well, but I knew him better than most."

He poked around in the fire, the shirt already burned to ash. "You and him are cut from the same mold—too emotional, too invested in life on the outside, and that can be dangerous. People will exploit it for an upper hand, and both of you share a weakness."

"What's that?"

Corrado looked at him like it was a stupid question. "Your women, Carmine."

"Doesn't everyone have that problem, though?"

Corrado shook his head. "Most are incapable of loving anyone. Their wives are like their cars and their houses. They feel like they've earned them, they take care of them, they show them off, but if push comes to shove, they'd sell them out to save themselves."

"Is that how you feel?" Carmine asked. "I always thought, you know, you and Celia . . ."

"I do love Celia," Corrado said. "The difference is I can't be manipulated. They used Maura to force your father to do their business, just as Haven will be used to get you to do what they want."

"You think that's why they kept me alive?"

"I'm sure of it. We're all pawns, Carmine, and if you aren't careful, you'll play into their hands. Exposure isn't good in our world. I hope, since you're so much like Vincent, you'll learn to put on that mask. I already helped him bury Maura. I don't want to go through that again." He turned to walk away. "And pack a bag, for God's sake. It looks suspicious to get on a plane with no luggage."

They landed in Chicago close to dusk that evening and made the twenty-five-minute journey from the airport to the Morettis' house in silence. Carmine watched out the window in a daze. He hadn't been back in years, but the neighborhood looked exactly like he recalled. They passed Tarullo's Pizzeria and Carmine closed his eyes, unable to look as they neared the alley where his life changed.

Corrado pulled into the driveway of the large brick house. A frazzled Celia stood in the doorway, and Corrado barely gave her a glance as he passed. She offered Vincent a sympathetic smile, and Carmine tried to slip by her, but she grabbed him for a hug.

He pulled away from her. "This is my fault."

Shaking her head, Celia cupped his chin. "You didn't cause this, kiddo. You would never do anything to hurt her. She's one of us . . . she's family. We'll find her."

"I hope you're right," he said, dropping his bag right inside the house. He headed for the front room, catching sight of his brother on the couch. Dominic had his head down, his hands covering his face. Tess sat beside him and glanced at Carmine, her eyes widening. She nudged Dominic. "Dom."

Dominic's head popped up, his mouth agape. "Look at you, bro."

"It looks worse than it is," he lied, sitting on the other side of him. The pain was unbearable, both inside and out. "She's all that matters right now."

Neither said anything more before Vincent walked in, setting up his laptop on the coffee table. He looked at Dominic, his voice stern. "I need you to locate her chip for me."

Carmine blanched. "You can't find it?"

"It won't connect."

When he left, a tense silence lingered in his wake. Tess sighed loudly as she paced the room, picking up things to keep busy as Dominic turned to the laptop. His fingers flew furiously across the keys as he typed in code, none of it making any sense to Carmine.

The clicking keys grated on Carmine's raw nerves. He was nearing forty hours without sleep. His head felt too heavy for his neck, his red-rimmed eyes burning from exhaustion. Running his hand through his hair, he clutched it tightly as he swayed in his seat. The ticking of a clock in the background blended with Dominic's typing, taunting Carmine. Every tick was one second longer without her, one more second of uncertainty. Tess continued to pace, her heels clacking against the wood floor. It was too much for him to take.

Pace, click, tick. Pace, click, tick. Pace, click, tick.

Carmine was losing his fucking mind.

Celia walked in with some sandwiches and set a plate in front of him. "You should eat."

"Do you think she's eating?" His voice cracked as the question came out. Was she eating? Were they taking care of her? Was she warm? Christ, where the fuck was she? He let out a shaky breath as his fear skyrocketed. Was she even alive?

Celia rubbed his back but he pulled away from her as Tess huffed again. "Do you have something you wanna say, Tess?" Carmine asked, standing. "Something you wanna get off your chest? Miss Goddamn Perfect always knows better than everyone. You never liked Haven, anyway. You're probably glad she's gone."

Tess gasped and covered her mouth as Dominic jumped up. He looked like he wanted to punch him, and for a moment, Carmine wished his brother would.

"I think you need some sleep," Dominic said. "Haven's like my sister. I'm upset, too, so don't act like you're the only one who cares."

Carmine tried to get himself under control. "I wasn't thinking."

"I know you weren't." Dominic sat back down, focusing his attention on the laptop. "And if you think you can help in your condition, you're wrong. So eat your sandwich and go close your damn eyes."

The nondescript cinder block building stood in the middle of an abandoned neighborhood. Rust coated the black metal door, elaborate graffiti sprayed indiscriminately on the outside. Inside, the building was just as neglected, the concrete floor cracked and the walls covered in grime. It was still wired for electricity, overhead lights flickering. A metal exhaust fan near the ceiling continuously ran.

In the center of the room was a large card table, surrounded by men in collapsible chairs. Thousands of dollars lay on the table, empty beer bottles scattered around as each man held a set of cards. They spoke animatedly, arguing and laughing as their game of poker wore on into the night.

They seemed oblivious to the girl in the shadows of the far corner, curled up on a torn, stained mattress. Haven was equally as oblivious to them, her breathing shallow. Noises occasionally filtered into her blackness, muffled, incoherent words spoken in unrecognizable voices.

Little by little, she came back around, and with the consciousness came pain. The voices grew louder when she tried to sit up, her head swimming from disorientation. Panic flooded her system when the door banged in the distance. A woman entered and started toward the others, but stopped as she looked in Haven's direction. "Why didn't you tell me the girl was awake?"

She had a tinge of a foreign accent that struck Haven as familiar, flashes of the accident coming back to her. It reminded her of the man who had held a gun to her head.

Everyone stopped speaking, shifting their focus to Haven. A pair of familiar eyes met hers, the sight of them making her stomach twist. Nunzio smirked before turning back to his cards, the rest of the men grumbling as they did the same.

The woman grabbed a bottle from a large cooler by the table and poured some of the liquid into a plastic cup before making her way across the room. Haven could make out her features as she approached, her long, stringy hair so blonde it was nearly white, the roots the color of midnight. Her blue eyes were large, her face round and full. She looked like an antique porcelain doll.

"I'm surprised to see you moving around," she said, her voice gentle as she held out the cup. Haven resisted, and the woman laughed lightly. "It's water, pretty girl. Drink."

A part of Haven screamed not to trust her, but there was a bigger part desperate to accept the drink. She gave in after a moment, the cold liquid soothing her burning chest.

"I thought he put you out for good," she said. "I told Nunzy that last dose was too much. I don't know why he never listens to me."

The woman scoured through her purse and pulled out a pack of saltine crackers. "You're going to want to eat these. There's no telling when you'll have another chance."

Although she didn't trust her, Haven didn't want her stubbornness to ruin a chance to get some strength. Her stomach hurt with familiar pangs of hunger, so she took the crackers and ate them.

Her eyelids grew heavy. She fought the sleepiness, but it took control of her. She was light-headed and had to lie down as the woman smiled.

"Sorry," she said, her voice a fading whisper, "but Nunzy won't bother you if you're asleep."

Haven realized, as the pain lifted and the sounds grew muffled, that she'd been drugged again.

47

Carmine groggily glanced around the spare bedroom, his eyes falling on a clock across the room. It took a second for the numbers to register, and he sat up when he realized it was already eight in the morning. Pain surged through every inch of him as he climbed to his feet and descended the stairs. He paused in the doorway of the living room, seeing Dominic still typing away at the laptop as Tess paced. Everything appeared how he had left it.

Nearly half a day had passed, but nothing had changed.

Celia stepped out of the kitchen at the sound of his footsteps, appearing as exhausted as everyone else. "How are you feeling, kiddo?"

How did she think he felt? He hurt, inside and out. His entire life was chaos. Was he supposed to tell her he felt like dying would be relief? Would that make her feel better?

"I feel fucking useless," he said, running his hand through his hair. "It's like I'm just waiting for the other shoe to drop, and I hate that goddamn feeling."

Celia opened her mouth to respond, but chaos erupted before she could get out a single word.

Dominic jumped to his feet. "It's connecting!"

Carmine's heart pounded rapidly as a door down the hall flung open and slammed against a wall. Carmine figured they had heard Dominic, but all hope disappeared when he made eye contact with his uncle. Corrado stared right past him at the door, his tanned skin seemingly void of all color.

Carmine's blood ran cold. Something was terribly wrong, but never in his wildest dreams could he have predicted what happened next.

"FBI! Search warrant! Get on the ground! Now!"

The shouting rang out from outside, multiple voices yelling at once. Carmine turned in disbelief as something slammed against the door, forcing it open. He flinched as the same noise echoed on the other side of the house, the back door torn from the hinges. Instinctively, he covered his head as a series of loud bangs ricocheted through the downstairs, bright lights blinding him as the police flash bombed the house.

An influx of men in SWAT gear burst through the doors, screaming for them to get down. Tess cried out from the living room as Dominic cursed, their voices muffled to Carmine's ringing ears. It happened fast, and Carmine was cemented in place as Celia dropped to the floor with her hands above her head.

"Get down!" an officer screamed, pointing his weapon at Carmine, but he couldn't move. He couldn't do anything. Celia grabbed his foot and yanked it, sending him stumbling. He dropped to his knees, and the officer shoved his face into the floor. They forced his arms behind him, and he cried out, trying to pull his hands away when they grabbed handcuffs.

"Don't resist," Celia said. "They need to detain us for their safety."

He relaxed his arms to let them secure the cuffs. The officer nearly cut off his circulation as he tightened them.

"Vincenzo Roman DeMarco, you're under arrest for violation of the RICO Acts, Title 18 of the United States Code, Section 1961," an officer declared as he walked down the hallway, leading Vincent to the front door. "You have the right to remain silent. Anything you say can and will be used against you in a court of law. You have the right to have an attorney present during questioning. If you cannot afford an attorney, one will be appointed for you."

Carmine grew frantic as they neared. "Dad!"

"Keep your mouth shut, Carmine," he said as they led him outside. Officers pulled Corrado off the floor next and read him the same rights, placing him under arrest too.

"Call the lawyers, Celia," Corrado said calmly. "I don't want them seizing anything without one present."

"I will," she said, her voice shaking a bit. "Stay strong."

"Don't worry about me," Corrado said. "I'll be fine."

An officer helped Celia off the ground and searched her before they walked away, and others led both Dominic and Tess out of the living room. They pulled Carmine to his feet last and pushed him against the wall, vehemently patting him down and taking everything out of his pockets.

Once they were satisfied he had no weapons, they led him through the front door. The street was blocked off and covered in police vehicles, dozens of FBI agents and local officers swarming the area. Carmine watched as they put his father and uncle in separate unmarked dark SUVs, his footsteps faltering as the reality of it hit him.

"Walk," the officer said, pushing him.

Carmine stumbled a few steps and winced as they shoved him down on the curb beside Celia. "Take it fucking easy, man! I'm hurt!"

"Do you need a medic, son?" an older man asked, stepping in their direction. Carmine narrowed his eyes, reading *Special Agent U.S. D.O.J.* written on his vest in bright yellow letters.

"I'm not your son," he said. "And what I need is to get the fuck out of here."

"Patience would be nice. I'm Special Agent Donald Cerone, head of the organized crime division."

Carmine cocked an eyebrow at his Italian name. "Cerone? Must be new slang for *traitor*."

The agent snickered, motioning for the other officer to give him Carmine's belongings. Carmine sighed when the agent opened his wallet, knowing what he would find.

"Ah, what's this?" he asked. "Carmine Marcello DeMarco. Tell me, son, what year were you born? We have two different IDs here with two different ages."

"*Vaffanculo.*"

"Carmine," Celia warned. "Stop goading him."

Agent Cerone just laughed again.

A female agent released Celia from her handcuffs and handed her a cell phone to call a lawyer. They gave her paperwork, explaining what they were doing as officers released Dominic and Tess from their restraints. Carmine watched as calmly as he could, but his patience was severely thin.

"Are you gonna take mine off?" he asked. "This is bullshit, Cerone."

Agent Cerone ignored Carmine's request and instead tried to ask him questions, which Carmine in turn ignored, refusing to say a word. He ached and shifted position, but every time he did a dozen agents eyed him like he was going to run.

He would. He would run if he could get away.

They brought boxes and bags out of the house, all of them tagged with evidence tape. Carmine leaned back on his elbows and stared at the ground until someone yanked him to his feet. "Should I release him now, boss? We're nearly done."

Agent Cerone shook his head. "Take him downtown."

"For what?" Carmine asked. "I didn't fucking do anything!"

The smirk returned to the agent's lips. "It's been a pleasure, Carmine Marcello DeMarco. I'm sure we'll see more of each other in the future."

―――――

When Haven regained consciousness for the second time, sunlight streamed through the cracks around the exhaust fan. She tried to block out the pain as she looked around, her eyes meeting the same woman from before. "Good morning, pretty girl."

Once again, everyone stopped talking and turned to her. Haven's heart rate accelerated when she spotted Nunzio. In the daylight she could see he had a bandage on his cheek.

"Ah, Sleeping Beauty is awake?" a man asked as he stood from one of the chairs. He was tall with thick muscles, his face rigid as if chiseled from stone. His hair was mainly gray and his nose too large for his face. He, too, had an accent.

Nunzio laughed. "Didn't even take a kiss from her prince to do it."

"How do you feel?" the man asked, ignoring Nunzio's comment. He dragged a chair across the room and sat down in front of Haven. Up close, she could see wrinkles covering his face. "Can you speak, *Princzessa?*"

Her brow furrowed at the word.

"Ah, confused? You are more comfortable with the Italians. Nunzy, boy, what word am I looking for?"

"*Principessa.*"

"Yes, do you know that one?" He raised his eyebrows, expecting some response. Haven nodded and cringed from the pain in her neck. "Are you hurting? You may speak. We are friends here."

She gave him an incredulous look, and the woman laughed. "I don't think she believes you, Papa."

"So it appears," he said, gazing at her curiously. "I cannot say I blame you. You should not trust people, especially the ones you associate with, but I will never deceive you as they have."

Haven's voice was scratchy. "What are you talking about?"

"Ah, she speaks!" His hard expression gave way to excitement. "What I am talking about is that your Italians have not been honest with you, nor have they treated you fairly, *Principessa.*"

He confused her. "Why do you keep calling me that?"

"Would you rather I call you by your slave name?"

"I, uh . . ." Did she? "I don't know."

He laughed. "I cannot believe you do not know."

"I told you," Nunzio said. "She's clueless."

The man leaned toward her, his hands clasped together in front of him. Haven tried to move away, her back pressed into the corner, his proximity nerve-racking.

"You are probably wondering what you are doing here," he said, his tone serious. "I will level with you—I do not wish to hurt you, but I will if you make me, so I am asking for cooperation. I know you have fight in you, considering you have twice scarred my son."

She gaped at him as he motioned toward Nunzio. *Son?*

"I should explain," he said. "I am Ivan Volkov, and I have been acquainted with the DeMarcos for many years. Vincent was a child the first time we met. He was a pretentious prick, much like I hear his youngest is."

He laughed, as did Nunzio, and Haven felt tears forming at the mention of Carmine.

"Did I strike a nerve, *Principessa*?" he asked. "I hear you care for the boy. It would be a pity if something happened to him, so let us hope it does not come to that."

"Don't," she whispered. "Please don't . . ."

"I do not wish to hurt him. If it helps, I have not heard of his death, so he is probably fine."

His voice taunted her. She tried to fight back tears, but it was too much to take.

"Aw, do not cry." He reached toward her but she recoiled. He dropped his hand without touching her. "Where was I?"

"You were talking about how much of a prick Vincent was," Nunzio said.

"Ah, yes. This was before he met his wife, of course. Shame what happened to her. I suppose I should feel guilty, but it was her fault." He shook his head. "Meddling bitch."

"You? *You* did it?"

"You can say I conducted that beautiful symphony."

"I don't understand," Haven said. "What do I have to do with any of this?"

"You have the power to bring down the enemy, and that is what you are going to do."

She tensed, Carmine's words from weeks before hitting her again. *I was born with enemies. My last name alone gives me more than I could ever earn.*

"I have laid the groundwork around Chicago, taking over businesses," he continued. "We have wiped out the competition, except for the Italians. People are loyal to them, and they have proven to be strong. I do not like being told where I can go and what I can do. I have found little ways in and turned a few, but I need something bigger, someone higher up. I need to crack the leadership, and Nunzy created a rift. They have held themselves together, but it is different now. Now I have you."

"Me? But I'm just . . . I'm no one."

"Oh, you are definitely someone," he insisted. "You are my golden ticket. If I kidnapped the DeMarco boy, the Italians would come with guns blazing, but you are trickier. Salvatore will be happy to have you gone, the complication removed, but the others will not give up. There is nothing I enjoy more than seeing them fight. And when the DeMarco boy demands action, someone will spill the truth about who you are, thinking it will make Salvatore want to help."

Ivan laughed long and hard, as if that were the funniest thing he had ever heard.

"Who am I?" She immediately regretted the question, but it was too late to take it back.

"I have been trying to tell you. You are the buried treasure, the one Salvatore thought would never be found, but I have dug you up." He reached out, his calloused finger drawing an *X* on her forehead. "When the dust settles and they have killed one another, everything will be mine for the taking . . . including you."

He stood and turned to the blond-haired woman. "Get her some water and something to eat, Natalia. Let her rest. You and your brother are on watch tonight."

Haven sat as still as possible, her eyes vigilantly darting around the room as everyone filtered out, leaving her and Nunzio alone. He strolled to her and knelt down, placing his hand on her knee.

She fought back a shudder as his hand roamed up her leg and came to rest on her thigh. He squeezed tightly, his fingers digging into her flesh, and she cringed as he pulled himself up. Leaning over, he paused with his mouth next to her ear. "Miss me?"

A chill shot down her spine when his tongue swirled around her earlobe. Panicking, she shoved him. He stumbled a few steps, and before he could react, she pulled her leg up and slammed it into his crotch. He hunched over as she jumped up, her vision blurring from the sudden movement. She sprinted for the metal door across the room, but barely made it halfway there when he grabbed her from behind.

"I like it when you fight," Nunzio said breathlessly. She cried for help as he dragged her across the room, grabbing a roll of duct tape from the card table.

She shook her head at the sight of it. "No!"

He smirked. "Yes."

She tried to move past him, shoving him again, but he grabbed her wrist and yanked her back. Pain ripped up her shoulder with such intensity that everything went black. He threw her on the mattress and straddled her.

Her brittle fingernails caught on his skin as she grasped at his face, pulling his bandage off and ripping the stitches underneath. Blood gushed from the wound, running down her arm.

Raising his fist, Nunzio slammed it into her face. Stars danced before her eyes. He tore off a piece of duct tape to cover her mouth. After muffling her cries, he jerked her onto her stomach. Pain radiated through her body as he forced her arms behind her, binding her hands and ankles together. He wiped his cheek, bringing his hand up to eye the blood, before storming outside.

Natalia returned with a bag of food and sat down on the mattress beside her. She unbound her and gently pulled the duct tape from Haven's mouth, feeding her until Haven turned away. Sickness churned in her stomach as Natalia patted her head. "You should not anger him. It isn't smart."

Eventually, Haven passed out from exhaustion, only to awaken later to Ivan kneeling in front of her. "I thought you were going to play nice, *Principessa*."

"I, uh, he was going to—"

"I do not need excuses," he said. "I need cooperation."

Before she could speak again, he jabbed her with a needle. "It will be easier this way."

———

The holding cells at Cook County Jail are overcrowded bullpens of chain-link fence, the sour, putrid smell inside strong enough to singe nose hair. Carmine sat in the corner of one with his head down, surrounded by dozens of murderers, druggies, and thieves. People bickered, scuffles breaking out between rival detainees. On edge, he tried to maintain his strength, but he was dangerously close to cracking.

It was after nightfall when they booked him into the system. He was taken to a small room where he sat across from a lady who asked a lot of questions he had no desire to answer. He humored her with the basics, like his name and date of birth, but when she asked how he felt or if he was suicidal, he remained silent.

The love of his life was missing and his ability to help was gone. Instead of being out there, searching, he was trapped in a room with this nosy bitch asking him if he felt angry. Of course he was angry. Wasn't he supposed to be?

They gave up and ordered him out, writing an identification

number on his arm in permanent marker before fingerprinting him and taking mug shots. He stared at the number the whole time, feeling sick at the sight of it. They had stripped him of his name. He was now number 2006-0903201.

An intake officer photographed Carmine's tattoos as he continued to glare at the number. "Are you affiliated with any gangs?"

"No."

"Are you sure? LCN counts as a gang."

"LCN?"

"You know, the Mafia?"

Carmine cut his eyes to him. "There is no Mafia."

The officer wrote something in his file before sending Carmine to be strip searched. By the time he put on that orange jumpsuit for protective custody, he felt like he had been thoroughly fucked.

They took him to division nine, placing him in a small cell on the top tier. It was closed in and suffocating, no bars or windows to the outside. The green paint on the thick metal door flaked, words scratched into it. He had nothing but a light and a threadbare blanket, the mattress no thicker than egg crate foam.

Hours slipped by while Carmine lay there, staring at the ceiling. Inmates yelled around him, sirens going off as guards ran by the door. He barely slept, tossing and turning in agony all night.

The next morning they came by with a breakfast tray, but he refused to eat their food, demanding they get him a lawyer. The same thing happened with lunch—he ignored their food, and they ignored his questions. He was infuriated by the time dinner rolled around, utterly exhausted and frantically pacing the cell. He heard someone walking up and expected another tray to be shoved inside but was surprised when two correctional officers unlocked his door.

"You have a visitor," one of them said, handcuffing and shackling him before leading him to a small holding room. A hefty balding man sat inside at a table, a briefcase open in front of him.

He looked up when Carmine entered and motioned for him to sit. The corrections officer secured Carmine before leaving them alone.

"My name's Rocco Borza, attorney at law. Celia Moretti contacted me about you." He pulled out some paperwork, sliding it across the table to Carmine along with a pen. "I need you to sign this, agreeing to let me handle your case, and anything you say is confidential."

Carmine scanned the papers and awkwardly signed the lines the best he could with his restraints, before sliding them back.

"First of all, I need to know if you've spoken to anyone," he said, slipping the papers into his briefcase. "Have they attempted to interrogate you?"

"No," he said. "They haven't even explained why I'm here."

"They charged you with possessing a fraudulent government document," he said. "It's a class-four felony but can easily be knocked down to a misdemeanor. You should've been given a probable cause hearing within a few hours and been released on bail."

"Then why am I sitting in that damn cell?"

"They can detain you for a reasonable amount of time," he said. "But truthfully? You're there because you're the son of Vincenzo Roman DeMarco, the nephew of Corrado Alphonse Moretti, and the godson of Salvatore Gerardo Capozzi. You don't get much more notorious than that."

"That's fucked up," Carmine said. "I have nothing to do with their business."

"Guilty by association," he said. "Having you released is my number one priority right now. Lucky for you, it shouldn't be more than a few days."

"Days? I'm supposed to stay in this place for *days*?"

"Unfortunately, yes. I'll request a hearing, but it'll take time to get in front of a judge."

Mr. Borza walked out as the corrections officer patted Carmine down before escorting him to his cell, where a tray of food awaited him. He conceded to hunger, grabbing the container of pudding and sitting on the lumpy bed.

––––––––––

The second day of Carmine's incarceration passed similar to the first. Sometime in the evening, an officer came by to tell him he had another visitor. Relief washed through him, as he figured Mr. Borza had news, but the familiar man waiting was clearly not his lawyer.

"Carmine DeMarco," Special Agent Cerone said. "Have a seat."

"I have nothing to say to you."

"But you don't even know why I'm here."

He laughed dryly. "It doesn't matter. I have nothing to say."

"Fair enough. You know your rights and can go back to your cell." Carmine turned to leave when the agent sighed exaggeratedly. "I just wanted to talk about a girl named Haven."

Carmine's heart pounded rapidly at the mention of her, the ache in his chest intensifying. "Why?"

"Her name came up a few times during the investigation," he said. "I tried locating her, but there's barely any evidence she exists. It's as if she's a *ghost*."

Carmine balked at the word. "Why are you asking me?"

"I figure if you help me, I can help you."

"I don't need your help," he said. "There's nothing I can tell you."

"You can't tell me who she is?"

"No." He desperately wished he fucking could.

"Strange. We made a trip to your hometown yesterday, and the people there are under the impression she's your girlfriend. I even came across this while I was there." He reached into his briefcase for a piece of paper, and Carmine's knees went weak when he saw it was the picture Haven had drawn for him, her name neatly written in the corner. "Does that jog your memory?"

"Fuck you."

"Where is she?" he asked. "She's not in Durante, and she wasn't with you in Chicago. One of the only other people this girl seems to talk to is a boy named Nicholas Barlow, who coincidentally is also missing."

"I don't know what you're talking about."

Special Agent Cerone was undeterred. "Did something happen to your girlfriend? You can tell me. I'm here to help—"

"You aren't here to help. You don't give a shit about me."

"Did she run off with Nicholas?" he asked. "Did she choose him over you?"

"That's ridiculous."

"Is she dead?"

He recoiled from his statement. "No."

"Is Nicholas dead?"

"Are you accusing me of something?"

He shook his head. "As I said, I want to help."

"There's nothing you can do for me."

"If she's missing or has been hurt—"

"I want my lawyer."

"Fine." Agent Cerone stuck the drawing back into his briefcase. "You know, the truth always prevails. At the end of the day, the truth is what sets you free."

48

Time drifted by in a haze, like curls of smoke obstructing Haven's surroundings. She would come to the surface to find food waiting, and she would eat what she could stomach before slipping back under. Jen appeared a few times with Nunzio to check her vitals but never spoke a word. In fact, people were always in and out of the building, but no one acknowledged her except for Natalia. She would bring her fresh clothes and offer words of encouragement, helping her up whenever she needed to use the bathroom.

Each day grew progressively worse. Haven's strength diminished as her body began to reject everything. She would vomit profusely whenever she tried to eat, her skin clammy and pale. A pounding in her head made it hard to focus, everything becoming a blur of nothingness.

It was about then that she started hallucinating, hearing voices and seeing faces she couldn't be sure were truly there. The nightmares were extreme, filled with flashbacks in an inconsistent loop. Dr. DeMarco haunted her with the piercing glare of hatred she had seen that day in his room. She could feel the gun pressed into her throat as she gasped for air. She screamed in the darkness, her chest vibrating with the high-pitched shrieks.

The moments of lucidity became few and far between. Unfamiliar people stood over her, having strange conversations that made little sense. Her monster even surfaced, his mangled face appearing as if it were melting away. He said nothing, just stared as the fire engulfed her from the inside out.

————————

The Metropolitan Correctional Center, a three-sided triangular skyscraper in the middle of downtown Chicago, has no barbed wire or electric fence, no armed guards standing in towers along the edge of the property. With its flat surface and narrow vertical windows, the front of the building resembles an old punch card. It appears harmless, indiscriminate, but some of the most dangerous people in the world call the place home.

Vincent sat in a small cell on the twentieth floor, a few yards from where Corrado was housed. The window was frosted, obstructing Vincent's view of the outside, so all he had to look at were the drab gray walls surrounding him.

Every day was the same: three meals, frequent head counts, occasional sirens, and little conversation. The guards watched their every move, all calls and visits monitored so none of them could risk communicating.

He sat there early one day, right after morning roll call, when a few corrections officers approached. They placed him in restraints and led him to a room, where Agent Cerone waited at a small table.

"Vincenzo DeMarco," he said, motioning toward the chair across from him. "Have a seat."

Vincent sat down, grateful to be out of that dreary cell. They tried to secure him to the table, but the agent stopped them. "That's unnecessary. We're both civilized human beings here."

The officers looked at him with disbelief but walked out, leaving Vincent unsecured. The agent folded his hands on the table. "You're probably wondering who—"

Vincent cut him off. "Doctor."

Agent Cerone's smile faltered. "Doctor?"

"And unless you're my mother or my priest, don't call me Vincenzo. It's Dr. *Vincent* DeMarco."

The agent stared at him before nodding. "Right. And I'm Special Agent Donald Cerone with the Justice Department . . . head of organized crime."

Vincent sighed exasperatedly. "I have nothing to say."

"I figured that much. You wouldn't have made it as far as you have if you weren't cunning. But truthfully, I'm not here about your case. I hoped we could discuss something I found." Reaching into his briefcase, Agent Cerone pulled out a black notebook. "Do you recognize this?"

Vincent didn't respond, having no intention of saying another word to the man.

"I'll take the lack of reaction as a no," he said. "We found this in a bedroom on the third floor of your residence."

He flipped it open, and Vincent saw the page was covered in barely legible juvenile scrawl. Realization hit him that it belonged to Haven. He tensed, concerned as to what information those pages might contain.

"The entire thing's engaging, but there were some passages I found particularly interesting. I thought I'd share them with you." He stopped on a bookmarked page and scanned the lines of writing with his finger before reading a passage out loud.

Katrina sometimes said she would kill me in my sleep. She told me to keep one eye open if I wanted to live. I stayed awake those nights in case she meant it. I wasn't afraid to die, but I didn't want to leave Mama alone. I didn't want Master Michael to hurt her more, and I thought Katrina would kill her next.

The agent flipped to a different page and read another one.

I called Master Michael daddy *once when he visited the ranch. I heard someone say that was what he was to me, but he got angry and beat me. Mama begged him not to kill me. He stopped because Frankie made him. Frankie hit Michael for it and I remember thinking we weren't the only people who got punished like that. I should've been scared, but it made me feel like maybe Frankie didn't hate me. He hit his son, but he still loved him, right?*

Agent Cerone glanced at him when he was finished. "The Antonellis? So unfortunate about their deaths."

Vincent sat still, not giving any indication he was panicking inside. Things were unraveling quickly.

"How about one more?" Agent Cerone asked, flipping to another page. "I think you'll personally find this one fascinating."

I'll never forget the look in his eyes. I was only trying to do what he told me to do, because I didn't want to get in trouble for not listening. I thought he was going to kill me, but he did something worse. He left me alone in the dark. He was nice to me, and I didn't want to disappoint him. I dream about the look on his face when he turned into a monster. I wish I could forget. I wish Dr. DeMarco liked me.

Vincent kept his expression blank, but the words hit him hard. The agent closed the notebook, shaking his head. "What did you do to the poor girl? Why don't you like her?"

"Reading that is an invasion of privacy," Vincent said. "I know the law, and I'm well aware of what you can confiscate during a search and seizure. A young girl's diary is off limits."

Special Agent Cerone slipped the notebook into his briefcase. "Like I said, cunning. I'd love to return it. Do you know where I can find her?"

"I'd like to speak to my lawyer."

He pushed his chair back. "I'm sure you would, Vincenzo. It's nice to officially meet you after spending so many months monitoring you from afar. If you decide you want to talk after all, I think you can figure out how to get ahold of me."

———

The orange jumpsuit was particularly bright under the fluorescent lights of the busy courtroom. Carmine listened to his lawyer argue that there was no probable cause to keep him incarcerated. The judge seemed bored, and as soon as Mr. Borza stopped speaking, he ordered Carmine released and the charges dropped.

He walked out the doors of the jail, finding Celia waiting for him. "Thanks for springing me."

She smiled. "You shouldn't have been in there in the first place. Let's just hope Mr. Borza has as much luck with Vincent and Corrado."

"How are they? Fuck, *where* are they?"

"They're being detained downtown at MCC. They have hearings next week, though, and the lawyers are confident they can get them released."

Carmine shook his head. "Another week?"

"Unfortunately."

A tense silence lingered in the car during the drive to the Morettis' house as that sunk in with Carmine. It wouldn't be easy, and he'd have to take some big risks if he was going to save Haven. He always said he would sacrifice for her, and that was exactly what he would have to do.

Celia pulled up to the house, but Carmine remained in the car. She realized he wasn't moving. "You coming inside?"

He could feel tears building up. "I can't. I, uh . . . There's somewhere I have to go."

"Carmine . . ."

"Look, I've made mistakes, but I'd never do anything to get any of you hurt."

"Okay." She handed him the car keys. "Just be careful, kiddo."

––––––

Carmine drove straight to Lincoln Park, parking in front of the five-bedroom mansion that sat alone on a hill. He took a deep breath as he made his way onto the porch, his nerves on edge.

He pressed the doorbell, hearing the chimes inside the house. The door was opened swiftly. Standing in front of him was Teresa Capozzi. "Carmine DeMarco? What a surprise! I thought you were locked up with the rest of them."

"They released me."

She brought her glass of wine to her lips and gulped the contents. "Well, then. I'm sure Salvatore will be ecstatic to see you. He's upstairs with Carlo. Do you know him? Lovely man. Second door on the right."

Carmine brushed by her without replying and headed upstairs. He hesitated in front of the closed door, hearing arguing inside. He couldn't make out their words, but Sal sounded irate. Carmine briefly reconsidered, unsure of how he would do what he had come to do, but forced himself to knock. He had no time to waste.

The bickering silenced immediately. The door was yanked open, an annoyed Salvatore appearing in the doorway. He froze, surprise flashing across his face. "*Principe!* I thought you were my dreadful wife coming to nag me some more. Come in."

Carmine stepped past him into the vast room, seeing a man in a chair off to the side. The guy stood and turned toward him, and Carmine balked at his disfigured face. A strange sensation hit Carmine, a rush of bitter cold running from his head down to his toes.

Lovely man? He didn't fucking think so.

Carlo left without a word, and Salvatore shut the door. "To what do I owe the pleasure of your visit?" he asked, sitting at his desk as Carmine slipped into an empty chair.

"I think you know why I'm here, so we can cut the bullshit."

Salvatore's smile fell. "You always were a bold one. Most people wouldn't dare come to me like this, but you have guts. That kind of commitment is rare nowadays."

"I have to find her," Carmine said. "No matter what."

"I respect that." Salvatore pulled out a cigar, lighting it and taking a deep puff before continuing. "I wish I could help you."

"You *wish* you could help? What does that mean?"

"It means as unfortunate as this situation is, I have more pressing matters to deal with right now. My men are turning quicker than I can keep track of. I have people being arrested, their houses invaded and property seized. Every day it's something new. I can't take on anything else."

Carmine stared at him. "But this is my girlfriend. She's been kidnapped by your people, and you're telling me you can't help?"

"I assure you, if anyone wants to locate Squint, it's me," Sal said. "I have people on the lookout for him, and when he's found he'll face the consequences. But I don't have the resources or the justification to focus on him when my entire organization is being attacked. I sympathize with you, *Principe*, because I've lost loved ones, but Haven means nothing to me."

His words hit Carmine hard, the callous, nonchalant tone sending his temper flaring. "She's not *nothing*. She's fucking family!"

Sal scoffed. "How did you come to that conclusion?"

Carmine hesitated for a split second, but he needed to cover his tracks. "I thought we were all family. You talk about loyalty and commitment, but where's yours? Am I nothing to you, too?"

"You chose not to be a part of my family," Salvatore said. "I'll always have a soft spot for you, but you need to understand the organization, *la famiglia*, is my family. I respect your choice not to be involved, but it's all I have. Just as you'll sacrifice to save what matters to you, I'll do whatever it takes to save what matters to me. We have the same type of loyalty, just for different things."

"So that's it?"

"That's it."

"And that's what it's gonna take. You're gonna make me—"

"I'm not making you do anything," he said. "You can walk out that door, and I wish you all the luck in the world, but if you're requesting my assistance—if you're demanding my loyalty—then it's only fair you give me yours in return. Without it, we have nothing."

Carmine's anger and heartbreak came together in that moment. It didn't take him long to respond, because deep down he already knew. Part of him knew it when he laid eyes on her that first day in the kitchen. "You got it," he said. "Whatever it takes."

Salvatore stared at him. "Are you sure?"

"She's the only thing I've ever been sure of."

"Great," Salvatore said, holding out his hand. Carmine hesitated before kissing the back of it obediently. "I'll make a few calls and see what I can do for you, *Principe*."

Vivid dreams turned into hallucinations, memories morphing back into nightmares. It all ravaged Haven as if it were flames, melting everything into molten lava of pain. She held on, clinging to the surface and fighting to survive. But no matter what, the blackness took her deeper . . . and deeper . . . and deeper . . . until one afternoon, it swallowed her whole.

Haven was certain she was dead then, because in front of her, wearing a flowing white dress, stood an angel.

Maura took Haven's hand and helped her to her feet in the filthy abandoned warehouse. The two of them strolled away, the walls crumbling as they stepped into a vast field of flowers. Sunlight streamed upon them, and Haven realized it was the clearing in Durante.

"Carmine brought me here," she said. "I think he came here when he was sad."

"I know," Maura said. "I'm always with him."

"Are you?"

"Of course. I'm his mother, and mothers never leave their children. We live in them, deep down in their hearts. Carmine can't see me, but I know he feels me all the time."

The thought comforted Haven. "Do you think he's okay?"

Maura smiled. "I'm sure he will be."

Haven wandered through the field and picked a dandelion puff, blowing on it. The fluffy seeds flew off and multiplied, exploding into hundreds surrounding her in the air.

"Is my mama with me, too?"

"Yes," Maura said. "Don't you feel her? She's right there."

Haven spun around so quick everything blurred. When it came back into focus, the dandelion seeds had morphed into snowflakes, falling from the sky like puffs of cotton. They coated everything in a layer of white, hindering her view of her mama a few feet away. She was twirling, the sound of her laughter encasing Haven in a blanket of love. For a moment, as she watched her mama dance, she forgot it wasn't real. She forgot her mama was dead. She forgot she must be, too.

But in a flash it all came back, as when she blinked, her mama started to fade.

Panicked, Haven ran toward her, but the snow came down heavier, blinding her with whiteness. Haven ran long and hard, her chest burning and legs weak, but she didn't seem to be getting anywhere. Exhausted, she collapsed to the ground in sobs, suddenly in Blackburn again. The desert ground burned her, scorching the soles of her feet.

After a moment, a voice rang out behind her, the smooth familiarity silencing her cries as goose bumps spread across her skin. "She's gone," Carmine said. "I'm sorry, hummingbird, but she isn't coming back."

Haven turned, desperate to see him, but instead of deep green eyes, all she saw was icy blue. Haven's stomach twisted as Number 33 stared through her, the paper still pinned to her shirt. "Never stop fighting," she said. "I didn't."

"But you're gone, too," Haven said. "I saw it. Frankie killed you in front of me."

"Some things in life are worse than death," Number 33 said, "and had I lived, those things would've happened to me. He took my life, but he didn't break my spirit. No one did, and no one ever will. Don't let them break you. Don't let them win. Fight the fight. It's the only way to be free."

Haven was jolted roughly from behind then, everything going black. Someone shook her as pain swept through her body, and she forced her eyes open, seeing Ivan. His voice was muffled as if her ears were clogged. "What is the code at the DeMarco house?"

"What?" she mouthed, no sound carrying out. It burned, stabbing her throat.

"The code for the house," he repeated. "If you do not want to die from dehydration, you will tell me what I want to know."

She turned her head, wishing he would disappear. "Go away."

Her disobedience sent him into a rage. He pulled out a knife as he grabbed her hand, twisting it violently. "Tell me the code, or I'll cut off your finger."

Every inch of her begged for relief. She squeezed her eyes shut, Dr. DeMarco flashing in her mind again. She could see his anger, but she couldn't feel the fear anymore as he pressed the gun to her throat. She understood how he felt, and as she lay there in agony, she almost wished Dr. DeMarco really had pulled the trigger. "Do it."

———

Night had fallen hours before, but Carmine no longer had any sense of time. He thought it was ten o'clock, maybe midnight, but it was nothing but a number to him now. He would simply go until he felt like he couldn't go anymore, and then he would push himself just a little more. He had moved past exhaustion and now teetered on the brink of a nervous breakdown. Sleep only happened when his body gave out, periods of blackouts tucked into the frantic spells.

Carmine knew nothing about Giovanni, besides the fact that he was Sicilian and he broke the law. They had only met a handful of times, and Giovanni was never friendly, but Carmine had a new-found respect for the man. The two of them stood in the small office at Giovanni's modest brick house, poring over a map of Chicago. They had been at it for so long that Carmine couldn't read the small print anymore and counted on Giovanni to keep everything straight.

"Are you sure it's this guy?" Carmine asked, picking up the small photograph. "He looks like someone's grandfather."

"I am certain," Giovanni said. "Do not be fooled. Ivan Volkov is dangerous."

Carmine stared at the photo, trying to focus. He remembered his father mentioning problems with the Russians months ago, but Carmine still didn't understand what any of it had to do with them. Giovanni had tried to explain it more than once, but the point was lost somewhere between the man's accent and Carmine's exhausted mind.

He set the picture down and glanced at the map. Giovanni was on his laptop researching addresses associated with the Volkov family. The map was littered with writing, random circles splattered on it like polka dots.

Carmine stared at it, overwhelmed.

"I thought Doc microchipped the girl," Giovanni said. "Why have you not found her that way?"

"We tried," Carmine said. "The chip isn't working."

"And what does that mean?"

Carmine looked at Giovanni. "Means she's probably underwater or in a windowless room."

"So we should circle Lake Michigan also?"

Carmine felt like he had been punched at those words. "I refuse to think that."

"I would not believe it, either," Giovanni said. "Volkov would not take her just to kill her. And in good news, we can cross out everywhere with a lot of windows."

"That'll still leave a dozen properties," Carmine said. "How do we know which one to go to?"

"We start at the top," Giovanni said, pointing at a location in the north side of the city. "Work our way down until we find her."

Sighing, Carmine ran his hands down his face in frustration. "Why are you helping me, anyway? Everyone else said it was a waste of time, that it was a suicide mission."

"They do not understand." Giovanni's voice was quiet as he sat down near Carmine. "I warned them the Russians would make a move, but they did not listen. The Russians invade our streets, and Sal does nothing. They harass our people, and Sal does nothing. They turn our people against us, and Sal does nothing. Now they kidnap a girl, and what does Sal do?"

"Nothing," Carmine said. "He doesn't do a damn thing."

Giovanni nodded. "If somebody does not do something, they will kill our people next. I, for one, cannot sit back and allow them to."

The day of the hearing, Vincent's stress level was at an all-time high. The U.S. Marshals drove him and Corrado in separate cars to the Dirksen Federal Building a few blocks away. Their team of lawyers waited when they walked into the courtroom, taking seats at the defendants' table. Corrado appeared calm and confident in his black Armani suit, the complete opposite of how Vincent felt. While it was a relief to be out of the prison attire, his button-up shirt choked him.

The government seemed confident, their lackadaisical attitudes making Vincent more nervous. A prosecutor stood, casually fixing his tie as he addressed the court. "Your Honor, we're talking about racketeering, gambling, extortion, fraud, and conspiracy to commit murder. Each defendant is facing thirty-five counts. Releasing them would be potentially unleashing more of this onto the community. The evidence clearly suggests neither man intends to stop."

Their lawyers argued their cases when the government was done, citing Fourth Amendment violations and unreasonable searches. They said the evidence was flimsy at best—no surveillance footage, no confessions, no DNA. The most they had were rumors and infamous names, and that wasn't enough to take a man away from his life. Rocco Borza went on a passionate tirade about how the RICO Acts were being used to railroad innocent individuals, and how much of an injustice it was that they weren't free. It took everything Vincent had not to laugh. He was guilty as charged, and the man beside him certainly was no saint.

The judge let out a long sigh when both sides were done. "While the government makes a good point, the Fifth Amendment guarantees no one should be deprived of life, liberty, or property without due process of law. We're innocent until proven guilty in this country, and the defendants have yet to be convicted of any crimes. They can't be remanded without bail simply because you believe they may commit a crime in the future. Therefore, the defendants' petition for bail is granted. Fifty thousand dollars, cash bond."

"Your honor," the prosecutor said, standing. "We ask that the defendants surrender their passports, and that neither be allowed to leave the state."

Mr. Borza interjected right away. "One of my clients is a well-known doctor in North Carolina, where his permanent residence is located. Demanding he stay in Illinois isn't fair."

"Both defendants will surrender their passports," the judge ordered. "If Dr. DeMarco chooses to return home, he'll have to submit to electronic monitoring."

Celia gathered the bail money as the men were processed out of the system. It was later that evening when Vincent walked out the front doors of the jail to come face-to-face with his sister, leaning against the side of her car, her face lined with worry as if she had aged a decade over night.

"Hey, little brother." She forced a smile. "You look like hell."

"Look who's talking," he said. "You're starting to look like Ma."

She laughed awkwardly. "Ouch, low blow. Speaking of Mom, you should call her. She's worried about you."

"That woman hates me," Vincent said. "She's probably worried I'll publicly disgrace the DeMarco name."

"She doesn't hate you. She just has a strange way of showing her love. I had to talk her out of calling the Department of Corrections to ask if the foot of your bed faced the door, since it's bad luck. She was worried your soul would slip out while you slept."

Despite his stress, he managed to smile. "Must be why I got lucky enough to be released today. The bed faced the other way."

Things grew tense as they drove toward Portage Park in silence. "Did Corrado get released?"

"Yes," she said. "He went home an hour ago."

Vincent turned to look out the window. He wanted to ask about Carmine, but it was an answer he wasn't ready to hear. It had been two weeks since the girl disappeared, and Vincent couldn't imagine what his son was going through.

When they reached the Moretti's house, Celia headed inside without waiting for him. He followed, his footsteps faltering when he heard her frantically whispering in Corrado's office.

"I couldn't do it," she said. "How am I supposed to tell him?"

"You know him better than anyone," Corrado said. "He'll take it better coming from you."

"It doesn't matter who it comes from—he's going to flip out."

"That may be true, but someone needs to tell Vincent."

Vincent stepped into the doorway. "Tell me what?"

Celia stammered. "Carmine was worried. Or, he is worried. He couldn't just sit around. I suspected what he was going to do, but I couldn't forbid him. I didn't even know if I should. He's an adult, and it's not what she would want for him, and I knew you'd be upset, but it's his life. And he was worried, Vincent. You were in jail, and he didn't know who else to turn to."

Her statements were disjointed, but the gist of them registered with him. "Don't tell me he . . . No, there's no way he went to them after everything I did to make sure it didn't happen."

"He did."

"You're wrong! He's not that stupid, Celia!"

Her eyes filled with tears. "I'm not wrong."

"Then you misunderstood."

"I didn't," she said. "Giovanni was here with him."

"Giovanni? You have to be kidding. If he—"

"Vincent," Corrado said, his harsh voice cutting him off. "You know there are things we cannot and should not say as men of honor, and you're teetering dangerously close to saying something you'll later regret."

"But this is Carmine we're talking about. This is my son!"

"Yes, and he's made his choice. He's in the life now, and nothing can change that fact."

"There has to be something! Carmine isn't cut out for this! He's throwing his life away and why, Corrado? For what?"

"For her," he said, giving him an incredulous look. "How soon you forget. You were once that eighteen-year-old boy, turning to *La Cosa Nostra* to save the woman you loved."

"But I didn't save her! She's dead, and if I would've never gotten involved in this, she'd—"

"She'd what?" Corrado asked, cutting him off again. "She'd be alive? Even you can't believe that! She'd still be dead today, but she would've died a slave. You gave her a chance. Her life was cut short, but it wasn't you or *La Cosa Nostra* that did it. Maura sacrificed herself. You think your son is so much like you, but what you fail to realize is he's his mother, too. There's nothing naïve about the decision he made."

Before he could respond, the phone in the office rang. Corrado grabbed the receiver off the desk in front of him. "Moretti." He paused. "Yes, we'll be there."

Vincent sighed when he hung up. "Salvatore."

"He wants to see us."

"Carmine's in too deep," Vincent said. "He has no idea what he's doing."

"Let's hope you're wrong." Corrado grabbed his keys. "How long until you need to report in?"

"Forty-eight hours." Vincent had two days to self-surrender to be fitted with an ankle monitor. It wasn't house arrest, with a curfew or a base restricting him to a certain location, but a precaution to make sure he didn't try to disappear. It also meant they could keep a log of everywhere he went, which put him in a precarious situation within the organization.

"I suppose that means we have forty-eight hours, then."

Corrado started for the door, but Celia stopped him. "It's good to have you home, so make sure you come back."

He brushed his hand across her cheek. "I always do, don't I?"

Anger festered inside Vincent as they drove to Salvatore's house. They went straight to the den when they arrived, where Salvatore sat with a few members of the organization. The younger ones stood out of respect, but Vincent ignored them and took his usual seat.

He ignored the glass of scotch someone tried to hand him, too.

"It's nice to see the two of you," Salvatore said. "I know you're both honorable, though, so I'm not worried about any future issues in this case."

Vincent stared at him. As usual, Salvatore's only concern was it coming back on him. He expected them to keep their mouths shut and accept whatever punishment, and the saddest part of all, Vincent thought, was they would do it. The *Omertà* vow of silence swore just that.

"Anyway, on to lighter business," Sal said. "I assume you've heard the good news by now."

"About Carmine?" Vincent clenched his hands into fists in his lap. There was nothing *light* or *good* about it.

"It's great to have another generation of DeMarcos working with us. You've raised a great son, a loyal man like you. You should be proud."

Vincent cleared his throat to force back the words he really wanted to say. "Where is he?"

"He's with Giovanni," Salvatore said. "They've been trying to track down that poor girl. Such a shame she hasn't been located."

"Have they gotten any information?"

Salvatore's insensitive laughter cut through the room. "Vincent, you know I've chosen to remain uninvolved. You'd have to ask them."

"Still? What did my son come to you for?"

"Carmine choosing this path is unrelated," he said, his lips still curved into a sinister smile. "Giovanni volunteered for his little mission, and they have our resources at their disposal, of course, but it has nothing to do with me."

"How can you say that? Our women are to be respected; we're supposed to protect them! It's part of the oath; it's one of our commandments! How is that not your problem? It's all of our problem!"

The room fell into a tense silence, and everyone stared at Vincent, stunned. Corrado spoke before the strain could grow. "If you don't mind, I think we should catch up with Carmine."

"Yes, do that," Salvatore said. "Use whatever you need."

Corrado stood. "Come on."

Vincent pushed his chair back and followed Corrado out of the room. Whispers started as he exited, but Salvatore demanded silence right away. Vincent shouldn't have reacted, but he was so disgusted he couldn't stop himself. Everything he had done had been in vain, a waste of time and energy, because Carmine ended up exactly where he had tried to keep him from going.

And the girl certainly hadn't been saved.

"You must want to die," Corrado said, walking through the house. "Speaking to him that way will get you killed."

Corrado opened a door to a back room and stepped inside. He opened cabinet doors and grabbed weapons, tossing Vincent two .45 Smith & Wessons before pulling out two guns for himself, slipping them into his coat along with more ammunition.

———

Giovanni lived not far from Salvatore. The house was empty when Corrado and Vincent arrived, so Corrado slipped around the back and kicked in the door. The two of them headed straight to Giovanni's office and rifled through drawers and files, looking for anything they might have dug up.

Corrado found a map of Chicago and unfolded it on the desk beside him. Areas of it were circled and crossed out, the entire thing riddled with writing. Vincent recognized some of it as his son's, the sloppy words scribbled with a frenzied hand.

"They have Ivan's properties pinpointed on the map, but there's no way they would've taken Haven somewhere with his name on the deed," Corrado said. "He's smarter than that. He would've found somewhere close to home but far enough away to keep the two separate. Somewhere remote where there's no chance of her being stumbled upon, but not so isolated that their traffic would draw curious eyes. Somewhere people mind their own business."

"You would've made a good detective," Vincent mused.

Corrado shot him an incredulous look. "Just because I understand the mind of a criminal doesn't mean I'd be a good cop."

"Yeah, maybe you're right," Vincent said, scrolling through the computer's history. "You wouldn't last a day before you got an excessive force complaint."

Corrado stared at him in silence for a moment before turning to the map, and Vincent focused his attention on Giovanni's computer. Numerous addresses and names had been searched, but nothing stood out as important.

Corrado pointed to a section of map circled with a pencil. "What's on this side of Austin?"

"Nothing that I know of," Vincent said. "Bad neighborhood, a lot of gang activity. Most of the businesses moved out of the area, so there are a lot of vacant buildings."

"That's what I thought," Corrado said. "It's a money pit, yet Natalia Volkov owns property there."

"Ivan's daughter? Isn't she still a teenager?"

"I believe she just turned nineteen."

"Sounds odd."

"It does," Corrado said. "It also sounds like a good place to start."

49

The sun had set, darkness falling over Chicago as Vincent and Corrado drove to the west side of the city. A full moon hovered in the sky, a ring of light surrounding it partially shielded by a thin cloud covering. The wind whipped a bit, vibrating the car with its unpredictable gusts.

The lack of communication wore on Vincent's nerves. He had no idea what his son was up to, what situation he was in, or if he was okay. Giovanni had never given Vincent reason to distrust him, but the fact that it was his *soldati* that had gone awry didn't sit well with him. If he had been paying attention, he should have seen it.

Corrado turned off the highway and cruised through the streets. Most of the buildings appeared abandoned, worn down and boarded up. Gang signs were strewn around with spray paint by street thugs who considered themselves hardcore. Men with no true loyalty, no respect within their orders.

Their lack of civility had always disgusted Antonio. He loathed their usage of the word *gangster*, cringed at their definition of *brotherhood*. Vincent couldn't count how many times his father had ranted about it, priding himself on the fact that his organization had respect. They may have committed heinous crimes, but in his mind, all of it was founded. His father took the oath seriously and believed, until the day he died, that they were a true family, *la famiglia*, with a bond stronger than blood.

Vincent never thought he would see the day where he wished his father was still in control.

"Are you all right, Vincent?" Corrado asked. "We can't afford second thoughts."

"I'm not having second thoughts," he said. "I'm thinking about how disturbed my father would be about this."

"None of this would be happening if your father were around," Corrado said. "He was an honorable man, as far as honor goes within our world. Antonio's organization was united."

"And now we're no better than the guys tagging these buildings."

"I wouldn't go *that* far. I think most of us still have our honor. What you've done for Haven, after what she's cost you, is honorable. I can't say I'd do the same if I were in your position. If it were my wife, I would've killed the girl a long time ago."

"I almost did," he said. "I wanted to."

"But you didn't," he said. "Instead, you're risking your life to find her, and that's where the honor is, Vincent. Sometimes you have to look at the bigger picture."

Vincent shook his head as Corrado pulled the car behind a vacant building, partially concealing it beside a Dumpster. "I never imagined you'd be the one to give me a pep talk about this."

"Well, you heard my wife," he said as he cut the engine. "She told me to come home, and I need you to have a level head for that to be possible."

They climbed out and walked alongside the building, staying out of sight. Corrado stopped when he reached the corner, and Vincent spotted a black Mercedes parked among some trees.

"Squint's car," Corrado said, reaching into his coat for one of his guns. "I'm going to check it out. Cover me."

Vincent pulled out a gun and flicked off the safety as Corrado jogged across the road. He peered into the car and tried the doors as Vincent watched for signs of movement. Corrado looked around, glancing into the windows of an old business, before returning. "It's empty."

Vincent started to speak when a loud noise rang out behind them, startling him into silence. He swung around, aiming his weapon, but Corrado pulled him around the corner instead. Multiple rushed voices blurred together, cutting through the night as they hid alongside the vacant building Corrado had checked out moments earlier.

Three men stepped out from a warehouse and paused in the spot Vincent and Corrado had been standing moments ago. Vincent recognized Squint, a guy with shaggy blond hair nonchalantly clutching an AK-47 beside him. It was one of Volkov's guys, one who had been in the pizzeria. The third man was vaguely familiar, but Vincent couldn't place him in the dark.

"Brazen," Corrado said. "Brave and careless. It's a dangerous combination."

"Demented is what they are," Vincent said as Squint pulled out a set of keys and tossed them to the third guy. He and the man with the AK-47 disappeared inside.

"Unlocked," Corrado observed. "I suppose we can add *stupid* to the list of adjectives."

The third guy sprinted across the street toward Squint's car as Corrado slipped around to the back of the building. Vincent took a few steps around to the front, remaining in the shadows. He reached the corner just as Corrado warded off the guy, pointing his gun at his head.

The guy threw up his hands as he dropped the keys. "Corrado."

The voice struck Vincent as familiar. His stomach sank. "Tarullo?"

The guy turned, fear flashing across his face. Dean Tarullo, the youngest son of the man who had saved Carmine's life.

"Uh, Vincent, sir," he said. "What are you doing here?"

Before Vincent could respond, Corrado threw the boy against the side of the building, patting him down. Pressing his gun into the boy's throat, his finger lightly touched the trigger. "You know why we're here. How many people are inside?"

"Five or six, I think. Maybe more."

"Not a good enough answer. Think harder."

"I saw six."

"Better," Corrado said. "Are they all armed?"

"The ones I saw were."

"Who are they?"

"I don't know."

"You better figure it out," Corrado said, "before I kill you."

"Shit! Okay! Nunzio's the only one I know. He talked me into this. I didn't realize what he was doing. I didn't know he was—"

His rambling was cut off when Corrado slammed his gun into the side of his head. "I'm only interested in names."

"Nunzio . . . that girl, the nurse."

Vincent's anger festered, seeping into his taut muscles. "Jen?"

"Yeah, her. There are some others I don't know, but an older man's in charge. Ivan, I think."

"And what about the girl?" Corrado asked. "Haven?"

"Oh, uh, I know they have her, but I haven't looked around. I've only gone in twice, and I never went past the doorway."

"You haven't seen her at all?"

He shook his head frantically as headlights of an approaching car flashed in their direction. They all tensed as the black BMW crept down the street. Vincent stalked to the front of the building cautiously, watching as it stopped less than a block away. The passenger door opened and a person hopped out before the car pulled out of sight.

Vincent's eyes widened when the person stepped under a streetlight, giving him a clear view of his son. Carmine haphazardly approached the building, clutching a gun in his shaking hand.

Corrado groaned. "Stop him."

Vincent sprinted across the street when Carmine went for the door. His hand grasped the handle as Vincent reached him, and Carmine turned in his direction.

"Da—" he started, but Vincent dragged him away before he

could react. He cursed and stumbled. "What the fuck? She might be in there!"

"Keep your voice down," Vincent said. "You can't just walk in."

"What else am I supposed to do?" he asked, frantic. "Do you know how long it's been? Do you know how long she's been gone? I have to find her!"

"I know. We're here, we're on it."

"About fucking time."

Groaning, Vincent grabbed his son's arm and dragged him across the street. Carmine resisted at first, but he was too exhausted to put up a fight. Vincent took him to where Corrado stood in the darkness, with Dean huddled against the wall at his feet.

Corrado shook his head. "You must not have any sense of self-preservation left."

"Fuck my life," Carmine said. "She's worth dying for."

"And what happens when you die?" Corrado gave him a pointed look. "Your carelessness is going to get her killed. You're in the fold now. You need to start thinking like one of us."

Carmine shot his father a panicked look. "Whatever, I need to save her, that's what I need to do." Frazzled, he motioned toward Dean. "Who's this?"

"He's a friend," Corrado said. "Although he's more of a friend to Nunzio, it seems."

"Wait, he's in on this?" Carmine rushed forward and grabbed Dean by the collar. "She better not be hurt! What did you do to her?"

"I didn't do anything to her!" Dean said. "I haven't seen her!"

"What the fuck do you mean you haven't seen her?" Carmine snapped, slamming the boy against the building. "You took my girl from me, and I want her back!"

"He's so much like you it's disturbing," Corrado said, glancing at Vincent as Carmine kicked Dean in the ribs.

"He'll kill him," Vincent warned.

Corrado grabbed Carmine, begrudgingly forcing him away. "Enough."

Vincent helped Dean to his feet. "Where were you going?"

"Uh, food," he said. "I was supposed to get food."

The brush nearby ruffled. Carmine and Vincent reached for their weapons as a precaution, but Corrado didn't move. He addressed the person without turning around. "Giovanni."

"Corrado, Vincent," Giovanni said, strolling up to them. "Nice to see you gentlemen again."

Carmine looked at his uncle. "How did you know it was him?"

"I always know my surroundings," Corrado said, his attention going back to Dean. "If you want me to show you any mercy, you're going to walk inside and say you were jumped. Say some thugs stole your money and Squint's keys. Understand?"

Dean staggered away as the four men positioned themselves beside the entrance. Vincent pulled his gun out as Carmine fidgeted, the tension coming from him intense. "You're pissed at me, aren't you? I had to do it. I needed to find her. I need her to be okay."

"I don't see how throwing your life away helps anything, but now isn't the time for this." He needed to remain calm, and dwelling on what his son did would get him riled up again. "We're going to go in here and end this, and no matter what we find, we'll deal with it."

Within a matter of seconds, the door burst open and a vaguely familiar Russian man with blond hair rushed out. He froze, raising his gun as Corrado and Giovanni ducked inside the building, but Vincent was faster. Aiming, Vincent fired off a round that hit him square between the eyes. The back of his head exploded, blood splattering, and he slammed to the ground. Vincent grabbed the door and slipped inside, momentarily stunned by what he saw. People clamored and dodged flying bullets, the sound of most of the noise muffled by silencers. Carmine came in behind him, ducking to the side in the flurry of gunfire.

Corrado stood by the front door, firing at a cowering Ivan, while Squint hid behind a table a few feet away, loading a gun. Vincent fired a few shots as Squint finished and pointed his weapon to fire back. Vincent's first two bullets barely missed as he shielded himself, but the third one struck Squint in the chest. A loud gasp escaped his mouth as he slumped backward.

Something nearby caught Vincent's attention as a bullet whizzed right by him, grazing his neck. He flinched at the searing pain, giving a wounded Squint barely enough time to get the upper hand. He fired off some back-to-back rounds, a bullet ripping through Vincent's left shoulder as more flew past him. His arm went numb, burning coursing through his upper body as his son screamed.

Vincent turned at the sound as Carmine grasped his right arm, blood flowing through his shirt. Carmine recovered and grabbed his gun as Vincent swung back around to Squint.

He had shot his son.

Firing quickly, Vincent took a few steps toward Squint, his vision narrowing with the flash of the gun barrel as he pumped bullet after bullet into him. Three slammed into Squint's chest, piercing his heart. Horrid gasps tore from him as he struggled to breathe.

Vincent paused over Squint, glaring down at his incapacitated form. He tried to pull himself away, straining to get ahold of his gun, but the life faded from him. Vincent aimed at his head and stared him in the eyes, seeing not an ounce of fear in Squint's expression as he stared back. Cold and heartless, even down to his last seconds. No remorse for what he had done.

"Arrivederci," Vincent said.

There was a flash of fire in Squint's eyes at the word as he picked up his gun. Vincent fired off rounds in succession, bullets ripping through his skull.

Squint's finger squeezed the trigger as a knee-jerk reaction, and a bullet flew off to the side as his body violently shook. Vincent didn't stop until the gun clicked, leaving the mangled form unrecognizable.

He didn't have any time to dwell before the deafening sound of an AK-47 ripped through the building, louder than the other muffled gunfire. Bullets slammed all around him, and Vincent ducked for cover as he grabbed his second gun. He flicked the safety off and fired at the man with the weapon, hitting him in the leg. The man stumbled but continued to shoot, another bullet grazing Vincent in the chaos.

Giovanni ran from the gunfire but couldn't dive for cover fast enough. Bullets tore into him, and he cried out, attempting a few wayward shots as he collapsed.

Vincent's gun clicked as he ran out of ammunition, and he struggled to reload as Carmine started shooting a few feet away. One of his bullets hit the man in the back, and he staggered, struggling to stay on his feet. Corrado aimed at that moment, finally turning his focus from Ivan, and fired three rounds into the man's head without hesitation. He collapsed, his finger clutching the trigger and wildly spraying bullets. Corrado stumbled a few steps as he was hit from the side, but he stayed on his feet, his attention going back to Ivan.

A female's piercing scream shattered the air, the sound sending a cold chill down Vincent's spine. Carmine immediately ran in the direction of the noise, and Vincent chased after him as Corrado covered them.

On the filthy mattress in the corner, a body folded into itself. Jen obstructed their view as she stood over it, her eyes wide with fear, her hands in the air as if to surrender. "I'm sorry!"

An eerie silence fell over them as they stared at her. It passed as quickly as it came, however, and Carmine reacted . . . but Vincent was faster. He blocked Carmine's line of sight and pulled the trigger, shooting Jen between the eyes. Riddled with shame, he stood over her as she dropped.

He couldn't let his son be the one to carry that burden.

Staggering, an injured Ivan grabbed a discarded AK-47 from the floor as a last ditch effort. Vincent lunged for Carmine, throwing him to the ground as the spray of bullets rang out. They fired back, bullets tearing into Ivan from all directions. Vincent watched in horror as Corrado was shot again and dropped to his knees.

Vincent jumped up, his rage taking over, and three bullets struck Ivan in the head. He rushed toward his brother-in-law as Ivan dropped hard, taking out a metal chair on his way down. Vincent glanced around cautiously to make sure it was safe before dropping his gun and crouching down. Corrado wheezed and clutched his bloody chest, his face pale.

"Let me see," Vincent said, prying Corrado's hands away. He ripped his shirt open, exposing three entrance wounds on his chest. "This isn't good, Corrado. We need to get you to the hospital."

"I'm fine," he said, pushing Vincent away as he struggled to get to his feet. He swayed a bit but stood on his own, refusing help.

. "Haven!" Carmine's voice pulled Vincent's attention away. His breath left him at the sight of Carmine sitting on the edge of the mattress, pulling the limp body into his arms.

Vincent approached, fearing the worst. She was barely recognizable from the girl who had stood in his house a few weeks earlier, instead resembling the girl he had picked up more than a year before. She had dropped a lot of weight, her skin blotchy and lips tinged blue.

Vincent grabbed her wrist. Her pulse was weak, her hand freezing and arm twisted in an odd direction. Vincent could see her chest moving rapidly with shallow breaths. Feverish, her pupils constricted, she didn't react with any of her reflexes, her neurological system not functioning normally.

In less than a minute, Vincent knew what was wrong. The problem was, he couldn't fix it.

"Is she okay?" Carmine caressed her face. "Christ, why isn't she waking up?"

"I'm assuming she's been drugged."

"But is she going to be all right?"

"I wish I knew."

"You're always trying to play doctor with me, and the one god-damn time I ask you for help, that's what you give me? You *wish* you knew?"

"I need to get her somewhere to assess her," he said. "She's alive."

"And she better stay that way," Carmine said. "Haven, I need you to wake up. Please, baby. You have to make it. I can't do this if you don't."

Vincent's chest ached at his son's outburst of emotion. "I'll do what I can for her."

"If she doesn't make it, I'll fucking kill them all. Every single one of them."

Corrado's voice rang out beside them. "Too late. They're already dead."

Carmine glared at his uncle. "Well, we'll bring those mother-fuckers back to life, then."

Corrado tried to take a step, but his knees buckled. Vincent grabbed him before he hit the floor. "I need to get you to a hospital right now."

He scoffed, pushing Vincent away. "I'll take myself and make something up. You need to get some men over here to clean up this mess before it takes us all down."

He limped away, his pain visible in his movements, but he didn't verbalize it. Corrado looked at the bodies scattered around, his eyes falling on Giovanni. *"Che peccato."*

"I know. It's a pity," Vincent said, pulling out his phone as Corrado staggered toward the door. He watched, worry eating away at him. "Are you sure about this? You're losing a lot of blood."

"Don't be ignorant, Vincent," he said. "Get Haven to my house and fix her before your son resorts to resuscitating people just to kill them again."

Corrado paused near the exit and pulled out his gun, turning back around. He glanced across the room to where young Dean sat quietly in shock and fired three times into the boy, startling Carmine. "Fuck! I thought you were going to show him some mercy!"

Corrado dropped his gun to the floor. "I did. Death is a lot more humane than what would've happened had he still been breathing when Salvatore arrived."

———

All Haven could see were fireworks.

Flashes of light broke through in the darkness, loud bangs ringing out in the distance. She didn't know what was real anymore, where she was or what was happening, but one thing she was sure about was the fireworks. It reminded her of the day Carmine had taken her to the party. She could still feel him, and a million butterflies invaded her system, leaving her weakened and dizzy.

"Just fireworks, *tesoro*. Nothing to be afraid of," he had said. "They won't hurt you."

She believed that as she lay there, just as she had the day he first spoke those words. She felt no fear and believed they couldn't harm her. Nothing would. Carmine would come for her, and he would save her, because that was what they did for each other. Although she was drowning, slipping further away, she knew she would be fine as long as she didn't give in.

They couldn't have her spirit. She wouldn't let them win.

So as she lay in the darkness, listening to the fireworks, she fought to hold on with what little strength she had left.

The fireworks faded, the moment lost, but his faint voice continued to register with her ears. The tiny hairs on her arms stood up as her skin tingled, the sensation so real she could smell his cologne. It drew her closer to the surface as it swirled all around. She wondered if it was a mirage, like a thirsty man in the midst of a hot, dry desert who saw a lake that wasn't there. Was she so desperate for him to come that her senses tricked her into believing he had?

Yes, she thought. She must be hallucinating again.

Light filtered through her eyelids as Carmine's voice grew louder. She forced her eyes open at the sound, blinking rapidly in an attempt to clear her vision. Everything was hazy, but she could make out the familiar face, the sight of it nearly stilling her weary heart.

It didn't even seem to want to beat right anymore.

Carmine turned his head, his eyes meeting hers. They were clearer than everything else, the green color striking amidst the fog. "Fuck!" he spat, sending chills through her body. Her vision blurred more, and she blinked rapidly, anxious to stay conscious. "Fucking *ninja*, you scared me!"

"Carmine?" She winced from the burn in her throat.

"Yeah, it's me. I told you I'd find you. I was never gonna give up." His voice was fueled with emotion as he ran his hand along her cheek. "God, I fucking love you."

She tried to reach for him, but the movement sapped every ounce of energy from her. Everything went black again as soon as her hand dropped, noises fading out as if she were drowning again.

"Happy new year," she whispered as he disappeared.

50

Haven had no way to gauge how much time had passed while she was out—it could have been hours or days, even months before she slowly started having moments of clarity, ones she knew were real because of the pain. She heard noises during one of her spells and pushed to regain consciousness. She was in a dark room, but she could make out a form standing a few feet away. "Dr. DeMarco?"

"Yes, it's me." He pulled out a stethoscope and pressed it against her chest. She jumped from the unexpected coldness, pain ricocheting through her from the movement. "Try not to move."

"It hurts," she said, tears falling.

"I know it does." He placed his hand against her forehead, and she lay as still as possible as he checked her over. The scene was dreamlike. "You're not real."

Dr. DeMarco's brow furrowed. "I'm not real?"

"You're not really here," she said. "I'm dreaming again."

"Oh, I'm really real." He paused as a small smile took over his lips. "At least, I think so."

She tried to smile in response, but she was weak and wasn't sure if it worked. "I don't understand. How did you get here? Where's Carmine?" Fear paralyzed her. "Did Nunzio kill him?"

She tried to sit up as she looked around the room frantically, but Dr. DeMarco blocked her. "Calm down, child."

"I can't." Her voice cracked. "Where is he? Is he hurt? Is that why he isn't here?"

"He's fine. He just had something to take care of."

She narrowed her eyes suspiciously as he averted his gaze. "What?"

"It's not important right now," he said. "Carmine will be back soon, and he'll be elated you're awake."

Nothing made sense. "I'm confused."

"I imagine you are." He gave her a wary look. "You were drugged when you were away."

"Drugged." Flashes of memory hit her. A man injecting her a few times, his voice unfamiliar.

"I assume it was their way of keeping you subdued. You probably don't remember much, and it's best you don't strain yourself trying to." His tone told her he meant business. "Your body overdosed on the medication, so when you came off it you went through withdrawal. It would've been best to take you to a hospital, but there was no way to explain your condition along with the thiopental and phenobarbital in your system."

"What are they?"

"They're some powerful drugs we use at the hospital. I'm assuming that's where Jen came into play. Thiopental is, uh . . ." He looked wracked with guilt. "It's what I've given you a few times. In low doses it will subdue someone, but higher doses result in a coma. The other slows brain function. With those two used together, I'll be shocked if you remember anything at all."

She started to reply but stopped abruptly when he pulled out a syringe. History told her nothing good came from needles.

"Morphine for the pain," he explained when he noticed her reaction, gently picking up her arm. She glanced at the IV attached to her, watching as Dr. DeMarco injected the drug into her vein. "You were in bad shape when we found you."

"How long has it been?" she asked.

"It's the twenty-ninth of October." He eyed her cautiously. "You disappeared September thirtieth."

A month had passed, and she had little recollection of it.

"They had you for two weeks," he said. "The other two you have spent recuperating here."

"Where's here?" Exhaustion crept in fast as numbness overtook her body.

"We're in Chicago at my sister's house."

"Chicago," she said, vaguely recalling a man telling her that before. She had no energy to make sense of it, especially considering she had already forgotten what she wanted to say in the first place.

The dim hospital corridor smelled strongly of antiseptic. The suffocating stench of misery hung in the air, thicker than the night before. The feel of death was stronger, the desperation greater. It was a sensation Vincent still hadn't gotten used to.

The sound of his footsteps bounced off the sterilized walls as he made his way to room 129. Pushing open the door, he stepped inside the darkened ICU room. As soon as his eyes adjusted, he saw his sister curled up in the gray chair. Her eyes were closed, her breathing steady. Quietly, he grabbed an extra blanket from the cabinet and covered her up. Waking her was pointless—she never went home when he told her to.

He turned to the bed, his blurry, tired eyes inspecting the numerous machines. The steady hum of the ventilator drowned out almost every noise, but the tube that had been taped in Corrado's mouth the past two weeks was no longer there. He had gotten a tracheotomy overnight, a tube now running straight into the front of his throat. The sight of it made Vincent's stomach sink.

More complications, one after another. Corrado couldn't catch a break.

He'd been dead on arrival, but a young ER doctor refused to write him off. After a valiant attempt, they had managed to get Corrado's heart beating again. It had remained steady since then, but he was in a coma, his body giving no indication it ever intended to wake up.

Vincent watched for a while, feeling helpless and entirely to blame. He couldn't bear to think of what would happen if Corrado never regained consciousness. But even if he did, Vincent was plagued with the possible side effects. There could be massive brain damage, seizures, or paralysis. If he woke up, he may never be the same.

And that terrified him more than the possibility of the man dying.

Celia stirred, her eyes opening and meeting Vincent's right away. She sat up, stretching. "How long have you been here?"

"Just a few minutes," he said. "I would've come sooner, but the girl woke up."

Optimism shined from Celia. It was out of place in the dismal hospital room. "How is she?"

"She's . . . alive. She has a long road of recovery ahead of her."

"I bet Carmine's relieved."

"He doesn't know," Vincent said. "He was at Sal's."

Celia cringed. "How did you explain that to her?"

"I didn't. It's time for Carmine to handle things on his own. Time for him to be a man."

"You sound like Dad," Celia said.

It was Vincent's turn to cringe, but he kept his opinion to himself. "It's after seven. You should go home and get some sleep."

"I already slept."

Stubborn woman. "Dozing in a chair doesn't count. If you keep it up, you'll end up in a bed on the floor below, committed for exhaustion."

Celia climbed to her feet and pressed a kiss on Corrado's forehead. "I'll go home when he can."

Vincent's chest constricted as he watched his sister care for her husband, lovingly smoothing his hair and fixing his hospital gown. "What if that doesn't happen?"

Celia's shoulders stiffened. "Don't say that."

"You have to consider the possibility."

Anger flared in her dark eyes. "He'll wake up."

"Yes, but . . . what if he doesn't? Corrado wouldn't want to be lying in a bed like this."

"He'd want to live, and he will. He's getting stronger every day."

His sister sounded certain, but Vincent knew too much to succumb to her hopeful words. "The longer he's unconscious, the less likely it is he'll—"

"I know," Celia said, cutting him off. "I've heard the doctors, but they don't know Corrado like I do. He'll come out of this."

"What makes you sure?"

"Because he told me he would. When he left the house, he said he'd come back to me. Corrado has never broken his word."

———

Haven awoke again to a bright room, squinting from the harsh light filtering in the window. She groaned as she turned away from the sunlight, her hand coming into contact with a body in bed beside her. Carmine was asleep, his chest rising and falling at a steady pace, his right arm wrapped from his fingers up past his elbow with an elastic bandage.

Clenching her jaw, she fought back the cry that threatened to come out as she rolled onto her side, the needle in her arm pulling when she reached toward Carmine. She hesitated an inch from his face, not wanting to disturb him, before running her fingertips along the bridge of his nose. There was a small bump that hadn't existed before, and she knew firsthand where something like that came from.

Carmine stirred, grumbling incoherently before his eyes drifted open. He jumped, nearly falling off the bed as she quickly pulled her hand away.

"Shit, you're awake!" he said. A smile spread across her face at the sound of his voice. She fought back her emotion, but it was too much to handle. Tears flowed down her cheeks, and he wiped them away. "Are you okay? Are you hurt? Wait, of course you're hurt!"

"I'm fine."

"You're not fine," he said. "You're hurt, *tesoro*. Do you know how much you scared me? I thought I was gonna lose you! When I woke up in that car and you were gone, I thought my life was over. But I swore I'd never give up, and I didn't. I couldn't think about going on if you were dead."

"I'm not dead," she said through her tears.

"Yes, but—"

"No buts," she interrupted. "I thought I was going to lose you, too. I begged them to leave you alone in the car."

"You begged them?"

"They were going to kill you." Her voice cracked as the memory resurfaced. "I told them I'd go with them, that I wouldn't fight as long as they let you live. I would've given up anything."

"You would've sacrificed yourself for me?" he asked, his expression serious. "You'd throw your life away if it meant I'd keep mine?"

"Yes. Wouldn't you do the same?"

"You know I would."

He tried to pull her into a hug, but it wasn't easy maneuvering around their injuries. They both groaned and cringed from pain, his bandaged arm making the embrace awkward. "Your arm," she said, nuzzling into his chest.

"The bone fractured when I was shot, so they had to splint it."

She tensed. "You were shot?"

"Yeah. It's not that serious, though."

"Not serious? Someone shot you!"

"Yeah, Nunzio did."

She gasped. "Oh God, where is he?"

"He's dead," Carmine said. "Him and the rest of them."

"They're dead?" He nodded. "All of them?" Another nod. "And you aren't?"

He cracked a smile at her question. "Last time I checked," he said, reaching for her hand and pressing it against his chest, over his heart. "I think it's still beating."

"It is." She stared into his eyes—eyes she worried she would never see again. "I missed you."

"Mi sei mancata," he said. "I'm glad you're awake now."

"Where were you earlier?"

He didn't respond right away. "I had an appointment."

"What kind of appointment?"

"That doesn't matter right now."

"That's the same thing your father said."

"Yeah, well, there you go. We should probably listen to him."

"You're a rebel," she said. "Since when do you listen?"

"I never did before and look where that got us. I figure it's time to start, since he seems to know what the hell he's talking about." He paused. "Sometimes, anyway. Other times I still think he's full of shit."

She laughed at his response. They both lay quietly, holding on to each other as she tried to clear the fog that settled in her brain. Her memory was sketchy, an odd tension mounting in the room as a result. "Is everything okay?"

"Why wouldn't it be?" he asked.

"I don't know. I was worried . . ."

"Well, stop worrying." His voice was firm. "You need to focus on getting better."

"You sound like your father again," she said, his evasive answer doing nothing to calm her fears.

"Apparently I'm more like him than we thought."

"You're nothing like him," she said. "You'll never be like him."

"I wouldn't be so sure."

She wondered what he meant when there was a knock on the door. Dr. DeMarco walked in, and Carmine groaned at his father's arrival. "We talked him up."

Dr. DeMarco raised his eyebrows. "It's not nice to talk about people."

"It's nothing I wouldn't say to your face."

"True, son. You've never been one to hold your tongue."

"Isn't that part of my charm?"

"I wouldn't call it charm," Dr. DeMarco said. "Your mouth gets you into trouble as often as it gets you out of it."

"Haven's never had any complaints about my mouth," Carmine said playfully. She blushed and jabbed him in the ribs. Even though her touch was light, Carmine clenched his teeth to muffle a cry.

"He has a fractured rib," Dr. DeMarco explained when she eyed Carmine peculiarly. "It would be fine by now if he'd learn to take it easy."

She felt guilty for hurting him. "Sorry."

"Don't apologize." Carmine turned his attention to his father. "Is there something you needed?"

"I got back from the hospital and wanted to check on her." He grabbed Haven's wrist to check her pulse before feeling her forehead. "How are you feeling?"

"Still mixed up, but I feel better than I did."

"You will be for a while as your body heals," he said. "I want you to try to eat something. Carmine can bring you some chicken broth."

"I can get my own," Haven said.

"Nonsense, child. You're far too weak for that right now," he said, shaking his head. "Anyway, I'm sure the two of you have a lot to talk about, but get some rest today. Carmine can also get you something for the pain. I know he knows where the narcotics are, considering he's been popping them like candy for weeks."

Haven stared at the door when Dr. DeMarco left. "He seems strange."

"I've noticed," Carmine muttered. "He's resolved, like he has some grand plan to save us all."

"Do we need to be saved?"

"Don't we always?"

Rhetorical question. Of course they did. "Is he working at the hospital here now?"

"No, he was just seeing about something."

"What?"

He sighed. "Christ, you're full of questions. It's not something you need to worry about."

"But I can't lie around, wondering what happened. I'll worry myself sick and never get better."

"Fine," he said. "I don't think it's a good idea to tell you yet, but I'm not gonna fight about it."

She listened as Carmine recounted waking up in the car. He explained what had happened in Durante, tears flowing from her eyes when he broke the news that Nicholas hadn't survived. Her mind drifted through scenarios, and she got lost in her thoughts, Carmine's words drifting into the background until he said something that caught her off guard. "Arrested?"

He sighed and stood, running his left hand awkwardly through his uncombed hair. It obviously hadn't been cut in more than a month, strands covering his neck and spilling over his forehead. There was a slight curl to it at that long length. "Yes, and for bullshit reasons. The feds raided with warrants for my father and Corrado, and some egotistical agent named Cerone threw me in jail along with them."

"I can't believe you went to jail," she said. "How did you find me? My chip?"

"I wish," he said. "It wouldn't work, and they were in jail, *tesoro*. I knew it would be at least another week until they got out, and I didn't know if you had that long. I had to do something."

"What did you do?" she asked, suspicious of his cryptic words. "Whatever it is, I'll understand."

He shook his head. "It doesn't matter."

"Why do you keep saying things don't matter?"

"Because there are some things you shouldn't know right now."

"You can't mean that," she said. "You said we'd tell each other everything."

"I know, but things change. There are some things I can't tell you . . . some things I won't be able to tell you. It's shit you won't wanna know anyway, Haven."

"What do you think you can't tell me?"

He started to respond, but the ringing of his phone silenced him. Groaning, he pulled it from his pocket and shot her a nervous look as he answered. "Yes, sir?" His tone was even, his demeanor instantly shifting. "But I don't . . . Yes, fine. I get it. I'll be there."

He sighed as he hung up and sat beside her. He took her hand, lightly placing a kiss on the back of it. "Nothing's more important to me than you, *tesoro*. I'd give my life for you."

"You're scaring me, Carmine."

"Don't be scared," he said. "I was desperate, baby. I needed to know you were alive, and now that you're safe, I can't regret it."

"You're not making sense."

"I'm not surprised," he said, letting go of her hand. "I have to go."

"Go?"

"Yeah, but I shouldn't be long. We'll talk when I get back, but I can't be late."

"You can't be late for what? Tell me what you did, Carmine!"

"I went to Sal, okay? Is that what you fucking wanna know? I asked him to help me, so now I owe him in return."

She stared at him, fighting back her panic. "Owe him what?"

"My loyalty."

She sat up, grimacing from her sudden movement. "Take it back!"

"I can't," he said. "It's too late."

"But you can't do that! You can't be like them! You can't do those things they do. We talked about this before!"

"Do you think I wanna be that person? That I wanna do those things? Of course I don't!"

"Then why'd you do it? How could you agree to that?"

"I didn't have a choice. I get it if you're upset, but it's done."

He stared at her imploringly, begging her to understand, but she couldn't in the moment. She averted her gaze when he reached over to wipe the tears from her cheeks. "We always have a choice."

His touch was gentle and should have been comforting, but it wasn't enough to extinguish her fears.

"Look, it's gonna be okay," he said. "Nothing's changed."

Her heart ached to believe his words, but she wasn't naïve. Not anymore. It was a life of crime, a world of violence where danger constantly forced its way in. It was a world that turned men cold and cynical as they did unspeakable things she couldn't fathom. It was a world that had taken both of their mamas and had nearly killed them, too. It was a world they had tried to escape, but one that sucked them in, anyway.

It wasn't the world she had envisioned for their future.

All she could think about were their plans slipping away. Going somewhere no one knew them, starting over fresh where he could just be him and she could just be her, untainted by slavery and the labels forced upon them. Going to college so he could play football while she studied art—all of it a distant dream. Getting married and having a family—the concept overshadowed by reality. She wasn't sure what was possible anymore, where they could go or what they could do. Would he be allowed to go to school? Could they bring children into that world?

More importantly, what would happen to Carmine? Could he live that life and be the same person she loved? Could someone do bad things, but not be a bad person? After being brutalized her entire life, how could she accept him becoming one of them?

How had Maura done it?

———

Vincent stood at the front of the dim church, staring at the flickering flame of the candle he had lit. It glowed brightly, illuminating his hand as he sullenly made the sign of the cross. There was a quiet shuffling behind him after a moment. Vincent turned to see

Father Alberto approaching, clutching a Bible. He nodded at the priest. "Father."

"How are you, my child?"

"I'm well."

Father Alberto shook his head. "There are certain people in life you can never fool, Vincenzo, and your priest is one of them."

"Who are the others?" he asked curiously. "My mother?"

The sober old priest actually barked with laughter. "I've known your mother for decades. I can safely say she sees and hears only what she wants, nothing more. It's a gift with that woman."

Vincent smiled. "Should you talk that way about people?"

"I'm not judging," he said. "I'm simply telling the truth. While in church. It's a nice concept. Would you like to give it a try?"

"Sure."

"Then I'll ask again. How are you, my child?"

Vincent hesitated. "Terrified."

There was no surprise in Father Alberto's expression. "What scares you, Vincenzo?"

"Corrado's in the hospital."

"I heard. Is he getting better?"

"Not that I can tell," he said. "Celia believes he'll be fine, that he'll wake up soon, but I don't see how. His brain went without oxygen for too long for him to walk away from this."

"How long was he without oxygen?"

"Almost four minutes."

"Is it impossible to recover after being down for four minutes?"

"Impossible? No, but it is improbable."

"A doctor would also say an Immaculate Conception is improbable."

"No, a doctor would say an Immaculate Conception is impossible."

"But yet Mother Mary had Jesus."

"She did."

"Miracles happen," he said. "There's a reason you don't see what Celia does."

"Because I'm a doctor?"

"No, because you've lost your faith."

Vincent looked at the priest with disbelief. "If that were true, I wouldn't come here."

"On the contrary, Vincenzo. You come here because you wish to find your faith again. You can't fool God, either. He knows everything, and it's okay, because He'll forgive you. The question is whether you're ready to be forgiven."

He was quiet, turning back to the lit candle. "I am."

"Then ask."

Vincent took a deep breath before speaking again. "Forgive me, Father, for I have sinned."

Father Alberto's voice was gentle. "Go on. You're safe here."

The word *safe* made him hesitate again. For the first time since he was that young boy, walking into the church and believing he belonged, he felt like he was truly safe there.

"The first time I killed a man, I was eighteen. I shot him once in the heart with my revolver. He lost consciousness instantly, but it took exactly a minute and twenty-nine seconds for him to stop breathing. I counted. Seems so quick in retrospect, but while I watched it happen, it felt like he'd never die. And the whole time I stood there, all I could think was how wrong it seemed."

"Wrong because you shouldn't have killed him?"

"No, wrong because there wasn't enough blood. Some seeped out onto his shirt, and his nose bled as he choked on a bit, but it was a relatively clean scene. He bled out internally. I thought a shot to the heart should've been messier."

Father Alberto was silent for a moment. "Why did you kill him?"

"He raped my wife," he said, his voice an octave above a whisper. "I was judge, jury, and executioner."

"You didn't think God would make him pay?"

"Yes," he said. "I just made it so he'd face God sooner."

"Why?"

Vincent's brow furrowed. "I told you why."

"You told me what this man did wrong, what sin he committed, but you didn't tell me why you killed him. I remember you at eighteen. I married you and Maura at eighteen. You weren't a vengeful person, and Maura wouldn't have wanted you to do it."

The priest was right, of course. "My father sanctioned it, called it my wedding present. I hadn't wanted to, but it wasn't open for negotiation. Permission to kill him was my first order, my first *test*. He thought he was doing me a favor."

"What other *favors* did your father do for you?"

Vincent shook his head. "I don't think there are enough hours in the day to tell you it all."

"I have time," the priest said. "Just as long as you're finished by Sunday morning."

Vincent laughed at that.

"Come on," Father Alberto said, motioning toward the confessional. "We will do this right."

The candle still flickered, and Vincent gazed at it before following him. The moment he sat down in the confessional, the words flooded from his lips. He spilled it all, every sinful thing he had done in his life—the men he had murdered, the places he had robbed, the people he had hurt. Every shameful act, every scornful word. Vincent didn't stop until it was all out in the open.

"How do you feel?" Father Alberto asked when he finished.

How did he feel? He felt relief. He felt at ease. He felt as if a burden had been lifted from his shoulders, a weight no longer pressing on his chest. He felt freer, lighter. He felt forgiveness. He felt peace. "I feel like painting a door blue today."

———

Shifting uncomfortably in the chair, Haven gazed through the large window at the world outside. It was close to dusk and dozens of kids wandered the street in costumes, stopping at houses with their colorful buckets for candy. She watched them, longing brewing inside her. They were all so young and carefree, ignorant to the dangers lurking a few feet from them. She had never known that type of innocence. When she was their age, the monsters in her life had been real.

"Hey, Twinkle Toes."

She turned at the unexpected voice and saw Dominic in the doorway. He smiled as he walked forward, pulling an orange pumpkin-shaped lollipop from his pocket. He handed it to her, and Carmine groaned from his spot on the bed. He hadn't left her side since going to his meeting with Salvatore days ago.

"She can barely keep soup down, and you're giving her candy?"

Dominic rolled his eyes. "When did you become her guardian? She's her own woman. Let her have a sucker. It won't kill her."

"Whatever," Carmine said, standing. "I'll get her something real to eat."

"Yeah, you do that, Martha Stewart," Dominic said. "Go knit her a scarf while you're at it. Maybe some booties, too."

"*Vaffanculo,*" Carmine hollered as he walked out.

Dominic turned to her. "That boy needs to chill before he bursts a blood vessel."

"He's trying to help," she said. "Give him a break."

"I know he's trying to help, but that's no excuse to deny someone candy on Halloween."

"Thank you for it," she said, pulling off the wrapper and sucking on it. "I didn't realize it was Halloween until I saw the treatsters."

He sat on the arm of the chair beside her and laughed. "They're called trick-or-treaters."

"Oh." She looked back out at the kids in costumes. "I didn't know, since I've never been. I didn't have a normal childhood."

"*Normal* is a relative term," he said. "Besides, it's never too late to trick-or-treat. Maybe we'll go one of these years."

She smiled, knowing Dominic would actually do it. "I'd like that."

"It's good to see you. I would've come sooner, but Tess made me promise to leave you alone."

"I'm glad you're here. It's nice to see friendly faces again."

He nodded. "So, how are you holding up? Can't be easy losing a month of your life."

"I'm alive," she said. "That's more than I can say for some people."

"Nicholas," he said quietly. "He didn't deserve what happened. He was a good friend, always had a joke for anyone who would listen."

"He did." Tears formed, guilt eating away at her. "It's dumb, but I can't stop thinking about the last joke he told me. He was telling one when he was shot, but he never got to say the answer."

"Yeah? What was the joke?"

"What's black, white, and red all over?"

Dominic laughed. "Classic Nicholas. He'd give a different bullshit answer every time he told that joke, like a penguin with sunburn or a zebra with chicken pox. The real answer is a newspaper, though. It's black and white, and *read* all over."

"Oh." She sat there for a moment before a light laugh escaped her lips. "I like that one."

"It's not stupid to think about it. He'd be honored to be remembered by his jokes," he said, patting her head. "I'm glad you're up and moving around. Everyone's been worried, but I never doubted everything would turn out all right."

"I wish I was as sure."

"As hard as it is, you have to have hope. Remember I told you before? What my brother did sucks, but if I was in his shoes, I would've done the same thing, and I know you would, too. So maybe I'm not the only one who needs to give Carmine a break. I'm sure somehow you guys will figure things out, and it won't be the ideal fairy tale, but when is life? Especially for the two of you."

"You're right."

"Anyway, I should go." Dominic stood and froze, clearing

his throat. "Damn, that was quick, bro. You're a regular ol' Betty Crocker these days."

"I didn't *make* it, motherfucker." Carmine handed Haven a bowl of vegetable soup. "I just poured it."

"Well, you did a damn fine job at that."

"Thanks, asshole," Carmine said, feigning annoyance as an amused smile formed on his lips. "Don't you have shit to go break with a sword or something? It's Halloween."

"Hey, that reminds me! Today's the anniversary of the first time you two crazy kids made out."

Haven smiled. "It was when I kissed him."

"I still can't believe you made the first move. Bet you're regretting that decision now, huh?"

Glancing at Carmine, she took in his solemn expression. "I'll never regret it."

His face lit up at her words, and she was immediately ashamed for her thoughts. She was still hurt, unsure of what the future held, but one thing Carmine had never done was give up on her. She mourned a life she thought she lost, but it was a life she would have never dreamed of having if he hadn't fought for her in the first place. He had sacrificed for her, his world irrevocably altered to give her a chance. Carmine deserved a life outside of the violence.

How would she forgive herself if he didn't get it?

She sighed after Dominic left, setting her bowl of soup down on the small table beside the chair. She got up, wincing from the pain in her wobbly legs, and Carmine rushed forward when he saw what she was doing. She held her hand up to stop him, taking a few weak steps on her own to him.

"I love you, Carmine DeMarco," she said, nuzzling into his chest. Her shoulder throbbed from where it had been dislocated and her knees felt as if they were going to give out, but she held on to him and ignored it all. None of those things mattered. They would fade, and with them the memory, but her love for Carmine would never go away.

He hugged her back, pulling her closer and resting his head on top of hers. Haven's smile grew. Despite everything, she still felt safest in his arms.

———————

Haven grew stronger, her injuries healing, but she still struggled mentally as days turned into weeks. She spent most days resting, but eventually ventured outside with Carmine. He held her hand the first time they strolled down the street, pointing out different landmarks from his childhood. They were about a block away from Celia's house when her legs grew tired, and the two of them stopped in front of a large white house. Carmine pulled her to it and sat on the front porch.

"I don't think you should sit on someone's steps like that," she said. "They might get angry."

"This is our house, *tesoro*," he said with a small smile, continuing as she took the seat beside him. "It's where I grew up, but it's been empty since my mom . . ."

Since she was murdered, Haven thought, finishing the sentence he still couldn't say. She glanced at the bright blue door, a stark contrast to the chipped red paint of the shutters.

"What are we going to do, Carmine?" she asked. "What happens now?"

"We go back to Durante. Sal's gonna give me some time before he expects me to move here. Other than that, I guess we figure it out as we go."

———————

And that was exactly what they did. A few days later, Dr. DeMarco rented a car, and the three of them made the journey back to Durante. She slept a lot, sprawled out in the backseat as Carmine and Dr. DeMarco took turns driving. They stopped so frequently it took a few days before they saw the brown wooden DURANTE WELCOMES YOU sign.

An odd sensation overcame Haven when they pulled off the faded highway and up to the familiar plantation house. It wasn't hurt or heartache, although it was deep within her chest, surrounding her heart and stealing her breath.

It wasn't until Carmine muttered the words that it struck her. "We're finally home."

Home. She got it now. For the first time in her life, something felt like home. It was the place they had come together. It was where they had found love.

She finally knew what that word meant.

51

Settling back in hadn't been easy. Memories haunted Haven's dreams and continued to follow her during her waking hours. Flashes of faces, horrific screams, and scathing words constantly ate away at her, and the worst part was she wasn't sure any of it was real.

She scribbled in notebooks again and sketched pictures of the images she saw in her mind. Her monster returned, taunting her with his scaly face and evil eyes. It reminded her that no matter where she went, that part of her life was never far away.

Carmine was just as distracted, nightmares infesting his sleep again. He would sneak out of bed at night, and sometimes she would follow, listening as he played the same song for hours on end.

They were two broken kids, desperate to be whole again, struggling to find balance in a world out of their control. What's black and white and red all over? Carmine was, Haven thought. A soul savagely ripped in half, bleeding out for all to see. The yin and yang, the good and evil, the love and pain all at odds with each other. Two sides, two vastly different worlds, but someday they would merge as one. They had to.

Il tempo guarisce tutti i mali. Time heals all wounds.

———

Some things in life only happen once, the memories lasting forever. They are moments that alter you, turning you into a person you never thought you would become, but someone you were destined to be. There's no magical rewind button in life, no take backs or do-overs to fix things you wish you could change.

If there were, Carmine would be eight years old again, demanding his mom wait for a car to pick them up. They wouldn't wind up in that alley, and his mom would live to see another day.

He'd go back to sixteen and put his gun away instead of driving to his best friend's house in anger. Bygones would be bygones, and there would be peace, instead of public rivalries that hurt everyone in the end.

He'd be in that kitchen at seventeen again, cleaning his spilled juice instead of frightening Haven so badly. He wouldn't have passed judgment on the strange girl, and maybe he would have known what love was a little sooner.

There were many places Carmine would go back to, many things he would have done differently, but one thing he wouldn't take back was what he had done to save her.

Sacrifice. It was something he learned from his mom, when she gave her life to save a young girl. He had learned it from his father, when he swore himself to an organization to be with the woman he loved. Even Corrado had put himself on the line, risking his safety to spare them more pain.

And he learned it from Nicholas, who helped a virtual stranger and got nothing in return. Nothing, that is, except a bullet to the chest, ending his short life.

If Carmine could go back, he would have truly apologized to him that day.

Life's a struggle, and it would be easy if it came with an eraser, but it didn't. What's done is done, as hard as that was to accept.

Sometimes, though, people get second chances. They get more tries. It was too late for others, but Carmine was blessed with more time. Time to try to make things right.

"Carmine?"

Carmine glanced at his American history teacher, Mrs. Anderson, and felt the strangest sense of déjà vu at her expectant look.

He had failed her class last time around and was back in it senior year, a requirement for graduation.

Not as if he counted on graduating. He had already missed more than a month of school.

"Yeah?"

"It's your turn."

Sighing, he strolled to the front of the room, the eyes of his peers fixed on him. They expected a show, but Carmine only had one thing on his mind.

Redemption.

"The Battle of Gettysburg was fought in Gettysburg, Pennsylvania in eighteen-something-or-other. The year doesn't matter."

Mrs. Anderson started to interrupt but closed her mouth when he continued. "They considered it the turning point of the war, and President Lincoln showed up to give his big speech. Who really cares what it was called? I don't. After it was all over and the North won, Congress passed the thirteenth amendment to free the slaves. It outlawed owning another person—yada, yada, yada—but it was a waste of time. All of it."

"Uh, Carmine?"

He ignored his teacher, continuing on as if she hadn't spoken. "All those people died and it didn't change anything, because it doesn't work if they don't enforce it. They turn their backs and say it's not their problem, but it is. It's everyone's problem. They can say slavery ended all they want, but that doesn't make it true. People lie. They'll tell you what they think you wanna hear, and you'll believe it. Whatever makes you feel better about your dismal little lives."

"That's enough, Carmine."

"So, whatever. Go on being naïve. Believe what the history books tell you if you want. Believe what Mrs. Anderson wants me to tell you about it. Believe the land of the free—blah, blah, blah— star-spangled-banner bullshit. Believe there aren't any slaves anymore because a tall guy in a big-ass top hat and a bunch of politicians said so. But I won't believe it, because if I do too, we'll all be fucking wrong, and someone has to be right here."

Mrs. Anderson stood, and Carmine smiled to himself. Maybe they got a show, after all.

He grabbed his belongings and headed for the door before she could tell him to get out of her classroom. The hallway was deserted, everything silent and still as he made his way to the front office. Principal Rutledge stood near the secretary's desk, and he looked at Carmine with surprise when he walked in. "Did you get in trouble?"

"Me? Of course not."

Principal Rutledge sighed. "It's been a while."

"I know, but don't worry . . . It's the last time you'll have to see me."

Haven stood in the kitchen making herself lunch when Dr. DeMarco walked in. "When you get a minute, can you come to my office?"

She nodded, nervous as to why he would want to see her. She wrapped up her sandwich, her appetite gone, and placed it in the refrigerator for later. Even though he rarely left the house, since the hospital had terminated his job after news of his arrest, she and Dr. DeMarco hadn't exchanged more than basic pleasantries in weeks.

She headed up to his office when she couldn't delay it any longer and softly knocked, opening the door when he told her to enter.

"Have a seat," he said, motioning toward the chair across from him. "How are you?"

She sat down, watching him cautiously. "I'm okay, sir."

"Are you?" He raised his eyebrows. "You don't seem okay."

She stared at him, debating how to respond. "I'm dealing."

"Are you starting to remember things?"

She was anxious about where the conversation was heading. "Yes, but I'm not sure how much of it to believe. I hallucinated a lot."

"It's not my place to press you for details, but if you have any questions, I can answer them."

She debated his offer. "Am I really a *Principessa*?"

He leaned back in his chair, giving her an interested look. "Technically speaking, yes. My wife got too close to discovering that, which is why she was murdered."

Guilt consumed her. "Because of me."

"No, not because of you," he said, his tone serious. "For you."

"Is there a difference?"

"Yes," he said. "I once blamed you, believed it was because of you, and it took me a long time to see my anger was unfounded. There are a few people I could reasonably blame, myself included, but you aren't one of them. If I would've realized that sooner, it could've saved us both a lot of hurt."

She stared at him with surprise, and he continued after a brief pause. "The day we found you in Chicago was October twelfth. I was so caught up in everything that it wasn't until the next afternoon that it dawned on me it had been the anniversary of Maura's death. Last year on that day, you didn't stand a chance. No matter what you did, I would've gotten you, because it wasn't about you—it was about her."

A chill shot down her spine at the memory of that afternoon.

"I want you to know I've never hated you. I couldn't hate you, because I never knew you. And I didn't want to know you because I didn't want to care about you. Nine years in a row, I spent October twelfth wishing I could punish you, but this year, all I could think about was rescuing you, which is what got her killed in the first place." He paused. "I'm talking in circles, and I'm not sure if you'll believe me, but I want you to know I've grown to care for you. And as for what I did to you last year, I don't expect forgiveness, but I am sorry about it. If I could take it back, I would."

He pushed his chair back and walked over to her, pulling up his pant leg to show his ankle bracelet. "Do you know what this is?"

"No."

"It's a GPS monitoring device. A stipulation of my bail was that I had to wear it." Her eyes widened, and he laughed at her expression. "It's something, isn't it? You don't know what it's like to have your every move watched until it happens to you. Somewhere there's a man watching to see where I am to insure I'm not trying to get away."

"Sounds familiar."

"I'm sure it does," he said. "I had my reasons for chipping you, but that doesn't mean what I did was right. I called in one last favor with a colleague of mine, the one who saw Carmine after the accident, and I made an appointment for you. I may be stuck with my monitoring device, but that doesn't mean I can't remove yours."

Her mouth fell open as she struggled to find words. "Thank you."

"You're welcome, but I don't deserve your gratitude. I'm only fixing my mistakes at this point." He sat in his chair as tears spilled down Haven's cheeks. "Anyway, one more thing. I want to give this to you before our guests arrive. It could be my last Christmas with my family, so I'd like to make the best of it."

His words made her stomach twist. "You think you'll go to prison?"

"I'm sure they'll get me one way or another," he said as he opened the top drawer of his desk and pulled out a familiar leather bound book. He set it in front of her. "My wife's journal. I think you should keep it."

"Me? Why?"

"She wrote a lot about adjusting to this life and her conflicting feelings about the world I belonged to," he said. "It might help you going forward."

She picked up the book cautiously. "Are you sure?"

"I'm positive. Maura would've wanted it this way."

Standing, Haven headed for the door, but she hesitated before she reached it. "Not long after I got here, you asked me not to call you *Master* because it made you feel like my father. Michael Antonelli was a horrible man, but despite everything, you've been kinder to me than he was. So I do forgive you for hurting me, because you've helped me more than anyone else. You're a good man, Vincent, and I think sometimes good men find themselves doing bad things."

His expression remained blank, but for the first time since meeting him, Haven saw his eyes gloss over with tears. "Thank you, Haven."

Haven. Her name on his lips sounded foreign as he finally said it. She wiped her tears as she walked out, knowing there was nothing left to say. She stepped out into the hallway at the same time Carmine came up the stairs. She eyed him peculiarly. "You're home early."

"Yeah, school was a bust," he said, shrugging. "How are you today?"

"Okay."

He cocked an eyebrow at her. "Okay? Is that an, 'Okay, I'm about two seconds away from finding a window to throw myself through, but I'm not gonna tell you because you'll stop me,' or is it an, 'Okay, I'm pretty fucking peachy, Carmine, so stop questioning me'?"

She laughed. "I'm just . . . okay. Especially now that you're here."

He kissed her before the two of them headed upstairs. Settling into the chairs in the library, Carmine grabbed his guitar as Haven gazed at the cover of the journal.

"You still reading *The Secret Garden*?" he asked.

"No, I finished that book months ago."

"Really? What happened in it?"

He didn't truly sound interested, his gaze on his fingers as he strummed the guitar, but she smiled at the fact that he would ask. "The girl comes to the conclusion that the mean man she lives with isn't as bad as she assumed. He's just grieving because he lost his wife. She makes friends with the son, who the father can't face for a long time, because he reminds him of his wife."

Carmine's fingers stilled, the music abruptly stopping as he looked at Haven. "No shit?"

She shook her head. "Nope."

"Fate," he said, his eyes drifting from her to the book on her lap. "My mom's journal."

"Uh, yeah. Your father gave it to me."

He turned back to his guitar and started strumming again, music filling the room as sunshine streamed in on them from the window. She watched him in silence, her chest swelling with love as her favorite passage from *The Secret Garden* sprang to mind.

> *One of the strangest things about living in the world is that it is only now and then one is quite sure one is going to live forever and ever and ever . . . sometimes a sound of far-off music makes it true; and sometimes a look in someone's eyes.*

Haven felt it then, sitting in the library with the scarred boy who had stolen her heart, his deep green eyes twinkling as the beautiful notes poured from his fingertips.

Sempre. No matter what happened next, or what went on tomorrow, nothing would ever take that away. Their love existed, despite everything else, and it was that love that would go on forever. The moment was etched in time, transcending the constraints put on them by life.

For even after they were gone, when life continued on, a part of them would always exist in everything—and everyone—they ever touched.

She turned back to the journal and opened it. Taking a deep breath, she read the first line:

> *Today is my first day as a free woman.*

ACKNOWLEDGMENTS

While *Sempre* is a work of fiction, the concept of modern-day slavery is not make-believe. There are an estimated twenty-seven million people in the world today who are coerced and forced into sexual or labor slavery. The majority of them are female, half being young girls. They're our mothers, our fathers, our sisters, our brothers. They're our friends, our lovers, our neighbors, our kids. They're us. It could happen to anyone, even you.

Become an abolitionist. If we don't fight for them, who will?

I have to first and foremost thank my family. I wouldn't be who I am today if not for their endless support and love. Even when I was floundering and seemed to have lost my way in the world, you never once gave up on me (even when I gave up on myself). To my father, whose love of reading and *The Godfather* I inherited. I could never thank you enough. And to my mother, who showed me what true strength was all about. I wish you were here to see this.

To my rock star of an agent, the incomparable Frank Weimann, for taking a chance on me and this story, and for not shuddering in fear when I sent over a crazy-long manuscript. To Kiele Raymond, Lauren McKenna, Jen Bergstrom, Kristin Dwyer, Jules Horbachevsky, and everyone else at Pocket Books/Simon & Schuster for the support and hard work. I'll never be able to adequately express how grateful I am for you all. You've helped make my dreams come true.

To my freshman high school English teacher, Melissa Agee, for being the first to say, "You could be someone someday." You made me believe in myself. And to my freshman college creative writing professor, who shall remain nameless, for telling me I'd never write anything worth reading. You made me strive to be a better word-slinger.

To Traci Blackwood, who spent countless hours going through plot and structure with me. You, my friend, are a wizard. Your help was invaluable. To Sarah Anderson, for always being willing to break out the pom-poms whenever I start getting down on myself. No one else speaks "wonky fingers" like you. I couldn't ask for a better writing friend. And to all who have read this story from the very beginning and commented, reviewed, questioned, and cheered (or jeered) . . . I learned so much from all of you, both the good and the bad. And to Vanessa Diaz, who I don't think realizes has been as influential as she has. To have someone love my words so much is a dream.

There are so many more I need to thank, but it would take another five hundred pages to get through all of them. I'm sure you know who you are. *Grazie mille.* But a very special thanks to Lion Shirdan, for reading and believing.

Finally, to Stephenie Meyer, J. K. Rowling, L. Frank Baum, Mario Puzo, and Richelle Mead . . . I have never had the pleasure of meeting any of you (and I most likely never will), but you've impacted my life more than words can express. You constantly inspire me to pick up a pen and write. And a very special shout-out to the *Twilight* fandom. We often get picked on for our love of a certain sparkly vampire, and we may not always get along or agree with each other, but no one can deny we're a force to be reckoned with. You'll forever hold a spot in my heart.